AF819388

Massacre at Midnight

A Novella of Medieval Intrigue

Massacre at Midnight

A Novella of Medieval Intrigue

Chaudhary Kaushal Kishore Thakur

PRABHAT PRAKASHAN

ISO 9001: 2008 Publishers

Published by
PRABHAT PRAKASHAN
4/19 Asaf Ali Road,
New Delhi-110 002 (INDIA)
Tele : +91-11-23289777
e-mail: prabhatbooks@gmail.com

ISBN 978-93-5186-735-7
MASSACRE AT MIDNIGHT
by Chaudhary Kaushal Kishore Thakur

Translated from original Hindi novel 'Bhavaanii Bahu'
by Priyadarshi Thakur 'Khayal'

Cover design
Sankarshan Thakur

Edition
First, 2016

Price
₹ 400.00 (Rupees Four Hundred only)

© C.K.K. Thakur

Printed at
R-Tech Offset Printers, Delhi

Dedicated to
Smt. Sita Rani Thakur

Contents

Author's Note

Although folklore does abound in legends of my ancestors Dharaadhar Thakur and Jagdambii Thakur, this is largely a work of fiction, and characters other than these two illustrious ancestors, and events as described in this book are all figments of my imagination based on the references to family lore by my elders since I was a boy some seventy odd years ago. Any resemblance to any person, living or dead, is purely a coincidence and should be ignored as such.

Indeed, according to legends Dharaadhar Thaakur was brutally murdered and his estate confiscated during Mughal times, and later his son Jagdambii, who enjoyed special blessings of Kshemkarii Vana-Durgaa, is believed to have won back his estate and was conferred the hereditary title of Chaudhary, though the exact historicity of events is difficult to ascertain at this distance of time.I would therefore request the readers to enjoy it simply as a story from the past.

I acknowledge my debt of gratitude to my nephew-in-law, Dr. Ratneshwar Mishra, formerly Professor and Head of the Department of History, L.N. Mithila University whose assistance has been immensely valuable in making this work worth publishing.

Chaudhary Kaushal Kishore Thakur

Translator's Note

First and foremost, I acknowledge my debt of gratitude to my elder brother Prof. Murari Madhusudan Thakur, a learned former professor of English and an erudite Sanskrit scholar, for his invaluable help and guidance at various stages and in different aspects of this work, particularly the translation of Sanskrit shlokas and preparation of the glossary. Himself a master translator, my brother has always been a source of inspiration and assistance to me in all my translation projects.

I am grateful to my nephews Vinayanand Jha and Sankarshan Thakur, my daughter Jaya, my niece Sona Thakur, my granddaughter Devyani, my friend and brother-in-law Parameshwar N. Jha and friend Raghavendra K. Dixit, who agreed to take the trouble of going through the manuscript, and gave me valuable suggestions, which have been of immense help to me in improving the final draft. In particular, I must thank Sankarshan for racking his head, not once but a second time as well, for finding the right title for the English version, and for designing the cover. My sincere thanks to Pawan K. Thakur, better known as Bambam, and my grand-nephew Subrat Thakur, grandson of the author, for their technical assistance in digitising the manuscript.

To Rekha, my wife, and Bhuvan and Soni, my son and daughter-in-law, not only do I owe a debt of gratitude for their constant support in my literary ventures, but also for the fortitude and patience with which they put up with me, silently working for long hours.

Last but not the least, I have to thank my elder cousin and the author of the original Hindi novel 'Bhavaanii Bahuu',

Chaudhary Kaushal Kishore Thakur of Singhwaar Deorhii, for asking me whether I would like to translate it into English for him, thus giving me the opportunity to discover what a wonderful story it held within its pages. I hope he likes my English rendering of his work. Regardless of whether anyone else likes it or not, if he does, that should be enough reward for my love's labour.

Priyadarshi Thakur 'Khayal'

Note on Phonetics-based Spellings of Sanskrit or Other Indian Words in the Text

The names of places, cities and persons, and of Sanskrit, Hindi, Maithilii and Urdu words in the text of this translation – of the original Hindi novel Bhavaanii Bahuu by Chaudhary Kaushal Kishore Thakur – have been spelt largely in line with a scheme of phonetics-based spellings of Urdu and ethnic words used by www.Rekhta.org, a noted Urdu poetry website, with just a few exceptions that prove the rule.

For the information of readers who are already used to a different set of spellings, and might raise their eyebrows in chagrin at these new ones, I wish to say that this phonetics-based method, odd as it might appear at first, is perhaps one of the most effective ways of conveying the correct pronunciation of such words to those unfamiliar with the names of people and places in India and other Indian words in question. Of course, Indophiles and former colonial-types, and, very likely, many Indian readers as well, who know these words from previous exposure are bound to find 'Baabaa' ridiculous, because they already know that Baba is simply Baba! More's the pity – for most of them still end up pronouncing 'Raam' as either 'Ram' as in a battering-ram, or 'Raamaa' as in "Hare Krishna Hare Rama"! Hence the need for a method that makes for a more efficient phonetic transcription of Indian words into Roman script, and can take such words, particularly for the novice, as close as possible to the correct native pronunciation, instead of taking the natives to anglicised mispronunciations. This is also the reason for such oddities as an upper case D or T or N cropping up in the middle of a word or at its end.

Indeed, it is not my case that the Rekhta method is a panacea for our difficulties in this regard; like all solutions to a rather complicated set of problems, it is far from perfect; for example, it does not yet have a formula, to my knowledge, for transcribing the hard sound of the combination of the hard 'Dh' with a touch of R, like PaDhnaa, meaning 'the act of reading' in Hindi and Urdu – as distinct from the simple hard sound of 'Dh' as in, let us say, 'Dhol', a musical instrument. But short of using diacritical marks – regarded as avoidable in works of fiction – it is perhaps the best option.

Enough by way of preamble, I think. For better or worse, this translator has made a conscious decision in favour of the Rekhta-style spellings in the hope that they will be more effective in communicating how the words are pronounced by the native speakers of the language.

The basic rules of the Rekhta method are summarised below:

- AA, or aa, wherever placed in a word is for the sound that A has, for example, in words like arm, art, dart and the like.
- Similarly, a stands for the sound that in English is made mostly by the letters like i or u or e or a in words like bird, urge, herd or westham. When 'a' in the lower case occurs at the end of proper nouns like Raama, Maheshvara, Ganesha, etc., it is mostly silent, or only to be left half articulated.
- I stands for short sound as in if, is or in itself.
- II equals the long sound made in English usually by double 'e' as in eery or coffee; and also by y as in guy, or by i as in ice when 'ii' is immediately preceded by AA or aa.

- U is meant for the short phonetic sound it makes in the word 'Ulema', now included in all standard English dictionaries.
- UU stand for the long phonetic sound normally made in English by OO, as in words like ooze or booze; and in boo, where 'uu' occur at the end of a word.
- D in the upper case stands for the hard sound of 'd' as in words like dart or done, wherever it might occur in a word.
- The letter 'd' in the lower case stands for the soft sound made by 'th' in English, as in words like 'the' or 'thus'; however, exceptions have had to be necessarily made in proper nouns like Devii, Durgaa, Dilli, Diidii, Daadaa, etc., though these are all soft sounding 'd's, or when the word happens to be placed at the beginning of a sentence.
- The word 'danDa'vat' in the text is a good example of both the hard and the soft sounds of the letter D.
- Similarly, T, wherever it occurs in the upper case, denotes the hard sound as in tea, task, etc. while 't' always stands for the soft sound of the letter quite commonly found in French and many other European languages. However, proper nouns starting with 't', and words placed at the beginning of a sentence, have been spelt with 'T' in the upper case.
- The word 'PaThet' in the text is a good example of the both the hard and soft sounds of the letter 'T'.
- Doubts, if any, between 'T' and 't', and 'D' and 'd' in any word used in the text can be resolved by referring to the Glossary that follows.
- The capital 'D' followed by 'h', and capital 'T' followed by 'h', wherever in a word these might occur, stand for the hard 'T' sound and hard 'D' sound with a touch of 'H' in either case.
- In line with the Rekhta precedent, 'V' has been preferred over 'W' for the phonetic sound associated

with English words like war, wage, way, etc. except for Nawaab and Waah-waah.

- Some of the longer words have been broken by apostrophe for easier articulation.
- And finally, the upper case 'N', whether occurring in the middle or at the end of a word, denotes the nasal sound as in the French pronunciation of Jean; but this is not so when it begins a word, where it is a full 'N'.

Glossary of Sanskrit, Hindi and Maithilii Words

A

Aachaarya-Guruu: A family elder chosen to help a boy through the rituals of his sacred-thread ceremony

Aadi-Shakti: Mother Goddess

Aashiish-mudraa: Gesture of blessing

Achkan: A long buttoned-up coat

Anna-daata: Bread-giver

Aaratii: A fire-service

Aaasana: a cloth/wool seat on the floor

Agni-deva: Fire-god

Airaavat: The heavenly elephant

Ajaraa: A name of the Mother Goddess

Allah-o-Akbar: The Muslim prayer call, lit. 'God is Great!'

AnushThaan: A special puujaa

Ardha-Naariishvara: Lord Shiva in his form of half male and half female

Ashok-vaaTikaa: The garden where Raavana kept Siitaa in Lanka

Asura: Demon

Avaleha: A medicinal paste

Avidyaa: State of delusion

B

Baabaa: Grandfather

Baabuu: A gentleman, usually suffixed to the first name

BaDee: Eldest or elder

BaiThak-khaanaa: A parlour or meeting hall

Bajrangbalii kii Jai: Victory to Hanumaan

Bachaao: Save me!
Bahuu: Daughter-in-law
Baidyanaath-dhaam: A famous Shiva shrine
Baraat: A wedding party
Baraatii: Wedding guests
Baruaa: A boy about to be initiated
Bastii: A human settlement
Begam: A Muslim lady; wife
Benaares: The famous pilgrim city of Varanasi
Benaaresii: Made in Benaares
BeTii: Daughter
Bhaabhii: Elder brother's or cousin's wife
Bhaai: Brother
Bhaai jii: Elder brother
Bhaara: A gift of food-stuff sent on ceremonial occasions
Bhagvatii: Mother Goddess
Bhagvatii ChanDikaa: A terrible aspect of Bhagvatii
Bhaiyaa: Elder brother or cousin
Bhajjaa: A name of Mother Goddess
Bhumihaar: A Braamhana sub-caste
Bidaaii: A parting gift to a guest
BiiDaa: A folded leaf, see paan
Bilva-patra: A fruit tree – wood apple – leaf sacred to Lord Shiva
Braahmana: The priestly class in the Hindu caste system, considered learned
Bramhaa: The creator-god of the Hindu pantheon
Braamhii: A name of Mother Goddess

C

Chakra: Lord Vishnu's serrated flying discus
ChhoTe Nawaab: Junior Nawaab
Chandramaa: The moon .
Chaur: Large open fields outlying a village
Chaturthii: The fourth night after the wedding
Chinvaar: Raised platform in the worship chamber of Hindu families
ChuuDiidaars: Tight fitting pajamas like breeches
Chuuran: Medicinal powder

D

daadaa-maulvii: A senior Muslim cleric respected like a grandfather

daastaan: A long tale; a saga

daastaan-e-Alif-Lailaa: The tale of Alif and Lailaa

dakshinaa: A money gift given after ceremonial feeding

danDa'vat: Prostrating to deities

dayaa: Mercy

darshan: A vision

darshan-shaastra: Philosophy

Deorhii: A seat and residence of landed gentry

Deraa: A temporary lodge

devii: Mother Goddess

devii-Bhaagvat: A scripture about Mother Goddess

devyah-kavacham: A coat of mail related to Mother Goddess; also a chapter in devii-Bhaagvat

dhaanuk: A lower sub-caste

dhoti: Several yards long piece of cloth – traditional male lower body garment

dharma'shaalaa: A charitable inn in a place of pilgrimage

dhuniyaa: A Muslim sub-group specializing in carding cotton

diidii: An elder sister or sister-in-law

dighvae'sannahpur: A Braamhana family stock

drishTi: Sight; view

durgaa: Another form of Mother Goddess

durgaa-Sapta'shatii: A seven hundred verse scripture devoted to Mother Goddess

dvaatrinsh'maalaa: A string of thirty-two names of Mother Goddess

dviraagaman: The maiden arrival of a bride at her in-laws'

Some of these words being proper nouns, e.g., Durgaa, Devii, Dilli, etc. have been spelt in the text with D in upper case, but in terms of sound, the letter 'd' in these is like the word 'the'. In this listing upper or lower case has been used on the basis of the correct phonetic sound.

F

Faqiir: A mendicant

Farmaan: A royal edict

Farsaa: An axe with a half-moon blade

Farshii-salaam: A salutation touching the floor, common in the courts of Muslim rulers

Fiil'khaanaa: Stable for elephants

G

Gaachhii: An orchard, usually of mango trees in Mithilaa

Gaddii: The seat of a businessman or a ruler

Ganesha: The elephant headed Hindu Deity, the lord of auspicious beginnings

Gangaa: The River Ganges

Gaurii: Consort of Lord Shiva

Gayaa: A pilgrim place known for terminal obsequies

Ghabraanaa mat ham tumhaare saath hain: Don't panic, here we come!

Giri'raaj: The Himalayas as a deity in the Hindu pantheon

Gotra: An original Hindu family-root or stock

Guptii: A long dagger hidden inside a baton

Guruu: The mentor-teacher

H

Hakiim: A traditional Muslim physician

Hanumaan: the Monkey-god in the Hindu pantheon

Har-har Mahaadeva: Hail Lord Shiva; also a Hindu war-cry

Havelii: A rambling mansion

Haudaa: A canopied seat for riding on elephant back

Himaalaya: The Himalayas

Huzuur: Your Honour

I

Indra: The Rain-god

IshTa-deva: One's preferred deity

J

Jalebii: An Indian sweet, usu. served hot

Jaanakii: Siitaa, the consort of Lord Raama

Jagdambaa: Mother Goddess

Jagmohan: The entrance porch of a Hindu temple

JahaaNpanaah: Emperoror's title, lit. 'Shelter of the world'

Jaraa: A name of Mother Goddess

Jii/jii: An honorific suffix for respected names/people

Julaahaa: a Muslim sub-group specializing in weaving cloth

Jyotishii: A Hindu astrologer or palmist

K

Kaafir: A non-Muslim; a un-believer (in Islam)

Kaakii-MaaN: Aunt

Kaal-darshii: clairvoyant

Kaamdeva: The Hindu god of Desire

Kaashyap: A Hindu stock

Kaauverii: A name of Mother Goddess

Kahaar: A palanquin bearer

Kakka jii: Uncle; father's brother'

Kalpa-vriksh: A mythical wishing-tree

Kangan: A thick bangle, usually golden

Kamandalu: A water container with in-built handle on top

Karna-vedha: The ceremony of piercing the ears

KaTkaa'ians: The residents of KaTkaa village

Katthaa: A measure of land, roughly 1/20 of an acre

Kaumod-gadaa: The mace of Lord Vishnu

Khaaltaa: Wide bottomed pajamas

Khavaas: A personal valet

Kiirti: Fame; Celebrity

Kimaam: A betel spice

Kimkhaab: Richly embroidered velvet, usually in golden threads

Kosa: A traditional measure of distance, approximately equaling two miles

Kripaa: Grace; blessing, usu. divine

Kubera: Lord of Wealth in the Hindu pantheon

Kula: Family line

Kula-mantra: A preferred mantra used by the family for initiation

Kuma'ram: Ceremony on the day prior to a sacred thread ceremony

Kumaarii: A maid; a virgin

Kunjraa: Vegetable/fruit growing Muslim sub-group

Kurtaa: A long tunic worn with dhotii

Kshamaa: Forgiveness; pardon

Kshatriya: Warrior caste, second in the hierarchy of Hindu caste system

Kshemkarii: One who blesses with or promotes well-being

Kshiir-saagar: Mythical Ocean of milk-pudding

L

LaaThii: A stick or staff, usu. bamboo

Lagna: A period conducive to a ceremony

Lajjaa: Shame or shyness

LaThait: A bamboo staff fighter

Loka: A world or realm

Lingam: A phallus, symbol of Lord Shiva

Lungii: A loose piece of cloth worn as lower body garment for males, popular among Muslims.

M

Maaheshvarii: A name of Mother Goddess

Maalik: Lord and master

MaaN: Mother

MaaN jii: Mother with honorific

Maatu: An affectionate address for Mother

Maatri-bhikshaa: Alms given by the Mother of the boy going through sacred thread ceremony/ceremony of senior ladies giving similar alms after the mother

Madhyamaa: A middle degree in Sanskrit

Mahaa-ashTamii: The eighth and the holiest day of Navratra puujaa

Mahaa-panDit: A man of great erudition/learning

Mahaaraaj: Lit. 'A great king'; also used to address a ruler or some important person

Mahaa-Shivaraatri: The Grand Night of Lord Shiva

Maheshvara: A name of Lord Shiva

Mahishaasura-mardinii: The name given to the Mother Goddess as the destroyer of Mahishaasura, the buffalo-demon

Mahuaa: A sweet-smelling fruit tree whose flower is used for wine-making

Maithil: An inhabitant of Mithilaa, the realm of Raajaa Janaka, located in northern Bihar

Malmal: Muslin; a fine cotton fabric usu. hand-woven

Mandaakinii: A tributary of the Ganges

Mandaar: A hill that was used for ocean churning according to Hindu mythology

ManDap: A thatched gazebo for ceremonies

Masnad: A bolster; a large pillow

Maulvii: A Muslim cleric

Medhaa: Brains or intellect

Mehfil: A ceremonial gathering, usu. associated with dancing-singing, poetry-readings etc. at royal courts

MiaaN: A form of address to male Muslims

Mithilaa: The realm of Raajaa Janak in ancient times-modern north Bihar

Mithyaa: falsehood, untruth; a lie

Muh-bajaaon: Ceremonial first speech of a bride with her husband

Mujraa: A professional singer's or dancer's performance, usu. by courtesans

Mukti: Deliverance; liberation from the cycle of birth and death

MunDan: A ceremonial head-shaving by razor as distinct from a hair-cut

Munshii: an accountant or a clerk

Mussalmaan: A follower of Islam

N

Naag-devataa: A serpent-deity

Naarsimhii: Related to Man-lion avatar

Namaskaar-mudraa: The gesture of Hindu salutation with palms together in front

Naubat-khaanaa: A raised chamber for drum or shehnaaii music, usu. atop the entrance to palaces or temples

Navaraatra: The nine days of Durgaa worship in the spring and autumn

Navaratna; Nine jewels; also a collective reference to the nine important advisers of Akbar, the Great Mughal

Nimitta: A medium or cause

Nuniaa: A sub-caste specializing in salt mining

O

Om Namah Shivaay: A mantra for invoking Lord Shiva, lit. Om obeisance to Shiva

P

Paag: A Maithil head gear

Paan: A betel leaf folded in a triangle with lime and other condiments incl. tobacco, if desired

Paarvatii: Lord Shiva's consort, the daughter of the Mountain

Paata'ir: Rice pudding offered to Mother Goddess on plantain leaves on ceremonial occasions

Paash: A weapon consisting of a huge net and thick rope

PaaTaliputra: Ancient Patna, seat of several empires

PaaTh: Religious reading/recitation

Paav: Abt. 250 grams

Padmaasana: A lotus posture in yogic practice

Pallu: The loose end of the saarii hanging over the shoulder

Panchaakshara: Formula of five letters/syllables

Panchaang: Hindu Almanac

Panch-tatva: The five elements in Hindu cosmology like the Earth, Water, Air etc.

PanDit: An erudite, learned scholar

Paraa: Lit. 'The One Beyond', of the Deity

Parikramaa: Circumambulation, usu. of a temple/idol

Pashyantii: A form of speech

PaTvaarii: A village revenue official

PaThet sarva bhayaan'mukto bhavishyati Na sanshayah: Have no doubts, whoever reads this shall be delivered from all fears

Pavan: Wind; Wind-god in the Hindu pantheon

PinDa-daan: A gift of cooked rice balls offered to departed ancestors

Pranaam: Respectful salutation with palms together and head bowed

Pranaam-mudra: The stance of pranaam

Prasaad: Sacred food distributed to devotees after first offering it to a deity

Preta-yoni: The state of being a wandering spirit in limbo

Prithvii: The Earth

Puaa: Deep-fried sweet flat bread made of ground wheat

Puujaa: Worship

Puujaa-ghar: A worship chamber in a house

Puraana: The post-Vedic Hindu scriptures; Mythology

Puurii: Deep-fried flat small, round flatbread of wheat

R

Raamaayana: The epic of Lord Raama

Rakta-biij: A self-multiplying demon from each drop of its blood, destroyed by Mother Goddess as Durgaa

Ras-bharii: A viscous and very sweet condiment for betel leaf

Rasanchowkii: a traditional percussion musical instrument akin to shehnaaii

Raudrii: A combative form of Mother Goddess

Rudra: A name of Lord Shiva, "The Terrible One'

Rudraaksha: A seed found in the mountains used as a sacred bead

S

Saadhuu: A holy man; a mendicant

Saarii: Six yard long traditional wear of Indian women, usu. Hindu ladies

SaaThaa paag: A traditional Mithilaa head-gear with sixty folds

Sakhii-MaaN: An honorific for mother's companion

Sandhyaa: Evening

Sandhyaa-aaratii: Evening Fire-service

Sanyaasii: One who has renounced worldly life

Samskaara: An initiation/religious ceremony

Satya-vaanii: Articulated truth

SeTh/SeTh jii: The owner of a substantial business; a rich businessman

ShaanDilya gotra: A Hindu family stock/root

Shaardiiya Navaraatra: The nine-day-long worship of Mother Goddess as Mahishaasura-mardinii every autumn

Shaayar: An Urdu poet

Shabkhuun: A surprise night raid

Shahanshaah-e-Hindostaan: Emperor of India

Shahnaaii: A well known percussion musical instrument

Shakti: Strength, power; the prowess of Mother Goddess

Shastra-puujaa: Ceremonial worship of weaponry in anticipation of combat/on special occasions

Shervaanii: A long buttoned-up coat traditionally worn by Muslim gentry

Shivaalaya: A Shiva temple

Shloka: A Sanskrit couplet

Shraddhaa: Reverence

Siitaa jii: Honorific for Siitaa, the consort of Lord Raama

Simha'vaahinii: A reference to Mother Goddess when riding her Lion

Singhwaarian: A resident of village Singhwara

Smriti: Memory; also a name of Mother Goddess

Sprihaa: A name of Mother Goddess

Srii: A name of Mother Goddess

Stotra: A hymn

Subedaar: Provincial Governor

Sudhaa: Ambrosia; a name of Mother Goddess

Syce: A servant who grooms the horses (in Indian sub-continent)

T

taagra: A demon, companion of Mahishaasura destroyed by Durgaa

taallukedaar: A landlord

tandraa: A name of Mother Goddess

tantra-mantra: Tantric magical practice

tamolii: A betel shop-owner

tasmaii: Rice-pudding

teja: Brilliant prowess

tejah-pradaan: The gift of brilliant prowess by gods of the Hindu pantheon to Mother Goddess

teja-samuuh: Hindu mythology – the brilliance from which the Mother Goddess emerged as Durgaa

teraai: The Himalayan foothills bordering Nepal

Tiikaa: A Hindu sacred mark on the forehead, usu. of sandal paste

tithi: A date, usu. reference to an auspicious date

Topii: A cap

trikaal-darshii: A clairvoyant who can see the past, present and the future

trishnaa: A name of Mother Goddess

tvachaa: Skin

tvashTaa: A Hindu Deity

'T' in upper case denotes the hard sound as in 'tea', while 't' in lower case signifies the soft phonetic sound of the letter often found in French and several other European languages.

U

UddishTa-puujaa: A ceremonial worship for a specific purpose

Udyog: The day marking the beginning of preparations for sacred thread ceremony

Upanayan: Sacred thread ceremony

V

Vaanchhaa-shakti: A name of Mother Goddess

Vaanii: A name of Mother Goddess
Vaaraahii: A name of Mother Goddess
Vaarunii: A name of Mother Goddess
Vaasu: A Hindu Deity
Vaidika: A Vedic scholar adept at chanting hymns
Vaijayantii: A fabled garland in Hindu mythology
Vaidya: A traditional Hindu physician
VaikunTh: The Heaven of Lord Vishnu
Vaishnavii: A name of Mother Goddess
Vajra: A thunderbolt; a weapon in Hindu mythology
Vana-Durgaa: A form of Mother Goddess
Varq: Ultra-thin, edible silver foil usu. to cover expensive paan
Varun: A Hindu deity
Vasaa: A name of Mother Goddess
Vidyaa: A name of Mother Goddess
Vidyaarambha: Ceremony to initiate a child into the alphabet
Vijal: A demon, companion of Mahishaasura
Vinaash Kaale vipariit buddhi: Losing one's mind when close to being annihilated
Vishvanaath: A name of Lord Shiva
Vishnu: The Supreme Lord of the Hindu pantheon
Vishvakarmaa: A Hindu deity

W

Waah-waah: Wow (repeated)

Y

Yamaraaj: The Lord of Death in the Hindu pantheon
Yajna: A ceremonial offering to deities with Vedic chanting; a ceremonial occasion or puujaa
Yajno'paviit: Sacred thread ceremony
Yogii: A Yoga practitioner; an ascetic

Z

Zenaanaa: The women's quarter in a Muslim household
Zill-e-Ilaahii: Lit. 'Reflection of the Almighty' – a title of Mughal emperors

Prologue

Bhavaanii had but only a few short years of her husband's company and their good life together in the big ancestral mansion when tragedy overtook them and she was forced to flee the *havelii*. At the time of leaving home, she was in the last stages of her pregnancy, eagerly awaiting the bliss of motherhood. Everyone at the big house had been impatiently looking forward to the big day. As a matter of fact, Bhavaanii decided to run away from home not so much on account of the unforeseen circumstances that had suddenly arisen, or the fear of losing her life, as the need to save the illustrious family-line of her husband from complete annihilation.

Bhavaanii exited the *havelii* from the rear entrance in the dead of the night and stood by the stream that flowed behind the big mansion. For a while, she stood perfectly still, staring absent-mindedly at the currents rippling on the river surface and turning to look back every once in a while towards the *havelii* silhouetted against the night sky, as if trying to make out something in the dark.

Hardly had a few minutes gone by when a cacophony of heart-rending shrieks of women and children – as though the whole lot of them had cried out together in sheer terror and agony – erupted from the house, shattering the silence of the night. Bhavaanii shivered. She went down or her knees gingerly, given her protruding belly, touching her forehead to the ground, perhaps as her last *pranaam* to the residents of the *havelii* whom she might never see again. Rising to her feet, she rushed off as fast as her unwieldy form would allow, in the general direction of the north, wiping the incessant flow of tears from her eyes with the *pallu* of her dishevelled *saarii* billowing in the breeze. Bhavaanii, who had never set foot outside the threshold of the *havelii*, was out abroad in the dark night, all alone, walking at a brisk pace but without a clue where she was headed, consumed only by the blind impulse to escape, to get away as far as she could. Soon she had left the habitation of Singhwaar behind and was out in the open fields, walking the boundaries of holdings that doubled as pedestrian walkways. She still had no idea where she was going.

A quarter of the night had gone by when Bhavaanii, still walking, reached the huge open *chaur* of KaTkaa, the village that bordered the Singhwaar estate to the north. But here her legs refused to keep going anymore. Unaccustomed as Bhavaanii was to walking such distances at a stretch, she now felt completely drained, besides being suddenly engulfed in labour pains that seemed to be tearing out her gut. She leaned against the trunk of a huge *mahuaa* tree with a round leafy canopy. The deep exhaustion soon took its toll and Bhavaanii slumped to the ground unconscious. While in that state, she gave birth to a male child. As she came to, she was again gripped by blind panic and the irresistible urge to get away. Even the infant she had just birthed in a fugue, as it were, was quite forgotten as she got to her feet and hurried off. Soon she was in the inhabited part of KaTkaa. It was nearly midnight; the village was deserted, as the inhabitants slept peacefully in their houses, most of them huts with mud-walls and thatched roofs, or on the porches facing the threshing yards in front of their houses, the quiet of night broken only by intermittent barking of dogs.

Bhavaanii waited in front of houses, as she passed them one after the other, as if she meant to wake up the master of the house and ask for shelter, but, in fact, she did nothing of the sort. She would stand before each house by turn, suspiciously casting an anxious glance all around, and then move on to the next. Destiny seemed to be propelling her in a particular direction.

If someone had happened to see Bhavaanii at the time, she would have been taken for nothing better than a crazy tramp. Her dishevelled and soiled clothes with dark splotches of dried blood; the deathly pallor of her haggard face, deeply lined by fatigue and anguish; her eyes glazed by the trauma of her ordeal that was by no means over yet; her dusty, cracked lips, all together defined her as crazy waif roaming the streets with nowhere to go.

Eventually, Bhavaanii reached the centre of the village, and stood once before the entrance to a house, this time a large one that dominated the village square and boasted of brick-walls and tiles on its roof. Once again she looked around suspiciously, except that on this occasion, she stepped forward to the entrance of the house.

The master of the house, sleeping on the porch of his front courtyard, was woken up by constant rattling of the metallic locking device of the main entrance. He was still in bed, wondering who the untimely caller might be, when something falling with a heavy thud brought things to a head. He got out of bed quickly, put on his wooden sandals and walked briskly to the entrance, with a silent prayer to Lord Shiva, his *ishTa-Deva.*

As the master of the house, Shambhuu Naath Thaakur, opened the door, he was dismayed to see an unknown woman lying unconscious on the ground. He jogged his memory trying to place her, but to no avail. Though a bit bewildered, he began to consider his options and soon concluded that he was morally obliged to protect the hapless woman, whatever her religion or caste or social standing, since she seemed to have sought succour at the doorsteps of his house preferring it over so many others around the square. Shambhuu Naath summoned his eldest son, calling out his name, "Kaashii Naath... arre o Kaashii Naath!"

Shortly, the door leading to the inner courtyard of the big house was unlocked from inside and Kaashii Naath rushed out, anxious to find out the reason for his father's untimely summons. Before he could ask anything of the older man, however, he noticed the unconscious woman and looked questioningly at his father. Meanwhile, Kaashii Naath's wife Paaro had also appeared on the scene. Shambhuu Nath eventually said looking towards Paaro, "I've no idea who this woman is or how come she's here. I can't recall having seen her ever before, but whoever she is, it's our duty to protect her."

By this time, other family members and the servants of the house had all gathered. *Baabaa* Shambhuu Naath finally took a deep breath and said, "Let's bring her inside and try to revive her."

His command drew immediate compliance: Bhavaanii was carried inside and laid down on a mattress and the family women began making efforts to revive the unconscious stranger. Shortly, Bhavaanii came to and groaned,

"Where am I?"

❋❋❋

The news of a woman found unconscious at the door-steps of the village headman spread through the village like a wildfire. The whole village was awake in a trice, as it were, and everyone rushed towards *Baabaa*'s house. Soon the large open area in front of the house and its front courtyard were packed with the denizens of KaTkaa, all waiting for the woman to regain consciousness and reveal her identity.

When Bhavaanii opened her eyes, she was quite disconcerted to find herself surrounded by so many strangers. She made a futile effort to sit up but being terribly weakened by the harrowing ordeal, she failed to sit up on her own and had to be propped up. She became instantly conscious of her dishevelled state and started to hastily rearrange her clothing, and covered half of her face with the *pallu* of her *saarii*. It didn't take long for *Baabaa* Shambhuu Naath, sitting with prominent village elders at the far end of the verandah, to make out that much as the stranger was caught up in a distressing situation, she was undoubtedly a lady from a respectable, very likely a noble family. His heart went out to her. Without moving from where he was, *Baabaa* addressed his eldest daughter-in-law, Paaro, in a loud voice, "*BaDii Bahuu*, arrange for her to take a small dose of *makaradhvaj* mixed in a glass of lukewarm milk sweetened with crystal sugar, and reassure her on behalf of the inhabitants of KaTkaa that she needn't worry for her safety anymore."

Before Shambhuu Naath could say anything more, an old village elder sitting by his side whispered something in his ear. The headman seemed to agree with his suggestion, and proceeded to address the stranger directly in a gentle, reassuring tone, looking closely in her direction,

"*BeTii*, there are so many of us gathered here but there's none that knows who you are. Would you be so good as to introduce yourself?"

Bhavaanii took a good look at the rather attractive man who had addressed her as 'daughter'. He appeared to be in excellent health, old age notwithstanding. Then casting her eyes down, she replied,

"I've no idea where I am, or who you all are. I cannot remember how I came to be here either, but all that can wait. At this moment, I'm dying to know the fate of my people at the *Deorhii* whom I deserted in terribly dire straits. God alone knows what's become of them!"

Bhavaanii hadn't yet said very much but whatever little she had, left the gathering deeply mystified, wondering what a plain commoner like her could possibly have to do with the *Deorhii* or its residents. Intrigued by curiosity, they wanted to find out who the woman really was, but they all waited in silence.

Bhavaanii went on to introduce herself, "In the family to which I belong, it's strictly forbidden for daughters-in-law to even utter the name of their in-laws or their husbands, and, in fact, the transgression of this unwritten code is regarded as a grave misdemeanour. But, in my present circumstances, I'm compelled to do so. I only hope that the gods will forgive me for this."

Bhavaanii glanced at Shambhuu Naath from under her veil and continued, "I am Bhavaanii, the wife of Dharaadhar Thaakur of the famed *Dighvae'Sannahpur* lineage of the Thaakurs of Singhwaar."

Everyone present was stunned at her revelation: many of them sprang to their feet, excitedly exclaiming in unison, "Who has reduced you to such a state, madam? Do tell us quickly what compelled you to leave the *Deorhii?*"

Baabaa Shambhuu Naath, who had stood up from his *aasana*, too, along with the others, added, "*BeTii*, tell us everything without any further delay. We are of the same blood-line; you may not know me but I am now fully aware of who you are. What on earth has happened to the people at the *Deorhii* to make you so anxious? We must know if we can be of help."

"What can I say, *Baabaa*?" Bhavaanii responded ruefully as if thinking aloud and fell silent again. After a pause, she briefly described the likely attack on the *Deorhii* by a Mughal army contingent and the consequent panic and anxiety there, and added in a voice choked by emotions,

"As my husband's life-long companion, it was my duty to have been at his side, whether I lived or died. But I shamed the family-lines of both my father and my husband by running away!"

It was then that Bhavaanii suddenly remembered about her newborn baby. In a tone of voice wretched with despair, she exclaimed, "Oh my God! Look at my rotten fate!! I fled the *Deorhii* to protect the illustrious lineage of my husband's family from extinction by saving its heir I was carrying in my womb, and now I have betrayed the very cause by leaving the infant unattended in the wilderness. How selfish of me that all I could think of was to run for my life. Oh, my baby! Surely I have no right to go on living after such cowardice!"

Having vented her anguish thus, Bhavaanii fell faint all over again.

By now, *Baabaa* Shambhuu Naath had fully grasped the overall situation. Addressing the assembled villagers, he said, "Listen, O residents of KaTkaa, there is no time to lose. Neither is there any time to think or plan. Pick up your weapons and go for them! None of you except the very old and infirm should remain here. Singhwaar is hardly any distance; go like a hurricane and decimate the barbarians who have dared to torture our kinsmen without provocation."

Suddenly, *Baabaa*'s eyes fell upon his eldest son, a contemporary of Dharaadhar's and his childhood playmate, standing to a side. He chided him gently, "Kaashii, you're still here! Go and lead the men and make the enemy pay heavily for coming at our kin. Hurry up, man, go now!"

The widely revered headman's exhortation filled the men with pulsating excitement, the night sky of KaTkaa reverberating with their chorussed war-cry of *Har-har Mahaadeva*. They hurriedly got hold of their weapons and began to march towards Singhwaar. As the core team of KaTkaa'ians moved along, more and more volunteers joined them on the way. Meanwhile, *Baabaa* Shambhuu Naath, leaving Bhavaanii in the care of his daughters-in-law, began to put together a search party to look for the infant scion of the Singhwaar branch of his family descended from common forebears, lying abandoned somewhere in the wilderness of KaTkaa *chaur*.

1
The Story of LaaDlii and Pyaare

Dharaadhar Thaakur had two younger brothers, Shri Raam and Radhey Shyaam; the three of them lived in a joint family in the sprawling *havelii* of the Singhwaar *Deorhii*, a minor principality in a remote corner of *Mithilaa* owing allegiance to the Mughal emperor.

Being the eldest, Dharaadhar was the one responsible for managing the affairs of the family estate and protecting the family fortune, which their ancestors had built brick by brick over generations by their sweat and blood, their learning and foresight. Dharaadhar Thaakur was a suave, cultured, soft-spoken and friendly sort of a person, very conscious of his moral bearings despite the feudal milieu in which he had been brought up. An upright and handsome man in his mid-thirties, Dharaadhar was quite a democrat for the era he lived in, rarely making his decisions on the basis of social standing of his people, and mingled pleasantly with one and all, whether high or low, the reason why he commanded respect in all hierarchies of social order. Having been born in a family of Maithil *Braahmanas*, Dharaadhar possessed a natural flair for learning common to that class, but he had also inherited the attributes of a *Kshatriya* – the warrior class – from his ancestors who had ruled the principality for generations. While he was gregarious and flexible, he was also a man of unbending principles and iron-will where family honour was concerned. All in all, Dharaadhar was a formidable man.

Dharaadhar was very fond of hunting but that didn't prevent him from being unusually attached to his domestic animals and pets. Apart from scores of oxen, milch animals and the like, usually found in the households of landed gentry of the times, his stables boasted of several thoroughbreds, one of which called Baadal, a dark tawny steed of Arabian bloodline, was his favourite personal mount. The Thaakurs of Singhwaar also owned a pair of canines, the female called LaaDlii and the male, Pyaare, both excellent hunting dogs. In Dharaadhar's frequent hunting expeditions, their main task was to sniff and ferret out the quarry and block its escape routes. Between the two of them, there was a unique relationship: Pyaare didn't move a muscle, remaining practically inert, until LaaDlii had taken the initiative, as if giving an invisible signal to him to get going; once she did that, Pyaare jumped into the fray with all his might, willing to stake even his life. Pyaare was worth precious little without LaaDlii to egg him on, the latter being the sole fount of Pyaare's prowess. Pyaare and LaaDlii were treated at par with family members and invariably accompanied the master on his hunting trips.

On one such occasion, as Dharaadhar and his friends entered a densely forested area, it started to rain heavily. The hunting party ran for cover every which way, taking shelter under trees and getting separated from one another in the process. Dharaadhar sheltered under the canopy of a tree, all by himself except Baadal, LaaDlii and Pyaare who were always with him. The downpour carried on for the longest time, a stiff westerly turning it into a nasty squall. The porous canopy, hardly enough protection against such heavy downpour, soon began to leak, leaving Dharaadhar drenched. He was beginning to feel cold despite Baadal trying to position its hulk over his crouching master to shield him from the rain swirling in the wind.

Pyaare and LaaDlii stood nearby trying to sniff out any unusual scent. Presently, they both ran off in a particular direction, defying the driving rain. One could hear them growling and barking in the distance. Dharaadhar was quite familiar to the nuances of their barking. He immediately sensed danger at hand, though he was yet unable to spot anything out of the ordinary. Soon LaaDlii ran back to him, and standing by his side, began to bark menacingly in the direction of the shrubs she had run off to while Pyaare continued to bark incessantly from behind them. Dharaadhar couldn't ignore it any longer. As he stood up, he saw a fearsome bison coming straight at him. Pyaare was trying his darndest to deter its progress like an old veteran. Having seen to it that the master was forewarned and up on his feet, LaaDlii ran up to reinforce Pyaare's effort to block the path of the beast which was going berserk with fury at their barking; indeed, it seemed bent upon taking the pair of them head on and tearing them apart on its huge horns. The eyes of the beast radiated blind rage, the corners of its mouth foaming and its nostrils flared.

Dharaadhar lost no time. In a flash, he lifted his heavy spear leaning against the tree, and whistling to Pyaare and LaaDlii to get out of the way, threw it at the beast, aiming to hit the soft spot between its eyes. The spear hit the target spot on and pierced the centre of the bison's forehead. The fearsome beast, stopped dead in its tracks, fell to the ground, its legs thrashing in the throes of death. Gradually, the skies cleared and it stopped raining. Soon the hunting party reassembled where Dharaadhar had felled the bison and seeing his marvellous trophy of the day, began offering their congratulations to him.

Such incidents were, however, an ordinary day's work for LaaDlii and Pyaare. They had saved the lives of many a hunter on previous expeditions as well. But this particular incident turned them into a real living legend. They became the talk of the town, as it were, and far more exaggerated and spiced up versions of their exploits began to circulate in hunting circles. So much so that many connoisseurs began to frequent the *Deorhii* only to have a look at the now famous pair of Pyaare and LaaDlii.

❋❋❋

The neighbouring Nawaabship of Waariaul was a seat of great power and influence those days. The ruling Nawaab, Salaamat Khaan, regardless of his advancing years, was debauchery personified, as full of vices as he was devoid of good sense; his perversions were so gross as to beggar description. Salaamat Khaan was a little over sixty years of age with a perfectly snow-white head of hair, in reality, but the magic of henna made sure that not a strand of his hair appeared to have turned gray. He was a barrel-chested, stocky man with stylishly trimmed beard and moustaches; a crude hedonist, he was almost invariably drunk and busy watching his nautch-girls swirling, or cavorting with courtesans.

Salaamat Khaan had three wives. The eldest was known as Raanii *Begam*, literally meaning the Lady Queen, but they had never got along as a couple. Raanii *Begam*, the only child of a wealthy father, was not dependent on the Nawaab for her keep; her dowry had been so large, it more than met her needs. In any case, her life-style was abstemious and pretty inexpensive. A quiet, devout woman, given to spiritual pursuits, she spent more on helping out the destitute and *faqiir*s than on herself. Indeed, she abhorred the Nawaab's debauchery and was repelled by her husband when occasionally they happened to see each other. Tired of frequent bickering, Salaamat Khaan had eventually stopped paying attention to her. As far as Raanii Begam was concerned, it was good riddance by divine intervention.

The other two wives of Salaamat, Raziaa *Begam* and Jamiilaa *Begam*, were forever cursing their rotten fate, too, for while they pined for the Nawaab's attention, he was always busy philandering elsewhere. His passions were apparently aroused more by seducing chamber-maids, charwomen and the like, the luxury of three wives notwithstanding. His harem provided livelihood to umpteen women, besides a regular turnover of visiting courtesans.

The Nawaab took enormous pride in the fact that one of his female cousins – his father's sister's daughter – was a fixture in the harem of the Mughal emperor, deeming himself a brother-in-law to none other than the *Shahanshaah-e-Hindostaan* himself. Every time he was in a fit of rage, he tended to thump his chest and declare that if he were ever to go complaining to Delhi, he would be back with a tornado of devastation; in such outbursts, he never forgot to claim to be from the same stock as the emperor's grand vizier.

The favourite confidant of Salaamat Khaan was Nusrat, the younger brother of Jamiilaa *Begam*, his third wife. He came with her as a young boy when the Nawaab married Jamiilaa, never to return home again. Indeed, Nusrat was much younger than the Nawaab, almost the same age as his son Shahnavaaz by Raanii *Begam*, but being his brother-in-law, he enjoyed Salaamat's favour. At the same time, he was friends with Shahnavaaz, as a contemporary of his. Nusrat was having a whale of a time at Salaamat's court, lording it over the closest aides of the ruler down to lowest menials, and was a special favourite of the courtesans as well. Ghulaam Sarvar, the Nawaab's vizier, however, thought Nusrat was a rogue and a trouble-maker and detested him, a sentiment shared in equal measure by Nusrat. There was little that the Vizier could do about it though.

Like any other evening, Salaamat Khaan sat reclining against heavy, ornately-clad bolsters on his elevated *masnad* in a quiet corner of his palace which few were allowed to enter. The Nawaab, wearing a *kurtaa* of the finest muslin from Dhaakaa on top of *ChuuDiidaars* and sporting a hand-crocheted cap, made for an impressive presence. The room was bathed in subdued light of candles burning in the chandelier hanging from the ceiling. A nubile and beautiful courtesan, sitting by the Nawaab's side, topped up his cup of wine from time to time, intermittently offering him *paan* when he asked for one, or the mouth-piece of the hookah pipe, affecting a graceful courtly mannerism.

The Nawaab appeared glum and quiet; probably the booze was acting as a depressant for a change. He turned to Nusrat, his ever-present courtier, and said, "Well, Nusrat, if you can't come up with any news, at least you could relate a *daastaan*! I can't bear this silence."

Whenever so commanded, Nusrat had hardly any option except to begin spouting whatever came to his mind on the spur of the moment. He would then carry on until the master shut him up, saying, 'What on earth are you going on and on about', or until the Nawaab slumped into an alcohol-induced oblivion for the night. This was a routine the twosome repeated every other evening. Presently, Nusrat began to recite *Daastaan-e-Alif-Lailaa* to his master. It was difficult to gauge whether Nawaab Saahib was paying much attention. As Nusrat paused, having completed the tale, Salaamat Khaan reclining on the *masnad*, his eyes closed, exclaimed, "So, what happened then?"

Nusrat didn't know what to say! How was he to explain that the *Dastaan* was done? While he was still wondering how best to put it across to the master, the latter impatiently snapped without opening his eyes, "Oh! Come on, old chap, do tell what happened next?"

With nothing ready at hand, Nusrat launched into a colourful account of the exploits of LaaDlii and Pyaare.

It wasn't as if Salaamat didn't know Dharaadhar Thaakur. The two families had had friendly relations with each other for generations. It was another matter that the standing, influence, wealth and pomp of the Nawaab's family far exceeded that of Dharaadhar Thaakur's, besides the political scene at the time being more favourable to the Nawaab. The country was ruled by the Great Mughal, and the Nawaab enjoyed easy access to the imperial court through his cousin. The Nawaab had, however, always treated the Thaakurs of Singhwaar well so far, and the two families even exchanged gifts on festivals and special occasions. Destiny, though, had other plans for the future.

Salaamat Khaan, quite sozzled and slumped against the bolsters in a near horizontal posture until then, seemed to suddenly recover his wits and sat up on hearing of the canine wonders of Dharaadhar. He motioned to the courtesan to refill his cup, and addressed Nusrat, "*MiaaN*, come again! What did you just say?"

Nusrat, sensing his master's interest aroused, began to wax eloquent, spicing up the exploits of Pyaare and LaaDlii with renewed vigour. Salaamat's eyes opened wide in amazement.

"Are they really so wonderful, Nusrat?" he exclaimed incredulously.

"They indeed are, Sire. The entire region is agog with their tales!" said Nusrat.

"In that case, they ought to be here rather than Singhwaar, don't you think?" said the Nawaab.

"Absolutely, Sire! Such an asset definitely belongs here. You just have to ask for it. After all, you have friendly relations with them. Surely, Dharaadhar wouldn't grudge you a dog if you asked for it. Just send a messenger over. I'm sure he wouldn't turn down your request," replied Nusrat.

"Well! Nusrat, you do talk some sense once in a while! Let me send for the Vizier this very moment," said the Nawaab smiling and clapped twice as a signal to summon an attendant. The servant came running, bent low, his head almost touching the ground and greeted the Nawaab with *farshii salaams* three times over. As he straightened, he was told to convey orders summoning the vizier. When the servant had gone, Nusrat piped up, "Look here, Nawaab Saahib, let me tell you something quite plainly: You must give us all a grand feast to celebrate the acquisition of such a rare dog as Pyaare."

"Nusrat MiaaN! replied the Nawaab, "What does a feast matter! You'll have everything you want, but first let's get hold of the dog."

"Oh, not to worry, Sire, Pyaare will be here in a jiffy!" Nusrat declared smiling confidently, "It will be ours the moment the messenger reaches Singhwaar with your request."

The Nawaab, stuffing a fresh *biiDaa* of *paan* in his mouth, warned Nusrat, wagging his finger at him, "Now, mind what you say, Nusrat! There is still time for you to think it over: you'll have hell to pay if Dharaadhar Thaakur turns down my request."

Nusrat felt his heart miss a beat, but deciding to remain in an optimistic frame of mind, said, "Don't you worry, Nawaab Saahib, nothing of the sort will happen. You'll see."

Vizier Ghulaam Sarvar said a silent prayer on receiving the untimely summons from the master. He had been having a sense of foreboding since the morning. As the day passed without incident, he had thanked the Almighty, but once again he was filled with a sense of doom, praying that all would be well. Anyhow, go to the master he must! As soon as he entered the room, Salaamat Khaan came to the point without preamble, "I've just been told that my brother *PanDit* Dharaadhar Thaakur has a priceless hunting dog, a most useful animal. I want you to get the dog for me, at all cost."

Ghulaam Sarvar was an experienced man who had seen a lot in his time. He glared at Nusrat fleetingly, and then addressed the master, "Sire, please bear with me if my advice appears a bit impertinent on the surface. Domestic animals, birds and pets of this nature come to be treated as family. It's quite possible that Dharaadhar Thaakur would be loath to part with his dog. You have just called the Thaakur your brother. If that be so, I wonder whether we shouldn't respect his sentiments!"

Ghulaam Sarvar's contrarian approach instantly raised the heckles of the Nawaab; he quipped sarcastically, "I called him my brother! That's not an expletive, is it? I don't intend to rob him of his fortune either. Hell, it's only a dog I'm asking for, man! Now, listen carefully, Ghulaam, I must have this dog, no matter what the cost. I'll even go to Delhi and seek the backing of the imperial court, if that is what it takes."

The old Nawaab was almost shouting at the vizier and all the excitement had left him short of breath. He paused for a moment to recover his composure, before resuming his tirade, "You call yourself a vizier! If you can't help your master with a small thing like this, what good are you then?"

Ghulaam Sarvar could see that it was pointless to argue with the Nawaab just then. Trying to buy time, he said to him with an exaggerated bow, "I'll make arrangements to get the dog as soon as possible, Your Highness."

'Arrangements?' retorted the Nawaab as if he couldn't believe his ears, "What arrangements are you talking about, Ghulaam? Just send a messenger with a letter, but make no mistake, I mean to have the dog forthwith, regardless of what it costs as I've repeated over and over." Having made his point in no unclear terms, Salaamat Khaan curtly dismissed the Vizier from his presence pointing his finger to the door imperiously, "You can go now, Ghulaam."

The Vizier left the room silently. There was little he could do in the face of such determined insistence of his employer. At the break of dawn the next morning, he handed over a letter, signed and sealed under his hand, to a trusted dispatch-rider to take it to Singhwaar *Deorhii*, instructing him to wait until a response was ready to bring back.

❋❋❋

It was some time between ten and eleven in the forenoon. Dharaadhar Thaakur, surrounded by five or six of his employees like the *Munshii*, his chief aide, some *paTvaariis*, and a couple of *ghumaashtaas*, sat disposing of routine papers concerning his estate in a large room in the outer annex of the *Deorhii* called the *BaiThak-Khaanaa*, an office room that also served the purpose of a formal audience-hall. An attendant came in and announced the arrival of a dispatch-rider with a letter from the Nawaab of Waariaul. Dharaadhar received letters of invitations to this or that event from Nawaab Saahib several times a year, and thought this must be something of the sort. He, however, asked the man to be shown in immediately as a courtesy to the Nawaab in absentia.

The messenger from Waariaul entered, greeted Dharaadhar, and handing over the letter, stood aside to wait while the Thaakur read the letter. The ageing chief aide, *Munshii* JaTeshvar Laal, a man of great experience and wisdom, was quick to notice the signs of tension appear on his young master's handsome face no sooner than he had started reading the Nawaab's missive, and did not take long to conclude that this was no ordinary letter. Glancing towards the man from Waariaul, he said, "It may take a while to draft a reply to Nawaab Saahib's letter. Meanwhile, why don't you rest for some time in the messengers' parlour?"

"As you wish, Sir," said the messenger and left the room, as did the others at a sign the old *Munshii* made. As soon as they had privacy, he addressed Dharaadhar, "Master, all's well I hope?"

Munshii JaTeshvar Laal was a princely aide in the same mould as Ghulaam Sarvar, except that he served a different and a good-hearted master. He had served several generations of the Singhwaar Thaakurs with distinction, and had been so close to his young master's late father that Dharaadhar and his brothers addressed him as Uncle *Munshii*. *Munshii* JaTeshvar Laal commanded universal respect and adulation in the region around Singhwaar.

Dharaadhar sighed wearily and said, "It's a letter from Vizier Ghulaam Sarvar written at Nawaab Saahib's behest; it says that he has heard great praise lavished on Pyaare's accomplishments as a hunting dog, and that he may be sent per messenger. What sort of a demand is this, Uncle *Munshii*! Why on earth should we send away Pyaare to him?"

Silence hung heavy in the air as neither said anything for a while. It was Dharaadhar who finally spoke, "Uncle *Munshii*, this is more of a family matter than something to do with the estate. We should also consult Shri Raam and Raadhey Shyaam before taking a final call."

"No harm at all. Let's talk to them," replied the *Munshii*.

The two younger siblings were sent for. Seating them near him, Dharaadhar brought them up to speed. For a few seconds that seemed to drag on forever, no one said a thing, but eventually Shri Raam burst out indignantly, "*Bhaiyaa*, this is absolutely preposterous! We mustn't give in to the Nawaab's demand, come what may. In fact, I'll go a step further; the matter doesn't merit any further discussion." Shri Raam paused for an instant, but soon pushed for closure, addressing JaTeshvar Laal, "Uncle *Munshii*, please send a reply on *Bhaiyaa*'s behalf, that he's in no position at all to send Pyaare."

Radhey Shyaam echoed Shri Raam's sentiments, "Pyaare might well be a mere dog for Nawaab Saahib, but for us, he is like a family member, and we all love him like one. There's no way we're going to part with him!"

Having heard his younger brothers out, Dharaadhar Thaakur turned thoughtful, pondering over the unusual predicament in which he found himself. Eventually, he said addressing his siblings pensively, "Shri Raam .... Raadhey, I'd like you to know that my view is no different from yours, but...."

"But what, *Bhaiyaa*?" Shri Raam, usually deferential to his elder brother, couldn't help interjecting for once.

In a tone of voice that clearly suggested a mature elder brother counselling younger siblings to dissuade them from a rash decision, Dharaadhar said, "Look, we can't ignore the fact that the country happens to be under Muslim rule. Given the implied predominance of that community, I don't consider it wise to make an enemy of the Nawaab."

Dharaadhar was still looking at their faces, trying to gauge their reaction, when *Munshii* JaTeshvar Laal spoke up to reinforce his voice of reason, "Pyaare has without doubt risked his life any number of times to prove his loyalty and devotion to you all, and we do indeed owe him a debt of gratitude for it. And yet, it would be unwise on our part to react without taking into account the realpolitik of the day, or the fact of Nawaab Saahib having access to the imperial court. Ancient texts also advise that in a situation such as this, one must act having due regard to the elements of time and space. I, for once, would think it wise not to get bogged down in sentiments, and so, would advise you similarly to make a compromise."

Listening to the old man's advice of prudence, which he obviously considered cowardly, Shri Raam was boiling over inside. Indeed, he felt that the suggested compromise involved a complete negation of principles. Yet, trying to keep his temper in check, he said, "Uncle *Munshii*, I hope you aren't suggesting that we handover Pyaare to the Nawaab's messenger."

Before the old aide could respond, Dharaadhar interjected, "Shri Raam, you said it! That's exactly what Uncle meant. We should let the messenger take Pyaare. As the family elder, I, too, think that this would be in our best interest." Shri Raam, short-tempered by nature, could no longer keep his cool and retorted tartly, "All right then, brother, go right ahead and do what you think best, but let me tell you something plainly: it's not just about Pyaare. I think it's an abject surrender to the Nawaab's unjust demand. Today he's enamoured of Pyaare and asking to have him, next he'll want to have LaaDlii, and then perhaps our family women...."

Dharaadhar hotly interrupted Shri Raam at this point, "What nonsense are you blabbering, Shri Raam. Are you out of your mind?"

Shri Raam said no more and walked out. Raadhey Shyaam also seemed to agree with him and left the audience-hall sullenly. The room was suddenly so quiet you could hear a pin drop. Dharaadhar sank deeper into his predicament. Being responsible for the entire family, he clearly didn't want to be carried away by sentiments which might put them all at grave risk. Sure enough, he was reluctant himself to part with Pyaare. He took great pride in Pyaare and LaaDlii and well knew that everyone in the family would hate to lose either of them. He had already had a measure of their likely reaction, having heard Shri Raam and Raadhey and seen their near-rebellious behaviour. Even so, he eventually decided to let Pyaare be made over to the Nawaab's man.

Uncanny as it might seem, Pyaare by this time had sensed what was in store for him. He was not letting anyone come anywhere near him, cleverly eluding several *Deorhii* servants desperately trying to catch hold of him. When cornered by them, he would run inside the *havelii* and cling to the legs of family ladies. So much so that breaking all rules, he even mounted *MaaN Jii*'s sacred platform in the inner courtyard – a transgression he had never before committed – trying to hole up there as if seeking asylum with her. *MaaN Jii*, Dharaadhar Thaakur's mother, was quite flabbergasted; what the devil could have happened to Pyaare for him to be behaving in this manner, she wondered. But when she wised up to the reason for Pyaare's unprecedented behaviour, her eyes welled up. Eventually, when all efforts to get the frightened beast had failed, Dharaadhar Thaakur was compelled to take matters in hand himself. He called out aloud to Pyaare by name twice. That was it! The dog ran to him without demur and started cowering at his feet, whimpering. Dharaadhar's eyes filled with tears; he collared Pyaare and, with a heavy heart, handed over the leash to the Nawaab's man. Indeed, he felt as if his heart would break at the silent protest in the pleading eyes and squirming torso of his pet. After seeing Pyaare off, he headed straight to his private quarters, and having secured the latch from inside, lay down on his bed hating himself for his helplessness.

No one touched a morsel of food in the *Deorhii* that day. Everyone seemed to grieve as though a dear family member had died. LaaDlii's condition was the most serious; she lay comatose in a remote corner of the house in self-imposed solitary confinement, refusing to eat or drink at all. Everyone worried for her, fearing she would die grieving for Pyaare. But time, they say, is a great healer. Within the space of a few days, everything seemed to have returned to 'business as usual'.

❋❋❋

It was late afternoon by the time the dispatch-rider arrived at the Nawaab's palace with Pyaare in tow. Salaamat Khaan was as usual ensconced in his private chamber, eagerly awaiting Pyaare. He was just about to lose patience when he was told that Pyaare was there. He jumped for joy like a child who had just got a much-awaited toy. Asking Nusrat to follow him, he said, "Let's go and welcome Pyaare. Having waited for him all day, we do deserve a glance at him straightaway."

They walked into the porch facing the forecourt of the palace where the messenger stood with Pyaare, leash in hand. Ghulaam Sarvar was already there. Seeing him, the Nawaab appeared about to say something to him but changed his mind and moved ahead. After taking a good look at the dog, he turned to Nusrat and said, "It does indeed appear to be a rare dog as you'd said. As for its exploits, we'll have to wait and see, won't we?"

The Nawaab then began to move slowly around Pyaare, apparently viewing his new acquisition from different angles. Then he stopped abruptly, seeming to remember something important and addressed the dispatch-rider who had brought Pyaare from Singhwaar, "This moment onwards you will take care of Pyaare; make sure he doesn't want for anything and is made so comfortable he forgets his old masters."

Having so instructed the servant, the Nawaab resumed circling around the dog, lovingly appreciating his new toy. After several more rounds, he told Pyaare's recently appointed handler, "He looks tired from the journey; go, make arrangements for him to rest. And give him what he wants to eat, whenever, whatever! We shall see to the rest later."

Salaamat Khaan then returned to the private pleasure-chamber where he usually spent his evenings, flopping down against the bolsters of his *masnad*. A few sips of wine and a *biiDaa* of *paan* later, he said to Nusrat in an elated tone, "*MiaaN*, I cannot tell you how happy I am today. The acquisition of something as rare as Pyaare does call for a celebration. But be forewarned, my brother, your hackneyed *Daastaan-e-Alif-Lailaa* just won't do!"

Nusrat, too, replied in an equally jubilant tone, "Of course, we must have a celebration, and indeed I've no intention of reciting a *daastaan*. I'm at your command, whom shall I present this evening – Chaand Baai or Rehaanaa or Nuurjahaan? Actually, for several days now, Rehaanaa has been pining to serve Your Highness. Shall I call her?"

Taking the pipe of the hookaah in hand, the Nawaab chuckled merrily and said, "They say the worth of one's wife's brother is more than the rest of the world, Nusrat *MiaaN*! I must defer to your preference then, mustn't I? And truth to tell, my dear man, Chaand Baai or Rehaanaa or Nuurjahaan, they are all the same to me." The Nawaab laughed out aloud as though he had cracked a joke.

Salaamat Khaan was indeed bursting at the seams in good cheer at having acquired Pyaare's ownership. In fact, the celebrations kicked off with Rehaanaa Baai reciting ghazals that evening, went on for weeks. The sequence of drinking bouts followed by feasts and *mujraas*, often overlapping one another, seemed endless. But as soon as it finally ended, it was time to put Pyaare to test. The Nawaab ordered an elaborate hunting expedition to be organised and invited all his friends and peers – the neighbouring Nawaabs, tallukedaars and landed gentry – to participate in it. He was dying to show off Pyaare's accomplishments and gather congratulations from connoisseurs. The way he had been going on about his wonderful new asset, his guests could hardly wait to watch Pyaare's exploits.

The hunting party left for the forest with each participant in his full regalia and retinue in keeping with his status. Pyaare expensively caparisoned and on a brand-new leash, trudged along too. But alas! Pyaare was no longer the Pyaare of yore; indeed, he was on the verge of belying the reason for all the attention being showered on him. Being separated from LaaDlii, the source of his inspiration and prowess, he had been reduced to a mere shadow of his former self. Besides, as the once active canine had been kept leashed night and day for quite some time past, his alertness had vanished for lack of exercise. He no longer possessed either the morale or the will to risk his all for the master. Indeed, he was so crestfallen, he didn't even look sharp, far less bark menacingly.

As the party entered dense jungle, Pyaare was unleashed, but after dawdling around for a bit, he went off to sit quietly by a shrub. No amount of goading could persuade him to show the least interest in the proceedings or get up to move from where he had chosen to lie. Salaamat Khaan's peers, waiting to witness the wonder canine in action, were sorely disappointed and some even began to snicker after a while. The Nawaab didn't quite know which way to look. The moment he was back in his palace, he blew a fuse and started berating Nusrat in the foulest of terms and choicest expletives, "Damn you, Nusrat! Do you think I provide for your entire bloody family so lavishly just for you to humiliate me before my friends?"

What could Nusrat say! He was quite stunned himself. Had all those tales of Pyaare's exploits been lies? No, that couldn't be right. He kept turning over the matter in his mind as he waited for the Nawaab's temper to cool off. The moment he thought he could edge a word in, he said gingerly, "Sire, I'm most ashamed of it all myself, but could I say that perhaps you didn't pay attention to all I'd said. You'd recall that I'd also mentioned a bitch along with Pyaare as its companion in his outings."

"Yes...you had at that, now that I think back. So?"

"Nawaab Saahib, allow me to explain. What if Pyaare is only a dog! Would he not be distraught at being parted with his beloved?"

Now Nusrat had his master's attention. Salaamat, who had so far been lying listless on his *masnad*, perked up at once on hearing of a likely amorous angle. Taking a few sips of wine, followed by a fresh *biiDaa* of *paan* stuffed in his mouth, the Nawaab said, "*MiaaN*, if that's the problem, then think of a way to get hold of the bitch as well. So, there you are!"

"Well, Sire, what's there to 'think' in it? Just send for the Vizier and order him to dispatch a rider post-haste to Singhwaar asking for the bitch as well. It has a lovely name... aaah... yes, LaaDlii it is! If Ghulaam can't handle even this, he's hardly worth his keep."

"You are damn right. I'll have him over this moment," said the Nawaab, clapping twice to call the attendant. After a while, Ghulaam Sarvar showed up and was ordered to send a messenger to Singhwaar, asking for LaaDlii this time.

The Vizier did not like the idea at all and tried his best to plead against it, but the Nawaab was adamant. Indeed, hearing the old Vizier say it would amount to insulting the Thaakurs of Singhwaar to ask for the bitch, he was so furious that he threatened him with immediate dismissal, his vast experience notwithstanding. Ghulaam was left with no option but to dispatch the letter to Singhwaar with a messenger asking for LaaDlii to be sent with him.

❋❋❋

When Dharaadhar Thaakur was informed of another messenger from Waariaul, he was assailed by worrisome apprehension. Having read the letter, the first thing that flashed through his mind was Shri Raam saying on the last occasion, 'Being enamoured of Pyaare's reputation today, he's asked for him; up next, he'll be demanding LaaDlii, and then perhaps…' The letter left Dharaadhar in a towering rage; he recoiled even from the thought of what Shri Raam had been about to say. Surrendering LaaDlii to the Nawaab's man, a compromise sans principles, was out of question. Everyone in the family down to the last man, or woman for that matter, was opposed to the very idea. This time around, *Munshii* JaTeshvar Laal also kept his counsel, saying nothing.

The Waariaul messenger went back with nothing to show for his trip to Singhwaar and back. As the Nawaab came to know of it, his fury knew no bounds; he simply went berserk. Summoning the poor Vizier, he pounced on him without giving him a chance to explain.

"A disloyal nincompoop, that's what you are, Ghulaam! I've left my realm for you to do as you please with it, never interfering. And what do I get in return for all that? Nothing at all! You can't even handle a simple errand like this. A messenger from the great Nawaab of Waariaul returning empty-handed! I feel as if I'm getting buried alive for shame. As for you, you have no shame at all. Well, let me then make it absolutely clear: I'm not letting this pass. Even if I have to travel all the way to Delhi to get help, I'll make these *kaafirs* pay for their insolence. Who do they think they are! I shall destroy them; wipe the entire lot of them from the face of the earth."

Shouting loudly in anger had left the Nawaab breathing heavily and coughing. He paused to regain his composure, and as usual, also to take a few sips of wine to help things along. Then he addressed his Vizier in a fairly even tone, 'Ghulaam Sarvar, you know what, you should visit

Dharaadhar in person and counsel him. It'd be in his own interest to maintain the cordial relations our two families have enjoyed for generations. He can't be so dumb as to ruin it all simply over a bitch!"

It was after ages that the old Vizier had seen his master in such a mad rage, and wanting to soothe him, he said, "Your Highness, I can't bear to see you so worried. As an old servant of yours, I wouldn't take your words to heart. Believe you me, Sire, and God is my witness, that I wouldn't hesitate a moment to risk even my life in your service. I swear my undying allegiance on the Holy Qur'aan."

By now the Nawaab had his temper under control and sat down on his *masnad*. Seeing him make his usual sign to the courtesan for a goblet of wine, the Vizier decided that this was his opportunity to ingratiate himself back into his master's favour.

"I know Your Highness must have the bitch," he said "and I shall be the one to bring it to you. I'll go to Singhwaar myself and persuade the Thaakur to yield whatever it takes. Rest assured, I'll come back with the bitch."

The Nawaab trusted the capabilities of his aide. He softened and said, "Why are you still standing, Ghulaam, do take a seat, my dear fellow! How can I help being mad. I didn't expect such bad form of the Thaakurs. You're a witness to the embarrassment this bastard Pyaare caused me in front of my peers. I can bear no more of it; I must have the bitch at all cost. I must show my friends that I'm nobody's fool; I have to retrieve my reputation as a connoisseur of rare things. Leave for Singhwaar as soon as you can, if possible, today. Try to reason with the Thaakurs, but don't hesitate to threaten them in case they refuse to listen. You could ask them to name a price if it's money they're after. They are welcome to have whatever they want but make sure you don't return without the bitch."

Ghulaam Sarvar had the uncomfortable sense of being placed between the devil and the deep sea. He was distressed at the prospect of bringing an insulting proposition to the Thaakurs, but he was in a no-win situation. Escorted by a posse of bodyguards, he left for Singhwaar at dawn the following day.

❋❋❋

Familiar as he was with the Nawaab Waariaul's traits, Dharaadhar Thaakur knew only too well that Salaamat Khaan was not the one to sit quiet for long at his man being sent back empty-handed. He was still waiting to see the Nawaab's next move, when he was told of the arrival of Ghulaam Sarvar. The Vizier was welcomed as a special guest and seated in the main audience hall of the *Deorhii*. As they faced each other, Dharaadhar asked after the well-being of Nawaab Saahib and his family, observing customary courtesies, and then politely asked the Vizier the reason for the 'pleasant surprise' of his visit.

The Vizier, obviously moved by the tenor of Dharaadhar Thaakur's reception, said plaintively, "Is this not my home to visit whenever I feel like it, Sir?"

Dharaadhar promptly parried, saying, "Of course, it is, but busy as you are with your numerous responsibilities, there has to be a reason for you to be taking the trouble to visit personally, Vizier Saahib."

"Sir, there is but one reason only," replied Ghulaam Sarvar.

Although Dharaadhar was well aware of what it was all about, he pretended otherwise, saying innocently, "Do please tell me, Vizier."

"Look Thaakur Saahib, I don't want to see the relations between your two families to be strained over petty issues. You're known for your wisdom; I'm sure you appreciate the sensitivities of the overall situation and would make your decision accordingly. The fact of the matter is, sir, that Nawaab Saahib was deeply offended at his messenger being sent back empty-handed. Indeed, he was so provoked that he'd have taken steps that would have proved irreparably detrimental to mutual relations."

Having made his preliminaries, the Vizier looked around the audience hall, his glance finally settling on an impressive, multicoloured fresco of *Mahishaasura-mardinii Durgaa* with ten arms, painted on one of the walls by a master hand. After seeming to scan the fresco for a while, Ghulaam Sarvar went on, "Thaakur Saahib, you're well aware of how dangerous Nawaab Salaamat Khaan's obstinacy can be. He's so stubborn as to be incapable of resting until he has what he wants, regardless of the consequences. You also know how difficult he can be when provoked. Indeed, it took me hours of counselling against hasty decisions, and to bring him around to see reason. Now, sir, the matter is entirely in your hands. I'd only request you to make your decision after due deliberation on your part."

Continuing the charade of ignorance, Dharaadhar parried, "I've no idea what you are talking about, Vizier Saahib!"

Ghulaam Sarvar said in a somewhat disappointed tone, "Sir, I was always told that a hint is enough for men of wisdom, but if plain-speaking is what you want, so be it. Nawaab Saahib wants the bitch without whose company the dog you sent proved worthless."

"Well, the bitch as you call her has a name, she's called LaaDlii. For you and your master, she may be a mere bitch but to us she's like a family member. As for our regard for Nawaab Saahib, if we didn't hold him in high esteem, would we have handed Pyaare over to your man? After all, true to name, he was also very dear to us," said Dharaadhar in an even tone.

"Why are you objecting to hand over the bitch then?" asked Ghulaam Sarvar.

"Precisely because she's a bitch!" replied Dharaadhar.

Ghulaam Sarvar was quite flummoxed. "Excuse me, I don't get you," he said.

Dharaadhar chuckled, giving him back a bit of his own medicine, "I thought you'd have got my hint since you said it usually suffices for men of wisdom. Well, if it didn't, let me come clean and state unambiguously that we will not hand over LaaDlii, regardless of the consequences."

"But I'm curious to know the reason that makes you so adamant," said the Vizier.

"Because I can't make a compromise that runs counter to my principles," said Dharaadhar.

"But, sir, I quite fail to understand what principle you are talking about here?" Ghulaam Sarvar looked genuinely confused.

Dharaadhar, looking at the Vizier in the eye, replied slowly, as though pointing at each word while explaining a theorem to a child, "The principle involved here is that LaaDlii is a female dog and we have brought her up in the family. Now, is it clear why we can't hand her over to you?"

The Vizier took a deep breath of understanding, and said, "Oh, so that's the case!"

"Yes sir, that's exactly the case," said Dharaadhar with finality, holding the gaze of the older man. Then reverting to his usual affability, he added, "You're like a family elder to me. Be fair and tell me, shouldn't Nawaab Saahib defer to our sentiments, or are we asking for too much?"

Sidestepping Dharaadhar's question, the Vizier assumed an ominous tone, saying, "Now, you listen to me, Nawaab Saahib has access to the imperial court in Delhi."

"I'm quite aware of it. Either his uncle's or his aunt's daughter is a resident of the imperial harem. So?" replied Dharaadhar.

"Thaakur Saahib, allow me for once to forewarn you: were I to return with nothing to show for this visit, like our messenger earlier on, God alone knows what might happen. I'm afraid it won't be possible then for anyone to rein in Nawaab Saahib's fury."

"You're not only a respected elder, Vizier Saahib, but also a man of considerable experience. I'm sure you're aware that we Hindus believe that the day of one's death is determined the very moment one is born. We aren't afraid of dying. It's inevitable that every living being must die sooner or later. A day will come when neither I nor you, nor Nawaab Saahib will be around; who has ever escaped the ultimate truth of mortality! Our ancestors always taught us to go through life holding one's head held high, or else regard it as a burden, ready to sacrifice it for the sake of family honour and principle."

"So long, then," said Ghulaam Sarvar, preparing to leave, "but beware you'll pay heavily for this."

Dharaadhar also rose to his feet, showing the departing envoy due courtesy to the hilt, and replied, "Well, allow me to say this, too, then: as long as I or any one of my brothers live, no power on earth can make us part with LaaDlii. Still I'd plead with you not to let Nawaab Saahib get carried away by trappings of wealth and power and hurt our sentiments. That won't be good for him either."

Having failed to get the job done, as he had confidently hoped he would, Ghulaam Sarvar started back for Waariaul in a terrible mood. Indeed, he was so put off with his failure, he began to feel as though Dharaadhar Thaakur had insulted him rather than his master. He had not expected to be refused so pointedly by him. All the way back home, he kept making plans to get even with the conceited Thaakur, as he now saw Dharaadhar, and by the time he reached Waariaul, he was ready with one.

After seeing Ghulaam Sarvar off, Dharaadhar followed by *Munshii* JaTeshvar Laal returned to the audience hall.

"This is not an ordinary matter any longer. We'll have to be on our guard now. The Vizier's attitude was worrisome," said the *Munshii*.

Dharaadhar tried to play down the seriousness of the matter.

"Uncle *Munshii*, you heard all that was said between us. Did I say anything improper to him?"

"There's hardly any point debating what's already done. The word that has exited the lips and the arrow that has left the bow are both beyond recall. We must focus on what lies ahead," advised JaTeshvar.

Deferring to the old aide's advice, Dharaadhar asked, "All right then, what do you suggest we do?"

"I think we should identify some intelligent and alert young fellows quickly and station them at Waariaul clandestinely for a time to keep us secretly posted on any suspicious developments there."

"Do you know of any such men willing to work for us?" asked Dharaadhar.

"Yes, I do know several such men, suitable not only for what we have in mind but also with relatives at Waariaul. They can go and stay with them and keep a close watch on whatever's new and report to us." Rising from his seat, the *Munshii* added, "I'll see to the arrangements and send them over to Waariaul as soon as possible."

Soon after he left, the younger brothers of Dharaadhar joined him in the audience hall.

"Come, sit," said Dharaadhar, welcoming them affectionately. The two came and sat down near him. For an awkwardly long moment, no one said anything. Finally, Shri Ram broke the ice, "*Bhaiyaa*, there's no point in worrying about it now. We must be prepared for the worst."

"You're right," said Dharaadhar looking at Shri Raam with appreciation. "What good is worrying? We'll cross the bridge when we come to it."

As word spread about the disagreement with Waariaul, the apprehension of events taking an ominous turn threw a pall of gloom over Singhwaar. The villagers worried about the possibility of an armed assault and its likely outcome. The security around the *Deorhii* was reinforced. The weaponry collected inside the *havelii* started being inspected and sharpened in anticipation of a possible assault. All customary festivities were put on hold for the time-being. Apart from his own family, Dharaadhar felt responsible for the well-being of the village-folk at large, and tended to worry all the time, regardless of what he had told Shri Raam.

***

Nawaab Salaamat Khaan was more furious than he had been in a long time when he was told that the Vizier had returned empty-handed, too. Shouting and cursing angrily, he caught hold of the lapels of the Vizier's robe, shaking him violently. Ghulaam Sarvar had little to say by way of explanation. He just stood there in silence, with a hangdog expression on his face.

"You had promised to bring the bitch with you. So, where the hell is it? Do you have nothing to say?" the Nawaab screamed at him. His aide's continuing silence provoked him even more. He shouted louder, "You think you're a Vizier, and take pride in your wisdom! Those piddly Thaakurs have insulted me; if you can't extract revenge for it, I'll wring your neck. I'll have you buried alive, Ghulaam!"

The old Nawaab was gasping for sheer rage and eventually slumped on his *masnad*, and as was his wont, after a few sips of wine and a fresh dose of *paan*, his temper began to cool down.

The Vizier had only been waiting for such an opportunity, and now launched his defense, saying, "Your Highness, I admit I was sadly mistaken as to the true character of the Singhwaar Thaakurs. I always took them for an unassuming, simple-minded lot, but I know better now. The Singhwaar *Deorhii* is nothing but a snake-pit!"

"Go, crush the viper's head before it raises its hood to strike," replied the Nawaab.

"That's what we'll do now," said the Vizier, sighing audibly as though in deep anguish, "I'm not sad to return empty-handed. What really hurt was the Thaakur's pomposity and all that he said while turning down our request. Who does he really think he is?"

"So, what exactly did say? I can't wait to hear it," said the Nawaab, apparently stung by curiosity.

"Dharaadhar Thakur said 'Unlike Pyaare, LaaDlii is a bitch; it's obvious she's a female, and having been brought up like a family member as she has been, how can we hand her over to you?" replied the Vizier.

This detail of Ghulaam Sarvar's conversation incensed the Nawaab even more. He went red in the face and erupted venomously, "How dare he? Is it a crime to be a *Mussalmaan*? So, we aren't good enough even for a bitch reared in a Hindu household? This is preposterous! Absolutely unacceptable! Ghulaam, take as many commandos as you please and leave this very moment for Singhwaar; order a no-holds-barred massacre. Let our elephants run amok in the *Deorhii*, reduce it to rubble and burn down the village. Before they have time to organise any defence, mount an attack and destroy them. I have access to the imperial court and shan't spare these *kaafirs*. Do you hear me, Ghulaam, go now!"

The Vizier raised his hand, palm outwards, grave as a Buddha and replied, "Sire, you needn't put yourself to avoidable strain. I'm determined to avenge the affront, and make such an example of them that no one will dare defy us ever again. Do please trust me; I shan't rest in peace until I have the bitch at your feet. But Your Highness, I need a little time to put my plan into action."

"All right," replied the Nawaab, mollified by the Vizier's vociferous assurance; the latter's policy of waiting for the opportune moment had paid off again. The Vizier now pressed his advantage, saying, "Your Highness, I've another little submission to make."

"Speak!" said the Nawaab.

"You will say no more on the subject to anyone. Just keep calm and let me handle everything at my own pace."

"Sarvar," said the Nawaab, quite pacified by now, "I've always trusted you. Do I ever interfere in what you do? I'll keep quiet in this matter as well. But don't forget, the Thaakur has insulted the whole community and we must have our revenge. Don't ever come back to me with excuses. Or I'll have your head instead!

"Sire, I have already thought of a plan. Just you wait and see how I go about it." With that the Vizier took leave of his master and left the room.

Days passed uneventfully and turned into placid months. Nothing out of the ordinary seemed to happen, the Vizier apparently engaged in his usual routine and the Nawaab lapsing back into his fun and frolics. As the under-cover agents, deputed by *Munshii* JaTeshvar Laal, had no training or previous experience of handling such assignments, they had little of consequence to report. To be fair to them, though, nothing much was actually happening on the surface, and it was quite simply beyond them to ferret out what a wily old fox like Ghulaam Sarvar was doing secretly. Eventually, with nothing much to report, they were recalled.

***

It was close to a year since the Vizier's visit to the *Deorhii*. Dharaadhar had almost forgotten his disagreement with Ghulaam Sarvar, and was beginning to think that the danger of retaliation had blown over. He was, however, sadly mistaken. Ghulaam Sarvar had over time persuaded himself to believe that the Thaakur had insulted him even more than his master and was determined on revenge, teaching him a lesson he would never forget. Stealth was a necessary part of his secret plan. He misled everyone into thinking that the whole thing had been forgotten, but he had been scheming secretly ever since his return from Singhwaar. He had a letter drafted from the Nawaab to the Mughal *Subedaar* at PaaTaliputra charging Dharaadhar Thakur with made-up allegations of such a communal nature as were bound to raise the heckles of any *Mussalmaan*. He had another letter ready from the Nawaab addressed to his cousin in the imperial harem, soliciting her help in putting down the Singhwaar Thaakurs.

Although Ghulaam Sarvar detested Nusrat, he selected him as the Nawaab's emissary to carry the letters and deliver them personally for the simple reason that as a member of his master's family, he would have easy access at both PaaTaliputra and the imperial capital.

As was to be expected, the provincial *Subedaar* was enraged on reading the Nawaab's letter depicting Dharaadhar Thaakur as a bigoted, seditious renegade who trampled upon the Muslims in his estate, clandestinely incited the Hindus in the Nawaab's domain and defaulted on remittances of revenues owed to the imperial treasury, besides secretly planning to raise the standard of revolt against the emperor. When the *Subedaar* learnt that Nusrat was on his way to deliver a letter to the Nawaab's cousin – of whom he had of course heard – he offered to go with Nusrat to facilitate his mission. Nusrat's life was made. The *Subedaar* took him straight to the highest echelons in the imperial bureaucracy and military, helping him paint Dharaadhar as a trouble-maker and a potential threat to imperial authority in the region. The response was swift, and far in excess of expectation, presumably on account of the personal intercession of provincial governor. A contingent of a hundred crack soldiers led by a veteran commander of the Mughal Army was deputed forthwith to go and 'see to the matter'.

After riding hard for almost a fortnight at breakneck speed, the Mughal contingent reached the outskirts of Singhwaar at sundown on the fourteenth day. The commander called a halt, ordering his troops to make camp there, and left with Nusrat to see the Nawaab and his Vizier; he was under orders to consult them before taking any action.

Meanwhile, the fact of a heavily armed contingent of Mughal soldiers camping at the village perimeter couldn't possibly remain a secret; it spread like wildfire. Alarmed village-folk began to gather at the *Deorhii*. Dharaadhar was momentarily overwhelmed with worry at the sudden turn of events which had taken him unawares. As things stood, he had only two options before him, to either surrender or take on the might of the Mughal troops. In reality, the latter was the sole option as he had no intention whatsoever of giving in to blackmail. Neither had he any illusions about what would happen even if he surrendered.

It was not as if Dharaadhar was unaware of the likely outcome of armed conflict with the highly trained and far better equipped Mughal troops, given the woefully limited resources at his command. Setting aside the thought of the intimidating prospect, however, he proceeded to address the gathering of villagers, "Folks, whether or not you're aware of the reason for the Mughals coming at us, I know it well enough. They are here to put me and my family to sword. It's also likely they want to plunder the *Deorhii*, and if that's not enough of revenge, they might even torch the village."

Before Dharaadhar could go on, an old villager, Bholaa Mandal by name, stood up leaning on his bamboo-staff, and asked, "*Anna-daataa*, what's your fault? What on earth have you done to harm them?"

"My fault?" Dharaadhar paused for a moment, thinking, and then briefly recapitulating the sequence of events, from the unjust demands of Nawaab Waariaul to sending back the Vizier without LaaDlii, he sighed and added, "I'm not as worried for myself as I am for you. You all are needlessly trapped in a potentially dangerous situation. I don't want you to perish with me. There's still time for those of you who wish to get out of harm's way; you're free to leave before the Mughals attack the village. My brothers and I shall, of course, defend the *Deorhii* to the last breath. If we ran away, the spirit of our ancestors would never forgive our cowardice." Bholaa Mandal, still leaning on his cane, exclaimed, "Master, you're our *anna-daataa*. Your ancestors were the ones who brought this settlement into being. For generations, we've lived on the bounty of this *Deorhii*. Now that we have a chance to repay our debt, how could we possibly flee the village, leaving you in the lurch? Anyone who even thinks of deserting you wouldn't find refuge even in hell!"

Dharaadhar was deeply moved at this show of solidarity, but before he could thank them, some fifty or so villagers stood up, chorusing in unison, "Master, we're all with you in this; the entire village is at your command; you just have to show us the way."

Having thanked them sincerely, Dharaadhar said, "Before we discuss our strategy, we must consider how to protect the lives and honour of our women-folk and children. There's no knowing what barbaric bestiality they might have to suffer if they were to fall into enemy hands. It would be best for you to send them away somewhere far, and the old or sick must leave forthwith to stay with relatives until this whole thing has passed over. They must also take with them all the valuables and cattle they can. Only able-bodied adults willing to risk their lives need stay here. Now, go home and carry out my instructions with dispatch. The Mughals might attack any time now. The time is short and there's so much to be done. I'll repeat, however, that only those of you prepared to lay down their lives defending our beloved village should remain. For all others, there's still plenty of time to get away."

Dharaadhar, accompanied by his two brothers, returned to the audience-hall where *Munshii* JaTeshvar Laal and the entire *Deorhii* retinue awaited them.

"Uncle *Munshii*, I must forewarn you that, in the circumstances, it's no longer safe to be here; it's as if you were courting death by choice. Those of you who wish to leave have my permission to do so," said Dharaadhar.

None of them, however, agreed to leave his side.

□

2
The Massacre at the Deorhii

A group of about two hundred fifty young men, led by Kaashii Nath and Sadaashiva, the two sons of *Baabaa* Shambhuu Naath, left KaTkaa to reinforce the defence of Singhwaar *Deorhii*, loudly chorusing slogans like *Har-har Mahaadeva, Bajrangbalii kii jai, Dharaadhar Bhaiyaa ghabraanaa mat, ham tumhaare saath hain* et al. The Katkaa contingent had swollen to twice its size by the time it reached the outskirts of Singhwaar.

Whether by chance or divine intervention, the Mughal commander decided on a *shabKhuun* assault, a stratagem of taking the quarry by surprise late at night, giving precious additional time to Dharaadhar to fine-tune his strategy of defending the *Deorhii*. He planned to surprise the attackers, too, by deploying a group to counter-attack from the rear.

The imperial troops met with far greater resistance than they had expected, many of the soldiers losing their lives or escaping with serious injuries that would incapacitate them for life.

The KaTkaa contingent closed on the *Deorhii* just as the attackers, having slaughtered the defenders to the last man, were about to begin plundering the big house. The Mughals heard the chorus of slogans, amplified by the silence of the night, loud and clear, though the KaTkkaa'ians were still some distance away. Having already suffered more casualties than they had imagined possible, the troopers were so disconcerted by this unexpected development, they decided discretion was the better part of valour and beat a hasty retreat, carrying the bodies of their slain, and injured comrades.

When the KaTkkaa'ians entered Singhwaar, it was eerily quiet and deserted, silent as a tomb. They wondered whether Dharaadhar Thaakur and his kin had abandoned the *Deorhii* and fled. They could only be sure one way or the other on reaching the *havelii*; so they quickly headed in that direction.

As the KaTkaa men set foot in the front courtyard of the *havelii*, they were petrified to find it thickly littered with dead bodies, innumerable rivulets of blood flowing in every direction. Kaashii Naath, leading the KaTkaa contingent, was so distressed by the gory sight, he all but threw up, besides feeling guilty for arriving too late to prevent the carnage. Alas! that was something in the past and could not be undone. He said to Sadaashiva, his younger brother, "I wonder why Dharaadhar didn't inform us in time. We would certainly have made it here in the time it took Bhavaanii Bahuu to walk to KaTkaa."

"Why he didn't and what might have happened if he had are like ifs and buts of history, *Bhaiyaa*! We would do well to concentrate on what lies ahead," replied the pragmatic Sadaashiva.

"What do you suggest then?"

"To begin with, we had better take a closer look at other parts of the *havelii*," replied Sadaashiva.

Kaashii Naath nodded in agreement, and asking the others to wait they went inside the sprawling *havelii* with Sadaashiva and Naageshvara, a close childhood friend.

Wherever they looked, there were heart-rending scenes of the aftermath of the most brutal carnage. Seemingly innumerable corpses of women and young children, blood still oozing out of their fatal wounds or severed heads or limbs, lay strewn all over the place in the inner apartments. On closer inspection, they noticed that most of them seemed to have been beheaded by a single, hefty stroke of a sword or some other sharp weapon. Kaashii Naath exclaimed, tears choking his voice, "If we had arrived even a few minutes later than we did, the Mughal soldiers would certainly have robbed the dead of their ornaments; the bodies of family ladies and children still having their jewellery on shows that they had no time for looting after the massacre."

"You're perhaps right, *Bhaiyaa*, but don't you think there's something very odd here?" asked Sadaashiva.

"What's that?"

"Well, if the Mughals killed them, they could also have robbed them simultaneously. Who else could be responsible for such ghastly mayhem if not them?"

"You might have a point, but at the moment, we have neither enough time, nor are we in a proper frame of mind to unravel this puzzle. Bhavaanii Bahuu is the only one who might perhaps have a clue," said Kaashii Naath, then sighing pensively, he added, "Let's go and have a look at the outer annex."

Walking towards the audience hall, suddenly Naageshvara gasped and exclaimed, "Kaashii, look .... Look at the porch there, it appears there's a headless body of a dog lying there... there to your right, can you see?" The three of them turned and walked towards it. Having looked at it closely, Sadaashiva said, "It's a bitch!" and proceeded to take a peek into the audience hall, crying out aloud in a horrified tone, "*Bhaiyyaaaa*...! Come and look at this. Good heavens!"

As Kaashii stepped inside the audience hall, he was so horrified at what he saw that his distress, building up since arriving at the *havelii*, burst forth like a breached dam. He ran to the mutilated body of Dharaadhar Thaakur and began to cry and lament inconsolably, taking the lifeless body of his kin in his arms. It was a hair-raising sight indeed. Dharaadhar's arms and legs had been bound by thick cords, used for hanging convicts, to the pillars set against the wall in the shape of the letter X and his head and torso had been cut right down the middle to the waist into two equal halves.

The two segments of his upper body sagged forward under their own weight in a horrendous bow.

Both Sadaashiva and Naageshvara stared at the gory tableau, stunned, as though cast in stone. For moments, that felt like centuries, they could think of nothing to say or do. Unlike Kaashii, they kept their composure intact, coping reasonably well in the circumstances. Kaashii, however, went on lamenting and weeping miserably; after a while, Sadaashiva and Naageshvar were beginning to worry over his mental state. It was with some difficulty that they finally brought him around to take heart.

The three of them unbound and brought down the body of Dharaadhar with reverent care owed to a martyred kinsman and laid it out alongside the bodies of his slain siblings and other defenders who had fought with them to their last breath, all laid out on the porch outside the audience hall. Kaashii Naath broke down again, unable to keep his recently regained composure. He sat down next to the dead bodies of Shri Raam and Radhey Shyaam and began to sob uncontrollably. Sadaashiva bore with it patiently for a while, but eventually he approached Kaashii, saying softly but in a firm tone, "*Bhaiyaa*!"

Kaashii looked up at him, his eyes reddened by so much crying. Exhorting him, Sadaashiva went on, "*Bhaiyaa*, the time to lament is over. If you carry on like this, how will we even give them a decent cremation? Take heart and be brave. Everyone's awaiting your instructions. Come on now, get up."

Naageshvar joined in, saying "Sadaashiva is right; whatever's happened can't be undone by lamenting. It's time for you to lead us. After all, *Baabaa* Shambhuu Naath himself entrusted you the responsibility. It's our sacred duty now to arrange for the cremation of these bravehearts according to custom."

Restraining himself with a Herculean effort, Kaashii Naath replied through tears, "Yes, you're right. Arranging for enough firewood for so many will be no mean task."

"We don't have far to go for that. Let's cut down the mango trees around the *havelii* and, of course, we'd have to level the ground by the river for the funeral pyres," said Naageshvara.

"Look here, I don't wish to impose any particular task on anyone; each one of you should decide on your own who's going to do what, and get going," said Kaashii Naath.

Someone among the men volunteered, "Where do we get axes and spades for cutting firewood and levelling the funeral site?"

Before Kaashii could respond, another man in the group replied, "Well, it's such a big mansion! Surely, it will have everything we need. Let's go and explore the cattle-sheds; there must be all varieties of tools in there."

Kaashii Naath breathed easy to find everyone ready to volunteer, rising to tasks in hand, and said to his brother, "Sadaashiva, go inside with some of the men; dead bodies are strewn all over the place, let's have some kind of order, and do make sure the valuables still on them are taken off and given to a trustworthy person for safe-keeping. Look each room over for anything of value. Go and see all this is done with due care."

Sadaashiva nodded his assent and left with some young men. They entered the inner courtyard as directed and placed the dead bodies by the *manDap* after taking off the jewellery on them which were placed in a cloth-bag and entrusted to one of his men. They then began to go through the rooms for other objects of value.

On entering a large room, they were shocked to find a headless female body lying on a fourposter, its severed head lying in a pool of blood underneath. It seemed she had been asleep when beheaded. Sadaashiva was bewildered; how could someone possibly sleep right through the hue and cry of a massacre! Although the clothes and jewellery of the dead woman were very like those of other victims, Sadaashiva found it hard to believe she was a daughter or daughter-in-law of the family. Intrigued, he peered at the corpse and noticed the name Mohini tattooed on the left forearm. It seemed to confirm his gut-feeling, for it was not customary then for women of upper-class families to have their person tattooed. Who this woman could have been, he wondered. He stood thinking about it for a moment, but there was no one about who could tell him anything more, and, in any case, this was hardly a time for an investigation. Eventually, Sadaashiva concluded that whoever Mohini had been, it was clear she must have had an important place in the family.

Having gone over the inner rooms, Sadaashiva and his team entered the *Puujaa-ghar* and were instantly struck dumb; on the raised platform for the family deity – covering nearly a third of the room – called the *Chinvaar*, lay the body of a fair-complexioned, imposing old woman face down on the floor. Of all the female bodies he had seen in the inner quarters, there was none that had its head intact. Unlike the others, a small dagger was embedded in the old lady's chest. It was stained in blood that was beginning to congeal. Sadaashiva felt sure that the imperious looking old woman must have been the mother of the proud Thaakurs of Singhwaar who had died fighting rather than surrender. Overwhelmed by emotion, he bent forward and plucked the dagger out. The dagger was small but very sharp. Before long, he found its sheath lying to a side on the floor; he re-sheathed it and stuck it in his waistband. They carried the old lady's body, and covering it in a white sheet, placed it alongside the others.

❋❋❋

It was afternoon by the time the cremation could begin on the bank of the river behind the *havelii*. It was not possible to arrange for individual pyres for everyone, but they unanimously agreed to have one for Dharaadhar Thaakur, in deference to his status as the head of the family. The rest of the pyres were categories clubbed together: one for other family males; another for family ladies including the lady in the *Puujaa-ghar* and Mohini; yet another for children; and eight more for other defenders who had laid down their lives fighting alongside the lord of the manor. In all, twelve pyres were lit on the site levelled for the purpose. Sadaashiva and his companions also dug a pit some distance away for LaaDlii to be buried.

In a matter of moments, the pyres were ablaze, making the atmosphere solemn and sombre. No one said a word as they stood around, their eyes welling up in grief over the death of so many of their kin.

The sun hung low on the western horizon as the living gathered in the courtyard after the cremation was over. Kaashii Naath thanked everyone for their support, adding, "It was only because of your assistance that we were able to get this important task accomplished, but there remains a lot more to be done before we can head home."

"What more can we do here?" asked Naageshvara.

"Naagesh, if we leave in a hurry without cleaning up the premises, the blood of martyrs is bound to be defiled by stray dogs and the like. Also, the wealth in the *Deorhii* treasury, accumulated over generations, would be easy loot for petty thieves and robbers. We must take care of these things, too, before departing." Then, turning to the men gathered around, he added politely, "Of, course, those of you who have any urgent family commitments are free to leave whenever you want. I'm only asking for a little more time from those who can spare it."

Naageshvara endorsed his friend's exhortation strongly, "I think Kaashii Naath is absolutely right; let's not even think of leaving before we've taken care of these. Alas! we couldn't save their lives; let us at least secure the inheritance of Bhavaanii Bahuu, who's now under our care."

The KaTkaa youth enthusiastically agreed to stay.

Kaashii Naath thanked them all again, and said, "The first thing is to make sure that we are not taken by surprise if the Mughal troops re-group and decide to return to plunder the *havelii*. Some of you should find a few vantage points around here and take turns to keep an eye out for any such movement. Then we must organise some fire-torches to light up the courtyards and porches, and get down to cleaning the place up. And yet another group must begin to cook because the living must eat in order to keep going on." Sadaashiva nodded, and suggested that a courier needed to be sent to KaTkaa to inform *Baabaa* of all that was happening, so that he didn't worry for them. Kaashii agreed, asking him to identify a man and send him over at once.

Soon they got busy with the identified tasks, different groups volunteering for sentry duty, cleaning up the premises and cooking food, while Kaashii Naath sat down with Sadaashiva and Naageshvara to confer on how to secure the large, heavy steel chests and lockers they had found in the *Deorhii* treasury. They surmised these must contain gold and other valuables of the family. Although the room-to-room search had yielded a bunch of keys that looked the right size for the padlocks on the lockers, they didn't think it would be right for them to open them. It was not possible to carry such heavy lockers with them, but they couldn't be left in plain sight either; or else they would be pried open and robbed by the first thief to enter the abandoned *havelii*. After considerable debate, they decided to bury the lockers underground. Accordingly, another team of volunteers was tasked to dig a deep cavernous pit in the inner courtyard that snaked in right underneath the foundations of the *Puujaa-ghar*. They toiled hard round the clock for close on two days but finally it was done. The heavy treasury lockers were put inside and the freshly dug patch was then patted down and camouflaged with shrubs and grass. Important documents, deeds and papers found in the treasury were tied up in a bundle to be taken back to KaTkaa.

After letting the funeral pyres cool for the customary period of three nights, Kaashii and Sadaashiva, being the nearest living blood relatives, gathered the ashes of Dharaadhar Thaakur and his family, and of the other defenders of the *Deorhii*, and putting it in cloth-bags, gave them to some *Braahmana* volunteers for immersion in *Gangaa* and other holy rivers.

The KaTkaa volunteers then began to trudge back home, an exhausted, sombre and leaden-footed lot, each man lost in his thoughts arising out of his background and station in life; some of them were still plagued by flashes of the horrendous scenes of carnage at the *havelii* while others admired the indomitable spirit of Dharaadhar Thaakur and his siblings. Also, several of them, unable to forget the heavy padlocked lockers buried underground, walked absentmindedly, silently estimating the amount of wealth that they must contain.

□

3
Under the Wings of Vana-Durgaa

It was a dark night. *Baabaa* Shambhuu Naath accompanied by five of his servants, all heavily armed, set out for the KaTkaa *chaur*. The men held aloft flaming fire-torches in their hands, as much to light up the way as an insurance against wild animals. None of them was very sanguine about Bhavaanii's new-born being found alive. Surely, by now the wild beasts would have finished with the infant, they thought to themselves. It was more out of a sense of duty than any real expectation that Shambhuu Naath was out with the search party so late in the night. They walked in the general direction given by Bhavaanii, the old man silently praying to his *IshTa-deva* Shiva, 'O Lord of the gods! I have rarely asked anything of you before but I do now. Make it happen that Bhavaanii's new-born is safe and we can restore it to her. You know what depths of despair will claim her should we fail to bring her baby back unharmed.'

Once in the *chaur*, they strode briskly towards the large *mahuaa* tree with a round leafy canopy under which Bhavaanii vaguely remembered to have lain down in labour. As they approached the tree, they spotted a large bird sitting underneath it with its wings spread out. *Baabaa* felt a shiver run down his spine, fearing that the bird might have mutilated the hapless infant with its long beak sharp as steel. Coming a bit closer, he saw that the bird had brown feathers with a ring of white downs around its neck, large eyes and a long curved beak. This wasn't an ordinary bird but a rare species that the locals revered as the embodiment of goddess *Jagdambaa*. The bird sat nonchalantly sheltering the infant's tiny form under its wings. It wasn't clear at that distance whether the baby still lived. As the bird noticed the approaching search party, it turned alert and hawkish.

Shambhuu Naath was closely observing every movement of the bird, too. Presently, it brought its beak to the side of the still form of the infant, as if whispering a secret in some esoteric language of its own. Then it flapped its wings close to the ground as though it was patting the sides of the babe. Shambhuu Naath had no issues with the bird's curious movements thus far, but when it jerked its head, sharply pecking the infant on the forehead, he was alarmed. However, it soon turned out to be a blessing in disguise; the infant, still and silent so far, began to bawl loudly, announcing to the world, as it were, that he was alive and kicking. *Baabaa* felt relief wash over him and his mood lifted. Paying a silent tribute to his *IshTa-deva* for answering his prayer, he strode forward towards Bhavaanii's child, elated. As the bird saw him approach, it took to wings disappearing instantly out of sight. *Baabaa* rushed to the infant and lifted it up, cradling it in his arms. Finding the baby unharmed, he was overwhelmed by tears of joy; and put a *tiikaa* on the infant's forehead from the trickle of blood that had oozed out from where the holy bird had pecked. He couldn't wait to reunite Bhavaanii with her little son, for she had given birth to a bonnie boy.

Shambhuu Naath looked up at the inky, star-spangled night sky and this time he gave his thanks aloud, invoking the goddess *Durgaa* by her various names:

"O Benevolent Mother, *Vana-Durgaa*, the goddess of the Wilderness, O *Bhagvatii Jagdambaa*! You're the one who's saved this child. I, therefore, name this protégé of yours, Jagdambii!"

Hailing *Vana-Durgaa*'s kindness and praising the omnipotence of Mahaadeva, his *IshTa-deva*, *Baabaa* and his men then retraced their steps to KaTkaa, overjoyed at finding Jagdambii not only alive but also unharmed, except for the smallest of cuts on his forehead that would heal in no time.

❋❋❋

It was the twelfth day after the massacre. In keeping with the Hindu tradition, after performing the last rites of the Eleventh and Twelfth days, a feast was organised in the honour of the departed. Most of those invited were the very same people who had been in the team that went to Singhwaar. *Baabaa* Shambhuu Naath stood on his front porch holding Jagdambii in his arms. He politely thanked the village-elders and others leaving after the meal, requesting them to bless the child with long life and to be ever victorious. The departing *Braahmana*s responded with 'Amen' in unison. Feeling deeply gratified, *Baabaa* turned inexplicably thoughtful, still holding baby Jagdambii in his arms. When he came out of his reverie he turned and walked back to the house.

It was close to midnight. The lone earthen wick-lamp on the verandah seemed to be fighting a losing battle against overwhelming darkness all around. The family members, exhausted by countless daily chores of a large rural household, had long retired to their rooms for the night.

As *Baabaa* entered the inner courtyard, he stopped abruptly noticing the silhouette of Bhavaanii sitting on the *manDap*, weeping silently into the night. She didn't hear *Baabaa* come in, being completely oblivious of the present, reliving the days gone by. She felt terribly guilty for having deserted her husband during a time of such adversity. Her conscience tormented her, bluntly repeating the same question over and over: 'Why had she not allowed her to be slain by her husband like the other daughters-in-law of the family?'

Baabaa stood watching her quietly for a few moments. When he could bear her despair no more, he accosted her, "Bahuu!" Bhavaanii turned with a start and stood up, wiping her eyes with her *palluu* and extending her arms to take the sleeping Jagdambii from *Baabaa.* Handing over the baby, Shambhuu Naath said to her, "Bahuu, I want to tell you something, you must heed my advice."

Bhavaanii looked at him, saying nothing, and cast her eyes down the very next instant. *Baabaa* went on, "Anxiety and anguish in a feeding mother are very harmful for the child's development. You've to live solely for Jagdambii now, forgetting the past and focusing on him alone. We're your kin and this is your home. It's very late. You ought to go to bed now. Sitting alone and grieving like this will harm you." With that *Baabaa* turned to leave, invoking the blessings of his *IshTa-Deva* once again. Just then he saw Paaro, his eldest daughter-in-law emerge from her room. Feeling reassured that she would take good care of Bhavaanii, Shambhuu Naath strode away to retire for the night.

Approaching Bhavaanii, Paaro said, "I was so tired from the day's chores I couldn't resist the urge to lie down for a while and was soon fast asleep. When I woke up some time ago and saw your bed empty, I came out directly to find you."

Bhavaanii laughed shyly and said, "Diidii, what did you think? That Bhavaanii has played truant all over again? There's not a chance of that happening, I assure you, Bhavaanii isn't going anywhere; she's here to stay! The support you all gave me in the hour of my great distress was nothing short of a divine intervention. But there's a question that keeps bothering me time and again."

"And what question is that, if I may ask?"

"Haven't I become a burden on your family?" replied Bhavaanii as though thinking aloud.

"Never say such a thing again, Bhavaanii. Do you hear me? Never! You've no idea how hurt *Baabaa* would be to hear you saying this, nor of how much more cheerful and alive he is since you came, particularly after he found and brought back Jagdambii. He had lost interest in worldly matters altogether until the two of you happened along. Now he's back into the thick of it again. He seems inseparable from Jagdambii, so fond he's become of the child. Don't you worry; you're no burden on us at all. It's quite late and time to get some sleep now," said Paaro, motioning Bhavaanii to follow her.

❋❋❋

Baabaa Shambhuu Naath must have been about seventy years of age, but he wore his years lightly and his skin glowed like a man much younger. His vegetarianism, abstemious habits, regularity of daily routine and exercise had all helped to keep him fitter than most men his age. *Baabaa* was quite a disciplinarian. In his younger days, he had had a flourishing business of buying and selling horses, and was a reputed connoisseur of equestrian stock. He was also an expert 'horse-whisperer' and trainer, a skill that opened to him the doors of many nawaabs, princes and other such wealthy and influential personages, who treated him with respect usually given to people with rare talents. Shambhuu Naath had leveraged his expertise to become fairly wealthy himself.

Shambhuu Naath had two sons – Kaashii Naath and Sadaashiva. Being the elder of the two, Kaashii looked after the family lands and property while Sadaashiva worked as a teacher in the local Sanskrit school. *Baabaa* was lucky to be the head of a flourishing household in every way – the family members were disciplined, deferential, polite and affectionate; the daughters-in-law came from good families and the house was cheerful with a host of well-mannered grandchildren. Maarkandeya, the eldest son of Kaashii Naath, already in his late teens, helped with agricultural chores besides looking after livestock and dairying.

Baabaa Shambhuu Naath had a sort of family council in his household. Whenever an issue of importance, big or small, came up, they all gathered with *Baabaa* as their chair; everyone was encouraged to freely air their views and decisions were taken unanimously after carefully considering all the suggestions. On learning that Bhavaanii had indicated her wish to live with them as part of the family, *Baabaa* decided it needed to be discussed in the family council. He had Maarkandeya inform them all of a meeting on the subject.

As *Baabaa* approached the family gathered on the *manDap* in the courtyard, they all rose to their feet to welcome him. After he had returned their greetings with his blessings, he took his seat, with Kaashii Naath, Sadaashiva and Maarkandeya to his right while the family women including Bhavaanii sat down to his left. As the patriarch took in the family, his eyes came to rest on little Jagdambii sleeping in Paaro's lap. Gazing fondly at him for a moment, he said, "Bahuu, can I have him in my lap for a while?" Paaro handed over the child gently to him. *Baabaa* still looking fascinated said to the sleeping baby softly, "You're so lovely, Jagdambii, you have me under a spell. I feel like living on some more. Let me see if I'm able to witness what I want to."

He then opened the discussion saying, "We're here to consider the likely inclusion of two new members. Does anyone have an objection to Bhavaanii Bahuu and Jagdambii living like family with us here for an indefinite period of time?" The gathering replied in the negative.

"Then it follows we'll have to make suitable arrangements for them," said *Baabaa*.

"That goes without saying, *Baabaa*. We'll, of course, have to see that they are made comfortable," rejoined Kaashii.

Thanking everyone, *Baabaa* said, "I expected no less of you. Well, that's why I have decided that Bhavaanii should henceforth use the larger room facing the courtyard."

The room that Shambhuu Naath mentioned had been used by his late wife in her life-time. It had two doors – one opening on the inner courtyard and the other into another room that adjoined the front porch where *Baabaa* spent most of his time. It was a relatively larger room, and also better ventilated and sunny.

"Now that we're all agreed on that, let it be understood that the additional expenses on their account will also be borne by us. Any comments on that?" asked *Baabaa*. They all agreed, but suddenly Bhavaanii spoke up in a small voice, scratchy with restrained emotions, "I wish to say something, too, *Baabaa*!"

"Sure, you'll have your chance, but before that I must ask Kaashii something and assign him an important task", said Shambhuu Naath turning to him. "Kaashii, what did the Mughals and Nawaab Waariaul get for going to all that trouble, besides, of course, slaughtering the Thaakurs?" asked *Baabaa*.

"Precious little by way of loot, I think," replied Kaashii.

"In that case, it's more than likely that they'd have confiscated Dharaadhar's family estate and the *havelii* by way of damages," said *Baabaa*, seeming to be thinking aloud.

"It's quite possible," replied Kaashii

"Hmmm ... Kaashii, I want you to visit Waariaul in cognito and find out the exact status, but take care to maintain total secrecy," said Shambhuu Naath.

"All right, *Baabaa*, I'll begin tomorrow."

"Well, now, it's your turn Bhavaanii Bahuu; go ahead and say what you want without any hesitation," said *Baabaa*, turning to look at her.

"*Baabaa*, the way you took me and my baby in at a time of great adversity and have been sheltering us so magnanimously and with so much affection is something I shan't forget for the rest of my life. But I do not wish to be a burden if I can help it ..." already sounding nasal for suppressed tears, Bhavaanii began to sob, using the *pallu* of her *saarii* to cover half her face and dab at her eyes as well.

They were all touched by her inconsolable sobbing.

"Don't lose heart, Bahuu. How long will you go on weeping! What happened to you was terribly unfortunate but lamenting endlessly is of no use. Nothing would change if you cried for the rest of your life. I tell you once again, forget everything else and live solely for Jagdambii, at least for now. And yes, you wanted to say something, go ahead, unburden yourself," said *Baabaa*.

Trying hard to get a hold on herself, Bhavaanii said, "The misfortune I've suffered, I wouldn't wish even upon an enemy. I lost everything I had: my prospering household, my husband, all my loved ones, all vanished with one cruel stroke of destiny. *Baabaa*, why were the gods so unkind, making me a queen for a handful of days only to be rendered a homeless dependent?" Everyone was deeply moved by her words, but she wasn't done yet, "What can I really say. I'm under your shelter and you must decide as you think fit. However, I'm keen that the expenses incurred on the last rites of my family are met by their own sources."

Then, glancing at Paaro who sat by her, she added, "I understand from Diidii that Kaashii *Baabuu* brought back some jewellery and valuables. Of course, I've no idea how much they might be worth, or whether it be might be enough to cover the expenses. But if it did...." Bhavaanii had to abruptly stop with tears choking her voice.

"Bahuu, what should I do to make you understand that you aren't a helpless woman at all? Who on earth would believe that a lady whose son is protected by none other than the Benevolent goddess *Vana-Durgaa* is helpless? From what Kaashii has told me, the wealth found in the *Deorhii* treasury is enough to last several generations of your family. So, you needn't worry on that score, and let me also tell you that the arrangements Kaashii's made to keep your inheritance secure were the very best possible in the circumstances. We may perhaps have to take steps for even better security, for hundreds of people saw where and how it was hidden. There's no telling who might get turned by temptation."

"It wouldn't be easy for anyone to carry it away. I don't think there's any need to tinker with the arrangement. Those heavy lockers could only be moved if fifty men kept digging day and night for several days," interjected Sadaashiva.

Kaashii also agreed with Sadaashiva, saying, "That's right. It wouldn't be easy for anyone to shift the treasure trove."

"It's reassuring to hear that, but what I really want to tell Bhavaanii Bahuu is that even the jewellery and valuables that Kaashii was able to bring back with him should be enough for a lifetime in comfort, and that I'm merely its custodian. She can have it all back whenever she wants. I've had an inventory made of the smallest of things that includes a complete account of the cash and gold and silver jewellery. We also recovered important documents relating to property, which might prove to be valuable in future," said *Baabaa* and added, pointing to Jagdambii, sleeping peacefully in his lap, "*Bahuu*, make no mistake. Your son is no ordinary child; you delivered and left him in the wilderness but the Benevolent goddess *Vana-Durgaa* saved him. Do you think she took all that trouble for nothing?"

Baabaa was clearly worked up by his own plea and went on, "You're after all Jagdambii's mother and he's with you for long hours; have you never noticed the scar on his forehead the *Devii* left?" As he tilted the sleeping infant's face for everyone to see, they all craned their necks forward to have a closer look. *Baabaa* continued, "This mark is like Lord Shiva's third eye. If it opened and turned on someone, he'd be reduced to ashes. Believe me, *Bahuu*, I'd never tell you a lie. No enemy, however powerful, would be able to withstand his might. The sacred bird, venerated as the embodiment of *Vana-Durgaa*, took your child under its wings and protected him. It made this mark on his forehead and spread its powerful wings over his body. I couldn't quite understand then why the bird did all that, but now that I think back to it, I can confidently tell you that much as Jagdambii might appear tender like any other baby, his body is as hard as *vajra*. Whatever weapons the enemy might possess, they'd all be ineffectual on him. The sacred bird also seemed to have whispered something into Jagdambii's ear. Whatever it was, it was all in bird lingo. I couldn't grasp it but who knows, Jagdambii might have."

The family members were visibly dismayed to hear all this, but clearly *Baabaa* wanted to tell them more,

"Jagdambii's still so small, but have you noticed his eyes? He appears to be kindliness and affection personified when he rolls his eyes, but the moment they are focused, they turn fearsome like the eyes of a tiger. I've had his horoscope made. It's truly unique. Truth to tell, it's only to see his faculties in full flow that I'm beginning to have this craving to live on until he comes of age." *Baabaa* paused for a moment, then continued with even greater conviction, "Mark my words, *Bahuu*, the Benevolent goddess did not shield your child in vain; there must be a greater purpose behind it. I know not whether I'll live to see the day but you all will certainly have occasion to witness this little boy here bring such great glory to his family-line that he will be remembered as the stuff of legend for generations to come."

Having played the soothsayer, Shambhuu Naath returned to the present, saying, "I'd like to bring today's proceedings of the family council to a close on a note of agreement with Bhavaanii Bahuu's sentiments: the expenses of the last rites of Singhwaar Thaakurs should be met by their own sources. I assure you, *Bahuu*, we'll go in this regard by your wishes."

The meeting over, Shambhuu Naath handed the sleeping baby over to Paaro, and hailing his *ishtTa-Deva*, walked away towards the front porch.

A few days later, Bhavaanii and the other two daughters-in-law, Paaro and Saavitri, sat on the courtyard verandah, chatting about *Baabaa*'s predictions on Jagdambii's future. Sadaashiva, seeing the three ladies together, also joined them in their conversation, asking Paaro, "*Bhaabhii*, haven't seen *Bhaiyaa* all day; has he gone out?"

"Yes, he's out seeing to the task *Baabaa* gave him in the family gathering the other day. He'll be back by sundown."

Sadaashiva then glanced at Bhavaanii tentatively, with an unspoken question in his eyes, silently debating whether it would be right to ask it. He addressed Bhavaanii as *Bahuu Bhaabhii* while *Baabaa* and Kaashii, being elder to Dharaadhar, called her Bhavaanii Bahuu; Saavitri addressed her as *Bahuu Diidii* and the children *Bahuu MaaN*; only Paaro called Bhavaanii by her given name.

Perhaps the manner of his looks gave Sadaashiva away. Bhavaanii sensed that he wanted to ask her something. "Go ahead, what's it you want to know?" she asked.

"I've been curious about certain things that appeared mysterious at the *Deorhii.* I was wondering whether you would help me unravel them."

"I'll try my best," said Bhavaanii sounding a bit concerned.

"Well, I've to say the scene at *Deorhii* in the aftermath of the massacre was a bit of a nightmare. We hadn't seen anything so horrendous and heart-rending ever before. The courtyards were strewn with dead bodies; the scene in the audience-hall, where the barbarians had brutally murdered Dharaadhar *Bhaiyaa* in captivity, was even more gruesome. In fact, it was so bad, Kaashii *Bhaiyaa* broke down and wept inconsolably for quite a while. Then I went inside with some men to take stock of the inner chambers. In the inner courtyard and the verandah facing it, I saw two headless female bodies, their heads lying in a pool of blood not far from where the body lay. There were numerous headless bodies of children lying around, too. One could see from their apparel and appearance, even in death, that they were members of the family. As we were looking through the rooms, in a large bed-chamber, we discovered another headless body of a woman lying in an ornate, finely carved fourposter. Apparently, she'd been asleep when beheaded. We were quite amazed how on earth could anyone continue to sleep in the hue and cry of a massacre taking place outside! Although she had expensive clothes and jewellery on, like the other family ladies, I couldn't bring myself to believe she was one of them. To begin with, this was just my instinct, but soon it was bolstered by bits of circumstantial evidence. Her hair was dry and uncared for; her skin lacked the sheen that other ladies had, even in death. Her body lay in a rather awkward posture under a duvet, clutching at a large pillow around her belly. The problem was I couldn't straightaway take her for a servant-woman, seeing the kind of clothes she had on and the bed she had been in, though only moments later we noticed that her left forearm had a tattoo that read 'Mohini' and knew for sure that she wasn't an upper-class lady. I still felt that she had enjoyed a special place in the family, regardless of her caste and station. I, therefore, decided to give her the same respect as the other ladies of the family and had her body placed alongside theirs."

The graphic description of the scene at the *Deorhii* in the wake of the carnage went like a spear through Bhavaanii's heart, her eyes welling up instantly. She lisped in a tearful voice, "You did just the right thing, Sadaashiva *Baabuu.*"

His curiosity whetted even more, Sadaashiva pointedly asked, "Who was Mohini?"

"Well," replied Bhavaanii, "Mohini was one of my many chamber-maids, but she really was more of a childhood companion to me. Our parents were from the same village. A while after my marriage into the Singhwaar family, she married a Singhwaarian, too. One day she came to the *Deorhii* to spend a day with me, and when leaving, she entreated me to employ her as one of my maids. I said I'd need my mother-in-law's permission for it. When *MaaN Jii*, my mother-in-law, came to know, she said I hardly needed her permission for such a small matter, and I could just go ahead and do as I pleased. So, Mohini once again became my constant companion; and that I'm still alive and amidst you with the last surviving male heir of the Singhwaar lineage was only made possible by the supreme sacrifice of Mohini. I shall forever be in her debt." Bhavaanii was totally overcome by emotion, but getting a hold on herself, she went on to tell them the entire sequence of events leading up to the massacre: how Salaamat Khaan had first sent a courier, and then his Vizier to get LaaDlii, and how, when Jagdambii's late father had refused, the Vizier tried to persuade him and ended up threatening him with dire consequences.

"Having failed to intimidate Jagdambii's father," said Bhavaanii, "finally, the Vizier tried to tempt him with his dirty lucre, 'How much do you want? Nawaab Saahib is prepared to give you whatever's your asking price', said Ghulaam Sarvar. But where principles came into the equation, the Thaakurs were just not ready to bend or bow. My husband made it clear he didn't want to pick up a needless fight with Nawaab Saahib. Or else, why would he have given up Pyaare when Salaamat Khaan had asked for him? But LaaDlii's case was different altogether. She was a 'girl'! Never mind if she was only a bitch; she had been brought up like family. How could they give her up to a *Mussalmaan*? Jagdambii's father had bluntly told the Vizier that as long as he or any one of his brothers was alive to defend LaaDlii, no power on earth could take her away from them. They were willing to lose their heads but not bow them. Nawaab took it as a grave insult and vowed to have his revenge, precisely as he had put it, by taking their heads!

"You know the rest," said Bhavaanii, concluding the recapitulation of events leading up to the calamity that had rendered her a homeless widow.

"Another mystery has been automatically solved from all that you just told us," said Sadaashiva.

"Which other mystery is that?" asked Bhavaanii.

"As we returned after having searched the inner rooms for things of value, we came upon the headless body of a bitch as well. I now know it must've been LaaDlii's, slain by the master so that the Nawaab's men couldn't lay their hands on her, though at the time we were left wondering why someone would behead a bitch."

"You're right, Sadaashiva; that must indeed have been LaaDlii," said Bhavaanii and began reminiscing again.

"We at the *Deorhii* were totally befooled by the Nawaab's guile. Initially, for a while, we did watch out for trouble from him, but eventually relaxed, thinking it had blown over. We couldn't have been more mistaken. The Vizier went quickly ahead with his plan of revenge in total secrecy. Within a year of his visit to the *Deorhii*, the Mughal contingent came thundering at the gates. The proud, even arrogant, Thaakurs hadn't a flexible bone that would allow them to bend. The three brothers got together in the *Puujaa-ghar* of the family deity for secret consultations on how to respond to the assault which appeared imminent. There was no simple solution.

"Mohini, a highly mobile chatterbox and newsy by nature, already knew about the Mughal troops camping at the outskirts of the village. She noticed the three Thaakur siblings entering the *Puujaa-ghar*, and unable to resist her curiosity, stood with her ear to the door. She overheard the three of them agreeing that they wouldn't surrender like cowards, whatever the consequences, nor would they abandon the *Deorhii* and run for their lives; taking on the attackers was the only honourable option. The question was whether they really stood a chance of making it alive with a rag-tag group of a hundred-odd part-time fighters in the face of well-equipped and highly-trained professional soldiers, or they should prepare to die fighting. They had no illusions about the outcome; they would likely be slaughtered like sheep in no time. Neither was it difficult for them to imagine the ghastly fate that would befall their women and children once they were finished. At the very mention of it, they all fell silent for a moment, but eventually they steeled their hearts and decided that each one of them would kill his wife and children himself rather than allow them to fall into enemy hands. There was very little time left as the attack could come anytime. Peeping inside the *Puujaa-ghar*, Mohini saw them begin to say their last prayers and the traditional *shastra-puujaa*. She ran to my chamber, distraught at what she'd learnt eavesdropping on my husband and his brothers, and began entreating that I flee the *havelii* without delay. Rejecting her suggestion I pushed her away, but truth be told, my heart sank to hear Mohini say that if I allowed myself to perish, it would also mean the end of the illustrious family line of my husband's. Still, for the longest time, I was in two minds: much as the child I carried was important, what would my husband think when he looked for me and I was nowhere to be found? If a search was mounted and I were brought back in shackles like an ordinary criminal, would I be able to look him in the eye? On the other hand, Mohini obstinately held her ground, "Mistress, I know what you're thinking, but please listen to me, your childhood friend and most devoted servant. Brushing aside all the inhibitions and apprehensions that assail your heart, you must leave here at once and save your distinguished family-line from extinction. I'll take care of everything here after you're gone, don't you worry. I'll take the consequences."

And then with an air of finality, she literally forced me to exchange our clothes, taking off my jewellery and putting them on as well. She then took my hand and said, "Let's go, Mistress!" and brought me out stealthily from the rear door opening on the riverside. By then I was quite dazed, my ambivalence having robbed me of all sense of time and space. Touching my feet in final greeting, Mohini said, "Mistress, now don't waste any more time worrying on what's to happen here. Go as far, as fast, as you possibly can." Bhavaanii took a deep, anguished breath before continuing, "Before I could even think of a befitting response, Mohini turned and strode away towards the rear entrance and was gone. For a few moments, I stood still, as if turned to stone. That's when I fell into a fugue: I have no recollection of what happened then, or how I reached here. When I came to, I found myself surrounded by you all."

Having described her escape from the *havelii* just before the massacre, Bhavaanii fell silent, staring sightlessly into mid-distance. Paaro, Saavitri and Sadaashiva could see that she was reliving that tragic evening, and that they ought not to intrude upon the privacy of her thoughts. After a while, Bhavaanii resumed her monologue in a voice thick with suppressed tears, "From what you told me about how and where you found Mohini's body, it's clear that having seen me off on the riverside that night, she must have gone and lain on my bed pretending to be fast asleep. Since I was carrying a full-term pregnancy, no one would have thought it odd that I was in bed so early, and Jagdambii's father must have mistaken Mohini for .....” Bhavaanii couldn’t speak any further, her voice drowned by tears.

After a while, Bhavaanii resumed, looking gratefully at Sadaashiva, “Much as Mohini was from a lower caste, her conduct and deportment was very like ladies of a noble house. You did me a great favour by having her last rites performed with other family women. I feel truly humbled by Mohini’s sacrifice to save our family-line from being wiped out. I can never repay her debt.” Bhavaanii broke down again, lamenting and sobbing her heart out behind her veil.

Sadaashiva tried to console her, saying, “*Bahuu Bhaabhii*, I’ve needlessly upset you by digging up painful memories of what can’t be changed. Believe me, I had no intention of causing you pain.”

“No. no, if you’re curious about anything else, just go ahead and ask,” replied Bhavaanii.

“Just one more thing: I’d like to be sure of the identity of the grand old lady whose body we found in the *Puujaa-ghar*, but it can wait as I’m already late for my classes at the school,” said Sadaashiva taking leave of them.

❋❋❋

Whenever Sadaashiva saw the small, finely hand-carved dagger lying on the table in his room, he was reminded of the imperious looking old lady whose body he had found lying on the *chinvaar* of *Puujaa-ghar* at the *Deorhii*. He vividly recalled her proud, noble face, impressive even in death. He soon got the chance to find out who she was. His school was closed that day. As he returned from his morning walk, he found the three ladies sitting on the courtyard verandah, chatting. Taking a seat near them, he asked Bhavaanii, “*Bahuu Bhaabhii*, if it’s all right with you, may I ask you about that old lady we assumed to be Dharaadhar Thaakur’s mother?”

Before Bhavaanii could reply, *Baabaa* Shambhuu Naath entered the courtyard calling out aloud to announce he was coming, “Bahuu, where’s Jagdambii? If he’s awake, could you bring him to me?" Jagdambii, sleeping in Paaro's lap, woke up on hearing *Baabaa*'s voice and began pumping his fists up jerkily and kicking the air with his tiny feet, as if he wanted to go to *Baabaa*.

Everyone rose to their feet to welcome the old patriarch. Saavitri brought an *aasana* for him to sit.

"I hadn't quite intended to sit but now that Saavitri *Bahuu's* brought me an *aasana*, I might as well be with you all for some time. I only hope my presence won't ruin your conversation!" said the old man.

"No.....no, father, you'd not be in the way," exclaimed Sadaashiva.

"That's fine then. You carry on while I have a little private chat with dear Jagdambii here," said *Baabaa*. Then, leaving the adults to their own devices, he began to make funny smoochy sounds at the baby, hearing which he squealed in delight, pumping the air with his tiny fists and legs even more vigorously. For a while, everyone looked on fascinated at *Baabaa*'s playful antics and the child's response. Then Shambhuu Naath asked, "What were you discussing when I interrupted you?"

"I was asking *Bahuu Bhaabhii* about the graceful old lady whose body we found in the *Puujaa-ghar* at Singhwaar. She appeared to have committed suicide with a small dagger. We assumed that she was the mother of the proud Thaakurs. But that was only guesswork. I was seeking confirmation," said Sadaashiva.

"You guessed it right, though. That must've been *MaaN Jii*, and the dagger that you speak of was a gift my father-in-law gave her as a memento of their *muh-bajaaon*, the first conversation they had as man and wife," said Bhavaanii.

"That's interesting, but how would you know that?" asked Paaro.

Bhavaanii smiled at her and continued, "Before starting my day, I used to go to *MaaN Jii's* private quarters to take her blessings. One morning she was sitting on the verandah adjoining her room. Before I could bend to touch her feet, she said, "Bhavaanii, first fetch me the tobacco-lime container; it must be under my pillow in the bedroom. As I looked under the pillow, I was startled to see a dagger lying alongside the carved silver lime-container. For one thing, I was curious about a dagger under my mother-in-law's pillow; for another, I was fascinated by the exquisite hand-carving on its handle and sheath. I just couldn't help picking it up for a closer look, but once I had it in my hands, a look wasn't enough; I unsheathed the dagger. It had a small but razor-sharp blade. Having satisfied my curiosity stealthily, I wanted to quickly restore it to its sheath, but it just wouldn't go back in. I wasn't aware then that a hidden button needed to be pressed while re-sheathing it. In my anxiety to return to *MaaN Jii*, I tried to force it in, causing a distinct metallic sound, with which she was quite familiar. She called out, '*Bahuu*, what's taking you so long? Can't you find my lime-container?' I panicked as if I'd been caught stealing something. Hurriedly putting the dagger back under the pillow, I rushed back. I was afraid that my mother-in-law would be annoyed, but she was very kind to me. She chuckled at seeing me so flustered and said, 'It appears you were taken aback to see the dagger lying under my pillow.' I touched her feet silently. Blessing me, she volunteered, 'Your father-in-law, while giving me the dagger as his first gift after our wedding, had asked me to promise him something.' I was instantly taken by curiosity to find out what the promise was; so, I asked her. My mother-in-law told me that he'd asked her to promise that she wouldn't ever part with his gift, that it would forever remind her of him, and God forbid, if ever she felt her honour as a woman so threatened that there was no other option left to her, she should put the dagger to heart without any hesitation. She told me that she had never parted with it since, nor would she ever do so while she lived."

"No wonder, when she knew there was no way out, she used the dagger to commit suicide," exclaimed Sadaashiva.

"That's what must've happened, but Sadaashiva *Baabuu*, can I ask you something?" said Bhavaanii.

"Sure, I'm willing to share everything I know," replied Sadaashiva.

"Like you noticed the dagger, do you remember seeing my husband's personal sword which was always at his side?" asked Bhavaanii anxiously.

"*Bahuu Bhaabhii*, there were so many swords lying around; unless you describe some distinguishing feature of Dharaadhar *Bhaiyaa's* sword, it'd be difficult for me to say anything with certainty," replied Sadaashiva.

"My husband's sword has a velvet-clad scabbard with the words '*Mahishaasura-mardinii*' artistically woven into the fabric; and unlike common swords, its blade is razor-sharp on both the sides."

"I do recall having seen the sword in Kaashii *Bhaiyaa's* hand. I'll have to ask him where it might be now. As for the dagger, it was so small and fascinating that I brought it along without telling anyone," said Sadaashiva.

"Wonderful! You did the right thing," said Bhavaanii happily, "but...."

"But, what?" Sadaashiva exclaimed.

Seemingly a bit embarrassed, Bhavaanii replied, "Knowing that you fancy the dagger so much, how do I tell you that I would like to keep it as a memento of my mother-in-law...."

Looking to relieve her of needless sense of guilt about it, Sadaashiva interrupted her, "Come off it, *Bahuu Bhaabhii*, that dagger is an heirloom; you have the first claim on it. I'll bring it over just now."

"No...no, there's no hurry, you can give it to me later. Of course, I'd have been far happier if you had also brought along the sword of Jagdambii's father. That sword has special significance for us in another way. There's been a long tradition in the family of the father passing on the sword to his eldest son on his eighteenth birthday. Jagdambii's grandfather had also handed it over to my husband the day he turned eighteen. My husband told me of it himself, and also that whoever had the good fortune of receiving this gift was in duty bound to worship the weapon observing elaborate time-honoured rituals, at midnight hour of *Mahaa-ashTamii* day of the autumanal *Nava-raatra* every year. The *shastra-puujaa* rituals required all doors, windows and other apertures of the *Puujaa-ghar* to be shut, with absolutely no one but the adult males of the family being allowed inside. The *shastra-puujaa*, performed in the dim light of earthen wick-lamps, began at the stroke of the midnight hour of the seventh night of *Nava-raatra*, and lasted several hours. The principal deity worshipped was *Mahishaasura-mardini*, *Durgaa*, who, as you know, is the main deity in *Shakti* worship. The ritual ended with the sacrifice of a year-old black goat-kid with the anointed sword. Then everyone touched the blood-smeared blade and put a *tiikaa* as *Prasaad*."

Bhavaanii paused to look gratefully at Sadaashiva, and resumed, "Sadaashiva *Baabuu*, I owe you for many a favour, but if you agreed to do me one more, I should be very obliged."

"What a strange way of asking me for it, though! *Bahuu Bhaabhii*, let's understand this clearly: If you adopt such fine manners, I would be loath to comply. On the other hand, just command Sadaashiva, and you'd straightaway get to see what he's capable of!" said Sadaashiva, smiling.

"If you could locate and bring me my husband's sword, it'd be a great solace to me. He's gone but I'm still around, and if I could hand it over to Jagdambii when he turns eighteen, I'd consider myself to be free of my obligation."

"I'll have to ask *Bhaiyaa* where the sword is, and as soon as I have done that, I'll bring it to you. These days he goes out at dawn and is back well past sundown."

Shambhuu Naath, who had only been listening to the conversation until now, joined in, "Sadaashiva, your conjecture that the lady in the *Puujaa-ghar* was Dharaadhar's mother and that she took her own life was correct on both counts."

"You say that rather confidently, Father! How'd you know for sure?" asked Sadaashiva.

"What I've said is based on Dharaadhar's last letter to me," replied *Baabaa*.

"Dharaadhar *Bhaiyaa's* last letter? Where did you get it?" asked Sadaashiva, amazed.

"Well, I sort of chanced upon it in the pile of property papers you guys brought back from the *Deorhii*," replied Shambhuu Naath, and paused, as if to reflect back on something admirable. Then he added, "That Dharaadhar Thaakur was able to write a letter with perfect composure even with the Mughal troops breathing down his neck, is a tribute to his character. It also shows that his equanimity was unimpaired by extreme danger. I was so impressed and touched by his letter that I've been carrying it around, reading and re-reading it since. Here, let me read it out to you all:

'I am very short of time. The Mughal contingent summoned by Nawaab Salaamat Khaan is camping at the village outskirts, and an assault on the Deorhii seems imminent. Alas! Having been taken unawares, I couldn't seek your assistance in time. In the circumstances, my brothers and I have decided to take the fight to the enemy, though we have only a small band of village youth to assist us. We know that we'll all go down fighting. Being fully aware of the outcome of this uneven battle to be, each one of us three has slain his wife and children to save them from a fate worse than death, should they fall into enemy hands, as they surely would after we've been slaughtered.

'My main purpose in writing you this letter is to ensure beyond any shadow of doubt that none of us three is seen as guilty of the mortal sin of matricide. Having steeled our hearts, when we started beheading our immediate families, our mother ran from one to the other in a frenzy, howling and protesting like someone going crazy with grief as she indeed must have felt, begging one of us to put her out of misery, too, but none of us was prepared to do that. I then asked my brothers to go out and see to whatever we had planned for defending the Deorhii, while I stayed back to protect our

mother until the very last. Seeing me torn between my duty to the Deorhii on the one hand and my loyalty to her on the other, however, she fell quiet and said to me, 'Dharaadhar, don't even think of neglecting your duty on my account; you must go out and lead your brothers and your men and fight until the last breath. It's been a glorious tradition in the family to give up all for the sake of honour. Now go, my son, keep it up! As for me, I'm going to meet your late father.'

'For a while, I stood still, nonplussed by my ambivalence, and then I saw her emerge from her bedroom, dagger in hand. She strode towards the Puujaa-ghar purposefully. I knew then what she was about to do, and frankly, I felt a sense of relief wash over me. I rushed out to the exit towards the audience hall, where the other defenders awaited me. On my way there, I saw LaaDlii sitting on the porch outside the hall, her eyes sunk in deep melancholy, as if she knew that she was at the root of the impending disaster. Tears flowed ceaselessly from her eyes, pleading silently to be slain like the rest of the family. Well, I couldn't allow her to fall in the hands of the invaders after all this, and so, beheaded her with one swift stroke of my sword.'

"The letter is signed Dharaadhar Thaakur," Shambhuu Naath stopped with an anguished sigh.

A sudden hush had fallen over the family group.

Meanwhile, Jagdambii, waking up after a long nap, now opened his eyes and began to throw about his limbs energetically, squealing with delight, while they all watched the adorable child.

□

4

Spying in Waariaul

Kaashii Naath's days were consumed by the task *Baabaa* had assigned him in the family council. For quite some time now, day after day, he had ridden off every morning, returning late at night. With little to show for his efforts, however, he was beginning to worry now. One day as he prepared to leave home as usual, Bhavaanii called out to Paaro from the verandah outside their room, "*Diidii*, can I see you for a minute." A bit anxious at Bhavaanii calling out to her rather early in the morning, Paaro came out instantly, asking, "Is everything all right? Why are you up so early," she asked.

"Not to worry, *Diidii*. I just came to say I've noticed Kaashii *Bhaiyaa* running around for several days now. I thought I'd suggest that he might like to rest for the day and review his efforts in his quiet moments at home, and see if it throws up any new ideas how to go about the whole thing. There's hardly any point in needlessly over-exerting oneself; it's possible some fresh angle might occur to him on reflection," said Bhavaanii.

Kaashii, overhearing the conversation between the two women, thought Bhavaanii's advice made sense, and decided to stay home that day. He did take her advice seriously, though, reflecting throughout the morning on the task at hand. His main problem was that he could neither reveal his identity nor let out the secret of Bhavaanii and her child being alive, and living with them.

Kaashii was still wondering what to do next when he saw a man approaching the house on horseback. Unable to place the rider at a distance, he wondered who he might be. As the man dismounted in the front yard, Kaashii saw it was his old friend Raam Iqbaal, who belonged to a well-to-do family of a neighbouring village. He was happy to see his friend and stepped forward to welcome him, "Hello there! It's been a long time. Good to see you, though."

A servant came to take the reins off Raam Iqbaal's hand and lead away his mount towards the stables. While the two friends ascended the steps to the porch, Raam Iqbaal replied, "Well, it's not that I don't remember you; I do, and fairly often too, but am unable to make time to see you. Lately, my old man hasn't been keeping too well, which naturally means a lot more work for me. But enough of me and mine now! How's everything with you these days? All well I hope?"

"We're all right, more or less," said Kaashii, and fell silent, wondering whether it'd be wise to share his predicament with his friend. Seeing him preoccupied, Raam Iqbaal said after a while, "Kaashii, you look worried, my friend! If it's something you can share with me, perhaps I might be able to help you."

Kaashii Naath's anxiety seemed contagious; Raam Iqbaal was beginning to feel uneasy himself after a while. Having waited for some time for his friend to open up, he eventually exclaimed, "Listen, old chap, it's painful for me to see you so worried. You have to tell me what's eating you!"

Kaashii eventually decided that Raam Iqbaal was trustworthy enough. He recapitulated the misfortune that had befallen his kin at Singhwaar *Deorhii*. Raam Iqbaal, who was already aware of the broad details of the Mughal attack on Singhwaar that the Nawaab had engineered, and deeply sympathetic, said, "Alas! By the time we came to know of the whole thing, it was already too late to do much. Our blood boiled but in vain! We did plan a counter-strike on Waariaul to teach a lesson to Salaamat but family elders thought it was foolhardy, and restrained us. They said there was no point shutting the stable-doors after the horses had bolted. Rushing off to succour a friend in distress would've made sense, but over-reacting after the event would only lead to avoidable blood-letting. Besides, one had to be realistic; after all, the country was ruled by the Mughals! In the circumstances, they said, it'd be best to wait patiently for divine justice, which would surely make the Nawaab pay heavily for the blood of innocents he had on his hands. We had to listen to our elders' advice." Raam Iqbaal paused a moment and then added, sadly, "I'm truly sorry that the Singhwaar branch of your lineage is extinct now."

Once again Kaashii Naath was in two minds whether he should come clean and let his friend in on the secret of Bhavaanii and Jagdambii being alive, or let the matter rest there. Raam Iqbaal sensed his hesitancy, "What's begun to bother you all over again? If it's something you can't share with me, I'll understand," he said.

That made up Kaashii's mind for him. "No....no, what's there to hide from you, my friend!" he said, and went on to briefly recount the events leading up to Bhavaanii and Jagdambii coming to live at KaTkaa. Raam Iqbaal, heaving a sigh of relief, said, "Thank heavens! By the blessings of Benevolent goddess *Durgaa,* that family-line has at least been spared extinction. I'm sure they'll continue to enjoy her grace. We must think positively."

Kaashii told his friend of the responsibility that *Baabaa* had entrusted him. Although Dharaadhar's family estate was very likely to have been confiscated as punitive damages, the exact position needed to be verified.

"So, what's the problem?" asked Raam Iqbaal.

"The difficulty is that we can't reveal the fact of Bhavaanii having survived the massacre, far less the existence of an heir to Dharaadhar Thaakur being alive," replied Kaashii

"Why is that?" asked Raam Iqbaal.

"There is no telling to what lengths the Nawaab might go to have his revenge. He might very well decide to have someone bump her and the child off," said Kaashii.

"Indeed so; the Nawaab is very devious and vengeful," agreed Raam Iqbaal.

"That's why it's so difficult to find out the status of Dharaadhar's family estate. There's no one trustworthy in Waariaul who can help us in the matter," said Kaashii ruefully.

"Well, that's not exactly correct. I do know someone who can be of great help in gathering intelligence quietly," said Raam Iqbaal smiling.

"Who's that?" asked Kaashii hopefully.

"His name's Gangeshvar Pandey; he's my wife's cousin," replied Raam Iqbaal, and then added chuckling, "You're aware that every caste has certain characteristics peculiar to it, good as well as some not so good!"

"Indeed so, but I don't quite get what you're hinting at," said Kaashii.

"What I mean is that we *Bhuumihaars* invariably keep our eyes, ears and noses open, and our mouths shut, no matter where we are. Besides, we're also pastmasters at talking glibly and casting a spell on folks by sheer bragging. Gangeshvar has insinuated himself into the Nawaab's favour precisely on account of such traits and has risen to the post of his principal *Munshii*. We can ask him to help."

Kaashii was delighted to hear this, and thanked his stars that he had taken Bhavaanii's advice and stayed home that day; or else, he would have missed Raam Iqbaal. He said he didn't know Gangeshvar, wondering whether he would spare time to help out someone he hardly knew.

"Listen, my friend, you needn't worry over such a small thing. I'd consider myself fortunate if I could be of the slightest help to you and Dharaadhar's widow. I'll take you to Waariaul myself, but let me tell you frankly that commuting everyday isn't my cup of tea. So, take an overnight bag and be prepared to spend a few days there," said Raam Iqbaal

"Why, that's very kind of you..." said Kaashii, beginning to thank him.

"Kind, my foot! What nonsense is this among friends, I say?" said Raam Iqbaal interrupting him.

"Fine, I take it back. I'm sorry I was being overly formal, but tell me something: busy as you are, how come you could find the time to visit us today," queried Kaashii.

"Well, there is a special reason, besides, of course, the pleasure of seeing you; my eldest boy, Raam Lohit is to be married three weeks from now. I came to personally invite you to join the *baraat*, and also ask whether I could borrow some of your horses for the occasion," said Raam Iqbaal.

"Oh, congratulations. It'd be a privilege to join the *baraat*. As for the horses, I'm afraid you'd have to ask *Baabaa* himself. He's out for a morning walk at the moment, but will be back soon. Meanwhile, let me order some refreshments for you", said Kaashii, and turning his head towards the inner courtyard, called out aloud to his manservant, "Fakiiraa…O Fakiiraa."

As they waited for Shambhuu Naath, the two of them engaged in small talk about the upcoming wedding. Raam Iqbaal said he was expecting about a hundred guests to join the *baraat*, and that he had already arranged for thirteen horses and seven elephants for the marriage party. Kaashii found the idea of such a large number of people and animals in a marriage party rather amusing. "Feeding the animals would likely cost more than feeding the *baraatiis*! It'd be really tough on the bride's family. Poor fellows!" he said in jest.

"Whatever! I don't care. My *baraat* has to have the pomp and paraphernalia customary in our caste. Certainly, it won't be like the staid, austere marriage parties of *Maithil Braahmana*s with just five or seven, or at best eleven *baraatiis* going and getting the whole thing done and dusted overnight, with the bare minimum fuss and food without salt. No music, no dancing girls either!" said Raam Iqbaal smiling broadly.

As Shambhuu Naath returned, Raam Iqbaal stepped forward and touched his feet in greeting, saying, "*Baabaa*, I hope you remember me. I'm Raam Iqbaal."

"Don't be silly, my boy! how can I forget my dear friend, Raam Sanehii's son? I believe he's been out of sorts lately. Better now?"

"You were informed right. His eyesight is nearly gone. He's able to see a little by daylight but next to nothing after it's dark; can't move around or go anywhere, and has turned very irritable; tends to fly off the handle at the drop of a hat."

Baabaa turned thoughtful, saddened to hear of his friend's condition. Trying to revive the conversation, Kaashii said, "*Baabaa*, Raam Iqbaal's here for a special reason." Raam Iqbaal proceeded to invite Shambhuu Naath to join the *baraat* and request for the loan of horses. While asking to be excused from personal participation, *Baabaa* readily granted his other request.

Raam Iqbaal thanked Shambhuu Naath, touching his feet again in parting, and took leave of him. Kaashii and he came out to the front-yard, where the syce was waiting with his horse; jumping into the saddle, Raam Iqbaal said, "Kaashii I'll come for you sometime the day after tomorrow and then we'll ride over together to Waariaul. Be prepared to leave at short notice."

As Kaashii returned after seeing his friend off, *Baabaa* said to him, "Do me a favour, son. See if Jagdambii is awake. If he is, could you ask someone to bring him to me. A few rounds in the fresh evening air will do him good."

❋❋❋

As promised, a day later, Raam Iqbaal returned to KaTkaa, this time a cloth bag hanging on the flank of his horse. As he mounted the front porch steps, he saw Shambhuu Naath at the far end of the verandah, still occupied with the rituals of his morning *puujaa*. He left his shoes and walked barefoot towards *Baabaa*, and when a few paces away from him, he kneeled and touched his head to the floor in a gesture that combined greetings to the patriarch as well as obeisance to the deity he was worshipping. *Baabaa*, pleased to see the old-world considerations of the younger man, raised his right forearm palm outwards to convey his silent blessings in response, and motioned him to take a seat.

Shambhuu Naath did not want his rather long morning rituals to come in the way of timely departure of Kaashii and Raam Iqbaal; so, taking a break at the end of a chapter of his *PaaTh*, he came over to them, and said, "Kaashii's made several trips to Waariaul without much avail, but there's no harm in trying once again. You must, however, remember to make sure that under no circumstance is the secret of Bhavaanii and the child being alive and living at KaTkaa revealed to anyone," said he in a forbidding tone, softening it with an invitation to Raam Iqbaal for the customary repast before departing on the day-long ride.

Having finished the light meal, Kaashii went to his room to get his overnight bag while Raam Iqbaal stood chatting with Paaro and Bhavaanii.

"*Bahuu Bhaabhii*, I seek your blessings for the success of our mission," he said, addressing Bhavaanii.

"Why only this, you have my blessings for all your missions in a good cause, including, of course, the upcoming wedding of your son," said Bhavaanii gracefully. Raam Iqbaal was ever more impressed with her as a noble lady.

Finally, the twosome was ready to depart. Going out of the inner courtyard, Kaashii halted abruptly, and called out aloud to Paaro, "Markandeya's mother, I'm going to town with Raam Iqbaal to help him with some shopping for his son's wedding, and would likely be gone for a couple of days." Paaro knew he was taking no chances, deliberately announcing a false destination to keep the real one secret.

Shambhuu Naath was waiting outside to see them off. They touched his feet to seek his blessings in parting.

"May the god of gods Mahaadeva protect you on your trip!" said the old man. The twosome replied in unison, "Har-har Mahaadeva!"

❋❋❋

It was late afternoon by the time Kaashii and Raam Iqbaal reached the outskirts of Waariaul. The two of them dismounted to rest awhile before entering the town. Kaashii, already familiar with its layout from his recent visits, said to his friend, "This is the main crossroads of Waariaul. Other than the road that brought us here, the one to the east takes you to the Nawaab's Palace; the one turning west goes straight to the main mosque, beyond which there are thickly populated Muslim *Bastii*s mainly inhabited by poorer sections, like the *kunjraas*, *julaahaas*, *dhuniyaas* and the like; the road to the north passes through the main bazaar and ends up in Hindu *Bastii*s."

"You do seem to have mastered the demographics and topography of Waariaul, but what we really need to decide now is what we do next," said Raam Iqbaal.

"If I knew that, wouldn't I have gone ahead by now? It's all in your hands now," replied Kaashii, acknowledging Raam Iqbaal as the leader despite being younger.

"Well, then let's play at being nawaabs for a while, since we're in a Nawaab's realm," said Raam Iqbaal.

Kaashii looked at his friend, intrigued, "I don't get your drift!" he said.

"Forget the drift! Let's go to that *tamolii's* kiosk over there and have some *paan* first," said Raam Iqbaal pointing to a *paan* shop nestling in the deep shade of a large, round tree by the roadside, and pulled at the reins of his horse to turn that way. Kaashii followed him.

Although the tamolii pretended to be preoccupied in delicately clipping away at *paan* leaves, he perked up to see gentlemen customers, astride expensive-looking horses, approaching his shop. As the twosome neared the kiosk, he greeted them courteously, "You are very welcome, *huzuur*! How can I be of service to you?"

The *tamolii*, in a snow-white *malmal kurtaa*, *khaaltaa* pajamas and a hand-embroidered *topii* on his head, was as impressive a specimen as they come. He would likely be a useful source of information, thought Raam Iqbaal to himself. He gave the *tamolii* an appraising look for one long moment, and said, "*Bhaai tamolii*, please make us two *biiDaas* of *paan*."

"As you wish, sir," said the *tamolii* carefully putting aside the pair of scissors in his hand, and said, "It won't take a moment, but you haven't told me what kind of *biiDaas* you want: sweet or plain; and whether with or without tobacco, *kimaam* and *varq*."

"My, what refreshing style! Even before having the *biiDaa*, I feel my exhaustion gone with your words alone," said Raam Iqbaal letting exaggerated admiration show in his eyes, and added, "Truly, it's a great pleasure meeting people like you."

The *tamolii* was delighted to hear such praise and bowed a salaam to them again.

"To tell you the truth, we're not used to having *paan*. We just fancied a *biiDaa* since we're in Nawaab Saahib's town, so, let's have a sweet *biiDaa* without tobacco," said Raam Iqbaal.

The *tamolii* was dismayed to see hale and hearty male customers asking for a *biiDaa* without tobacco. He looked curiously at Raam Iqbaal and said, "I do beg to be excused, sir, but may I tell you something?"

"Consider yourself excused! Feel free to say what you want," said Raam Iqbaal.

"Better to go to a confectioner's and have sweets than a sweet *paan*; it's something only lasses ask for! What man can enjoy his *paan* without tobacco and *kimaam* in it!" said the *tamolii*, and seeing that he had his customers attention now, he went on, "*Paan* is something commonplace, most people have it and there are *paan* shops at every nook and corner of this town, but may God save me from lying, the *biiDaa* prepared by yours truly is something else!"

"But what exactly makes your *biiDaa* so special?" said Raam Iqbaal, exhibiting much curiosity.

"I don't sell *paan* only for people to paint their lips red, sir. If that were so, I might as well have dealt in henna leaves. My *biiDaa* has an aspect of romance in it." Taking a deep breath, the *tamolii* ploughed on, "What can I really say? It's so embarrassing to pat your own back, but if I don't beat my own drum, who else will, sir! The fact is that after having one *biiDaa* from me once, people just fall in love with it forever. After all, this is a nawaab's capital frequented by other nawaabs, emirs, princes and rich folks. Many of them come rushing straight to my shop the moment they arrive in Waariaul, and they come reciting my own couplet:

> You can ask for my heart, it's yours
> With all the cravings that it stores;
> Why, you can have the entire world
> For just a *biiDaa* of *paan*, it's yours.

As the *tamolii* recited the couplet affecting a *shaayar*'s style, Raam Iqbaal showered him with praise, "*Waah-waah*, what lovely poetry! You're fantastic. What's your name?"

Preening and readjusting his *topii* at an angle, the *tamolii* replied, "My name? Pyaare Laal 'Nafiis' at your service, sir. 'Nafiis' is my nom-de-plume."

"Wonderful! Just as you're Nafiis, so is your shop. No praise would be too high."

As Pyaare Laal busied himself to prove his skills, Raam Iqbaal jumped the question he'd been waiting to ask, "*Bhaai tamolii*, could you tell me where and when one could possibly meet Gangeshvar Paandey?"

Pyaare Laal gulped nervously at hearing the name of the Nawaab's *Munshii* from a stranger; he looked at Raam Iqbaal with renewed interest, and asked, "Which Gangeshvar Paandey, sir? Are you referring to our Nawaab Saahib's *Munshii Jii*?"

"Yes. Yes, I'm here to see him; he's my wife's cousin. Do you know him?"

"You must be joking, sir. Who doesn't know *Munshii Jii*! He must be at the Nawaab's Palace at this hour. He is there from early morning until late at night. Where would he get the time to relax, after all he's Nawaab Saahib's favourite."

"All right, can you make it a bit fast; we're getting late," said Raam Iqbaal, suddenly in a hurry to leave.

Although the *tamolii* had now turned even more deferential to his new customer, he wasn't about to compromise on his repute. He rejoined pertly, "Sir, please be a little patient; making a *biiDaa* is no joke. I've just put lime on the leaves, now I'll apply a patina of *katthaa* over it and mix the two nicely together. Then some arecanut will go on to them, followed by a few grains of cardamom and a few drops of *ras-bharii*. Indeed, sir, all this is bound to take some time!"

Continuing to be absorbed by his task, the *tamolii* went on, "I've yet to see a person nicer than *Munshii Jii*. He's truly kind-hearted. May God give him even greater success! Lately, he's been specially kind to me, sir." By this time, the *biiDaas* were done. The *tamolii* put them on a hand-carved silver plate and proffered it to the gentlemen with a flourish. Raam Iqbaal took one and offered the other to Kaashii standing by his side, quietly listening to the exchange between the *tamolii* and his crafty friend.

"How much do I owe you?" Raam Iqbaal asked.

"Look at you, sir! I can't accept any payment from you," said Pyaare Laal.

"Why is that?"

"You're our *Munshii Jii*'s brother-in-law. If he were to even hear of it, I'd be done for," replied the *tamolii* with a feigned shudder.

"Why would I even mention it to him, my dear?" said Raam Iqbaal and, taking a silver crown from his pocket, offered it to him, "You've got to take this."

Pyaare, greedily eyeing the coin, gulped, "But this is too much, sir!" he said.

"Don't worry, just take it. I'm going to be in town for a few days and will keep coming back," assured Raam Iqbaal, but the *tamolii*, overcoming his temptation, said submissively, "I'm a small fry, sir, completely at *Munshii Jii*'s mercy!"

"Your fears are wholly misplaced, my dear fellow. Haven't I assured you already that I'll do nothing that might harm you? Now, just tell me how I get to meet your *Munshii Jii*. Surely, Nawaab Saahib's place would be guarded like a fortress," said Raam Iqbaal.

"Sir, the main entrance to the palace is guarded by a bouncer called Mustafaa. He's a rogue of the first order, but since the day he married a good-looking young lass, he's lost his marbles. All he can think of these days is how to keep her in good humour," said Pyaare Laal and went on to add warily in a whisper, "I've heard that Mustafaa's wife is very fond of crisp *jalebiis* just out of the frying pan; if he doesn't listen to you, just slip a couple of silver pieces to him, and you can be sure he'll arrange for you to meet not *Munshii Jii* alone, but perhaps even Nawaab Saahib himself. Anyhow, the state of affairs at the palace has been so lousy lately, it appears that an evil eye has come to haunt it!"

Raam Iqbaal's ears pricked at the last comment of the *tamolii*.

"What evil eye? What do you mean?" asked Raam Iqbaal.

Pyaare bit his tongue for being overly generous in sharing confidences with a near stranger and hastened to make amends, "Sir, you'll be meeting *Munshii Jii* soon; you might as well ask him for the details. I'd only be repeating a hearsay at best," he said diplomatically.

"So long then, we'll meet again," said Raam Iqbaal to him, and then turning to Kaashii, "Shall we go now?"

The two of them started for the Nawaab's palace, chewing Pyaare's delicious *biiDaa*.

❋❋❋

The Nawaab's palace was a sprawling two-storeyed fortress-like affair, with numerous domes, turrets and battlements. One wing of it was the *zenaanaa* where the Nawaab's *Begam*s lived; the other was occupied by the Nawaab, and included the audience hall and public offices of the realm. This is where Gangeshvar Paandey as his principal *Munshii* had a seat. The palace was fronted by a huge forecourt, with an arched entrance so high that a caparisoned elephant with a *haudaa* could easily pass through it. The arched structure had wooden shutters, thick and strong, studded with prickly bas relief flower patterns in beaten-brass that made the gate not only look grand, but also difficult to storm. The main gate to the palace was only opened for the elephants and cavalcades of the Nawaab or his heir-apparent Shahnavaaz Khaan, also known as the *ChhoTe Nawaab*. One of the big shutters had a smaller man-size shutter built into it for the use of the staff and others allowed access to the palace.

At a vantage point outside the palace gates, sat a stocky, barrel-chested man wearing a *lungii* and a round-necked vest with a hand-towel on his shoulder, busy priming chewing-tobacco with lime in his palm and humming the latest hit-number sung by a courtesan in her *mujraa* in Nawaab Saahib's honour. Though the man warily noted the two gentlemen on horse-back coming towards the gate, he neither got up from his perch nor stopped humming. Raam Iqbaal and Kaashii Naath dismounted well short of the gate, tied their horses to a nearby tree and advanced towards him. Raam Iqbaal, walking a couple of paces ahead, accosted the guard, "Khaan Saahib!"

Mustafaa, the bouncer, delighted to hear himself addressed deferentially as if he were part of the local gentry, but still not bothering to get up, acknowledged Raam Iqbaal with a gruff, "Yes, please?" Raam Iqbaal, moving a step closer, said in a low tone, "It's like this; I've come to see someone who is inside the palace. I'd be very obliged if you could help me with it."

Throwing the now primed tobacco into his mouth with a jerk of the palm, Mustafaa fired a salvo of multiple questions at the stranger, "Who have you come to see? Is it a man or a woman? What's your business and where are you from, and who's this with you?", all in the same breath! Slightly put off by the guard's officious attitude, Raam Iqbaal decided to come to the point, "I'm here to see Gangeshvar Paandey; he's my wife's cousin."

Mustafaa's face suddenly lost colour. He stood up hastily, saying, "Sir, why are you still standing? Please have a seat." He instantly realised his faux pas: there was but a single stool there that he had been occupying himself. Instead of taking advantage of his discomfiture, Raam Iqbaal said, "Don't worry about arranging seats for us. Just do me the favour of informing *Munshii Jii* that we're waiting here."

"Very well, sir, I'll go and inform him right away. Please wait here until I return," said Mustafaa with alacrity, disappearing through the small gate. Within moments, however, he came rushing back, and said panting, "Sir, I forgot to ask your name. Who shall I say is here if *Munshii Jii* were to ask?"

"Tell him it's Raam Iqbaal Thaakur of Ratanpur."

For fear of forgetting the names of the visitor and his village, Mustafaa left mumbling them both repeatedly as though trying to memorise them, and walked hurriedly back.

Shortly, Gangeshvar came out and embraced Raam Iqbaal, saying, "Well…well! It's been a long time. To what do we owe this unexpected pleasure after so many years?"

Before Raam Iqbaal could reply, Gangeshvar noticed his companion, and fearing he'd be considered rude for ignoring him, asked his brother-in-law, "I don't think I've ever met the gentleman with you before. Won't you introduce him to me?"

"Well, shall we say we've have both been busy with our lives," replied Raam Iqbaal. He, however, didn't think it wise to reveal Kaashii Naath's identity in the presence of Mustafaa; so, he added, "The gentleman here is like a brother to me. I'll introduce him at length later."

Gangeshvar greeted Kaashii and turned to Raam Iqbaal, "We have so much to catch up, but I'm afraid I can neither leave my seat just now to go with you, nor entertain you here. I'm sorry."

"Don't even think of it. My worries are over now that we're in touch. I'd only request you to try and return as early as you can after you're done with your day's work," said Raam Iqbaal reassuringly.

"Of course!" said Gangeshvar, apologising again, and suggested that they go to his place and rest awhile.

"My wife, Giitaa, has seen you before and is bound to remember you. You'll be very welcome even without me accompanying," he said, but after a pause, added as if wondering aloud, "Hey, how will you reach my place, though? You don't know where I live."

Raam Iqbaal smiled broadly and replied, "That's not much of a problem in such a small town. Anybody will be able to guide us to your place once we reach the Hindu *Bastii* on the other side of the bazaar. Now go, take care of your work. In any case, it's bad form to chat for long on the roadside."

"All right then; see you soon," said Gangeshvara. As he disappeared through the gate, Raam Iqbaal took Mustafaa aside, saying, "Khaan Saahib, I have no words to express my gratitude for your assistance. It's taken care of all my worries. I had been wondering throughout our long ride here whether I'd be able to connect with my brother-in-law who's so busy attending to Nawaab Saahib." With that, he took out a silver coin from his pocket and proffered it to the bouncer, "Please accept this as a token of my appreciation," he said. As Mustafaa extended his hand to take the coin, belying his own protest that the tip was hardly necessary, Raam Iqbaal pressed home his advantage, "If it were not necessary, why would one offer it? Say, can I suggest something, if you don't mind; whatever else you do with it, you must take at least a *paav* of hot *jalebiis* home for your wife, or she would be most upset with you!"

Mustafaa gaped in dismay at Raam Iqbaal; "Sir, can I ask you something?" he asked, gulping.

"Sure, go right ahead!" Raam Iqbaal knew his shot in the dark had hit the mark.

"Would you be so kind as to tell me how you learnt about my wife's fondness for hot *jalebiis*? Fact is, she asked me for *jalebiis* again this morning," said Mustafaa.

"Well, my friend, you had better ask what I don't know. I can even tell you what she finds most irritating about you and which of your habits she finds the most obnoxious. Would you like me to tell you?" said Raam Iqbaal playing the clairvoyant.

"If you please, sir, do tell," pleaded Mustafaa extremely curious now.

"Since you seem skeptical, I might as well tell you then: she's most put off by your unkempt, scruffy moustaches and she detests your addiction to tobacco chewing," Raam Iqbaal, a bit of a mind-reader and a confidence-trickster rolled into one, had made an intelligent guess, but it hit the mark. Mustafaa stared at Raam Iqbaal, his eyes widened in disbelief.

"*Huzuur*, you're a seer with the gift of clairvoyance! That's exactly what my wife says, that the odor of tobacco is nauseating and my scruffy moustaches make her feel like sneezing when I try to kiss her. I've often thought I'd have them shaved off and give up chewing tobacco as well!"

Raam Iqbaal smiled benignly and said, "Moustaches are the hallmark of a virile man; I wouldn't advise you to do away with them. Of course, tobacco is harmful for health. Give it up if you can. May I tell you something else, Khaan Saahib?"

"*Huzuur*, you're welcome to say whatever you want," said Mustafaa obsequiously.

"Then listen to me, and listen good," said Raam Iqbaal, whispering close to his ear, as if sharing a closely guarded secret, "Merely standing at the gates I've divined that of late the state of affairs in the Palace has been simply terrible. I rather suspect the ominous shadow of Saturn has fallen on it!"

Clearly amazed once again, Mustafa said reverently, "You're spot on, *huzuur*, things here have really been messy, but how on earth would you know about it?"

"You never paid attention, did you? I've already told you that I know everything that's worth knowing. Anyway, forget it all except that you have to bring hot *jalebiis* to your *Begam*. Now I must be going. So long, then!"

Raam Iqbaal and Kaashii Naath turned and walked away towards the tree to which they had tethered their horses. Mustafaa, the bouncer, looked at the departing visitors, spellbound, as if he had just seen a ghost.

❋❋❋

Raam Iqbaal had never really stopped thirsting for revenge from the Nawaab of Waariaul for having been at the root of the massacre and destruction of Singhwaar. After meeting Bhavaanii, a graceful lady widowed in her prime, his feelings were exacerbated all over again. He felt like launching a frontal attack on the Nawaab's Palace, but he knew that he had to play his cards carefully.

Meanwhile, the two of them were approaching the Waariaul bazaar. Raam Iqbaal noticed two confectionary shops opposite each other and was struck by the sharp contrast in their fortunes. The relatively larger of the two was heavily padlocked with seals on them, as if closed down for an indefinite period of time, while the smaller establishment on the other side of the street was flushed with customers. Raam Iqbaal was tempted to check it out and see if he could con someone there and pick up some more intelligence. He turned to Kaashii and said that it would be impolite to arrive at Gangeshvar's place without a little something by way of gift for the lady of the house, and suggested they stop and buy some sweets and also take the opportunity to eat something themselves, for it was equally inadvisable to arrive hungry at a new household.

They tethered their horses outside the shop and went inside. The shop seemed to be doing roaring business, with a steady stream of customers coming and going. The owner, Nathunii Saah, sat against a bolster on his *gaddii*, wearing a hand-embroidered round velvet cap that must have cost a packet and an expensive silk *kurtaa*, his small eyes flickering and shifting ceaselessly as he watched customers come and go. A glance at him was all Raam Iqbaal needed to conclude that Nathunii was a shifty character, exceedingly cunning and lustful despite being elderly. He motioned Kaashii to take a seat while he went and stood in front of the owner's *gaddii*; having stared at him for a long moment, he exclaimed in a serious tone, "*SeTh Jii*, you're about to hit a jackpot!"

Nathunii Saah was taken aback at a well-dressed, seemingly upper-class gentleman coming up with an inanity apropos nothing, and peering at him curiously, he said, "Pardon me, sir, but what's this all about?"

"It seems you are unable to place me. I didn't expect you would, for your eyes are hardly still even for a moment. Well, to answer your question, as a *Braahmana* I have the gift to divine a lot of things on account of my *samskaara*. On top of that, since my father was a *trikaal-darshii PanDit* who could see the past, present and the future, I've inherited some of his powers and am able to see at least one of these in respect of anyone before me."

Unable to restrain his curiosity, Nathunii Saah asked, "What did you say your father's name was?"

"I'm sure you'd have heard of him; his name was Bhairav Naath *trikaal-darshii*. He was so famous in his time that most royal houses would have no one but him prepare the horoscope for their new-born. He would diligently study every nuance of the position of stars and celestial bodies before he drew up his charts, and if he found something inauspicious, he would also suggest ways and means to take care of it. Fame and prosperity lay at his feet: he left behind so much wealth that for generations we can afford to have all the luxuries of life without exerting ourselves. I'm decidedly unlucky that even though I'm the son of such a gifted father, I could not pick up anything much from him. Still, I'm indebted to him that before he departed, he made me at least one-dimensional *kaal-darshii* that I am."

Looking closely at the owner for the impact of his self-introduction, Raam Iqbaal confidently went on, "Whatever little I learnt from my father clearly tells me that your fortunes are on the rise. If there are any inauspicious impediments of your stars, I can easily suggest effective remedies. I can give you a written guarantee, if you like."

Impressed by the confidence of the stranger, Nathunii invited him to take a seat. Thanking him, Raam Iqbaal made himself comfortable by his side and went on, "Now listen attentively, I'm going to ask you a question. You have to answer it truthfully. If you don't, I'll lose nothing: only my predictions would be rendered inaccurate and your future would be ruined. So, keep that in mind while answering the question." By now curious beyond measure to find out what the stranger would say, the *SeTh* asked him to go ahead.

Making sure no one could overhear, Raam Iqbaal asked in a low whisper, "Tell me the numbers of properly wedded wives you have and amorous liaisons you are simultaneously indulging in on the side?"

Nathunii Saah was aghast! He just didn't know what to say. Raam Iqbaal said, chuckling, "If this is your response to my first question, I wonder what will happen to you when I ask the second one."

Disconcerted by the mocking tone of the *PanDit*, Nathunii said in a hoarse whisper, "Let me have the second one as well."

"Who's the lass you're currently wooing and desperately wanting in your bed?" asked Raam Iqbaal in a serious, measured tone, making it clear he wasn't joking. Nathunii was no longer in doubt that the *PanDit* had the gift of clairvoyance, and turned thoughtful.

"Say, what reverie did I push you into?" asked Raam Iqbaal.

Finally, Nathunii decided to take the plunge, and looking around to see that no one was eavesdropping on them, he said in a frayed voice, "I've as many as three wives but no child with any one of them. Heck! I'm without a single successor,

Mahaaraaj. I consulted any number of *vaidyas*, *hakiims* and must have lapped up hundreds of kilos of *avalehas*, and got my wives to take *chuurans* by the sack-full, but all to no avail. At the end of it all, I thought there was hardly any point in accumulating wealth if there was no one to inherit and enjoy it. I began to distract myself with seducing pretty women and gradually got sucked into a vortex of lust; hunting around for variety has now become such an addiction, I just can't rid myself of it!"

"I understand, and you don't need to worry in the least now that the Almighty has sent me to take care of every ominous aspect in your stars."

With the *SeTh* practically eating out of his hands now, Raam Iqbaal asked pointing to the locked confectionary store across the street, "Whose shop is that? Looks like it's been locked up for good! You've any idea, why?"

The question left Nathunii wondering whether it would be prudent to share the secret of the locked store of his erstwhile competitor across the street. Raam Iqbaal was quick to gauge that there had to be a reason why Nathunii was hesitant. He nudged him in a roundabout manner, "*SeTh Jii*, don't you see that the locks on the shutters of that store are the key to the new treasures of fortune about to open up for you?"

Nathunii replied in a subdued tone, "That store belonged to one Khairaatii Saah, though his name was a misnomer, for never once in his life did he part with a farthing by way of charity. His store was confiscated and sealed by the orders of *ChhoTe Nawaab*, Shahnavaaz Khaan."

"What did he do?" asked Raam Iqbaal.

"Khairaatii Saah died several months ago; so, no question of him doing anything to bring on the recent closure. The reason for *ChhoTe Nawaab*'s wrath was altogether different." Nathunii was again hesitant to go on. Looking around to see whether anyone was taking unusual interest in their conversation, he went on, "Khairaatii made a fortune from that shop to add to the substantial family wealth he had inherited. He only had a daughter for an heir, no sons, and no other close relatives either; his wife had died years ago. Khairaatii was about eighty when he took seriously ill. He needed someone to attend on him all the time; so, he called his daughter, Belaa, who lived with her in-laws, to come and help him out. Her husband Ganeshii came escorting her on the journey, but he wasn't in a position to stay long as he had a job in the city he didn't want to lose. He left Belaa with her father and went back to it. Belaa had returned to Waariaul after a gap of several years. A lanky teenager when matrimony took her away, she had grown into a full woman now. Marriage seemed to have agreed with her. She was so lovely, soft and plump, and true to her name, seemed to spread an enticing fragrance wherever she went. Her breasts pushed at her chemise in such a way...." Nathunii would perhaps have gone on dreamily describing Belaa's beauty had Raam Iqbaal not interrupted him, "*SeTh Jii*, are you all right? You seem to be spouting poetry like some love-lorn lunatic."

Startled by the interruption, Nathunii looked around to check again if they were being watched, and said absent-mindedly, "So, where were we?"

"Oh, forget where we were! Belaa's hardly likely to take the bait from an old fogey like you. Now, tell me, why did *ChhoTe Nawaab* close down Khairaatii's shop?"

"That's what I was going to tell you," said Nathunii, exasperated, "After her father died, she started to manage the shop herself, not wanting to let go of the lucrative set-up she had inherited. She thought she'd have Ganeshii come over and join her, too, as soon as she had settled down a bit. After all, running one's own business was way better than serving someone else's. But fate had other plans! Anyway, to begin with, her business prospered. Khairaatii's shop had never wanted for customers, but now that there was the added lure of an attractive woman to ogle at, and occasionally to exchange a few words with, customers seemed to come in droves to her store.

"Folks bought even more than they actually needed, just to impress the comely proprietor who kept flashing smiles and chirping to egg them on. If she'd gone on like that a little longer, I would have no option but to close shop, for people had quit even looking at mine. I prayed fervently for something to happen, and finally one day my prayers were answered; *ChhoTe Nawaab* ordered her shop sealed and shut down!"

"But you haven't yet told me why!" said Raam Iqbaal.

"That's what I was getting at. Shahnavaaz Khaan happened to catch a glimpse of Belaa when his cavalcade on an evening round passed by Khairaatii's store. The next thing anyone knew was that a Palace sepoy came to the store and was seen talking to her. No one has a clue what was said between them. What people actually remember seeing was that soon after the sepoy's visit, Belaa left in a palanquin sent from the Palace. No sooner had she left than the store was sealed, shut down, and has remained so ever since."

All of a sudden, Raam Iqbaal recalled in a flash Pyaare, the *tamolii's* remark that things at the Palace were getting out of hand. Keen to find out more, he pumped Nathunii, "So, what happened then?"

"What do you expect? Belaa began to spread her fragrance at *ChhoTe Nawaab*'s, what else!" said Nathunii, beginning to tire of it all. Raam Iqbaal could see in his face, though, that he had more to tell. He asked persuasively, "Is that how the matter ended? Rather a tame affair then, I say!"

"Oh, they would have been extremely lucky had it ended there, but it turned into a real scandal."

Hardly had the word 'scandal' escaped Nathunii's lips, one of his servants, roughly his own age, jumped out of nowhere and said sharply, "*SeTh Jii*, I've been watching you for some time. Have you nothing better to do than let your tongue wag every which way and get the better of you?"

Nathunii was stunned at being spoken to so rudely by a servant. Raam Iqbaal, on the other hand, was annoyed beyond measure at the sudden interruption. He gave the interloper a dirty look and said to him sharply, "You think you're a well-wisher of your master, don't you? But tell me something: isn't it you who procures for him and takes him around to tarts?"

Raam Iqbaal had accurately guessed the reason for such a hold that alone could embolden a servant to reprimand his master like an errant child. The waiter in question, Bholaa, had fallen silent after the visitor snapped at him. Taking advantage of his momentary set-back, Raam Iqbaal raised his pitch, "Do you know who I am. I'm the sole heir of *PanDit* Bahirav Naath *trikaaldarshii*, an *ek-kaaldarshii jyotishii* myself. If I were to bless you, your life might get back on the rails!" Then, guessing again, he concluded that all of Bholaa's sons were wasters, the reason why he was still at work in his sunset years, he said, "All your sons are worthless scoundrels, aren't they? Admit to it!"

"Yes, all my four sons are useless," said Bholaa.

"They do nothing all day but loiter around, don't they? Come on, answer me!" said Raam Iqbaal.

"That's right."

"Does anyone of them listen to your counsel."

"No, every one of them threatens to commit suicide the moment I open my mouth."

"Your wife's health is failing, she's often unwell and confined to bed, isn't that so?"

"That's right," said Bholaa, his voice choked with emotions flowing from the thought of his depressing family life.

Grinning sardonically, Raam Iqbaal finally nailed Bholaa, "And look at yourself; imagine, having to wait upon people and wash their dirty plates at this stage of life! But don't worry, it can all be sorted out even now if you care to listen."

Bholaa suddenly rushed forward and fell at Raam Iqbaal's feet, whimpering, "*Mahaaraaj*, please do help me out. I'm yours to command!"

"All right, let me see what's possible." With that, Raam Iqbaal sat erect in *padmaasana* and started taking deep breaths, his eyes closed. After a while, he opened his eyes and exclaimed, "Look here, you'll have to take me home. I'll need to take a look at your place, it seems that the ominous Saturn has taken hold of the oven in your kitchen. That's where the problem has its roots."

Bowing reverently with his palms together in front, Bholaa pleaded, "*Mahaaraaj*, let's go immediately."

"Learn to be patient, Bholaa," said Raam Iqbaal as if chiding an over-eager child, "We'll go to your place on Tuesday; it's *Hanumaan Jii*'s special day and would be more auspicious. Now that I've agreed to the propitiation of your wayward stars, it will happen in good time. Meanwhile, go, take care of my friend over there while I solve *SeTh Jii*'s problems."

As soon as Bholaa was out of earshot, Raam Iqbaal turned to Nathunii, "Carry on. What happened after Belaa went to *ChhoTe Nawaab*'s palace?"

"Well, it turned into a daily routine. Every evening, the Palace palanquin would come to fetch her; what time of the night she returned from there, no one knew."

"Is her liaison with the prince consensual, or she goes under duress?"

"Well, that's a question only Belaa can answer," said Nathunii, and once again swivelling his shifty eyes all around to check for possible eavesdroppers, went on to volunteer, "Some time ago, a rumour had gone wild that Nawaab Salaamat Khaan had been having erazy panic attacks; he hallucinated snakes coming at him from all sides and fell unconscious, crying out to be saved from the vipers that apparently only he could see. Alas, the grand old Vizier, Ghulaam Sarvar, had gone missing at such a difficult time. If he were around, he would certainly have taken Nawaab Saahib in hand, but I also heard that, after a while, Nawaab Saahib recovered on his own and stopped having those crazy fits. For some time past, I believe he's been well-enough to have resumed his routine of evening *mehfil*s of booze and nautch."

"What happened then?" Raam Iqbaal prodded Nathunii.

"Well, might as well ask what didn't happen! It's

embarrassing even to recall it," said Nathunii and fell silent again.

Raam Iqbaal, beside himself for curiosity, said, "Come on now, tell me anyway!"

"It was all Nusrat's fault. He was at the root of the imbroglio," said Nathunii.

"Now, who's Nusrat?"

"Nusrat's the brother of the Nawaab's third wife and his favourite courtier," said Nathunii and stopped again.

Exasperated by Nathunii's stop and go, Raam Iqbaal chided him, "What's it with you, I say! Why don't you come clean?"

"*Mahaaraaj*, if I speak continuously for long, I get short of breath. After all, I happen to be an elderly....."

"Look here, Nathunii," interrupted Raam Iqbaal, clearly annoyed now, "Elderly or not, if you don't cooperate, it might happen that you'd have breathed your last instead of just being short of breath! Take care not to test my patience too hard. Now, you had better tell me where Nusrat fits in all this."

Nathunii cowered at the open threat and plunged into the narrative in right earnest, "*Mahaaraaj*, please spare me your wrath, I'll tell you everthing I know."

"It's common knowledge that Nawaab Saahib spends his evenings in a secluded part of the Palace, which few except trusted attendants and his pet courtiers are allowed to enter. It was such an evening, some time after *ChhoTe Nawaab* had commandeered Belaa's company. As usual, Nawaab Saahib sat in his private chamber enjoying the haze induced by alcohol while Nusrat, a permanent fixture in such evening *mehfils*, silently watched his master, waiting for his command. Eventually, the Nawaab said, 'Nusrat *miaaN*, don't be so glum, say something. I have begun to be scared of silence, and you know that! If nothing else, let's have your the blessed *Daastaan-e-Alif-Lailaa* again for all I care, but for heaven's sake, don't remain silent."

"This was their daily routine, but having run out of ideas that evening, Nusrat started singing paean of the unbelievable beauty of Belaa, little realising what a monumental mischief he was making.

"Nawaab Saahib was soon so enamoured of the beauty Nusrat described, he began to pressure him to somehow get Belaa for him, promising a carte blanch as his reward. Knowing Shahnavaaz's temper, Nusrat realised he had shot himself in the foot, but knew the ruler would not be denied. So, he started scheming.

"One night, as the palanquin carrying Belaa back home emerged from the *ChhoTe Nawaab*'s palace, an armed band of *laThii*-wielding goons staked out at Nusrat's behest ambushed it. The *kahaar*s carrying the palanquin abandoned it and ran for their lives. Belaa was whisked away to Salaamat Khaan's private quarters. The news of Belaa's kidnapping and the identity of likely perpetrators reached the *ChhoTe Nawaab* through the *kahaar*s who feared for their lives either way. The prince was incensed beyond words; picking up his leather hunter, he rushed out in a blind rage.

"He sought out Nusrat and began belting him mercilessly. Nusrat hadn't imagined he would have to face something so drastic. He fell to his knees at Shahnavaaz's feet, whimpering and pleading it wasn't his fault, he was merely carrying out Nawaab Saahib's bidding. The *ChhoTe Nawaab*, clearly unconvinced, kicked the cowering courtier, threatening to whip him until there was no skin left on his body.

'Tell me where Belaa is, or else you're dead meat', said Shahnavaaz, and raising his hunter, delivered another lusty crack. Nusrat couldn't take any more of it. He silently pointed in the direction of the Nawaab's private apartment.

"Belaa, mortally scared of the bizarre turn of events, stood trembling in front of Salaamat Khaan, her head bowed and tears flowing from her eyes. The Nawaab tried to lustily pull her into his arms, promising her untold fortunes in return for her favours. Shahnavaaz halted a moment at the door watching the awkward amorous advances of his drunken father through the gap in the velvet curtains, his temper rising by the second. When he couldn't stand it anymore, he entered the room thundering, 'Hey you old bugger! Stop this moment or I'll kill you. Do you know this woman you want to take to bed is mine. You've had her abducted and surely you deserve to be punished', said the frenzied prince gnashing his teeth, and lunged forward to start brutally lashing his father. The drunken old man, completely unmanned by the sudden assault, fell to the ground groaning. Within moments, the Palace was abuzz with a thousand whispered rumours, but no one had the gumption to confront Shahnavaaz, who had already jumped into the driver's seat with his brazen act of defiance. Nusrat was banished from the Palace with immediate effect. The Nawaab was placed under house-arrest in his private apartment; he was neither allowed to receive visitors nor go out of his rooms." Nathunii paused, and then said, as if wondering aloud, "Where the old Vizier was during the whole crisis remains a real mystery!" Curious to dig deeper, Raam Iqbaal asked, "For how long has Ghulaam Sarvar been missing?"

"Quite some time, I reckon. He was reported to have been sent on some kind of a secret mission. But how important could any mission be compared to the melt-down that was shaking the very foundations of the Palace!" replied Nathunii.

Raam Iqbaal turned thoughtful, wondering whether the Vizier's secret assignment could possibly involve a threat to the safety of Bhavaanii and Jagdambii. Then, preparing to take leave of Nathunii Saah, he said, "Now answer my last question truthfully and then I must be on my way. How're you so well-informed on Belaa's travails?"

"It's quite obvious. Don't you recall the old adage: 'Even walls have ears!' There are any number of servants, attendants and the like serving the rulers. Besides, there are courtiers who come and go, and listen at closed doors. How can anything of their lives remain secret for long? Wherever you go in this town today, you'll find young lads huddled together only chatting of Belaa and all that happened to her. Whatever I've told you is indeed based on hearsay, but I believe it to be true."

"Now, I'd like to take leave of you," said Raam Iqbaal, rising to his feet, "Allow me, however, to give you some good advice in parting: there's no end to hankering after material things. You need to be conscious of your elderly status and be done with chasing skirts now. In fact, it's time now for you to be preparing to meet your Maker. All your problems will be sorted out on their own if you follow my advice."

By then Kashii, refreshed by a repast of *puurii* and sweetmeats, also joined them and asked Raam Iqbaal to find out about payment.

"Oh, I had missed out on that. How much do I owe you?" Raam Iqbaal asked turning to Nathunii, who looked genuinely hurt. "*Mahaaraaj*, don't be so unkind! Do you think I'm going to accept payment for refreshments after you've done so much for me?"

"As you wish," said Raam Iqbaal.

The two friends exited the store and got on to their horses.

❋❋❋

Raam Iqbaal and Kashii rode together in silence through the bazaar towards *Munshii* Gangeshvar *Paan*dey's place, lost in their individual thoughts. Kaashii was amazed at the versatility of his friend; while he had little to show for his several visits to Waariaul on his own, Raam Iqbaal had within the space of a few hours unearthed a whole lot of inside information on how things were going inside the Nawaab's Palace. On the other hand, Raam Iqbaal was thinking of ways and means to unravel the mystery surrounding the Vizier's sudden disappearance; though not fully satisfied with the progress made, he brimmed with confidence for having conned Nathunii into revealing valuable information.

As they reached the heart of the shopping district, Raam Iqbaal abruptly motioned Kaashii to halt, saying,

"Gangeshvar's unlikely to be home until much later. Meanwhile, we can do but little more than twiddle our thumbs at his place. Let's talk to some more people instead, shall we?" he said.

"Well, you're the best judge; if I were any good at this kind of stuff, why would I need to bother you," said Kaashii.

They found the shade of a tree and tethered their horses. Raam Iqbaal pointed to a large, prosperous looking cloth merchant's store and said, "Let's go."

Seeing two well-attired gentlemen enter, the cloth merchant occupying the owner's *gaddii* smiled and said, "Welcome to the store, sir. What can I do for you?" That was enough of an opening for Raam Iqbaal to begin spinning his yarn.

"Well," he said, "I'm also into textile trading; we're based in Benares. Actually, I'm here with my partner to explore the possibility of setting up a branch dealing in Benares fabrics and stuff. We've heard a lot about Nawaab Salaamat Khaan's patronage."

Impressed by Raam Iqbaal's personality and manners, the *SeTh* responded positively, "You're welcome. I'm happy to make your acquaintance, but I seriously doubt that there would be enough demand of such expensive goods here. Only the Palace could afford it, but how much can they buy!"

Raam Iqbaal made himself comfortable on one side of the *gaddii*, patting the place at his side for Kaashii to do likewise, and replied, "You're right, *SeTh Jii*, but I can't reveal my trade secrets all at once; you know very well, it's simply not done. However, being in a similar line of business, we're like brothers, aren't we? So, let me make an exception for once and tell you everything."

Then, dropping his voice to a whisper, as if guarding his secret from eavesdroppers, Raam Iqbaal said, "Tell me something: haven't you ever heard of fakes coexisting with the genuine, and so skilfully produced that it's hard for anyone to tell the difference, except perhaps a connoisseur once in a blue moon?"

"I'm now beginning to get a hang of what you're saying," replied the shop-owner, and asked where the two were staying in Waariaul.

Affecting a sigh of sadness, Raam Iqbaal said, "This is my third visit here. On both the previous occasions, I stayed at Khairaatii Saah's place, but on arrival this time, I learnt that he's no more. So, I went across the street to the other confectioner. But if I may be frank with you, I didn't quite like this other guy, Nathunii."

"Fie on him, sir; you did well to decide against staying with him. Nathunii is a wretched womaniser!" remarked the *SeTh*, with obvious distaste.

"In the circumstances," continued Raam Iqbaal, "I think we'll stay at *Munshii* Gangeshvar Paandey's place this time. I haven't been able to see him yet on this visit, but the rather pleasant vibes of our past meetings make me think he would be happy to accommodate us. The last time I was here, I even brought his wife a gift of *Benaresii saariis* and jewellery for which my city is famous."

The *SeTh* was obviously bowled over at the mention of stranger's proximity to the Nawaab's *Munshii*, thinking he was talking to a man of substance. Raam Iqbaal decided it was time to throw the calculated provocation at him.

"In fact, I was on my way to *Munshii Jii*'s place when I happened to notice your shop, suddenly remembering that this was the very shop he'd promised he would persuade you to vacate for me, if I ever decided to set up a branch here."

The *SeTh* went red in the face at the presumptuous remark, but Raam Iqbaal ploughed on regardless, "*Munshii Jii* also promised to introduce me to Vizier Ghulaam Sarvar, who rules the roost here, as you no doubt know. Even the Nawaab himself wouldn't turn down his recommendation, and, of course, I have the means to make the Vizier happy. I'm sure you know what I mean," said Raam Iqbaal in a deliberately offensive tone.

An acrimonious exchange followed between the *SeTh* and Raam Iqbaal, the former contending that his store prospered because of his business acumen and hard work while the latter insisted it was entirely on account of the prominent, eye-catching location of the store that automatically brought him hordes of customers.

"How can I let go of such a vantage point?" said Raam Iqbaal with an air of finality.

"But where will I go then? I'll be ruined if I'm compelled to yield. I can't let that happen!"

"What can you possibly do? Can you imagine yourself resisting the combined might of *Munshii Jii* and the Vizier? You had better find a suitable alternative while there is still time," retorted Raam Iqbaal provoking him even more. That proved to be the last straw on the camel's back! The *SeTh* lost his cool precisely as Raam Iqbaal had intended, hoping that he would really get talking when enraged.

"Enough, I say! Who do you think you are, threatening me with eviction like this? The Vizier, who you think will get you this shop is no longer alive for your information, and as for the *Munshii*, his days are numbered as well," shot back the *SeTh*.

Feigning surprise, Raam Iqbaal exclaimed, "How can that be possible!"

"I'm not talking of possibilities, Mister; it's already happened!" said the *SeTh* sarcastically, "Even Nawaab Salaamat Khaan is no longer relevant. The *ChhoTe Nawaab*, Shahnavaaz Khaan is incharge now."

Raam Iqbaal now assumed a conciliatory tone, "Well, I'm quite shocked to hear that, but never mind. Being traders, we're used to such political turmoil. I'm sure we can work out an agreement that's profitable for us both."

"Like what?" said the *SeTh*, a little mollified but still on his guard.

"I can suggest a mutually acceptable arrangement if you wish," said Raam Iqbaal.

"All right, let's have it on the table, but you can be sure of one thing: of your two champions, one has departed the world and the other is about to lose his authority," declared the *SeTh* triumphantly.

"Oh, let them go to hell for all I care. I'm essentially a trader, used to shifting my loyalty as may be most profitable to me," said Raam Iqbaal.

"Now you're talking! As traders, we must only think of our profit and loss," gloated the *SeTh*.

"That's right. Well, can we then think of a business partnership in which I make the supplies and you manage the sales here. We'll split the profits evenly."

The proposal sounded too good to be true; the *SeTh* eagerly asked Raam Iqbaal whether he thought it was a feasible proposition.

"Sure, we can do it!" said Raam Iqbaal firmly, adding, "On my return to *Benaares*, I'll send you the first lot of goods worth, let's say, about fifteen to twenty thousand rupiahs, and then modulate supplies according to off-take and demand."

The *SeTh* couldn't believe his ears. A first instalment of goods worth fifteen thousand rupees was beyond his wildest dream!

"Are you serious?" he asked.

"Of course! In the holy city of *Benaares*, we don't deal in lies, my friend," said Raam Iqbaal with a confident smile on his lips. Then, after a pause, he added, "Now, before I take your leave, would you be so good as to tell me how the Vizier died? Just curious, you know!"

The *SeTh* glanced around suspiciously, and lowering his voice, replied, "I don't know how he died but I'm sure he didn't die in Waariaul; what's more, it wasn't a natural death either."

"On what basis are you saying so?" asked Raam Iqbaal.

"Well, if he had died of natural causes, Nawaab Saahib wouldn't have fallen prey to the strange fits that he did. He went kind of crazy, they say. He would see deadly snakes coming at him everywhere in the Palace. When he was a little better, he got into this nasty fracas with his son over Khairaatii Saah's daughter. The latest is that the old Nawaab has been confined to his private apartment. He isn't allowed to see anyone. As for the *Munshii*, *ChhoTe Nawaab* simply can't stand him. I'm sure he's about to be shown the door. But really, how does any of this concern us!"

"Indeed so! Palace intrigue isn't our cup of tea," Raam Iqbaal agreed emphatically, and added, "So then, I'll send the first consignment as soon as I get back, and will also return myself, if possible, but...." he let the sentence hang in the middle.

"But what?" queried the *SeTh*.

"*SeTh Jii*, you well know how messy business partnerships lacking clarity can turn out. I was thinking maybe we should reduce our understanding into a written agreement to help us sort out any possible differences of opinion later."

"Yes, of course. Let's do it," said the *SeTh*.

Raam Iqbaal had already got more out of the cloth-merchant than he had hoped for; he didn't want to push his luck too far.

"I must be on my way, *SeTh Jii*. We'll hopefully meet again soon by the blessings of *Baabaa Vishvanaath*," he said.

"As you wish, sir," said the *SeTh*, rising to his feet to see them off. They walked together to the tree to which Raam Iqbaal and Kaashii had tethered their horses. As they took hold of the reins, the *SeTh* bowed and said obsequiously, "I'll look forward to receiving your blessings."

"Please don't embarrass me, *SeTh Jii*! We are partners now, and friends as well," said Raam Iqbaal, jumping into the saddle.

As they moved out of earshot, Kaashii, amazed once again by his friend's manipulative skills, asked him uncertainly, "Do you really mean to send him a consignment, Raam?"

Raam Iqbaal simply guffawed at Kaashii Naath's innocence.

❋❋❋

They had no problem finding Gangeshvar's place. Giitaa readily recognised Raam Iqbaal from earlier meetings, hastening to roll out the red carpet for her husband's brother-in-law the 'gainer', as Indians term a sister's husband. The twosome was comfortably put up in a guestroom furnished with luxuriously upholstered beds with silk bed-linen. As dinner time approached, Giitaa persuaded them to eat without waiting for Gangeshvar, who was expected to be very late. After the meal, Giitaa escorted them back to the guest room. She said bantering with her brother-in-law, "I've had drinking water put in your room: it'll help you take care of insomnia!"

Giving up the hope of being able to have a chat with Gangeshvar that night, Raam Iqbaal and Kaashii Naath decided to turn in early, but Giitaa's words proved prophetic; Raam Iqbaal lay tossing and turning. His head, buzzing with the information he had picked up during the course of the day, refused to get turned off for the night. Sensing his unease, Kaashii said, "Why don't you take Giitaa's advice and have a glass of water?"

"That's poppycock! What can water do? How can one go to sleep when the mind's racked by anxiety!"

"But what's making you feel so anxious?" asked Kaashii naively.

Raam Iqbaal sat up in bed, saying, "Well, for one thing, I can't fathom the mystery surrounding the mission on which Ghulaam Sarvar was sent; for another, I can't make head or tail of the Nawaab imagining snakes coming at him."

"But how does any of that concern us?"

"Well, coming close on heels of the massacre at Singhwaar as they did, all these events may be linked to it in some way."

Before Kaashii could say anything, there was a knock on the door followed by Gangeshvar entering, apologising profusely for coming so late.

"All right...all right, you're duly forgiven, but first go and have your dinner. Giitaa poor girl must be famished. But after that, come right back and answer some questions that have been bothering me all evening. I can hardly sleep for curiosity until I get the answers," said Raam Iqbaal.

"Sure! I'll be right back and do my best," replied Gangeshvar. When he returned, Raam Iqbaal first introduced Kaashii Naath to him, as promised at the Palace gates.

After formally greeting Kaashii, Gangeshvar said, "I think I've seen you before."

It was Raam Iqbaal who replied on his friend's behalf and told him of his recent visits to Waariaul for a specific purpose.

"Would you like to tell me about it?" asked Gangeshvar, eyeing them with open curiosity.

While Kaashii was still wondering how much he could share with Gangeshvar, Raam Iqbaal spoke up on their behalf, "You must have heard about Dharaadhar Thaakur of Singhwaar."

"Oh the Singhwaar Thaakur!" the *Munshii*'s face clouded over instantly at the mention of Dharaadhar Thaakur. "Nusrat and the Vizier were at the root of the imbroglio. They could have brought Nawaab Saahib around if they wanted to, but they chose not to do so. On the contrary, they plotted against the *Deorhii* so secretly, no one was any the wiser for it until it was too late. Even I was kept out of the loop; if I had got the slightest inkling of what was cooking, I would certainly have forewarned the Thaakurs. With the blood of that innocent *Braahmana* family on his hands, Nawaab Saahib hasn't had a moment's peace since."

"Well," said Raam Iqbaal, "we're now reconciled to what happened as being God's will. Of course, we'll forever regret not getting to know of the evil secret plan in time. Anyway, my friend here, descended from the *Dighvae'Sannahpur* stock, is a kinsman of the Singhwaar Thaakurs. He has been trying to ascertain the status of their family estate, but hasn't had any success despite making several trips here. When I learnt about it, I decided to bring him to you."

"I'm afraid I can only bring you bad news on that account. Of course, the imperial authorities confiscated their estate and properties by way of damages," said Gangeshvar.

"Don't worry, we already kind of knew that," said Kaashii Naath, taking the bad news in his stride. Meanwhile, Raam Iqbaal jumped another question at Gangeshvar, "What was the mission that cost Ghulaam Sarvar his life and from which he only returned as a dead body?" Gangeshvar Paandey looked at his brother-in-law, his eyes widening in amazement.

"How did you find that out?" he asked.

"Ganguu," replied Raam Iqbaal, addressing him patronisingly by his nickname, "If you take us for innocent babes in the woods, you're sadly mistaken! We keep our eyes and ears open and can sniff around a bit, too. Now, tell me where did the Vizier go and how did he die."

"There's a Sanskrit adage '*Vinaash-kaale vipariit buddhi*'. That's what happened to the lot of them. A few weeks after the attack on the Singhwaar *Deorhii*, Nawaab Saahib summoned the Vizier, and gnashing his teeth, said to him peevishly, 'The imperial authorities confiscated the estate and immovable properties of the Thaakurs, but what did we get in return for our trouble? Take as many men as you like and lead them personally to make a thorough search of Singhwaar *Deorhii*. Go, grab whatever cash, jewellery and other valuables you can find and bring them all here.'

"Ghulaam Sarvar was reluctant to go, meekly pointing out that nothing of value was likely to be found after such a long gap. The abandoned mansion must have been scavenged to the bone by now. Salaamat Khaan thought that he was just being lazy, and flared up, 'Why wouldn't anything of value be there? You'd reported to me yourself that those who cremated the Thaakurs took back nothing but the ashes of their dead. So, where did the wealth accumulated over generations go then? Must still be there! Go now, and make a thorough search, mind you! You are free to handpick your team and take as many veterans as you like!'

"What could poor Ghulaam Sarvar do! He had to go. So, he left for Singhwaar, taking four daredevil veterans with him. They went over the *havelii* from one end to the other with a tooth-comb, as it were, but failed to turn up anything of much value. At last they entered the *Puujaa-ghar*, only to be confronted all of a sudden by two deadly king cobras, hissing ominously, their hoods tautly erect. Before they could even react and take evasive action, two of the veterans and the Vizier were bitten, and died instantaneously. The other two veterans, following them a few paces behind, witnessed the horrendous scene and wanted to run for their lives as fast as they could, but being trained professional soldiers, they couldn't very well leave the dead bodies of the Vizier and their comrades. Trembling in fear, somehow they retrieved the corpses, loaded them on their horses and brought them back to Waariaul in the dead of the night. The fiasco was reported to the Nawaab. The old man was terrified at what had happened. He ordered the bodies quietly buried with bare religious rites. He was, however, so troubled from that moment onwards, he soon began to suffer strange fits: he would see snakes everywhere in the Palace, coming at him with their hoods out; he would cry out '*bachaao...bachaao*' and faint. This went on for the longest time. Elders and *maulvii*s consoled; innumerable *vaidya*s and *hakiim*s were consulted. Eventually, he began to feel a little better, but how long could it last! He neither cared for his advancing years, nor was he bothered about the consequences of his excesses. Once again Nusrat played the villain, plying such bawdy description of the allures of Belaa that the old lech was left salivating. He promised to make Nusrat his Vizier if he brought her to his bed. Nusrat was so tempted, he didn't even pause to consider the consequences of taking the volatile *ChhoTe Nawaab* head on, ultimately causing the explosion that shook the Palace to its very foundations. The Nawaab had a massive row with his son leading to the virtual coup."

"Where's Belaa now?" asked Raam Iqbaal.

"But where did you get so much information from," countered Gangeshvar.

"Let's leave that alone for now, shall we? First answer my question," Raam Iqbaal persisted.

"After she was abducted by Nusrat's goons, *ChhoTe Nawaab* refuses to let her out of his sight. She lives in his palace now."

"Is she there by choice, do you think?" asked Raam Iqbaal.

"That's a question only she can answer."

"Thanks a ton, my dear," said Raam Iqbaal. Then, handing over a letter of invitation to Gangeshvar, he added, "My eldest son, Raam Lohit, is to be married soon. The dates, venues and all other coordinates are in here. I should be greatly honoured if you could join the *baraat* and other festivities."

Skimming through the invite, Gangeshvar said, "Raam Iqbaal *Bhaai*, you already know how difficult things are in the Palace right now. Nonetheless, I shall try my very best to join you for a day. Please accept my congratulations anyway."

"All right then, it's past midnight, and time for everyone to catch a few winks. Have a good night."

"Good night!" returning Raam Iqbaal's greeting, Gangeshvar rose to his feet and left the room.

Kaashii fell asleep no sooner than he hit the bed while Raam Iqbaal closed his eyes and prayed to his *IshTa-Deva*, Shiva, for courage and strength to do whatever he could to avenge the brutal destruction of Singhwaar *Deorhii* engineered by Salaamat Khaan and his Vizier.

❋❋❋

At first light the next morning, while Kaashii Naath and Gangeshvar were still asleep, Raam Iqbaal got through his morning ablutions and left for a morning walk. He had no pre-meditated agenda but the idea of revenge still simmered in his mind. He was determined to do something tangible about it before he left Waariaul. He walked briskly, praying silently again to his *IshTa-Deva* for guidance and strength.

Lost in his thoughts, Raam Iqbaal wound up in the heart of the Hindu *Bastii*. As he neared what appeared to be sort of a clearing surrounded by a maze of narrow lanes radiating out, he noticed a sizable group of men chatting animatedly. On seeing a well-appointed stranger approaching, a sudden hush fell over the group. Coming closer, Raam Iqbaal accosted them, "Folks, I'm indeed a stranger without any connections or relatives here. I'd heard a lot of praise for the Nawaab's patronage to meritorious people. Being educated and industrious, I thought I was bound to find a decent job here, but alas...." he deliberately fell silent mid-way through the sentence.

Dukhii Raam, a cobbler with salt and pepper hair that contrasted oddly with his lustrous black moustaches, feeling a bit concerned about the pained expression on the stranger's face, asked, "*Baabuu Jii*, why did you abruptly stop? Do tell us if there is something we can do to help."

"What can I really say! I'm now regretting my decision to come here at all. Truth to tell, I'm deeply ashamed to be breathing in the corruption and degradation that envelops this place and cursing myself."

Pausing for effect, he mollified them by adding that he shouldn't be misunderstood for his view of their town as he found his conscience chafing to be in a place so steeped in debauchery.

Dukhii Raam politely asked the stranger to take a seat. Raam Iqbaal thanked him and sat down, shaking his head sadly in the manner of someone regretting a bad decision.

"The moment I reached Waariaul, my hopes of finding employment were dashed, and now I'm under an ultimatum to leave the town without delay," he said.

"But why? Who's forcing you to leave?" asked Dukhii Raam, beside himself with curiosity by now.

"I came here with a letter of recommendation addressed to the Vizier. Upon my arrival, I learnt that Ghulaam Sarvar had died on some mission he was assigned, and the Nawaab was so upset, he lost his balance and started having crazy fits. I approached *Munshii* Gangeshvar Paandey for help but he told me bluntly that he could do nothing as the Palace was going through some kind of a crisis." Raam Iqbaal paused to gauge the reaction of his audience. None of them seemed to believe him in the least, and looked incredulously at one another. Eventually, Dukhii Raam spoke for them all, "But sir, our *Bastii* is situated so close to Nawaab Saahib's Palace, we can almost smell the aromas of the palace kitchens, and yet none of us has ever heard anything of the sort."

"I can swear by all that's holy that I've told you nothing but the truth. In fact, there are some more things that have caused me extreme anguish and shame, and these will undoubtedly be the cause for shame to you all, particularly the Hindus," said Raam Iqbaal with a weary sigh.

The men stared at the stranger, eagerly waiting for him to reveal the details of his claim. Dukhii Raam again voiced their anxiety, "Sir, instead of beating about the bush, why don't you tell us plainly what it is that's causing you such distress. In fact, you must, because you seem to be suggesting that our self-respect is compromised."

"Well, looking to the insulting manner in which the *Munshii* ordered me to leave, I ought to have left last night, but I deliberately decided to wait until the morning to fulfil my obligation to inform you all of the disturbing facts that I had learnt."

Pausing dramatically again to emphasise what he was about to say, Raam Iqbaal continued, "Who can deny that the Mughals hold sway over India! Who can wish away this political reality by closing his eyes? But are we, therefore, to assume that nothing's left of our identity and pride? That we are mere slaves dependent on their mercy? Does it mean that they can have their way with our women while we look on helplessly? I, for one, would rather die than cling on to such a despicable existence!" Having made his provocative little speech, Raam Iqbaal sighed mournfully, his face reddening in outrage that was partly contrived.

"Sir, if you're hinting at Khairaatii Saah's daughter, Belaa, I'll have you know that we've already resolved not to remain silent anymore. Our tolerance is at its breaking point and we couldn't care less about the consequences. In fact, we were discussing the very issue when you happened to arrive," said Dukhii Raam.

"I'm happy to hear you say that, but listen carefully to what I'm going to tell you now," said Raam Iqbaal, "Some time ago, your Nawaab Saahib had called for the assistance of a contingent of the imperial army..."

Several voices piped up from the gathering to interrupt him, saying that they had seen Mughal soldiers lounging around in Waariaul.

"But the question is: why did your Nawaab need to summon such a military contingent from Delhi?" asked Raam Iqbaal.

"Well," replied Dukhii Raam, "we reckoned they halted here on their way to some other place."

"Is that all? Didn't you try to find out more about the reason for their camping here?" asked Raam Iqbaal rhetorically.

They said they thought it wasn't any of their business. Raam Iqbaal whetted their appetite, asking whether they would like to know the real reason for the imperial troops' presence; they were all ears, they said. Raam Iqbaal then proceeded to relate the entire episode of the attack on Singhwaar *Deorhii* and the brutal assassination of the Thaakur siblings and their men.

"It's inevitable that all living beings must die one day, but those who die defending their integrity, pride and honour never really die. Immortalised by their valour, they turn into icons worthy of emulation for generations to come. The Thaakurs of Singhwaar, too, sacrificed their all for pride and honour," said Raam Iqbaal.

"Is all that really true?" asked a man in the gathering.

"Why would I tell you a lie? And, in any case, Singhwaar is not very far from here, you can easily go there and verify the facts for yourself."

"What do you expect us to do about it, though?" asked Dukhii Raam.

"Well, in such matters, it's no good trying to do anything in a hurry. A great deal of deliberation is needed before making a decision. All I can ask of you is to ponder over it all and be guided by your conscience, but whatever your decision, thorough preparation must precede action. Total secrecy and unity of purpose are of the essence. To succeed, you must hold your cards close to the chest and take the opposition by surprise. I've just told you how the Vizier used the element of stealth to his advantage. All said and done, however, this might be your best chance to teach a lesson to your rulers that they cannot take liberties with our women-folk at will; the old Nawaab's under house-arrest, *ChhoTe Nawaab* is busy doting over Belaa and the wily Vizier is simply no more! What more could you ask for by way of a weakened opposition? But beware, should you fail for want of adequate preparation, retribution will be swift and brutal, and many of you might even lose your lives," replied Raam Iqbaal, playing Machiavelli to the hilt.

An old man, who appeared to be the oldest of the lot and had been listening to Raam Iqbaal attentively, asked, "Master, you'd said yourself that you have no friends or family here; how come you're so well-informed, may I ask?" Some other murmurs of doubt arose from the gathering: how could they accept a stranger's claim to be better-informed than the locals living here for generations?

Smiling sardonically, Raam Iqbaal replied it was entirely up to them to believe what they liked, but they did indeed need to seriously reflect on how a total stranger could have discovered so much while they remained in the dark. Then, looking them all in the eye, he answered his own question, "The answer to the question is really quite simple. I'm afraid you haven't bothered to apply your mind to it; if you had, you could've found a good deal. Have you ever thought why the Almighty only endowed the humans with celebral faculties in addition to other simpler sensory ones? If we don't use this unique divine gift, it's bound to get atrophied. You all know that there's sweet sap in sugar-cane but it doesn't come out unless the cane is crushed. Similarly, without the brain grinding and analysing what the eyes see and ears hear, one can't know what might in fact be fairly obvious."

Encouraged by the rapt attention that his audience was now giving him regardless of his monologue being long-winded, Raam Iqbaal pressed his advantage, "Why only humans, even animals and birds use their various faculties intelligently in tandem. A dog can find out a whole lot of things by its sense of smell. An eagle can spot its food on the ground, no matter how high it's flying in the sky. No one need tell the ants where the sweets are kept. A human being is by far a superior creature. If he wants to find out something and is willing to work towards it, there's no reason why he won't succeed."

Concluding his long sermon, Raam Iqbaal served a fascinating cocktail of caution and provocation rolled into one, "I must be on my way, folks, as I've far to go. But before I leave, I'd caution you again not to jump into the fray in a hurry. Whatever you do, you'd be well advised to act only after careful deliberation. There is, however, a limit to tolerating injustice. If you go on being mute spectators, you can be sure that soon there will be nothing left of either your honour or self-esteem. How long can you hide like an ostrich? When Belaa's husband and her in-laws come looking for her, what will you say to them? All that has happened would surely tumble out into the open. Would anyone come to ask for your daughters' hands ever again? Just use your heads, folks!"

Leaving the gathering lost in reflecting over his discourse, Raam Iqbaal abruptly rose to his feet, and bringing his palms together in the *namaskaar-mudraa*, strode away towards the crossroads he had passed coming into the Hindu *Bastii*, without so much as a backward glance at the group he had just been addressing.

❋❋❋

As Raam Iqbaal approached the crossroads, his eyes were instinctively drawn to Khairaatii Saah's shop. He abruptly stopped when he saw a young man sitting weeping bitterly on the steps in front of the store. Raam Iqbaal wondered whether this could be Belaa's husband. He decided to ask the man himself.

"Are you all right, son? Why are you crying in front of this shuttered store?" he asked.

The young man, sobbing with his head held in his hands, raised his tearful eyes to see who had spoken to him so compassionately, and replied, "*Baabuu Jii*, I'm Ganeshii, son-in-law of Khairaatii Saah, his daughter Belaa's husband. I'd left her here some time ago to tend to her ailing father and gone back to my job in the city. When I learnt that the old man had passed away, I returned and found the house locked. Thinking Belaa would be at the store, I came here, only to find the shop locked as well. No one seemed to have any idea where she was. I was at my wit's end, but reckoned that the confectioner across the road, Nathunii Saah, being from our community and in the same line of business, might know where she was. So, I went and asked him, 'You have any idea where I might find Belaa?' Can you imagine his reply? He scornfully dismissed me, saying, 'In hell!' But that wasn't all; he called his servants and had me thrown out of his store! His outrageous rudeness broke my heart. What should I do if not weep, sir?"

Raam Iqbaal's heart went out to the fellow; he stroked his back to console him, "Calm down, Ganeshii. Weeping isn't going to be of any help. Much as I'm a stranger in this town, I could still tell you Belaa's whereabouts," he said.

"Oh sir, please...please tell me where she is... now, don't take so long," Ganeshii beseeched him, taking hold of his hands, "Why are the shop and the house both locked? I'm going crazy for anxiety...is she all right, sir?"

Raam Iqbaal was in two minds. He didn't quite like the idea of bringing bad news to the poor soul, but, on the other hand, he was reluctant to let go of a chance destiny seemed to have thrown his way. He began to break it gently, "Since you insist, I'll tell you, but clearly you won't be able to get your wife back now; even if you did, perhaps you wouldn't own her up."

"Sir, you can't imagine what I'm going through; for heaven's sake, don't talk in riddles! What did you mean by saying 'you won't be able to get your wife back'? I'm sure if she were to know I'm here, she'd drop everything else and come running to me, no matter what stood in her way!" said Ganeshii, intrigued by the stranger's assertion. Raam Iqbaal decided it was time to come clean, "Your wife's in *ChhoTe Nawaab*'s palace." Ganeshii couldn't believe he'd heard right, "What? What on earth are you trying to say?" he exclaimed, outraged.

"It's for you to choose whether to believe me or not, but what I've told you is true," replied Raam Iqbaal.

"But that's not possible!" said the desperate man in denial.

"It's the truth, but you tell me something, are you willing to own up Belaa after all this? Will your parents and family accept a tainted woman and give her the respect owed to a daughter-in-law?" countered Raam Iqbaal.

Ganeshii seized his arms, and shaking him gently, pleaded, "Please, sir, tell me that all this is a bad dream, nothing of what you said has actually happened!" Raam Iqbaal somehow disengaged himself from his insistent grip. Ganeshii slumped onto the stairs, lamenting bitterly, his head back into his palms. Raam Iqbaal tried to console him, "So, is that how far your courage for your wife goes? What do you really hope to achieve by crying like a coward? If you care even a little for her, get back on your feet and take up the cudgels! Go, knock at the doors of every household and ask them whether it's their custom to send married daughters come to visit parents to the Nawaab's palace. Go and spit on Nathunii's face for humiliating you so! This might be the only way you would have some peace of mind, and who knows, it might even lead to something more!"

Raam Iqbaal could see that he now had Ganeshii's attention. He went on, "It is entirely possible that Belaa, too, like *Siitaa Jii* surrounded by demons in *Ashok vaatikaa*, is waiting for her Raam to come to her rescue. Maybe she's as anxious to see you as you are to find her. You must be brave. I'm a stranger here and can't be of as much assistance as local residents. Acting alone, you're unlikely to be able to do anything much besides weeping and lamenting. Take my advice, go to every Hindu in Waariaul and prick his conscience."

Suddenly, Ganeshii sprang to his feet, his eyes burning like hot coals, and said, "You're right, sir, that's the only way to go for me. In any case, I can't possibly return without Belaa. What would I say when my folks back home ask me why I didn't bring their daughter-in-law back? Yes, I care not a fig if I die, but I must destroy the monster who has snatched my wife."

Raam Iqbaal, a bit surprised at the transformation, said, "I'm a total stranger to you. Do you trust me enough to have told you the truth?"

"Sir, don't call yourself a stranger; you're like a Messiah the Almighty sent down to guide me with words of wisdom," replied Ganeshii, looking gratefully at Raam Iqbaal.

"Then come with me!"

"Where are we going?" asked Ganeshii, surprised.

"Well, it isn't going to be easy to get Belaa out of the clutches of the evil prince. All we can do is to try our best."

Seeing Ganeshii was prepared to go with him, Raam Iqbaal raised his index finger, wagging it to warn him, and said, "Mind you, though, you won't utter a word where we're going; I'll do all the talking! Agreed?"

"All right, sir, I won't open my mouth at all."

❋❋❋

A while later, Raam Iqbaal, with Ganeshii in tow, approached the *paan* kiosk of Pyaare Laal 'Nafiis'. Pyaare, who hadn't forgotten his generous tip, greeted him with an enthusiastic smile and asked whether he could make *biiDaas* for them.

"Not at the moment, Pyaare, but you could do something else for me instead. Can you tell me who the most respected elderly Muslim resident in Waariaul is, except, of course, Nawaab Saahib himself?"

"Mohammed Zaqiuddin Khaan Saahib, sir," replied the *tamolii* without any hesitation, and volunteered, "He's popularly known as *Daadaa Maulvii*; a devout old man, he's widely respected for his learning and wisdom, and is also the Imaam of the main mosque here. Why, Nawaab Saahib himself holds him in the highest esteem and treats him with great courtesy. If you want to see him, he's almost always there at the mosque, and if by some chance he isn't, his residence is in the very next lane nearby. Anyone you ask will guide you to him. Oh, what a good, compassionate man he is!"

Thanking Pyaare, Raam Iqbaal left for the mosque. As luck would have it, they ran into Zaqiuddin himself as they reached its entrance, though initially they mistook him for just another *maulvii* coming out after the prayers. When they asked him for the Imaam, he smiled and replied, "Well, I'm Zaqiuddin. What can I do for you gentlmen?"

"We gather you're a kind and compassionate man who understands the feelings of others, sir. We've come to seek your advice and assistance in a rather sensitive matter."

"That's fine, but how could I possibly promise anything until you've told me what it's all about! And let me forewarn you at the outset, I won't stand for any blasphemy against my *Allah* or our Prophet or the Holy Qur'aan," said Zaqiuddin.

"Rest assured, *Daadaa-Maulvii*, we shan't even think of such a thing," said Raam Iqbaal.

"Then go ahead," said the Imaam.

"This young man here is the son-in-law of Khairaatii Saah," said Raam Iqbaal, nodding towards Ganeshii. The cleric's face suddenly lost colour the moment he mentioned Khairaatii Saah. Before he could say anything more, the Imaam said, "Let's go to my place, we can talk more comfortably there."

Once they were at the Imaam's, Zaqiuddin sat down on a divan on the front verandah, and invited them to sit down as well. He then asked Raam Iqbaal to go ahead.

"*Daadaa-Maulvii,* as I said, Ganeshii is Khairaatii Saah's son-in-law. He has a job in the city. Some time ago, he came to visit his parents and learnt that his wife, Belaa, had neither returned from her father's place nor been in touch with them for quite some time, which was indeed worrisome. He then came here intending to escort her back if her ailing father had recovered. But Belaa was nowhere to be found. Khairaatii Saah's house and his shop were both locked, and no one seemed to know where Belaa was. He made enquiries, and though no one said anything in so many words, he heard some disturbing innuendos; he got the sense that something was definitely wrong. He also overheard some unsavoury rumours that were floating around about his wife and was bursting with suppressed rage. Fortunately, he happened to run into me. I could see that if he kept running from pillar to post, searching for his missing wife, it might ruffle Hindu sentiments and cause avoidable communal tension. I suggested to him that we seek your advice and assistance as you're known for your kindness. I told him that if his wife was still in town, you would not only help him find her whereabouts but also see that she was reunited with him if she so wished.

"You did the right thing, but you haven't introduced yourself yet. However, since you called me *Daadaa-Maulvii,* you're like a son to me," said Zaqiuddin, and then turning towards Ganeshii, added, "And I'll treat this young man as a son-in-law since he's married to a girl from our town. Unfortunately, he's in a tough spot. To tell you the truth, I'm a bit embarrassed myself; it's rather difficult for me to help him, and yet, it'd be unethical to refuse to help him since his cause is just. I can only assure you that if his wife wishes to be restored to him, so shall it be!"

"That's exactly what we were hoping for, too," said Raam Iqbaal.

"Well, I'll be returning to the mosque for namaaz in a short while and will speak with my brethren gathered there about Ganeshii's matter. Let's see what comes of it," said Zaqiuddin.

"The will of *Allah* shall be done, but may I make a submission for your consideration?" asked Raam Iqbaal gravely.

"Go ahead," said Zaqiuddin agreeably.

"While deliberating on the subject, would you be so kind as to try and strike a balance between the Islamic tenets, on the one hand, and the sensitivities of the Hindus, on the other? I think that would help the cause of communal harmony."

"You're indeed an intelligent and right-thinking man. I greatly appreciate your concern for communal harmony, and will certainly keep your advice in mind. It's almost time for the next namaaz. Wait here until I return from the mosque," replied the cleric.

About an hour later, a man came and told Raam Iqbaal that Zaqiuddin had gone to *ChhoTe Nawaab*'s palace with a delegation of five other community elders, and had left word for Ganeshii and Raam Iqbaal to wait until they returned.

Raam Iqbaal felt his patience tested but there was little he could do except wait. He consoled himself with the thought that the cleric's visit to the palace would likely throw some light on the prince's intentions. Meanwhile, a sizable number of Muslim residents of the *Bastii* had gathered outside the Imaam's house, eagerly waiting to find out *ChhoTe Nawaab*'s response. Tongues wagged and whispers flew around in the gathering. It was deeply gratifying for Raam Iqbaal to find that they were more or less unanimous in their support to Ganeshii; they felt if they did not throw their weight behind his protest, it could be anyone's wife or daughter next, and that they needed to rise above considerations of caste and community on this occasion. Raam Iqbaal seized the opportunity to share his views with some of them, "I think it's for Belaa to decide whether or not she wishes to be reunited with her husband. She should be enabled to speak her mind without fear or favour. If she'd rather not go with her husband, she can say so in the presence of five elders from each of the two communities and terminate her relationship with Ganeshii. At least, this poor man here will know for sure that his wife wasn't taken by force, that she chose to be disloyal." He fell silent as he saw Zaqiuddin and his delegation return from the Palace.

Mohammed Zaqiuddin and his elderly associates returned from the long walk to the Palace looking completely crushed and crestfallen; they flopped down on the large divan on the cleric's porch. A hush had descended on the gathering that had been awaiting their return. Eventually, the Imaam began, "My brothers of the Faith! I'll come straight to the point: *ChhoTe Nawaab* isn't prepared to let go of Belaa. He cares neither for the community nor for our Faith. He doesn't care about consequences." Several voices of protest and consternation erupted from the crowd: 'So, the *ChhoTe Nawaab* has cut himself off from the community!'; 'Has he lost his faith in *Allah* and the Prophet and the Holy Qur'aan?' The Imaam raised his hands, gesturing for quiet as he delivered his punch-line. "We tried our best to reason with him, but far from giving us a patient hearing, he called out his goons and had us thrown out!" said the Imaam, trembling with suppressed rage.

Raam Iqbaal couldn't help feeling secretly elated at the sense of chagrin and disbelief in the congregation, even larger in size now as more and more people had joined it in a steady trickle. Meanwhile, several more voices of outrage and protest arose, overlapping one another, 'So, what should we do then?'; 'Should we meekly submit to the excesses of *ChhoTe Nawaab*!'; 'Isn't he ashamed of himself!'; 'At this rate, no one's women will ever be safe in future!'

The humiliation that the elderly cleric had suffered at the Palace suddenly welled up in his eyes; in a choked voice, he said, "What can I say to you, brethren! I'm feeling so small myself; never before in my life have I had to suffer such humiliation."

Several prominent community leaders tried to console the aged cleric, "*Daadaa-Maulvii*, please do not take it to heart. This is an insult not only to you but also to the community at large, and rest assured, we shan't let it pass!"

Zaqiuddin stood up, waving his hands again for silence, in an effort to reassert his leadership, "Don't get so excitable, my brothers! Whatever we do, let's do it with a cool head, but come to think of it, all we need to do, in any case, is to teach a lesson to this wayward offspring of Salaamat Khaan! He must be made to understand that the community won't be cowed down so easily, and that he is the ruler not because he commands a bunch of *LaaThii*-wielding goons but because of the support that the community gives to him. He can hardly make do without us!" Pausing to take a deep breath, Imaam Zaqiuddin concluded, "Now, what's to be done, where and when, are questions that we'll discuss amongst ourselves at the mosque."

As the crowd began to disperse, Raam Iqbaal rose to his feet and said, "*Daadaa-Maulvii*, we must also take leave of you now."

"All right, may *Allah* be with you! Rest assured, the sympathy of our entire community is squarely with Ganeshii."

Raam Iqbaal thanked everyone and left, Ganeshii following him quietly. As they moved towards the main square, he told Ganeshii to be wary of being ambushed by *ChhoTe Nawaab*'s *laThaits* and also advised him against complacency, or relying solely on the support of Muslim community; he told Ganeshii that he should go around lobbying with Hindu households and somehow cajole them into supporting him.

"If you truly are in love with Belaa and want to win her back, do precisely as I'm telling you to," said Raam Iqbaal.

"It matters little if I die fighting to rescue her, but I won't give up!" replied Ganeshii with conviction.

"May Lord Shiva protect you, my son! If you succeed in your mission, it would be immensely gratifying for me as well. So long then," said Raam Iqbaal as he turned and left for *Munshii* Gangeshvar Paandey's place.

❋❋❋

Kaashii Naath had been asleep when Raam Iqbaal had left that morning and had no idea where his friend had gone. To begin with, he thought he must be out for his usual morning walk and would return within the next hour or so. But when several hours passed and Raam Iqbaal didn't show up, Kaashii began to worry, wondering why he had disappeared without a word to anyone, and where to look for him. Giitaa also came asking where her brother-in-law might have gone but from Kaashii Naath's expression, she could see that he had no idea himself of his friend's wherabouts. There was little either of them could do except waiting for him to turn up.

Eventually, at about four in the afternoon, Raam Iqbaal trudged in, looking thoroughly spent. Kaashii Naath, at once relieved and curious, asked him where he had been all this while. Learning that he had finally arrived, Giitaa came in, too, with a barrage of questions and said plaintively, "Your friend was so anxious he hasn't eaten the whole day."

"Well, I'm sorry about that. In fact, I had only gone out for a short morning walk, but ran into a group of men from Hindu *Bastii* and started chatting with them. One thing led to another and I got so caught up with them that I lost track of time." He paused for a moment, then added mysteriously, "I've set up the fishing-rod with bait and all, let's see if the fish takes it!" Giitaa couldn't make out what he meant. In any case, her priority was to arrange for refreshments for her guests. Kaashii, on the other hand, recalled Raam Iqbaal telling him the previous night of his determination to avenge the Singhwaar outrage. He got the sense his friend had been working towards that end. Curious to find out more, he asked, "What are the chances of fish taking the bait?"

Seeing that Kaashii had rightly guessed the nature of his morning's activities, Raam Iqbaal continued the charade,

"Well, as usual, the Almighty has the last say. However, I'm hopeful, rather confidently hopeful, that our hard work won't go to waste. To have run into Ganeshii can't be a mere coincidence; it has to be a bit of divine intervention, and if that be so, surely the bait would be taken, and by a big fish, too."

Finally, the day was over. Once again Giitaa persuaded her guests to have their dinner without waiting for Gangeshvar. Just as well! because it was nearly midnight and yet Gangeshvar hadn't returned from the Palace. Kaashii fell asleep as soon as he lay down, but Raam Iqbaal, like the previous night, was restless and unable to go to sleep. He was beginning to suspect all his efforts had been in vain.

A little after midnight, he heard the sound of galloping hooves approaching the house and surmised that it must be Gangeshvar returning home. He had been waiting for him, hoping that he would bring back encouraging news from the Palace. He walked out to the front porch as Gangeshvar was dismounting. He looked distraught, a dark frown creasing his forehead. He strode towards Raam Iqbaal like someone in a tearing hurry and whispered to him, "The situation in the town's suddenly become very tense. Anything can happen! It's very embarrassing for me to say this, but in the circumstances, you must leave immediately."

"But what is it that makes you so distraught?" asked Raam Iqbaal with exaggerated surprise.

"There's no time to lose discussing that now. You must go at once. I hate to have to ask an honoured guest like you to leave my house in the middle of the night, but the situation is so grave, I have little choice!" said Gangeshvar.

"At least, tell me briefly what has happened," insisted Raam Iqbaal.

"I will, I promise, but it'll have to wait. For now, you must get away from this town as fast as you can. Where's your friend? You'd better wake him up quickly."

"All right," said Raam Iqbaal, giving up.

For a while, he did consider other options, but eventually he decided that it would be best to go by his host's advice. He woke up Kaashii Naath and asked him to quickly get ready for departure.

As he came out with his bag, he ran into Giitaa standing on the front veranda, bewildered at the sudden turn of events.

"Don't tell me you're leaving at such an unearthly hour. You can go at dawn, if you have to!" she said.

As Raam Iqbaal was explaining the situation, they were joined by Kaashii and Gangeshvar. The latter was apologetic but firm, "I'm afraid I can't jeopardise your safety over social niceties. You'd better go now!"

After seeing his guests off, Gangeshvar asked Giitaa and his men to remain on guard and galloped away towards the Palace.

As Raam Iqbaal and Kaashii approached the main road outside the town limits, they heard the sound of a thousand voices pierce the night sky with belligerent slogans like *Har-har Mahaadeva* and *Allah-o-Akbar* coming from the town behind them. They heeled their horses for extra speed, with only a fleeting backward glance – the whole of Waariaul seemed like an inferno, tall columns of orange flames and grey clouds of smoke painting the horizon into a surreal tableau. Raam Iqbaal looked up to the heavens as though to send a silent prayer skywards, as their horses carried them away to safety.

□

5
The Sword of Singhwaar

It was late afternoon when Kaashii Naath finally reached home. Markandeya, his teen-aged son, had heard him call out. He ran out, saying the servants were all out on various errands, and took the reins from his father's hand, leading the horse to the stables.

Kaashii Naath ascended the steps to the front porch and touched the feet of his father, who had come out hearing his son's voice, and stood waiting there. *Baabaa* Shambhuu Naath blessed him and asked, "Did you succeed in your mission?"

"Your apprehension turned out to be right. The imperial authorities have confiscated the estate of Dharaadhar Thaakur by way of damages, but...," Kaashii fell silent midway.

"But what?" asked Shambhuu Naath.

"I had no idea Raam Iqbaal's so gifted and clever. All on his own, he set in motion something that left the Nawaab's town in shambles. It would take a whole generation for Waariaul to get back on its feet again. They won't forget the blow for a long time to come."

Holding his curiosity in check, *Baabaa* said, "Well, you've just arrived after a long ride. Go, freshen up, have a bit of rest, then you can fill me in on the details."

That evening they had a family gathering for Kaashii to give a full account of his visit to Waariaul in the presence of Bhavaanii. Shambhuu Naath deliberately cleared his throat noisily and called out "Shiva...Shiva! to announce his arrival as he entered the inner courtyard, giving the ladies enough time to get properly organised to welcome him. Everyone stepped forward to touch his feet by turns. As they took their usual seats, *Baabaa* gazed fondly at little Jagdambii sleeping peacefully in Saavitrii's lap. Then, he turned to Kaashii and asked him to begin.

"Father," said Kaashii, "let me begin by delivering a message Raam Iqbaal requested me to bring to Bhavaanii Bahuu when we were parting at the end of our trip. He asked me to thank Bhavaanii Bahuu for her blessings, which he thought played an important part in, and the success of our mission beyond all expectation."

Giving the credit of their successful mission entirely to the brilliant tactics of Raam Iqbaal, Kaashii continued, "After going over the sequence of events from the massacre at the *Deorhii* down to what we unearthed in Waariaul, I've come to feel that some higher power is protecting not only the Singhwaar lineage but also their treasures we hid underground."

Shambhuu Naath, who had been listening intently to Kaashii, asked, "The lineage, yes, but what makes you say that about the hidden valuables?"

"I'll tell you something you will find hard to believe, but certainly worth celebrating; the scheming Vizier's dead; Salaamat Khaan went crazy and has now been overthrown by his son, and is languishing in house-arrest. No more fun and games for the old man!"

"What? Go on, tell us all about it, I say!" said Shambhuu Naath, silently offering a prayer of thanks to his *IshTa-Deva*. They were all ears, avidly waiting for the details. Kaashii then went on to tell them all they had learnt at Waariaul, thanks to the cunning of Raam Iqbaal and the generous help of Gangeshvar; how the Vizier and two of his henchmen, looking for hidden treasures in the *Deorhii Puujaa-ghar*, had been bitten by snakes and died; how Salaamat Khaan went crazy for fear of snakes he hallucinated; and how he and Shahnavaaz fought over Belaa leading to the Palace coup; and how they'd seen Waariaul go up in flames like a tinder-box, with blood-thirsty hordes of Hindus and Muslims roaming its streets raising communal war-cries.

Everyone listening was convinced that a higher power must be protecting the *Deorhii*, for no ordinary snake could bite to death three persons in an instant, and two of them trained veterans of the imperial army at that. Some of them wondered if it was a freak accident or a divine intervention.

After Kaashii Naath had finished, Sadaashiva sought *Baabaa*'s permission to speak, and on the latter nodding his assent, said, "*Bhaiyaa* has done his bit to avenge the brutal assassination of Dharaadhar *Bhaai Jii*, but I'm yet to fulfil my promise to *Bahuu Bhaabhii*!" Everyone listening looked at him for elaboration; even Bhavaanii could not remember what he was referring to.

Sadaashiva saw that he needed to explain, "While going over inner areas of the *Deorhii* after the massacre, I had found a beautifully hand-carved dagger. I picked it up and decided to bring it back with me. One day when I happened to mention it to *Bahuu Bhaabhii*, she told me it was given to her mother-in-law by her father-in-law as *muh-bajaaon* on their wedding day, and added that she would like to have it as a keepsake. So, I gave it to her. Then she asked whether I'd seen Dharaadhar *Bhaai Jii*'s personal sword which had a velvet sheath on its scabbard with *Bhagvatii*'s name embroidered on it. I told her that though I'd had the occasion to see it, only *Bhaiyaa* could say for sure where it was kept. She asked me if I could bring her that sword as well, and seeing how keen she was to have it, I promised her that I sure would as soon as I had ascertained where it is." Then, turning to Kaashii, he said, "*Bhaiyaa*, can you remember where you kept it?"

"Of course! That scabbard with '*Mahishaasura-mardinii*' embroidered on it is indeed quite unforgettable."

Bhavaanii blurted out excitedly, "Yes, yes! That's the one."

"I had leaned it to the wall in a corner of the *chinvaar* at the *Deorhi,*" said Kaashii Naath.

"*Bahuu Bhaabhii*, if you permit, I'll go and bring that sword for you," said Sadaashiva with such alacrity as if he would depart that very moment, if permitted.

But who would readily allow Sadaashiva to go to the *Deorhii* after what Kaashii Naath had just revealed! No one spoke.

"It seems you're all too scared to be able to think straight since learning of the Vizier's fate. Well! There's a huge difference between Vizier's trespass and my proposed visit; Ghulaam Sarvar had entered the *Puujaa-ghar* with evil intent while I would be going in to carry out a specific task assigned by the rightful owner of the *Deorhii*. Surely the deity guarding the place, whether it's *gandharva* or *naag-deva*, wouldn't stand in the way of something desired by the mistress of the *Deorhii* herself!"

Before anyone could speak, Maarkandeya offered enthusiastically, "*Kakkaa Jii*, if you wish, I could come along and assist you!"

"That's what they call a cart before the horse! Even I haven't been allowed yet!" replied Sadaashiva.

"Well, knowing what happened to the Vizier and his soldiers, I can't allow either of you to go to the *Deorhii*. Let the sword lie where it is; I'd hate to put your lives in danger for the sake of my sentiments and a family ceremony," said Bhavaanii.

Shambhuu Naath, who had been listening silently, now joined in the conversation, "*Bahuu*, are you keen to have that sword?"

"Well, to tell you the truth, I'd be happy to have it; besides being associated with my husband's memories, it's also needed for me to keep up an unbroken family tradition. Jagdambii, having lost his father can't possibly receive the sword from him, but if I can hand it over to him on his behalf when he enters his eighteenth, I'd have fulfilled an important family obligation," replied Bhavaanii.

"I quite agree with you, and in any case, it wouldn't be right to altogether abandon the *Deorhii* treating it as a dangerous place. If Sadaashiva and Maarkandeya are willing to go and bring the sword back, I, for one, have no objection to their doing so. But they can only go if specifically permitted by you," said *Baabaa*.

Bhavaanii's eyes widened at his generous offer as she exclaimed in astonishment, "*Baabaa*!"

Shambhuu Naath could make out how torn she was by conflicting emotions, and hastened to reassure her, "There's no need to worry; your permission would protect them from harm like body-armour."

❋❋❋

Bhavaanii sat on her bed feeding Jagdambii the next morning as Sadaashiva and Maarkandeya came to take leave of her. She was assailed by dilemma once again, whether to give them permission or simply refuse it. Sensing her ambivalence, Sadaashiva said, "*Bahuu Bhaabhii*, you needn't worry in the least; just say yes, and we'll go and fetch the sword."

Presently, Paaro and Saavitrii joined them; Paaro said, too, "Don't worry, let them go."

"*Diidii*! How can I help worrying? I've lost so many of my loved ones, I can't bear to think of losing any more!"

"I understand your apprehension. Anyone in your place would be worried, too, but I still think you should allow them to go. They already have *Baabaa*'s blessings, and if they had yours as well, no harm would come their way. They'll be back safely in hardly any time, you'll see," said Paaro.

Eventually, Bhavaanii said in a strangled voice, "May the gods protect you! But make sure you're back here by sundown. Until I know that you've returned safely, I'll think of nothing else!"

"We shall definitely return before it's dark," replied Sadaashiva, as the two of them bent to touch her feet for blessings.

Baabaa and Kaashii Naath were waiting on the front porch to see them off while the syce stood holding the reins of their horses, already saddled, in the front yard. The two of them touched the elders' feet and mounted their horses.

It was a pleasant ride in the mild morning sun of early spring, through verdant fields with patches of bright yellow of the mustard crop beginning to flower. As they closed on Singhwaar, they could see the domes and turrets of the *havelii* in the distance, and a little short of it, a small hamlet of a few huts that looked like a recent settlement. They decided to acquaint themselves with its dwellers before going on, just in case they needed some help later.

The hamlet had, indeed, come up lately as a result of some old family retainers of Singhwaar Thakurs deciding to resettle as close as possible to the *Deorhii*. The tiny settlement hummed at the moment with the usual morning routine of its inhabitants. They were a bit alarmed to see two armed men on horseback moving towards them, the women scurrying indoors and the men huddling together in a group. As soon as Sadaashiva and Maarkandeya reached the hamlet, the men surrounded them, their demeanour certainly less than friendly, if not openly hostile. Sensing the potential threat, Sadaashiva was quick to take preemptive action.

"We're no strangers, folks," he said to them. "We've been sent here by Dharaadhar Thaakur's widow for a specific purpose."

The hamlet dwellers were momentarily struck dumb at the mention of their late Master's widow being alive. Taking advantage of their stupefied silence, Sadaashiva and Maarkandeya dismounted. Sadaashiva pressed his advantage home; assuming a superior tone, he asked one of the men surrounding them to take their horses and tether them to a nearby tree. Then, motioning Maarkandeya to follow him, he began to walk towards the place where an elderly invalid lay resting on a mat. The old man tried to sit up by way of courtesy, pleading with the strangers to identify themselves in order that the villagers might feel reassured.

"You may have heard of Sri Shambhuu Naath Thaakur of KaTkaa village. I'm his son, Sadaashiva," he said.

The old man, Parameshvar, perked up to learn who he was.

"Oh, that would make you a cousin of my late Master then!" he exclaimed.

"That's right. Our families are like two branches of a tree. His ancestors came from Sannahpur and settled down in Singhwaar while mine migrated from there to KaTkaa." As Sadaashiva said this, the old man began to sob inconsolably.

"Why are you crying?" he asked.

"I miss my Master so bad, it hurts. I don't even feel like living here without him looking after us, but we've nowhere else to go. I can't bear to see the desolation of the *Deorhii*. Believe me, I constantly pray to the Almighty to reunite me with my Master up above in heaven," said Parameshvar.

Sadaashiva himself was stung by the old man's emotions, but tried to console him, "Who has ever succeeded in evading his karma! We must submit even to our misfortune as God's will and move on bravely. If we have His blessings, the *Deorhii* will soon be inhabited, and prosper again," said Sadaashiva.

The tension that had gripped the hamlet for a while had eased by now; women came out of the huts and stood in a huddle gaping at the gentlemen from KaTkaa chatting with village elders; the men, now reassured, heaved a sigh of relief. Most of them were either old or middle-aged, their younger siblings and offsprings having lost their lives fighting alongside the Master, and were prone to be easily rattled.

Wiping away his tears, Parameshvar called out to his son, JhagDuu, chiding him, "Can't you see the two young masters chatting with me are still standing. Go and quickly bring a cot for them to sit on."

JhagDuu ran to a nearby hut and came back with a cot made from bamboo pieces for its legs and webbing woven from a local variety of wild grass. As the two of them made themselves comfortable on the cot, Parameshvar asked,

"Master, please pardon me my curiosity, but may I ask the purpose of your visit?"

Sadaashiva did not think it would be wise to share the exact reason.

"Well, we've only come to have a look at *havelii* inside out. That's all."

The gathered hamlet dwellers silently quaked at the idea of someone entering the *Deorhii*. Finally, Parameshvar spoke up, "I would strongly advise you against going inside. You might consider returning home, having seen the *havelii* from here."

"But why? Why are you advising us not to go inside?" asked Sadaashiva, feigning surprise. Parameshvar, instead of giving a straight answer, prevaricated, "What's left to see inside the *havelii*? Now that all the owners have passed on, what's the point of exploring it anyway."

Sadaashiva could not hold himself back from countering, "Don't utter inauspicious words, man! Dharaadhar *Bhaai Jii*'s family-line isn't extinct by a long shot; his heir is very much alive and kicking. May God give him a long life!"

The revelation seemed to bring an instant sparkle of joy to the old man's eyes. He wanted to be sure he had heard it right.

"Master, are you telling me the truth?"

"Yes. As you're all old and trusted retainers of the family, I think I can share this with you: that night of the massacre, Dharaadhar *Bhaai Jii*'s wife, then in the final stage of her pregnancy, fled the *havelii* to save the family-line, and later gave birth to a healthy male heir."

"Where are they? Why don't they come and live in the *Deorhii* then?" asked an excited Parameshvar.

"Just think, man! Would it be safe for her to live here all alone with an infant? She's waiting for her boy to grow up. Meanwhile, they are living like respected family members at our place in KaTkaa. When the child comes of age and can take care of the *Deorhii*, they'll certainty return to live here, but that may take a while. Meanwhile, we've to wait patiently, haven't we?" said Sadaashiva.

The old family retainer, who had seemed terminally ill only a while ago, was so excited at the good news that he got to his feet, and called out to the others, smiling and animatedly waving his hands for them to come closer, "Did'ya hear that, folks? Our late Master's been reborn! Let's celebrate with fanfare."

"Don't even think of such a thing!" exclaimed Sadaashiva, before the old man could say anything more.

"Why so, master?" asked Parameshvar with a hint of dejection in his tone.

"We've got to keep this a closely guarded secret for now. It's entirely possible that the vengeful Nawaab would go after their lives if he were to get wind of the existence of an heir. He must still be fuming at the subsequent fiasco. I don't know whether you're aware of what happened later...." Sadaashiva paused for a moment to consider how much information could be safely shared, but went on to tell them of the ill-fated treasure hunting expedition of Vizier Ghulaam Sarvar to the *Deorhii*.

The villagers, beginning to exchange surreptitious glances with one another, were utterly terrified to hear of the Vizier's episode.

"You're right, master Sadaashiva," said Parameshvar, "the Nawaab is, indeed, unpredictable and ruthless, capable of stooping down to any level of insanity. We'll make sure no one gets even a whiff of what you've told us in confidence," assured Parameshvar solemnly.

"I've told you all this because being old and loyal retainers of the family, you shouldn't remain under the impression that the family line ended with Dharaadhar *Bhaai Jii*. Now, we're going to the *havelii*, leaving behind our horses here in your care; please look after them until we return," said Sadaashiva, beckoning to Maarkandeya to follow him.

Parameshvar, again impelled by his sense of loyalty, began to dissuade them from going inside the *havelii*.

"The *havelii,*" he said, "is a terrible place, master. No one comes out of it alive. After learning of the Vizier's fate, I'm convinced that stepping inside the place is no less than throwing a challenge to *Yamaraaj* himself. Please, sir, don't go in there, I beg of you!"

Intrigued by the desperation in Parameshvar's plea, Sadaashiva asked him, "Did anyone from among you go in and didn't return?"

"No, none of my people ever went in there," replied Parameshvar firmly but without meeting Sadaashiva's eyes.

"Well, then tell me the basis for your assertion that those who go don't come out alive?" said Sadaashiva, a degree of irritation beginning to creep into his voice.

Instead of answering the question himself, Parameshvar said to his son, JhagDuu, "Why don't you tell the gentlemen what happened soon after we returned to live here?"

JhagDuu, squatting on the ground nearby, launched into a long-winded account of the incident his father had mentioned, "It's only been a few weeks since we settled down here. We were the first to come, and then I persuaded some other of our kinsmen to come and join us. My father didn't want to go anywhere else; he said, 'we'd rather be here like loyal dogs by the gate-post of the Masters, whose 'salt we've eaten for generations', than go anywhere else. He wasn't doing so poorly at the time; in fact, I'd say he was in good health, given his age. But then, the attack on the *havelii* and the gruesome end of the Master had been such a shock, he never quite recovered from it. His health began to deteriorate by the day after we came back here. When the attack on the *Deorhii* was imminent, our late Master had called him and said, 'Parameshvar, it's impossible to predict the outcome of our resistance. You'd better leave immediately; taking all the livestock you can with you, and go away somewhere, as far from the *havelii* as possible. Later, you can decide and do what you think right in the circumstances. If none of us survives the battle, which seems inevitable, you'll still take good care of the *havelii*, won't you?'"

JhagDuu paused for a moment to catch his breath, resuming his narrative instantly, "Well, as instructed, we left with all the livestock and went deep into the forests of the Himalayan *teraii*. But since returning here, all we do is to regret bringing the livestock back; when there are no masters left, what good can come of these poor beasts!"

"Do all these cattle belong to the *Deorhii*?" asked Sadaashiva.

"I've no idea who owns these anymore. The livestock, used to having the best feed, have nothing but dry grass now for survival. But yes, until they are able to stand on all fours, they do belong to the masters of the *Deorhii*," said Parameshvar nodding his head sorrowfully.

Maarkandeya, who had seen through Parameshvar's ploy, burst out impatiently, "Now look here fellows, we're getting very late; we've to return home before it's dark, after finishing our task here. So, why don't you come to the point and tell us the reason for your insistence that we shouldn't enter the *havelii*?"

"I was just coming to that," said JhagDuu, resuming his narrative, "we'd only been here a few days at the time; no one knows how a gang of seven men sneaked into the *havelii*, four of them were *nuniaas* and remaining three, *dhaanuks*. We only came to know of the trespass when four of them stumbled out, carrying a fifth in an unconscious state. We later learnt that the unconscious man's name was Kaarii Mandal. All four of them were terribly distraught, kind of shell-shocked I should say, and had reached our hamlet with considerable difficulty. We ourselves lived at the time in constant fear of strangers – we still do – but we surrounded them, though they were in no condition to do us any harm, and began to interrogate them. Kaarii Mandal was already dead by then. The other four looked to have come pretty close, too. To begin with, they could hardly answer our questions coherently, but after a bit of consoling and water to drink, they broke down and told us that they were professional earth-diggers from the *Nuniaa* caste, known for its expertise in this line of work. Two men, Kaarii Mandal and Subodh Yaadav had engaged them, saying that they had been contracted by the masters for some urgent digging work at the *Deorhii*. The *nuniaas* were offered generous terms – daily wages at twice the going rates and food on the house – and thought that if the contractors were offering such lucrative terms, perhaps on account of express service desired by the masters, why shouldn't they go for it. Another man called Dhanessar joined Subodh and Kaarii en-route to the *Deorhii*, and it was then that they overheard Kaarii telling Dhanessar that if their mission was successful, they would be fabulously rich overnight. That left the *nuniaas* rather uneasy, wondering what Kaarii and Subodh were really up to! Something smelled fishy, but the panache with which the three of them entered the premises, without any stealth or hesitation, and the fact that once inside, they headed straight for the *Puujaa-ghar* purposefully as though they knew precisely what was to be done, lulled the *nuniaas* into believing that they had needlessly suspected their motives. So, they said nothing and followed them.

"Subodh and Dhanessar were in the lead, with Kaarii following a couple of steps behind them while the *Nuniaas*, a few paces further behind, brought up the rear. As soon as the three contractors entered the *Puujaa-ghar*, a pair of fearsome black cobras suddenly materialied, as if out of nowhere; Subodh and Dhanessar were felled in a flash. Kaarii desperately tried to withdraw, but apparently, he wasn't fast enough to avoid being bitten. The four *Nuniaas*, who stood just outside the *Puujaa-ghar* entrance watching all this horror, somehow dragged out Kaarii Mandal, still breathing scratchily. Thinking he might just make it, they heaved him up and ran for their lives. By the time they reached us, Kaarii had died. Now, it's for you to decide whether or not it would be safe to enter the *havelii*," JhagDuu, having related the incident, looked at their faces anxiously.

"The revelation of another incident of snakebite deaths in the *Puujaa-ghar* left Sadaashiva and Maarkandeya deeply concerned. Everyone had fallen silent. Finally, it was Maarkandeya who broke the silence with a question, "What was the total number of men who stole into the *havelii*?"

"The four *nuniaas* who survived said it was seven," replied JhagDuu.

"The four survivors and Kaarii Mandal, whose body they brought back, makes a total of five, right? So, where are the remaining two then?" asked Maarkandeya.

"From what the *Nuniaas* told us, they fell down and died instantaneously inside the *Puujaa-ghar*. It follows that their bodies must still be there," replied JhagDuu.

Maarkandeya turned over the snakebite incidents in his mind, silently debating the level of risk involved. Going into the *havelii*, particularly the *Puujaa-ghar*, which they must enter in order to retrieve the sword, seemed to be a perilous venture indeed. There was, however, no comparison between their proposed entry and the trespass by treasure-hunting robbers who had perished there. While the trespassers had gone in with evil intent, their hands were clean. In fact, it occurred to him that if they did not make an earnest effort to go in and bring the sword, it would amount to breach of trust. That made up his mind for him. Turning to his uncle, he said, "Let's go, *Kakkaa Jii*, there's no point in dithering endlessly. We shouldn't lose any more time. Let's not forget we have to return home by sundown."

"You're right. Let's invoke the blessings of *Ganesh Jii* and go. Having come this far, it would be cowardly on our part not to go in," said Sadaashiva, then turning to JhagDuu, he added, "we're going now. God willing, we'll see you again soon, but in case we don't come back by sundown, please go and inform my father that we went in and didn't come out."

With that, Sadaashiva and Maarkandeya walked away towards the deserted *havelii* bathed in afternoon sun. The hamlet dwellers watched the receding figures of the twosome and marvelled at their determination, silently praying that the gods would keep them safe.

❋❋❋

Soon Sadaashiva and Maarkandeya stood in the forecourt of the *havelii* in front of its arched entrance. The shutters were open. They cast a careful glance all around and entered inside. The front courtyard and the verandahs along its three sides, quiet as a graveyard and thick with cobwebs everywhere, were deserted. The open shutters of doors and windows lurched outward on rusty hinges, giving the structure a kind of gaping aspect; the courtyard, overgrown with wild cacti, was covered in layers of dry leaves; and the edges of verandahs were encrusted with pigeon droppings.

Watching their steps warily and looking all around for potential or real trouble, they eventually made it to the verandah of *Puujaa-ghar* in the inner courtyard. They hadn't encountered anything scary, or even out of the ordinary so far.

Most parts of the *Puujaa-ghar* were visible through the door with its shutters wide open. They could clearly see two corpses in an advanced stage of decay lying on the floor not very far from the entrance, and didn't need any verification to know that this was all that remained of Subodh and Dhanessar. The entire place stank to high heavens with a nasty, putrefying stench. Covering their noses with the loose end of their *dhotii*s, they stood mesmerised, watching the horrendous tableau when suddenly they felt the bodies stir for the fraction of an instant, and the next thing they knew was that a pair of black cobras had materialised, seemingly out of nowhere. If asked, neither Sadaashiva nor Maarkandeya could tell from where the vipers had suddenly appeared, but there they were now, sitting with their hoods erect in readiness to strike, on either side of the remains of the two bodies, as if standing guard on them. Sadaashiva and Maarkandeya both shivered to notice that their fiery eyes seemed to be trained on them.

Unable to come up with anything better, Sadaashiva fell to his knees and put his head down on the threshold of *Puujaa-ghar* in a gesture of obeisance and unconditional surrender. Then, continuing to be on his knees, he sat up and brought his palms together in front of his chest in the *pranaam-mudraa* and began to address the cobras with conviction, "I know not which deity you are, whether *Gandharva* or *Naag-devataa* himself. Regardless of who you are, I've no doubt in my mind that you're well-wishers protecting the family fortunes of my Singhwaar kin. Had it not been so, surely the unscrupulous Vizier would have succeeded in robbing, within a few hours, the treasures that took the family generations to accumulate. Instead of the treasures, only his dead body went back from here! What the Vizier failed to do, Kaarii might have done but for your intervention. But listen, O divines! Unlike those others, we're not thieves or robbers, nor have we come here with any ill intent."

Sadaashiva paused and took a deep breath to hold his nerves in check, keeping his eyes focused on the cobras, and resumed his petition, "As you're capable of divining what anyone's thinking or planning to do, you must already know why we're here. Even so, I think it's necessary to formally apprise you of the purpose of our visit, Bhavaanii Thakuraain, the widow of Dharaadhar Thaakur, the late Master of this *Deorhii*, is living respectably at KaTkaa with us, her kinsmen from another branch of the family. You would, no doubt, be aware of the circumstances that compelled her to leave. It's at her behest that we're here today to fetch the personal sword of Dharaadhar Thaakur, which she wishes to have as a keepsake until it's time, in line with family tradition, to hand it over to Jagdambii, Dharaadhar Thaakur's heir, born posthumously. We've only come to take that one sword out of here, *Prabhu*, nothing more! I'm sure that having regard to the sentiments of the Mistress of the *Deorhii*, you'd grant us your permission to do that."

As Sadaashiva concluded his submission, he saw that the two serpents, who had so far been incessantly glaring at him and Maarkandeya, turned their hoods towards each other, as if silently consulting with the other in some sort of a sign language. A moment later, they put their heads down, swiftly slithering away in opposite directions, and disappeared. It seemed Sadaashiva's prayer had been granted.

Sadaashiva kneeling all this while now stood up and making a sign to Maarkandeya to remain where he was, entered the *Puujaa-ghar*, announcing loudly, "*Prabhu*, I'm going in now to get the sword." Taking care to avoid the dead bodies, he quickly moved to the *chinvaar*, and bowing low, touched his forehead to the edge of the platform in obeisance to the family deity. As he raised his head, he saw the sword leaning against the wall on the *chinvaar*. He reached out to pick it up, reverently touching it to his forehead. Then, he carefully retraced his steps. Going out, once again he announced loudly, "*Prabhu*! thanks to your *kripaa*, I've accomplished my task. We'll soon leave the *Deorhii*. Please accept our grateful *pranaam*s."

Walking back towards the main entrance, they found that the serpents now sat on the *manDap* in the middle of the courtyard, their erect hoods gently oscillating from side to side, as if they were keeping an eye on everything all around. Sadaashiva and Maarkandeya came to an abrupt halt on seeing the pair of cobras, and forgetting their hurry, stood watching them for the longest time, mesmerised by their hypnotic eyes glinting in the afternoon sun. There was no doubt in their minds now that while the two vipers were harmless guardian-angels to well-wishers of the family, they turned into *Yamaraaj* himself for those who dared to trespass with evil intentions.

All of a sudden, Sadaashiva was overcome by an impulse to do a good turn to the old family retainers living on the margins of extreme poverty, and even now swearing allegiance to their late Master.

Once again Sadaashiva stood before *Naag-devataa* in the formal *pranaam-mudraa*, palms together in front of his chest with fingers pointing upwards, and began to make a new petition, "*Prabhu*, I know we ought to leave the premises forthwith, but before we go, I have to make just one more submission. Since you can divine whatever is happening all around, I'm sure you already know that Parameshvar, the trusted personal servant of Dharaadhar *Bhaai Jii* and some other old family retainers are trying to make a new beginning in the hamlet that's come up near the gate of the *Deorhii* compound. They are in dire straits, living from day to day in abject poverty with their master no longer there to take care of them. I'm afraid many of them might starve to death while huge amounts of grain locked up in *havelii* stores go rotten and become unedible. I'm seeking your permission to open the store and have the grain distributed to these people, whose families have served our kin for generations. *Prabhu*, you're omniscient, so it's useless for me to pretend that I have any prior instructions from the Mistress for this, but I assure you, being a compassionate soul, she'd be very pleased to learn that you blessed this good deed. I hope you'd agree, but it's all up to you as I know that it's impossible to even move a pin out of here without your permission."

Once again the two cobras seemed to consult each other; a moment later they slithered away towards the *Puujaa-ghar*. Sadaashiva flashed a jubilant smile to Maarkandeya and said, "Go to the hamlet and get them all to quickly come here."

The hamlet dwellers were shocked to see Maarkandeya rushing back all by himself, assuming that Sadaashiva had been killed in another snakebite incident. As soon as he was in their midst, a thousand anxious questions concerning the cobras and Sadaashiva greeted him; he raised his hand for patience, and as the hubbub subsided, said, "We did encounter the cobras but apparently they only attack those who enter the *Deorhii* with dishonest intent. You needn't worry for *Kakkaa Jii*; he's fine, as you'll see for yourself shortly. He wants you all there. Have no fears, come with me."

As was to be expected, villagers were reluctant to go with Maarkandeya; eventually, he repeated to them, word for word, his uncle's second petition to *Naag-devataa* in order to reassure them. They still hemmed and hawed, not quite sure that it was safe for them to go inside the *havelii*. Finally, Parameshvar, instinctively convinced that Maarkandeya was telling them the truth, settled the issue by chiding his son for being churlish, "I don't know what you're making such big fuss about, I say! The young master has explained everything in such detail. What's your problem now? Would you rather starve? All of you should go at once and take the women as well, so you can bring back as much grain as possible. I'm prepared to go myself, if you want me to."

"No, no *Baabuu*, you needn't bother; we'll go and see to it," said JhagDuu sheepishly.

As the old *Deorhii* servants nervously followed Maarkandeya inside the front courtyard, they found Sadaashiva waiting by the entrance to the grain-store.

"I have the permission of *Naag-devataa*, the guardian-angel of the premises, for what we are about to do: you have until sunset to take out as much grain from here as you possibly can, and your time starts now," said Sadaashiva, and broke the lock that fastened the shutters of the grain-store.

Delighted at the windfall, JhagDuu and his clan began to carry out grain by the sackful, carrying on for at least a couple of hours, during which the pair of cobras was seen appearing and vanishing like an apparition at different spots, but they neither came near them nor interfered with what was going on. As the sun neared the western horizon, Sadaashiva raised his hand and said, "That's it for now, folks! It's close to sunset, we must go now."

He then turned his head in the direction of the *Puujaa-ghar* and mumbled his thanks again to the guardian-angels for having allowed him to not only get the sword but also give the much-needed support to old family servants. He felt overwhelmed by a deep sense of satisfaction and gratitude.

Parameshvar was so grateful for Sadaashiva's thoughtfulness that he had tears in his eyes as he thanked his late Master's cousin from KaTkaa, "How could I ever thank you enough for your generosity, sir? We would surely have starved to death but for your timely assistance." Sadaashiva shrugged it off, modestly saying, it was all God's will; he, at best, was the *nimitta* for carrying it out.

Sadaashiva and Maarkandeya were now ready to leave for KaTkaa. In parting, Sadaashiva left instructions with JhagDuu to herd the *Deorhii* livestock to KaTkaa, where it would be possible to take better care of them; he, however, allowed him to retain one milch cow whose milk, he said, would help Parameshvar to recover his strength faster. Then, raising his index finger in warning, he added, "And yes, make sure no one enters the *havelii*. If anyone does, he's bound to meet the same fate as the Vizier and Kaarii Mandal's gang, of that you can be sure! If any such incident takes place nonetheless, don't forget to inform us as soon as you come to know of it."

JhagDuu promised him that his instructions would be followed to the letter. Sadaashiva asked him to bring the horses and turned to Parameshvar, "Don't worry, man, you'll recover soon. Take good care of yourself; I'm sure you would like to be around when the heir brings the *Deorhii* back to life again."

"To tell you the truth, I had lost all hope of that happening, but you've given me something to look forward to. Do be so kind as to give the Mistress my regard and bless my infant Master for me, sir," said Parameshvar.

Meanwhile, JhagDuu had returned with their horses. Sadaashiva and Maarkandeya jumped into the saddle, raising their hands in silent blessings to the assembled hamlet dwellers as they heeled their mounts. Soon they were galloping away towards KaTkaa.

At KaTkaa, everyone waited for them anxiously. It was nearly sunset time and the two were not back yet. Much as they tried to keep negative thoughts at bay, the details of the Vizier's misadventure kept popping up in their minds.

Although Paaro and Saavitrii were themselves worried for the safety of Sadaashiva and Maarkandeya, they knew Bhavaanii was twice as anxious because of her sense of guilt for having agreed to let them go. As the three of them sat on the *manDap* in the courtyard, Paaro and Saavitrii tried to divert her mind by small talk about everyday chores but Bhavaanii continued to be downcast.

Baabaa and Kaashii waited at the edge of the front porch, instinctively scanning the pathway to Singhwaar every once in a while. *Baabaa* was the first to spot the twosome riding in side by side, and said excitedly, "Look, Kaashii, there they are!" Kaashii, whose eyesight was better, replied, "Yes, that's them all right, and looks like they got hold of the sword as well."

Presently, Sadaashiva and Maarkandeya reached the front yard. Getting down from their horses, they touched the feet of *Baabaa* and Kaashii Naath and received their blessings. *Baabaa* hugged Sadaashiva, smiling, and said, "Well, well! Seeing you both back safe, and with Dharaadhar's sword, too, I need hardly ask you whether you had a good trip. Still, tell us, How did it go?"

"Marvellous! Successful beyond expectation, *Baabaa*," said Sadaashiva.

Shambhuu Naath told them that the details could wait and that they should first go into the courtyard and relieve the ladies of their anxiety.

The household, silent with suppressed anxiety all day, was agog with excitement within moments of their arrival. Sadaashiva approached Bhavaanii, the heavy sword of Singhwaar in its velvet-clad scabbard held horizontally in his hands, bowed to her with a touch of ceremony and handed it to her, saying, "*Bahuu Bhaabhii*, I've no doubt now in my mind that your *havelii* is fully protected from miscreants and treasure-hunters. Anyone who dares to enter it is sure to lose his life."

Bhavaanii took the sword from him, and touching it to her forehead reverently, she said, "I shall forever be obliged to you for this favour. But can I ask you something, what makes you so sure the *havelii*'s so securely guarded?"

"You're very welcome, and what's more, you don't even have to be so formal. As regarding the *havelii*, the Vizier's ill-fated misadventure could perhaps have been dismissed as a freak accident, but that wasn't an isolated incident. Some time ago another gang entered the *Deorhii* to dig for buried treasures and three of them were killed of snakebite while the others had to run for their lives. By all accounts, the *havelii* is protected by a deity that appears in the form of a pair of cobras."

Sadaashiva and Maarkandeya then took turns to fill them in on the details of their eventful day at the *Deorhii*, right down to the distribution of grain to the old servants. Everyone was amazed at their unusual and effective communication with the serpents, and *Baabaa* recognising it as a good omen, silently bowed to the unknown deity for his kindness.

As Sadaashiva had anticipated, Bhavaanii was delighted to learn of the distribution of grain to the old family retainers and thanked him for his ingenuity. Above all, she was grateful to him for bringing her husband's sword and once again began to thank him for it. Sadaashiva on his part shrugged it off, saying, "There's no need at all to be so formal, *Bahuu Bhaabhii*; all I need is your blessings."

"That's something you will always have," said Bhavaanii.

Meanwhile, Jagdambii had woken up and begun exercising his tiny limbs, happily squealing away, as if celebrating a momentous victory.

□

6
Belaa – The Apple of Discord

As Raam Iqbaal had planned, the wedding ceremony and celebrations of his son concluded with the usual pomp and splendour of such occasions in his community. *Munshii* Gangeshvar Paandey and Kaashii Naath were among the invitees, and stayed over at his place for several days, attending the festivities. Eventually, it was time for them to take leave of their host, but Raam Iqbaal wasn't prepared to let go of them yet, and insisted they stay for at least another day.

As Gangeshvar and Kaashii sat chatting after the evening meal, Raam Iqbaal also joined them. He was keen to find out the outcome of the seeds of discontent he had sown during his visit to Waariaul. Above all else, he was most curious to know whether Belaa and Ganeshii were eventually reunited or not.

"Ganguu, I can't forget how you drove us out of your house in the middle of the night. I've been meaning to ask you whether the trouble that seemed to be brewing there died down or it really took the serious turn you thought it might," said Raam Iqbaal in a pleasant, light-hearted tone, trying to nudge Gangeshvar along.

"O man! Don't even mention it. Just to think of that night gives me goosebumps. All hell broke loose after you left; it was worse by far than anyone could have imagined."

"Was it really so bad? I'd only heard of a minor clash between the two communities," prodded Raam Iqbaal.

"A minor clash, indeed! For days on end after that wretched night, people kept searching for the bodies of their loved ones who perished in the carnage. The whole town was virtually reduced to a heap of rubble, with no one in sight, so deserted it was! Those who survived somehow, hiding somewhere, were so scared they wouldn't venture out even to fetch drinking water. I can only say that it would perhaps take a decade for Waariaul to recover from the setback. And behind all this death and destruction there was but one reason alone – the intransigence of Shahnavaaz about Belaa and the crude insult he flung in the face of *Daadaa-Maulvii*. It wouldn't have mattered if he'd simply refused to take his advice but the least people expected of him was to treat the elderly cleric with some decency. It was his atrocious behaviour with him that left the Muslim community baying for his blood."

"But what happened to Ganeshii?" asked Raam Iqbaal, seeking to bring back Gangeshvar on track.

"Well, Ganeshii, on the other hand, hit the right chords and succeeded in stoking Hindu sentiments. I'm, however, sure that up until that point in time, the two communities had no intention of confrontation with each other. They both wanted to show Shahnavaaz his place by taking Belaa away from him and restoring her to Ganeshii, but both were so secretive about their respective plans that the right hand didn't know what the left was about to do. And it didn't help that both scheduled their strike for exactly the same time. Mobs from both sides, armed to the teeth, advanced on the Nawaab's Palace precisely at midnight hour, around the time you left my place that night."

Gangeshvar took a deep breath before going on, "This is what they call Destiny! Mobs are driven by a queer, unpredictable logic of their own; they entirely misread the situation in this instance. In their frenzy neither side could understand that their respective rally-cries, though articulated along communal lines, were not directed at each other. The Hindus imagined that the entire Muslim community was supporting 'their' Nawaab, and was out to teach them a lesson for presuming they could snatch Belaa from the Nawaab's Palace. The Muslims, on the other hand, were enraged that rather than be grateful for their solidarity in a common cause, the Hindus were targeting them as though they were *ChhoTe Nawaab*'s minions. Thousands of voices praising their *Allah* on the one hand, and their Shiva on the other, shouting as loudly as they could, and the inevitable confusion of a melee in the dark muddied the waters even more; no one quite knew what was going on! It could only result in total chaos and mindless killing. This is exactly what followed!

"Things at the Palace took a serious turn when a break-away group of Hindu lads including Ganeshii sneaked into the Palace, and then shouting *Har-har Mahaadeva* stormed into *ChhoTe Nawaab*'s wing. A massive confrontation ensued, with Shahnavaaz forcibly restraining Belaa from flying into Ganeshii's arms and the latter throwing challenges thick with expletives at the hot-headed prince, both of them brandishing their swords.

"Eventually, Ganeshii was the one who took the offensive with a blind, amateurish swipe but Shahnavaaz, obviously more skilled at fencing, ducked niftily, foiling Ganeshii's blow. Poor Ganeshii was still a bit off-balance from that all-or-nothing blow he'd tried to land when Shahnavaaz, embarrassed by the defensive ploy he had just been compelled to use, launched a determined counter-attack, beheading Ganeshii within moments.

"Horrified to see the headless body of her husband convulsing on the floor, Belaa erupted like a sleeping volcano suddenly come alive: she lunged forward, and picking up Ganeshii's sword, rushed at Shahnavaaz, roaring like a wounded tigress:

"Enough, you bastard! You've had your way with me far too long; and now, you're going to die for it!" she screamed and struck.

Shahnavaaz, taken by complete surprise, was slashed on the arm, and fell back awkwardly on to the bed, clutching the bleeding gash on his arm and howling in pain.

Belaa could not believe what she'd done and just wanted to flee, but Mustafaa had come running in and now stood blocking her way. Taking heart at the appearance of his henchman, the injured Nawaab-zaadaa shouted, "Mustafaa, get the bitch and lock her up!"

Mustafaa lunged forward; Belaa quickly veered and slipped through his fingers, as the saying goes, but only just! She knew this was the end of the road for her; making her decision like a flash of lightning, she upended the sword she still held in her hand and threw her torso down on it, killing herself almost instantaneously. Her convulsing body fell upon the headless corpse of Ganeshii, now gone cold."

The recounting of the tragic end of Belaa and Ganeshii in such graphic detail had turned the mood sombre, and they all sat in silence for a while. Kaashii and Raam Iqbaal, who had hoped for some lucky break for Ganeshii, were sorely disappointed to hear that, after all, his bid to get his wife back had only resulted in both of them losing their lives. Raam Iqbaal was, however, curious for more, "What happened then?" he asked.

"Meanwhile," said Gangeshvar, picking up the threads of his narrative, "Hindus got word of a Muslims mob seen heading towards their *bastii*. The Hindu lads rushed to defend their homes. Their shortest route was through the main bazaar, and in passing, they set fire to every shop owned by a Muslim, perhaps as an act of anticipatory revenge. Little did they realise that fire doesn't make a distinction between shops owned by Hindus from those belonging to Muslims! The entire shopping district was reduced to ashes in a trice, as it were. Earlier on, mobs from both sides had set fire to different wings of the Palace, gutting down nearly a half of it and leaving the other with big cracks all over; it would have to be virtually rebuilt."

"How did Salaamat Khaan fare through all this?" asked Raam Iqbaal.

"He was found dead in his private chamber, his personal dagger embedded in his chest," said Gangeshvar.

"But who killed him? Were they able to find out?" asked Raam Iqbaal.

"Difficult to say, really; some people believe that Ganeshii, while searching for Belaa, must have come upon the old Nawaab, lying as usual in a drunken stupor, and killed him; but then, there are as many others who think *ChhoTe Nawaab* bribed Mustafaa to get rid of his old man and spread the rumour about Ganeshii being the culprit. They argue it couldn't have been Ganeshii as he had a sword to hand with which he later attacked Shahnavaaz; so, why would he kill the Nawaab with his dagger? It had to have been done by someone else at the behest of Shahnavaaz, they say," said Gangeshvar, sighing wearily, and then abruptly added, "That's the time I was dismissed from service!"

"What? Why would they do that to you?" exclaimed Raam Iqbaal, surprised.

"Well, I was missing from the Palace when such a terrible incident happened! There was a coterie around *ChhoTe Nawaab* which poisoned his ear that I, being a Hindu, was mixed up with Hindu mobs. Besides, I had enjoyed the confidence of the old Nawaab. In the circumstances, I was a sitting duck for those jealous of me."

"But after persuading us to leave that night, you did intend to return to the Palace, didn't you?" asked Raam Iqbaal, feeling a tinge of guilt.

"Indeed so, but I couldn't reach it because by that time the streets were swarming with mobs looting and killing," replied Gangeshvar.

"I'm truly sorry that you lost your job because of us. I do sincerely apologise," said Raam Iqbaal sheepishly.

"Don't worry. Things will mend in due course. It shouldn't be difficult for me to sneak back into Shahnavaaz's favour," replied Gangeshvar.

Kaashii Naath, who had been listening silently to the conversation so far, now joined in, "The more I think of the whole affair, beginning with the machinations of the Vizier against the *Deorhii*, the more convinced I am that the misfortunes of Salaamat Khaan started the very day he had Singhwaar attacked by the Mughals. First, he lost his trusted Vizier, then he began to have those mysterious hallucinations, and then he fought with his only son over a chit of a girl, leading to his house-arrest, eventually getting killed with his own dagger. Waariaul, his much-vaunted seat, was ravaged in a communal conflagration largely of his own making, just as Singhwaar was laid waste at his instigation."

"I couldn't agree more with you. Such poetic justice invariably follows the atrocities and excesses of evil ones. It's divine retribution!" said Gangeshvar.

"Whether or not it was divine, I can't say, but Salaamat Khaan did get his just desserts for sure. Anyhow, it's awfully late; high time to catch a few winks, I think," said Raam Iqbaal, rising to his feet and bidding his guests a good night's rest.

□

7
Conversations with the Devii

Jagdambii was now about to turn five, but he was relatively bigger built and more cerebral than most children his age. He was a soft-spoken, quiet sort of a boy. Nonetheless, he impressed everyone with his brilliance. People wanted to hear him talk more often, but he preferred silence. He had a gravitas about him unusual at such an early age, and what he enjoyed most was to be left alone to himself. While his contemporaries were busy playing outdoors, he would sit in solitude, pondering one knew not what! Many a time, sitting in the yard, he would gaze endlessly at the sky, without blinking or uttering a word; if someone asked what it was he looked at up above in the heavens, he would only smile shyly and say, "The lovely blue expanse of the sky, the clouds floating by in the breeze and the birds free to roam the skies, that's all!"

Bhavaanii found his quiet aloofness worrisome. She was afraid Jagdambii might get drawn to spiritual pursuits, ending up as a *yogii* or *sannyaasii*. *Baabaa* Shambhuu Naath would console her: "Stop worrying and listen to what I've been saying for years, and it'll bear repetition: Jagdambii's no ordinary boy, so there's little point in comparing him with other children. You haven't lost faith in horoscopes the *jyotishiis* made after carefully studying the planetary positions at the time of his birth, have you? The boy is destined for miraculous feats that would leave people gasping. Truth to tell, I only want to live on for some more time in order to see Jagdambii's exploits."

At the end of his daily morning *puujaa*, *Baabaa* Shambhuu Naath chanted in a loud singing voice the hymns enumerating the one thousand different names of his *ishTa-deva* Shiva. As soon as he began chanting, Jagdambii would come and sit next to him, listening with unusual interest for someone so young. One day, as *Baabaa* concluded his *paaTh*, Jagdambii asked him, "*Baabaa*, may I ask you something?"

"Why not? Go right ahead," said *Baabaa*.

"What is it that you sing aloud at the end of your *puujaa* everyday?"

Baabaa laughed pleasantly and said, "Well, I *sing* the hymns containing the thousand names of my *ishTa-deva* Lord of the lords, Mahaadeva Shiva who is the Father of the Universe. And for your information, it's called chanting, not singing."

Jagdambii seemed to think through his answer and said, as if wondering aloud, "But, *Baabaa*, you only have one name, Shambhuu Naath Thaakur, as have I, Jagdambii, just the one, too. The same is true of practically everyone I know. Why, then, is just one not enough for Mahaadeva? Besides, when you do your evening *paaTh* at twilight time, you only say *Om Namah Shivaay* over and over and no other names? I was wondering why the morning *paaTh* has to be different!"

Shambhuu Naath turned thoughtful, pondering on how to respond to Jagdambii's rather unusual query, when the latter exclaimed, "Did I say something I shouldn't have, *Baabaa*?"

Baabaa hastened to reassure him, "No, no; in fact, it's a very good question."

Emboldened by *Baabaa*'s comment, Jagdambii asked if he might ask another question, and on *Baabaa* saying he sure could, he said, "*Baabaa*, you just said Shiva is the *Father of the Universe;* now, if that be so, I wonder who the *Mother of the Universe* is, because no one can be a father without there being a mother, right?"

Baabaa was amazed at Jagdambii's logic and analytical ability, and replied admiringly, "Absolutely, there can be no father unless there's a mother, too. Indeed, the Universe has a mother as well, my boy."

"Who is she?" asked Jagdambii.

"*Jagdambaa* is the *Mother of the Universe,* the reason we decided to name you Jagdambii."

"Does the *Mother of the Universe* also have a large number of names like its *Father*?"

"Yes, she's known by countless other names as well."

The moment *Baabaa* said that, Jagdambii began to pester him with childlike insistence, "*Baabaa*, please recite to me all those names of *Jagdambaa* now, please, *Baabaa*. I want to learn all her names, *now*."

Baabaa was in a fix; he didn't know all the thousand names of *Jagdambaa* by heart; obviously, he could not very well recite them from memory. He began to look for a sop to mollify the child, who had waited patiently so far but was beginning to be petulant now. Finding *Baabaa* still silent, Jagdambii began to plead again, "*Baabaa*, please! You know very well I've never seen my father. Mother's all I have!"

Shambhuu Naath was moved by the sentimental pitch of the boy. He didn't want to disappoint him; so, he began to speak to him on related issues: "Other than the one thousand names formally on record in the scriptures, *Jagdambaa* is also known by many other epithets, some of which are even more popular among her devotees. The briefest and the best loved of these is *MaaN*. It also occurs at the beginning and the end of the formal list of her names. *Jagdambaa* herself likes it the best and is most pleased when addressed as *MaaN*. Instead of her one thousand names, let me to recite to you her thirty-two select names, and a holy episode from the *Puraanas* to do with it. Now pay attention:

"Eons ago, *Bramhaa* and the other gods performed an elaborate *yajna* to honour *Devii Maaheshvarii Durgaa*, showering her with flower petals. Pleased with their devotion,

Durgaa, the destroyer of all things evil, appeared in person, and said:

"O Deities! I'm so pleased with your worship, I'll grant you anything, however rare, that you may wish to ask of me."

The gods replied:

"Devii! You've already done us all a great favour by destroying the demon, Mahishaasura, the scourge of all the three lokas, rendering us free of fear and restoring us to our divine authority. You're like a kalpa-vriksh; underneath your shelter, we have everything we could ever want. There's nothing more to ask of you. Still, for the sake of continuing calm and security of the Universe, pray tell us what rites of worship would please you the most if a devotee needed to invoke you for succour in a time of adversity. Deveshvarii, do tell us this, even if it is a highly guarded secret."

On the divine lords petitioning her thus, *Durgaa,* the kind goddess, said:

"O Deities, what you ask for is a rare secret shrouded in mystery; nonetheless, I shall share it with you. In all the three lokas of the Universe, there's no invocation as potent an antidote to distress as the chanting of my thirty-two names. Pay attention as I recite these to you."

The *Devii* then went on to recite the mysterious hymns comprising her thirty-two names she favours above all the rest."

After explaining the mythological origin of *Durgaa-dvaatrinsh'maalaa,* contained in the *Durgaa-sapt'shatii,* Shambhuu Naath went on to chant the hymn for Jagdambii's benefit. As he concluded, touching the sacred text to his forehead, the boy asked, "*Baabaa,* what benefits can one expect from chanting this hymn?"

"The *Devii* herself has made that clear towards the end: *PaThet sarva'bhayaanmukto bhavishyati na sansha'yah,* meaning, those who chant this string of my names shall, without doubt, be liberated from all fears."

Jagdambii seemed to ponder on *Baabaa*'s explanation, his head bowed; then he looked up to ask, "*Baabaa,* what does goddess *Bhagvatii* look like?"

Baabaa felt he was almost at his tether's end, but decided to go on explaining patiently, "Just as she has countless names, she has innumerable aspects and forms, too. She could appear to have two arms, or four or eight or ten, or for that matter, any number of arms. Similarly, she could be with four heads, or many more in some other form of hers. Sometimes she might have ten feet."

Baabaa was immensely gratified to observe that Jagdambii was listening to all this with intense concentration. He went on, "Let me tell you, Jagdambii, whoever chants the names of *Bhagvatii,* the goddess with countless names, aspects and forms, is bound to rise and prevail against all odds, no matter how adverse his circumstances. She invariably protects all those who think of her with deep devotion. The segment entitled *devyah kavacham* in *Durgaa-sapt'shatii* describes how she never allows a devotee to come to harm, whether he's surrounded by towering flames, or by foes in battlefield, or the most trying of circumstances. He is never assailed, far less overwhelmed, by fear, or sorrow, or morbidity."

Jagdambii not only listened to these mythological tales *Baabaa* told him from time to time, but also thought through these in his own way, sitting all by himself. With the exception of his mother, he was the most attached to *Baabaa* and spent most of his time with him. Shambhuu Naath, being a person of a religious bent of mind himself, often told him stories from *Raamaayan, Mahaabhaarat, Shiva-Puraana, Vishnuu-Puraana,* etc. During these storytelling sessions, Shambhuu Naath noticed that Jagdambii's face tended to light up like a lotus-bloom in the sun whenever he happened to mention *Devii Bhagvatii* or describe her appearance in any particular form of hers. *Baabaa* thought he would indulge the child and began to frequently choose anecdotes from the *Devii Bhaagvat.*

He told him of how *Mahishaasura* and *Rakta-biij* came into being and waged war against the gods with the assistance of *Vijal* and *Taagra*; of how the gods were eventually vanquished and had to retreat to *VaikunTh*; of how the Supreme Godhead, Lord *Vishnu* had then agreed to do *tejah-pradaan* to the divines and *Bhagvatii ChanDikaa* had materialised from the *tej-samuuha*; and finally, of how *Bhagvatii* destroyed *Mahishaasura,* thereby acquiring another epithet – *Mahishaasura-mardinii.*

Then one day, *Baabaa* told Jagdambii that lord *Bramhaa* is the Creator of the Universe, Lord *Vishnu* its Keeper, and *Rudra* is the one who controls its Destruction, but they all derive their *Shakti* from *Mahishaasura-mardinii Bhagvatii,* who is the sole fount of all faculties and properties like *Buddhi, Srii, Dhriti, Kiirti, Smriti, Shraddhaa, Medhaa, dayaa, Lajjaa, Sudhaa, trishnaa, Kshamaa, Kaanti, Shaanti, Pipaasaa, Nidraa, tandraa, Jaraa, Ajaraa, Vidyaa, Avidyaa, Sprihaa, Vaanchhaa-shakti, Vasaa, Bhajjaa, tvachaa, drishTi, Mithyaa, Satya-vaanii, Paraa, Madhyamaa, Pashyantii, Vaanii* and many more. *Bhagvatii* has even claimed that all other gods are nothing but She herself in different forms. She represents valour in the form of *Shakti* but *Gaurii, Braamhii, Raudrii, Vaaraahii, Vaishnavii, Vaarunii, Kaauverii* and *Naarsimhii* are all nothing but her other facets.

While Jagdambii was busy absorbing all this mythology, Bhavaanii continued to worry for her son. At times, when she couldn't bear it any more, she would gently say to him, "Why are you so glum and aloof, my son? Look, how the other children your age are having a good time playing together while you sit alone, looking too thoughtful for my liking! What's the matter with you, son?" When so cajoled, he would rush to her, and throwing his little arms as far around her as he could, say to her, "*MaaN*, I so keenly want to see *Devii Bhagvatii* in her full regalia, at least once in my lifetime!" Bhavaanii would feel a cold shiver run down her spine to hear him talk like that. Her mind would be plagued by myriad dark apprehensions. Drawing Jagdambii into her lap, she'd try to reason with him, "Look, you're too young to think of such things right now; when you're older, you can think through them. For now, all you need to do is to eat well and play with your friends."

To comfort his mother Jagdambii would pretend he had understood, and even go and play with neighbourhood children for some time, but his heart was not into fun and games. He just couldn't help his natural disposition, and would soon return to his lonely ways to be reclaimed by his obsessive ponderings.

❋❋❋

It was shortly before midnight. Bhavaanii was asleep in her room, with Jagdambii in deep slumber on the other half of the bed. The room was bathed in a weak, yellowish light from a single earthen wick-lamp burning on the rack built into one of the walls. All of a sudden, Bhavaanii had the sensation of someone standing very close to her, calling out her name. She came awake with a start and sat up a bit alarmed. As she turned to look in the direction from which the voice seemed to have come, she saw a statuesque lady standing; she wore a deep red *saarii* with a golden border and all manner of jewellery that glittered like the rays of sun, and had a sort of a halo around her. Indeed, the lady in red *saarii* was so resplendent that Bhavaanii's eyes were dazzled and she couldn't quite look straight at her as she wanted, but she could sense that the lady was still there. By now, Bhavaanii had begun to feel a bit scared, and instinctively asked her who she was and what she was doing in her room. The figure replied there was nothing to worry and that Bhavaanii should listen attentively to what she had to say. Bhavaanii made bold to stand firm; she would only do so after the lady had introduced herself and revealed the purpose of her visit.

"Oh, didn't you recognise me? I'm *Kshemkarii Vana-Durgaa* who protected your son. I come here every night to see my protégé whom you call Jagdambii. But seeing how you're neglecting your duty towards him, I have had to appear in person tonight to remind you of it. Your son's born in a *Braahmana kula* and he's going to be five soon. Still, he remains uninitiated in appropriate *samskaaras*. You must make amends and have the ceremonies organised in accordance with Vedic traditions without any further delay, or else your child's growth will be stymied."

Bhavaanii hastened to bow her head, bringing her palms together in the *pranaam-mudraa* and said reverently, "*Maatu!* I feel truly blessed to see your affection for my boy."

"Oh!" said the *Devii* with a quick little laugh, "Is that all? Wouldn't you like to know why I, the omnipotent *Vana-Durgaa,* who happily stood guard on your new-born, could not protect your husband?"

"Certainly I would," said Bhavaanii.

"Well, Destiny is irresistible! The lines on your palms are cast in stone, in a manner of speaking. Even for the gods, it is not possible to change them. Besides, if such events never took place at all, how would ideals be set for emulation? Why would I have to visit the mortal world in different forms and incarnations over and over again? But you must know this, too: the credit for my special favour to your son goes to your husband; while showing respect to the female gender, he cared not whether he lived or died and preferred to sacrifice his life rather than let his principles be compromised. Much as I may be divine, I still have a feminine form. How could I allow the lineage of a principled man like your husband's to be wiped out of existence. This child of yours was still in the womb at the time I made my decision to protect him. It was I who inspired your maid, Mohini, to persuade you to flee the *havelii.* When she returned after seeing you off at the riverside, I put her in a deep slumber; she didn't feel any pain when she was beheaded. And since you were so distraught, I guided you all the way here to this household where you could have a respectable existence."

Bhavaanii, who had been trying to look at the miraculous form all the time despite her dazzled eyes, now saw it gradually move away towards the open flame of the wick-lamp. Meanwhile, the *Devii* had resumed speaking to Bhavaanii in a tone of mild reprimand, "Bhavaanii, what's it with you, dear! You neither offer *puujaa* to your family deity nor ever chant the *kula-mantra.* It's not good to be neglecting your duties to the family deity. Maybe you're under some mistaken notion that you can't offer *puujaa* to the deity at Singhwaar from a distance. But I'm sure you're not so clueless as to be unaware of the specific ritual of *UddishTa puujaa* that'd enable you to invoke your deity wherever you happen to be."

Chastened by the reprimand and yet elated on receiving advice from none other than *Vana-Durgaa* herself, Bhavaanii said, "*Maatu!* I'm grateful to you for saving my husband's family-line from extinction and shall forever be indebted to you for your favours. May I have your permission to worship you everyday alongside our family deity?"

"Why not? I see no reason to object to that. Do as you wish," said the *Devii,* but after a pause, she hesitantly added, "There's something that I need to tell you, though. You might know that I'm fond of blood-red flowers, red sandalwood paste, red raiments and other red-coloured offerings, but I'm afraid that from your family I shan't be able to accept anything in red, not even *sinduur*, which is an offering most commonly made to me."

Feeling a trifle snubbed by the *Devii's* injunction, Bhavaanii couldn't help asking plaintively, "What have we done to be excluded from the privilege of offering you your favourite things, particularly when you've otherwise been so partial to our family, *Maatu*?"

Vana-Durgaa gave her a look of deep compassion and replied, "I was helpless about what happened to your husband, Bhavaanii; as I said, even we, the Divines, are unable to change the destiny of mortals. What's fated must happen, and we aren't supposed to interfere. Nonetheless, because of what happened, the beautiful red line of vermilion disappeared from the parting of your hair, the red *bindii* vanished from your forehead and so did the red bangles that adorned your wrists, and all this came to pass in the middle of your prime! I don't have the heart, Bhavaanii, to accept anything red in colour from you."

"But, *MaaN,* we'll forever be deprived of the chance to offer you the things you like best!" exclaimed Bhavaanii in a voice pitifully close to tears.

"Well, I could possibly reconsider, but it would be a rather limited window of opportunity at best," said the *Devii* after a pause.

"I'll take it!" said Bhavaanii, jumping at the offer, "When can we do it, *MaaN?*"

"Whenever a son is born in the family, or one of them is initiated through the *yajno'paviit samskaara,* you may make such offerings. In your family, animal sacrifice has been a custom since time immemorial. But remember, henceforth you shall only make such sacrifice under open sky, somewhere like a courtyard perhaps. Mark my words, never under a roof."

"We shall follow your instructions to the letter, *Maatu!*" said Bhavaanii.

Bhavaanii, who had been gazing at the *Devii's* resplendent image for some time now, her dazzled eyes notwithstanding, noticed that it was beginning to shrink in size, besides moving farther away from her. The goddess now addressed her one last time, "Bhavaanii, like I have forms without count, I also have innumerable aspects. One of them is compassion. I am *karunaa* personified; besides, you also happen to be the one who gave birth to my favoured protégé, Jagdambii. That's what made me decide to appear before you in person and remind you of your duty. It would otherwise have been impossible for you to see me. But I could not have allowed my protégé's growth to be stifled for want of timely initiation into appropriate *samskaaras*. Now, don't you allow any further delay to take place! I hope you won't forget anything of all that I've told you tonight."

And with that, the *Devii* seemed to shrink into a tiny point of light that kind of merged with the flame of the wick-lamp on the rack. The flame flickered for an instant before steadying itself. Bhavaanii gazed at it for the longest time, as if in a trance, wondering whether it had all been for real, or she had been dreaming all along. But if it was all just a dream, how come an ethereal fragrance now filled the room. Had *Kshemkarii Vana-Durgaa,* drawn irresistibly by her affection for Jagdambii and compassion for the widow of a principled martyr, really visited her? She was at once overwhelmed by the possibility of having had a real *darshan* of *Bhagvatii* as well as a deep sense of loss; it was unlikely that she would ever see her again. As the certainty of it hit her, Bhavaanii let out a wail to recall her, "*Maatuuu...!*"

Baabaa Shambhuu Naath, hearing Bhavaanii cry out aloud in the middle of the night, came awake alarmed. He got out of bed quickly, and entering the inner courtyard through his room, knocked at her door, "What happened, *Bahuu*? Open the door." Bhavaanii opened the door and returned to stand near Jagdambii, fast asleep on the bed.

Baabaa entered the room; he first looked to see where Jagdambii was, and seeing him sleeping safely, heaved a sigh of relief. He was about to ask Bhavaanii what had made her cry out when he sensed the fragrance that filled the room. "What's this fragrance in the room, Bahuu?" he asked.

Bhavaanii had by then regained her composure and wondered how to explain it. Presently, Paaro, who had woken up on hearing the commotion, joined them, straightaway expressing curiosity about the exquisite fragrance.

Bhavaanii described to them her vision and the conversation she'd had with her divine visitor (whether real or dreamt she couldn't be sure, she said), and pleaded with Shambhuu Naath in a voice gone hoarse with emotion, "*Baabaa*, please ascertain an auspicious date and arrange for the *mundan* and *karna-vedha samskaaras* of Jagdambii at the earliest. Don't misunderstand me; this is what *Kshemkarii Vana-Durgaa* has expressly desired."

"I do see now that we've been a bit remiss not thinking about it on our own. By rights, he should have been put through these *samskaaras* by now, but you needn't worry;

I shall consult the *PanDit*s the first thing tomorrow morning and have necessary arrangements made. It's a long time until then; close the door and go back to sleep," said Shambhuu Naath.

As *Baabaa* left the room, Paaro shut the door and returned to lie down by Jagdambii's side. She thought Bhavaanii might be better off for her company for the rest of the night.

The family *panDit* and *jyotishii* were consulted the next morning, and the *tithi* and *shubh-muhurt* determined. Accordingly, Jagdambii was put through the initiation rites of *munDan, karna-vedha* and *Vidyaa'rambh.* The village elders assembled at *Baabaa*'s place, and at the end of the ceremony, they stood around the *mànDap* to shower soaked-rice grains mixed with twigs of *duurva* grass on the boy's head, blessing him with a long life. To mark the special occasion, *paatair* of *tasmaii, puaa* and other sweetmeats was offered to the goddess *Bhagvatii*; virgin girls were pampered as embodiments of *aadi-shakti*, being fed sumptuous meals on green plantain-leaves and given gifts of new clothes. At the end of the meal, the hosts gave them money by way of *dakshinaa,* and even elders touched their feet for blessings, treating them as *Bhagvatii* personified. From that day on, Bhavaanii also began to offer *UddishTa puuja* to the family deity and *Vana-Durgaa* in a corner of her room.

After the ceremony, Jagdambii began to regularly attend the village Sanskrit school, the one at which Sadaashiva taught. In his solitary moments, the boy was already used to mulling over things he had picked up from *Baabaa.* Now, he did the same with things he learnt from his teachers at school. He had a phenomenal memory that didn't need to be propped up by rote learning. He simply never forgot a word of what he had read, or been told, just once.

The school was a bit far from Shambhuu Naath's house. There were two routes to it; one, a public thoroughfare that passed through the village, and the other, through the private mango-orchard of Shambhuu Naath, a short-cut that halved the distance. Jagdambii liked to use the latter to walk to school, not only because it was much shorter but also for the reason that he was rather fond of *Baabaa*'s orchard with its neat rows of mango trees and dense foliage overhead. In the middle of the orchard was a large *mahuaa* tree with a shady canopy that stood out conspicuously, being the only tree of a species other than mango. Jagdambii fancied the *mahuaa* for its cool shade and unique distinction, frequently stopping by it while on his way to school or returning from there. He would sit underneath it and recite aloud the *shlokas* he had learnt either from *Baabaa* or at school. This had almost become a part of his daily routine, even on days on which the school was off. He loved the quiet sprawl of the *gaachhii,* koels calling sweetly in its silent solitude. One day, as Jagdambii was about to close his loud rhythmic recitation of a *shloka* from *Devii-Bhaag'vat* and brought his palms together bowing his head in salutation to the goddess, he heard a female voice call out to him by name, a voice that sounded very like his mother's. "Can't be her, though! She hardly ever stirs out of *Baabaa*'s courtyard. How could she be here, in this deserted orchard rather far from the house?" thought Jagdambii to himself.

However, he responded instinctively, looking all around in curiosity, "*MaaN*, I'm here." Then he saw her, a lady he had never met before, looking at him with just the hint of an affectionate smile. He couldn't help staring at her for a second, eventually asking, "Who are you? And why are you looking at me like *that*?"

Bhagvatii Vana-Durgaa – for that is who she was, though Jagdambii did not know – now smiled broadly. Jagdambii, even more dismayed now, peppered the lady with several questions all at once, "How come you know my name? I can't remember having met you before; what do you want with me?"

"I found your song very pleasing to the ear. I thought maybe I could spend some time with you and have a chat," replied the lady.

Jagdambii chuckled and said, "What? You're so grown-up to look at, but apparently you can't tell a *shloka* from a song! I wasn't singing a song; it was a *shloka* from *Devii Bhaag'vat* I was chanting."

"You're right; I'm grown-up and still couldn't understand that it wasn't a song. But how is it that in spite of being so young, you know a *shloka* to be different from a song?" asked the lady.

"I'll explain," replied Jagdambii, "but why are you still standing? Do sit down."

Fascinated by the maturity of his manners, the *Devii* came closer and sat by his side. Looking closely at her, Jagdambii launched into his explanation, "My *Baabaa* once related to me an anecdote from *Devii-Bhhag'vat*:

Once the great sage Naarada went to Srii ManNaaraayana, the Supreme Lord of the Divines, who holds the shankha, chakra, gadaa and padma in his four hands, and asked him, 'My Lord, what are the rituals that please Bhagvatii the most?' Srii ManNaaraayana explained to Naarada the various ways of offering worship to her and the rituals appropriate for different occasions, concluding, 'One thing is certain: Bhagvatii relieves the suffering of her devotees and protects anyone in the world who worships her with pure devotion.'"

Jagdambii raised his eyes to the radiant, handsome face of the lady, and said innocently, "Since I'm still a child, I can't possibly manage the elaborate rituals *Naaraayana* described to the Sage; so, I recite the texts cited by Him instead. Who knows, *Devii Bhagvatii,* full of compassion, kindness and mother-like affection as she is, might melt at my modest offering and decide to give me her blessings. In any event, that's what I'm hoping for."

Vana-Durgaa looked at the boy in utter disbelief, "Look at you! Talking like a *mahaa-panDit*, and you call yourself 'still a child'. I'll admit, though, that your innocence is charming, Jagdambii. Believe me, I'm fascinated to hear you talk," said she.

"Go away," said Jagdambii with a degree of petulance, "If I tell you now that it's uncivil to praise someone to his face, you'd perhaps pretend ignorance, and say that you'd bear it in mind in future. I don't want to talk to you anymore!"

"But why won't you, my dear?"

"My mother says children ought not to talk to strangers for long. You haven't even introduced yourself yet, or told me your whereabouts. How can I go on talking to you?" said Jagdambii.

Bhagvatii looked at him, amazed, "Don't tell me you haven't recognised me. I'm your mother, Jagdambii!" "Another lie! You're so big, adult-like and yet you tell a lie to a child. Now don't go telling me you're unaware that it's seriously sinful to tell a lie," said Jagdambii sarcastically. "But I never tell a lie..."

Before she could complete her sentence, Jagdambii interrupted her firmly,

"My mother must be in the courtyard at *Baabaa*'s place. She never goes out, and yet you claim to be her! What is it if not a lie?"

The *Devii* smiled sweetly and said, "Now, let's try this then."

"What?" exclaimed Jagdambii.

"Shut your eyes for a moment and open them again, then tell me whether I'm your mother, or not."

"All right, that doesn't seem difficult," said Jagdambii, and went through the motion. As he opened his eyes, he was astonished to find that her face was rather like his mother's. He gazed at her quietly for a few seconds, moving involuntarily towards a grudging admission,

"Well, this is rather strange! You do look a lot like my mother..." He stopped midway through it, though, wondering whether what he saw was an illusion.

Seeing the little boy struggle with conflicting thoughts, *Vana-Durga* asked, "What are you thinking, Jagdambii?" "Well, I think you do look very like my mother in terms of age, height, complexion and all. You're beautiful like her and even your voice is like hers. But my mother never wears such expensive-looking clothes or jewellery as you have on," said Jagdambii.

"It's possible that your mother who, as you said, is mostly homebound and never leaves the courtyard doesn't have such clothes and ornaments," suggested *Bhagvatii.*

"No. No, she has them; perhaps not as fancy as yours, but I do know that she owns a whole lot of wonderful clothes and jewellery lying locked in *Baabaa*'s big wooden chest," said the boy.

"Why doesn't she wear them then?"

"I asked her the same question myself," said the boy in a subdued voice.

"So, what did she tell you?" asked his mother's look-a-like. "She said, a mother with a wonderful son like me needn't cover herself in ostentatious clothes and things. But I have often wondered whether that's really all there is to it. A little while ago, you said you were my mother, and you have such fine clothes and jewellery on. It's really puzzling!"

"What your mother said is absolutely right, though. The mother of a son like you has no need for such ostentation. I shall myself stop wearing such extravagant stuff in future," declared *Bhagvatii* trying to reassure the child. To the contrary, however, Jagdambii, seemingly upset by what she'd said, hastened to plead, "Oh no; please don't ever give up your fine clothes and all. I didn't mean to criticise you for them. Please!"

"But why should you be so upset? Why can't I opt for simpler things if that's what I want?" asked the *Devii.*

"I like my own mother just the way she is, I mean my mother at home; on the other hand, I would like to see you in your expensive clothes and glittering jewels, just the way they are now. But I won't talk to you anymore," said Jagdambii, turning his face away from her.

"Now what? Why are you cross with me again, my dear?" asked the *Devii* in a worried tone.

"Why shouldn't I be cross with you? You haven't told me even till now who you are. How will I tell my mother who I met today on my way back from school?"

"I'll tell you everything – my name, my whereabouts, everything, but I'm afraid it will have to be another time. For now, it's enough for you to know that I'm your mother. There's something that you must never forget, though."

"What?"

"If you wish me to come again and spend time chatting with you, as we're doing now, you'll have to keep all this to yourself. Were you to reveal it to anyone even by mistake, you'd have lost me forever."

A shadow of disappointment fell over Jagdambii's face. Looking a bit disheartened, he said to the lady, "Do you mean I've to keep our meeting a secret from even my mother who's at home?"

"Well, I'm afraid so!" said the *Devii* firmly.

"I never tell a lie to my mother, nor hide anything from her, but if I promise to keep our meetings secret, will you come again?" asked Jagdambii.

"I certainly will. But now you must go. We've been chatting for quite a while. All the other children must have reached home by now, and your mother would be worried for you," replied the lady.

"All right, I'll go now, but you'll come again tomorrow, won't you?" Jagdambii asked, picking up his school bag.

"Yes, I'll definitely come," she said, vanishing instantly, like a digital image folding up.

The very first meeting with the *Devii* left Jagdambii totally distracted, unable to concentrate on anything at home or school. After a few more such engagements, all he wanted was to be back with his 'orchard mother' as conversations with her filled him with a sense of pure joy. Of course, she still intrigued him and scores of puzzling questions, apprehensions and random thoughts concerning her flitted through his mind in his solitary moments: 'Who is she? Where does she live? She says she's my mother and looks like her, too, but she's always vague about herself, saying unintelligible things like being all-pervading, without a beginning or an end and stuff like that. Whenever I call out to her, she appears, but I see her neither come nor go! Am I being conned by this lady? Is she practising some sort of sorcery, creating illusions and luring me away from my real mother through *mohini mantra*? Regardless of who she is, though, it feels so wonderful to be with her. She loves me like a mother, and I also have feelings for her similar to those I have for my own mother. I feel so restless and out of sorts if don't see her every once in while. What to do? It's impossible to even ask someone for advice for the simple reason that I would be violating my promise and might lose her for ever. How do I find out then who she really is?'

Almost every day he resolved that when next they met, he would ask her bluntly, and insist that she disclose her identity and see to it that she did so clearly. But when they actually met, absorbed in their utterly delightful conversation he either forgot about his decision or he just couldn't find a suitable opening for broaching the subject without causing offense.

❋❋❋

Jagdambii had just turned eight. This time around *Baabaa* Shambuu Naath wanted to make sure that he was put through the *yajno'paviit samskaara* and received his sacred threads exactly at the age customarily regarded as the most appropriate. As soon as the *tithi* and *muhurta* were determined, the family launched into elaborate preparations. The entire household bustled in a festive mood but for Jagdambii, who sat in a corner, morose and grumpy, because in keeping with the prevalent custom he was forbidden from leaving the house after the rituals of '*Udyog*', or the formal launching of preparations, usually about a fortnight before the day of the main ceremony. Jagdambii felt as if he was serving a jail sentence; he craved to have a glimpse of his 'orchard mother' and have a few words with her, but just couldn't get away. Bhavaanii was concerned to see him so downcast, and in a variety of gentle ways, she tried to coax out the reason, but he could neither reveal his secret, nor openly defy the ban and hurt his mother. So, he bided his time, making various excuses; however, his urge to somehow go out and see his 'orchard mother' was far from forgotten. One day, seizing upon an opportunity to steal away without being missed for a while, he ran out to the *mahuaa* tree in the orchard, frantically calling out to his 'orchard mother', "*MaaN*, where are you? I can't stay long because someone is bound to notice that I'm missing. Please understand my difficulty."

The *Devii* materialised, straightaway addressing him with more than a hint of reprimand in her tone, "Jagdambii! What are you doing here? You're to have your *Upanayan* soon, and as you know, the *baruaa* is strictly forbidden to move out of doors."

"How come you already know about my *Upanayan*? I can't remember having told you about it!" exclaimed Jagdambii in surprise.

The *Devii* chuckled merrily, "Haven't I told you more than once that nothing is hidden from me; I know all there is to know! Now, don't you go telling me you only came here to inform me of your upcoming *samskaara*," she said.

"That was the idea, but there's another reason, too," said Jagdambii.

"Go ahead then. Why are you hesitant?"

"Well, as you wanted, I've been keeping you a total secret. No one in the family including my mother knows about our chat sessions. Obviously, your name's missing from the list of guests invited for the ceremony. There are a whole lot of them, but no mention of you, imagine! So, I thought let me go out and invite my 'orchard mother' in person. You'll come and bless me, won't you?" said Jagdambii, expectantly looking up at her face with pleading eyes.

"I certainly will, my dear boy. Who will give *Maatri-bhikshaa,* if the mother's missing from her son's *Upanayan*? But I'll only come on the condition that neither you nor anyone else there would be able to see me."

"How will I know then that you didn't just accept my invitation but actually came to the event?" said Jagdambii, clearly disappointed.

"Don't be so disheartened, my son. This will be the occasion when all your doubts about me will be resolved, and that goes for my participation in your ceremony as well. You'll come to know everything that's been a mystery to you up until now, I assure you," said the *Devii.*

"But how is that going to happen?" said Jagdambii, wide-eyed in anticipation.

"Well, look inside the satchel meant for *Maatri-bhikshaa* just before approaching your own mother for *bhikshaa*, and you'll have all the proof you need to have that I was actually there," said the lady of the orchard.

"I shall anxiously wait for it then," said Jagdambii and ran to get home before he was discovered.

Jagdambii's sacred-thread ceremony was completed in accordance with Vedic rites. *Baabaa* Shambhuu Naath officiated as his *Aachaarya-Guruu* and guided him through the rituals. When it was finally time for *Maatri-bhikshaa*, *Baabaa* handed him a make-shift satchel made from a piece of cloth dyed yellow with turmeric paste dissolved in water, and instructed him, "Jagdambii, now you've to go around asking for alms from all the ladies, beginning with your mother."

Jagdambii stood up surveying the gathering, satchel in hand. He surreptitiously put his hand inside to feel if there was something in it already, but apparently it was still empty. He thought bitterly that his 'orchard mother' had let him down despite having accepted his invitation. However, he knew he had to fulfil the customary expectations. He began to walk towards the verandah where his mother stood, surrounded by other ladies. But as he came closer to her, he was startled to see that she appeared to be his 'orchard mother' instead. He was still peering at her face to make sure he wasn't hallucinating when he sensed something drop into the satchel in his hands. He exclaimed involuntarily,

"Mother, wait a second, let me see what my 'orchard mother' has given me by way of *Maatri-bhikshaa*."

As Jagdambii dipped his hand into the satchel and took it out, everyone gasped; he held in his right hand an extremely rare species of blood-red hibiscus bloom, leaving everyone wondering at the miracle.

The moment Jagdambii bowed, touching the flower to his forehead in salutation to his 'orchard mother', he felt a wave of understanding come flooding into his head. All his doubts, questions and suspicions of possible sorcery that had plagued his mind melted away, as if someone had snapped dust-covers off crystal-clear comprehension. In that one instant, he knew everything that had been going on and the suddenness of it overwhelmed him. Quite unmindful of what people might think, he broke down, lamenting and deprecating himself, "O how stupid of me, *MaaN*! In your own way you'd told me everything that needed to be said, holding nothing back, and yet, the fool that I am, I kept seeing you time after time without realising who you really were, harbouring silly doubts in my mind. Now that I know everything, I don't know whether you'll ever want to see me again. O *MaaN*, what have I done!" Finally, unable to bear the weight of the revelation, Jagdambii flung the *Maatri-bhikshaa* satchel on to the ground in a gesture of disgust at his stupidity and ran out of the courtyard.

Appalled by the misconduct of her son on a solemn ceremonial occasion in front of the village elite, Bhavaanii didn't know which way to look. It hit her like an unexpected body-blow, given that Jagdambii had all along been a thoughtful and well-behaved child. Looking distressed, she glanced at Shambhuu Naath and let out an anguished plea for something to be done, saying just, "Oh *Baabaa*!" *Baabaa*, watching all that had happened, rose to his feet from Aacharya's *aasana* on the *manDap*. He had more or less grasped what was going on. Reassuring Bhavaanii not to worry, he rushed out after the boy. Many of the village elders, mystified by the turn of events towards the end of an otherwise well-organised ceremony, also followed him out of curiosity. Jagdambii ran to the orchard, and standing underneath the *mahuaa*, began to cry out in a loud voice, choking with tears, "Where are you, *MaaN*? Please let me look at you one last time. Now that you've revealed it all to me with your blessings, I know who you are. Let your favoured protégé have one last *darshan*, that's all I ask for." The benevolent goddess eventually yielded to his pleading and materialised.

"Jagdambii, do you know what you've done? You've broken your promise by speaking of our secret in front of everyone." Jagdambii fell to his knees, bringing his palms together in the *pranaam-mudraa*, signifying total and unconditional surrender. "*MaaN*," he said, "I know that it was a serious breach of trust, and that I've offended you, but you're *Kshama* personified; surely, there can be nothing that you can't forgive; and I didn't do it on purpose, either. I was so overwhelmed, it just happened, irresistibly. Reprimand me, penalise me, do what you like, but please do not forsake me, *MaaN*! Or else your favoured son will die of a broken heart."

Seeing Jagdambii repent thus, *Vana-Durgaa* softened; she raised her right forearm in the *Aashiish-mudraa* and said, "Jagdambii, my son, now calm down and tell me why you're here leaving your ceremony incomplete. I've attended it and already given you *Maatri-bhikshaa*. What more could you want? However, if you do have an unfulfilled wish, you just have to ask. I won't disappoint you. So, go ahead and tell me."

Jagdambii stood up and said as if praying, "*MaaN*, you're right, you have given me, with little effort on my part, all that devotees worship you for life after life, and yet only the most pious of them get blessed with. But since the time I was a toddler I've had one craving that remains unfulfilled. Please show me the *ruupa* in which you emerged out of *tejah-punj* to help the vanquished Divines." In her meetings with Jagdambii so far, *Bhagvatii* had always appeared in the form of *Prithvii-Devii*.

"Son, close your eyes and open them after a moment," she said.

As Jagdambii opened his eyes, he was mesmerised by what he now saw: the *Mahishaasura-mardini* aspect of *Bhagvatii*, right there in front of him. He gazed at it all; her lotus-shaped face radiating the *teja* of Shiva; her long curly tresses derived from the prowess of *Yamaraaj*a; her three eyes that sported the red, white and black colours made from the *teja* of *Agni*; her arched eyebrows like the bow of *Kaamadeva* provided by *Sandhya*; her ears possessing the velocity of *Pavan*; her comely nose, adorned by the glitter of *Kubera*; her shining teeth, reflecting the fine workmanship of *Prajaapati*; her beautifully full lips, a gift from *Varuna*; her eighteen arms made from the *teja* of *Vishnu*; her fingers endowed with the *teja* of *Vaasu*s; her bosom, radiant like the rays of *Chandramaa*; her waist, a homage of *Indra*; the thighs, created from the *teja* of *Varun*; and her back, derived from the *teja* of *Prithvii*. His hands folded in the *pranaam-mudraa*, Jagdambii circled around the celestial vision, peering at each of its features. He noticed her everlasting red habit, her resplendent crown and necklace, her pair of opulent ear-rings and enchanting bracelets, set with jewels radiating the brilliance of a billion suns, gifted in gratitude by *Kshiir-saagara*; the arm-bands and *kangan*s set with precious stones, happily crafted for her by *Vishvakarmaa*; the delicate anklets and be-jewelled finger rings rendered unto her by *TvashTaa*; and the fabled *Vaijayantii*, a garland of ever-fresh and fragrant blooms of lotus, presented by *Varun*a – all adorning the *Devii* in her sublime magnificence. Continuing his *parikramaa* reverently, Jagdambii went on to note the celestial weapons and equippage generously gifted by the divine lords to the goddess for the destruction of demons: the luminous, revolving disc, the deadly *Chakra*, with thousands of serrations around it, that *Vishnu* had lent; the equally lethal Trident of Shiva; the shiny, clean Conch-shell brought by *Varuna*; the Shataagni made available by *Agni-deva* for the annihilation of the *Asuras*; the sturdy Bow and quiver-full of arrows from *Pavan*a-*deva*; the *Vajra* from *Indra*; the shapely Bell with a sonorous sound taken down from *Airaavat*, the celestial elephant; the dark powers of penal Death rendered at her feet by *Yamaraaj*; the celestial *Kamandalu*, a container with an arched handle on top, filled with holy water from the *Gangaa*, presented by *Bramhaa*; the *Paash*, the penal cord rendered by *Varuna*; the dazzling Sword and Shield, presented by *Kaala*; the *Farsaa*, an axe with a half-moon blade, honed to perfection by *Vishvakarmaa*; and the golden Goblet of celestial Honey, furnished by *Kubera*. Jagdambii was enchanted to see the *Kaumod-gadaa* in her hand and the impenetrable body-armour of gold, provided by *TvashTaa*. Every pore of *Mahishaasura-mardini* radiated the brilliance of *Surya*, the Sun-god. Jagdambii thought he wanted nothing more from life after this gorgeous *darshan* the *Devii* had granted him. Completing his final *parikramaa* with this thought, Jagdambii halted and stood in the *pranaam-mudraa* before her. The *Devii* smiled and said sweetly, "You're quite a clever little fellow, aren't you? I see that you completed one hundred eight rounds of *parikramaa* in such a short time, earning for yourself a lifetime of my patronage. Now, tell me whether that's all, or you want anything more."

Continuing to gaze at her lovely visage, Jagdambii said gratefully, "*MaaN*, my life's already made, but since you asked, may I request you for just one more favour?"

"You may, but you must hurry up, for I can already see your grandfather and some others coming towards us," said the *Devii*.

Jagdambii looked over his shoulder to see how much more time they had. He couldn't see *Baabaa* anywhere yet. So, he took a deep breath and plunged, "I'm greatly beholden to you for the *darshan* of your *Mahishaasura-mardini* avatar in full regalia. However, all my life I've heard my elders also refer to you as *Simha'vaahinii*, the goddess astride her lion, but I'm yet to see your golden lion assigned as your *vaahana* by *Giriraaja Himaalaya*. Just one more favour, *MaaN*, grant me a *darshan* of your *Simha'vaahinii ruupa*."

"I didn't bring my lion along, lest you get too scared for comfort, my son!" said the *Devii*, chuckling. Jagdambii laughed, too, and said, "You must be joking! Do you think your son, with your blessings at his back, could be scared of an animal, even if it happens to be *your* lion?"

"Well, well! I now see that you're quick-witted to boot. All right, close your eyes for a moment again," said she, continuing to smile affectionately.

When Jagdambii opened his eyes, there she was: *Bhagvatii* in her *Simha'vaahini ruupa* with ten arms, riding her ferocious lion with a golden mane. "*MaaN*, do I have your permission to rest my head on your feet for a moment and seek your blessings?" asked Jagdambii, his eyes glistening with tears of joy.

"Yes, I'll grant you this last wish, too, but first listen to me; this will be the last time I shall meet you in person, like now. I want you to understand this clearly before your grandfather arrives."

Clearly, Jagdambii had hoped for a reprieve. "Why, *MaaN*? Have I offended you again?" he asked innocently.

"No, you haven't. On the contrary, I'm rather pleased with you, but you must realise I have my own rules that I must observe, and limitations that bind me down."

"But you needn't worry, whenever you need my help and recall me fervently I'll be there at your side, even if you can't see me. I am with you and will always be there for you. No one will be able to cause the least bit of harm to you." Then, after a pause, she added with finality, "Hurry up now, and get your last wish out of the way quickly before your pursuers are upon you."

Taking a step forward, Jagdambii laid his head on the lotus-feet of the *Devii*.

Baabaa Shambhuu Naath, after exiting the courtyard in hot pursuit, asked a few bystanders which way Jagdambii was seen heading and concluded he must have gone to the orchard. Accompanied by a score of his friends and peers, he started to walk towards it, taking long strides. As they reached the edge of the *gaachhii*, he could make out Jagdambii, lying face-down underneath the *mahuaa*, his arms extended as far as they would reach beyond the head. Fearing the worst, *Baabaa* ran towards the boy who, at that distance, appeared to be lying prone, as though he might have fainted while stretching. As he came closer, however, Shambhuu Naath realised that far from being unconscious, Jagdambii was actually lying in the *saashTaang pranaam-mudraa*, chanting a *shloka* from *Durga Saptashatii*. Realisation suddenly dawned on the wise, old man, wiping away his fears and apprehensions, as Jagdambii's sonorous recitation rang out in the quiet of the *gaachhii*. In any case, *Baabaa* had long been convinced that Jagdambii was destined for great things.

Although Shambhuu Naath and his companions were not so fortunate as to have an actual *darshan*, the *Devii* soon treated them to a second miracle within the hour. As Jagdambii finished his chanting, the *mahuaa* tree seemed to shake itself, without the slightest bit of breeze in the air, and showered a basket-full of its sweet smelling flowers on him. The flowers, falling like rain, seemed to wake him up from his trance-like state; he sat up with a start and looked around, dazed, trying to get his focus back. That's when he noticed *Baabaa* standing above him, and exclaimed with a start, "*Baabaa*! How did you get here?"

Overwhelmed by pride, Shambhuu Naath picked up the boy by his shoulders, and embracing him heartily, said, "Jagdambii, my boy, it's a rare privilege to know you! Sages and seers, *yogiis* and *sanyaasiis* go through a lifetime of the most trying meditation, fasting and abstentions to get a mere glimpse of the one whose bountiful blessings you've received with little ado, as if by a child's play. You're wealthy in the truest sense. Let's go back and complete the remainder of your ceremony. Your mother must be anxiously awaiting our return."

Jagdambii, looking at the trunk of the old *mahuaa*, offered it a *pranaam*, solemnly bowing his head; then he turned and began to walk back to the house alongside his *Aacharya-Guruu*.

□

8
Conversations with Wandering Spirits

Jagdambii was now fifteen.

Whatever he'd been able to gather over the years about his father and other ancestors had stirred in him an irrepressible desire to honourably regain his inheritance, acquired by them through their valour and learning. He was also determined to avenge the brutal murder of his father, challenging the Mughal commander who had killed him, to a duel. But before doing any of this, he wanted to visit his ancestral family home, the *havelii* at Singhwaar, and he wanted to do it all by himself. He, however, well knew that if he asked his doting, overprotective mother for permission, she'd never allow it, and even if he were to somehow persuade her to agree, she'd without doubt depute an escort, an idea that was unacceptable to Jagdambii. After debating the matter in his mind long, he concluded that he'd just have to sneak out someday. For if he asked his mother, and she refused, he'd have to simply forget it. Defying her blatantly was something he could not even imagine.

So, one morning he awoke at dawn, as usual, and having got ready for the day, he sought out Mangluu, the syce, who was busy cleaning the stables and feeding the horses. "Mangluu, old chap, I see that Baadal, my late father's favourite mount is wasting away for want of exercise. I think I'll take him out for a few rounds. Could you please saddle him for me?"

The syce nodded, and presently brought out the horse readied for the ride. Jagdambii took the reins in his hand, and making much of the horse, whispered in his ear, "Come Baadal, let's go out for a long ride today."

Baadal neighed loudly, rearing up on his hind legs, as if he'd understood Jagdambii, and was raring to go, too. Jagdambii affectionately patted Baadal's back, delighted at his response, and jumped into the saddle. To begin with, the horse trotted slowly, as if letting the young master get a feel of him, but as soon as heeled, he started galloping. Within moments he was going so fast, Mangluu, who stood watching them in the far distance now, felt as if the horse were airborne, its hooves barely touching the ground. Soon they were lost to sight over the horizon.

Jagdambii had no idea of the way to Singhwaar, and soon began wondering how he'd ever get to his destination without directions. His wondering turned into a serious dilemma as they came to a fork in the pathway, as he had no clue which one to take for Singhwaar. There was not a soul anywhere in sight whom he could ask for directions. Feeling baffled, Jagdambii put his head down on the mane of his mount in despair and said softly, "Baadal, I've no idea which of two would take us to Singhwaar. Do you, by any chance, remember the way to the *Deorhii*?"

The horse neighed, and bent his head to the ground, snorting, as if trying to sniff out the way forward; then taking the pathway going straight ahead it began to trot, increasing its speed as he went along. Jagdambii was still wondering whether they were heading in the right direction when he spotted a small hamlet, a cluster of barely ten to fifteen small huts. Jagdambii heaved a sigh of relief, heading straight for it; there was bound to be someone there who could guide him.

Meanwhile, the vigilant hamlet-dwellers had also noticed the stranger astride a fine horse coming towards their huts, a little away from the main pathway. JhagDuu was also among them, and didn't take long to recognise the favourite horse of the late Master, exclaiming excitedly, "Hey guys, surely this is Baadal, our late Master's favourite horse." Baadal also seemed to recognise JhagDuu, snorting and shaking its head. Jagdambii knew then that his father's horse had brought him to the right place. Dismounting, he said to JhagDuu, "You're right. Indeed, this is my father's favourite horse, Baadal."

JhagDuu could hardly believe he'd heard right; gaping at the handsome, young lad, he began to tentatively formulate his question, "Are you..."

Before he could complete it, though, Jagdambii smiled pleasantly and said, "Yes, I'm Dharaadhar Thaakur's son, Jagdambii Thaakur."

As he introduced himself, he could see a wave of great good cheer wash over the hamlet residents, their faces wreathed in toothy smiles all around. JhagDuu stepped forward to take the reins from his hands, and his ten-year-old boy ran to a hut to bring out one of those bamboo-and-*muunj* cots for him to sit on. The residents, men, women and children, all lined up to touch the feet of the young master for his blessings. Jagdambii was quite taken by their warmth and loyalty towards him.

JhagDuu apologised for taking time to place him, saying that he had only seen him once at KaTkaa, as a little child many years ago. He told Jagdambii of the visit of Sadaashiva and Maarkandeya to the *havelii* and his own subsequent trip to KaTkaa, herding the *Deorhii* cattle. He fondly recalled meeting the Mistress, who had given him a meal, clothes and a generous tip. The joy of seeing the young master tended to make JhagDuu garrulous. "*Maalik*, you may not recognise me. I'm JhagDuu, son of Parmeshvar, the trusted *khavaas* of your late father. You can ask the Mistress about him. He would have been so, so happy to see you, but unfortunately he passed away last year. Until the very day he died, he only kept lamenting your father's gruesome murder; he was never again quite the same after that," said JhagDuu.

"I know of him. My mother often mentions Parmeshvar Kakkaa when reminiscing over her days at the *Deorhii*. I'm truly sorry for your loss and mine as well, for I'll never be able to meet him now."

JhagDuu flushed with bashful joy to hear the young master speak deferentially of his father; his eyes welled up. In a tone of great longing, he asked Jagdambii, "*Maalik*, when will you return to live here?"

Jagdambii turned thoughtful; after a few moments of reflection, he replied, sighing, "I'm not sure exactly when that would be, but believe me, the day is not far. I shall certainly make my ancestral home come alive again."

Then, Jagdambii rose to his feet to take leave of them. He told Jhagduu that he was happy to have run into them and find them still loyally guarding the *Deorhii* gates. He asked him if they needed anything and offered his assistance. JhagDuu reassured him that they made ends meet nicely for now, and that he would go directly to him if they were stuck. "All right then. I'll go and have a look at the *havelii*," said Jagdambii, beginning to walk towards his horse. JhagDuu couldn't help feeling alarmed at the idea of his young master going inside the long-abandoned mansion, which no one, to his knowledge, had entered after the two gentlemen from KaTkaa many years ago. He ventured in a tremulous, pleading tone, "*Maalik*, is it necessary for you to go inside the *havelii* just yet?"

"Don't worry, JhagDuu. Nothing will happen to me."

Jagdambii got on to his horse and trotted out towards the massive structure a few hundred yards to the east. As he entered the *Deorhii* forecourt, looking around cautiously, all of a sudden Baadal neighed loudly and reared up on its hind legs. The horse's reaction to something it had sensed in the air was so abrupt that if Jagdambii hadn't his thighs clamped to the sides of his mount, like the expert horseman that he indeed was, he would have been certainly thrown off the saddle. Pulling at the reins with all his might, he calmed the horse down by a sharp reprimand. Then he dismounted and tethered Baadal, hidden behind a tree surrounded by shrubs. As Jagdambii turned to face the *havelii*, a crumbling shadow of its former self, he had an uncomfortable feeling of being watched by someone unseen; he no longer felt quite so self-assured as a few minutes before when he'd told JhagDuu that nothing would happen to him.

The *havelii* was deserted. It was beginning to crumble in several places, particularly in parts like balconies, window-canopies and the like that jutted out beyond the main walls; paint had peeled off from the walls, and the plaster, corroded for the most part, was cracking up; the entrance courtyard had been taken over almost entirely by a particularly aggressive species of thorny shrub. The whole place was desolate, and silent as a grave. Jagdambii was overcome by emotion at the sight of his ancestral home reduced to such a state, and feared he might break down sobbing.

Reminding himself that he was a big boy now, he reined in his emotions and moved on towards the big audience-hall where his father had been cleaved to death. As he entered it, he felt a chill run down his spine: this time he had an unmistakable feeling that he wasn't the only one there, a distinct sense of another presence in the room. Startled, he looked over his shoulder and all around to see if anyone hiding behind a piece of furniture was observing him; it also afforded him the chance to study the various features and fixtures of the room. Everything appeared to be faded and covered in thick layers of dust. For a long moment, Jagdambii's unblinking gaze rested on the fresco of *Mahishaasura-mardini*; indeed, the colours had faded but it was still an imposing painting. He bowed to the image, saluting his mentor, the Benevolent goddess *Vana-Durgaa*, who had so kindly given him a *darshan* of her *Mahishaasura-mardinii* facet as well.

Eventually, Jagdambii turned around, moving towards the exit. As he did so, he heard a male voice, with a distinct undertone of affection to it, call out his given name. Once again he looked all around to see who had accosted him, but was amazed to find no one, no matter how hard he looked. He was sure he wasn't mistaken, though. He finally decided to ascertain by speaking to the disembodied voice.

"Who is this? Who called out my name?" he said.

"It's me," replied the voice that seemed to come out of nowhere, "Dharaadhar Thaakur. Although my body was consigned to the flames of my funeral-pyre and restored into the *pancha-tatva* long years ago, my indestructible soul's still trapped in this *havelii* of our forebears. I know not how long I'm condemned to flit around this crumbling, desolate mansion."

Jagdambii, struck dumb by the enormity of the revelation, fell silent, but his fear was gone. He knew he was safe and wanted the conversation with his father's spirit to continue. He was perturbed by the despair in his voice and needed to know what he could do for him.

"Is there a way, I mean, for you to be released from your present state?" he asked.

"Jagdambii, my son, I can't find *mukti* from this *preta-yoni* until you've restored the *Deorhii* to its lost glory by your prowess and valour and returned to live here."

It occurred to Jagdambii that flustered by the unexpected turn of events, he hadn't yet properly greeted his father's spirit; adopting the *pranaam-mudraa*, he said in a submissive tone, "Father, I can hear you all right, but can't see you. Why are you invisible? Please show yourself to me."

"That's not possible, my son," the voice replied, "my present form is so minuscule, like an atom, that it's impossible for you to see me. But I can see you as well as hear your voice. To tell you the truth, it's an indescribable pleasure for me to be seeing you," said his father's ghost

"I'm no less delighted that you're so pleased to see me, Father," said Jagdambii.

"But what's your purpose in coming here all by yourself?" asked the spirit.

"Are you telling me that you don't approve of my coming here, Father?" asked Jagdambii in a small voice.

"No, no; nothing of the sort. In fact, it's difficult to express what a great solace it is for my desperate soul to be able to see you. When I first entered my present state after they killed me, I wandered restless and anguished that our family deity would never again be worshipped by an heir, that there wouldn't be anyone after me to light even a single *diip* on the *chinvaar* of the *Deorhii Puujaa-ghar*, far less offer an *aartii* every evening. I felt shattered – though I must say I was hardly in a form that could be shattered – and I began to drift aimlessly from one corner to the other. Then, one day I met another kindred spirit in a similar situation and this other spirit told me how your then pregnant mother had fled the *havelii* in the nick of time and saved our family line from annihilation, and how she and the son born posthumously of my seed were living in a generous family of another branch of our lineage settled in KaTkaa. That other spirit and I then decided to pass the rest of our time until our *mukti* exclusively in the *Deorhii*. Now, both of us are waiting for you to make this place come alive with real living people again and set us free."

"Father, I solemnly promise you that if I continue to have *MaaN Jagdambaa*'s patronage, I shall soon restore both this ancestral homestead as well as our family to their past glory. I need your blessings, too, Father," said Jagdambii in an humble tone.

"My blessings will always be with you, my son."

"Can I ask you something, Father?" 'Go ahead'.

"Are you aware that Nawaab Salaamat Khaan sent his Vizier to rob the treasure hidden here?"

"Of course, I am. I also know that the veterans who survived managed to somehow drag out the dead bodies of Ghulaam Sarvar and their two comrades, and took them back to Waariaul."

"Then, perhaps you also know of the low-life villains who trespassed with similar intention and entered the *Puujaa-ghar*?"

"I do; two of them were killed but their mates couldn't retrieve their bodies. Their skeletons are still lying in *Puuja-ghar*. You can take a look if you want," said the spirit.

"My foster-grandfather, *Baabaa* Shambhuu Naath, with whom mother and I have lived since my birth, had sent his son and grandson here to fetch your sword for mother. This was several years ago. They had also seen a pair of fearsome black cobras that seemed to be guarding the hard-earned treasures of our ancestors from fortune-hunters and thieves. Father, can you tell me who those cobras really were?" asked Jagdambii in a pleading voice.

A prolonged silence ensued, compelling Jagdambii to wonder whether he had unwittingly asked something that had offended his father's spirit. Or maybe it was a closely guarded secret he wasn't inclined to share with him. "If I've caused any offense by asking you that question, I beg to be forgiven, Father," he said.

"No, I'm not offended in the least. It's only natural for you to be curious. Why only you, my son, practically everyone would like to know who these guardian-angels, appearing as *Naag-devtaa*, really are. Well, I'll let you into the secret: it's actually me!"

"You, father?" exclaimed Jagdambii incredulously.

"Yes, I myself!"

"But didn't you say only a while ago that a wandering soul has no material form that human eyes can see?"

"Yes, I did. You're right to think that I have no material form," said the voice of his father.

"What are those fearsome cobras then?"

"Mere illusion!"

Utterly dismayed, Jagdambii echoed the words back, "Mere illusion?"

"Yes, Jagdambii. It's an illusion created to deter robbers and thieves; some of the trespassers were so scared that they died of heart-failure caused by the shock of a cobra striking. If someone had bothered to examine their dead bodies carefully, it would have been obvious they didn't die of snakebite. Those incidents and the wildfire-like rumours that spread about them have helped me protect the *Deorhii* from intruders all these years. After all, this is my close preserve until I'm released from limbo, but don't forget that all this must remain strictly between us. It is necessary for people to go on believing in the myth to keep the *havelii* safe from rogues."

"You're right, Father, I'll keep it to myself. But there's another thing I find intriguing. Why are there two snakes in the illusion that you create? You are just the one, aren't you?" asked Jagdambii.

"The other one is the kindred spirit who told me about you and your mother having survived the massacre. Although she wasn't, strictly speaking, a family member when she lived, yet the role she played in saving our family-line needs to be cherished for ever. She sacrificed her own life for it."

"Who was this, Father?"

"Well, in the eyes of the world she was a mere chamber-maid in your mother's apartment, but she was actually her childhood playmate, rather close to her. She was the one who persuaded your mother to flee when there was no other way to save you. Then, to mislead everyone, including me, she pretended to be your mother sleeping in her bed, knowing full well that she would be slain by me in the bargain. Her name was Mohini, and her soul, like mine, is stuck in the *havelii*."

"But why is her spirit necessarily bound to our ancestral homestead?"

"I'm afraid only she can answer that question;" said the spirit.

"Can she come and answer my question?"

"Why not!" replied the voice.

"I would be happy to have the chance to speak to her," said Jagdambii.

Hardly had he finished when a feminine voice joined the conversation. "I'm here," it said, "I was your mother's personal maid when I lived."

Jagdambii, assuming the *pranaam-mudraa* in formal greeting to Mohini's spirit, said with great politeness, "*Devii* Mohini, you were no maid; you were my mother's best friend, and almost like a sister to her. I'll never forget your great favour to the family and to me in particular. Do you mind if I call you *Sakhii-MaaN*?"

"Don't be silly, my son! '*MaaN*' is the loveliest word in the Universe. It would be both a pleasure and privilege to be so addressed by the future Thaakur of Singhwaar *Deorhii*," replied Mohini's spirit.

"Then, *Sakhii-MaaN*, first and foremost, please be so kind as to accept the *Pranaam* and eternal gratitude of Jagdambii Thaakur."

"May you live long happily, son, and be remembered as one of the leading lights of your illustrious lineage," said Mohini.

"*Sakhii-MaaN*, I'm very curious about something," said Jagdambii, "May I ask you a question?"

"By all means, go right ahead."

"There could be any number of reasons for my father's soul to be partial to the *havelii*, but pray tell me what it is that binds you to it," asked Jagdambii.

"Son, when you get back to KaTkaa, please convey my *pranaam* to your mother and tell her that her Mohini's spirit restlessly awaits her return to the *Deorhii*. It will only be released from limbo the day she starts living here again. There's no other way."

"All right," said Jagdambii, "I'll give her your message. But *Sakhii-MaaN*, I must take your leave now. Since I'm here, I might as well take a round of the entire *havelii*."

"That's a must. Do remember to go to the *Puuja-ghar* and pay obeisance to your family deity," said the disembodied female voice.

Jagdambii exited the audience-hall, and as suggested by Mohini, decided to first go to the *Puujaa-ghar*. As he entered it, leaving his shoes outside the entrance, he felt a wave of nausea wash over him at the sight of crumbling pieces of the skeletons of Subodh and Dhanessar, which had disintegrated over time and lay strewn all over the floor. Circumventing the litter somehow, he made it to the edge of the *chinvaar*, kneeled and put his forehead down on it. Moved to tears by the state of utter neglect of the sactum sanctorum of his family deity, Jagdambii both prayed and lamented at once, "*Prabhu*, how much more of this agony do we have to bear? When can we return here to worship you regularly? Do give me the strength to win back my ancestors' legacy so that I can live here and worship you myself morning and evening every single day, as did my father in happier times before I was born."

Having taken a round of the *havelii*, Jagdambii eventually wound up in the room that had once been his parents' bed chamber. As he entered the room, he heard his father's voice address him again, "Jagdambii, do you know something? The contingent that came from KaTkaa to help us out arrived a bit too late. By that time the carnage was over. Alas! I was clubbed from behind and captured alive, and was taken to the audience-hall; they strung me up against the wall on a hook, my hands and feet bound with thick cords, and hacked me down the middle, from the head to the waist, into two equal halves. The courtyards and verandahs were thickly littered by dead bodies of our men who'd died defending the *Deorhii*, and of women and children whom we ourselves had beheaded to save them from a fate worse than death. Rivulets of blood flowed in every direction you looked. In the circumstances, the guys from KaTkaa did a fine job, giving us a decent funeral and burying the *Deorhii* treasury-chests underground. Very thorough, I must say! They went through the entire *havelii* with a tooth-comb, as it were, and picked up everything of value for safe-keeping. But, thorough as they were, they did overlook something precious, and that 'something' is what I want to gift you to mark this special occasion, your maiden visit to our ancestral homestead, my son."

"It'd be a privilege to receive anything as a gift from you, father, no matter whether it's valuable or not," said Jagdambii smiling brightly.

"Do you see the fourposter in front of you?"

"Indeed, I do, Father."

"Well, the mattress is too moldy to touch, but push it aside anyhow. If you look closely at the wood plank underneath, you'll notice a cabinet built into it with a small switch to its side, like a nail sticking out a bit."

By this time, Jagdambii, enthusiastically following the instructions, had located the box concealed in the plank, but he still couldn't see the switch.

"Look a little harder and you'll see it, just a wee bit to the right of where you're looking for it," said the voice.

"Yesss!" said Jagdambii excitedly as he found the switch.

"Now, pull it up a bit and a cabinet will come out."

Jagdambii did as told; and as he removed the cover, he gasped: in it was an ebony baton clad in silver with the finest filigree work that he had ever seen. Jagdambii took it out and was still inspecting it when his father's voice rang out, "It only appears to be a baton covered in hand-carved silver filigree, but it can also be used as a hand weapon in an emergency."

"How can a baton be much of a weapon in an emergency, Father?" said Jagdambii.

"Well, just turn the knob at its top to the left, pulling it out simultaneously, and you'll see for yourself how it works. It's called *guptii* – a secret weapon."

As Jagdambii went through the motions, out came a sleek hand weapon with the sliver knob as its fist-hold; it was something like a mini-fence, just over a foot long, with a razor-sharp blade made of shining, tempered steel. Having inspected the blade, Jagdambii slid it back inside its silver-clad sheath, and with a soft click, it went back to being an ordinary baton, albeit an expensive one.

Delighted with the gift – from his father who had passed on before he was even born – Jagdambii thanked his father's spirit.

"I feel truly blessed to receive such a wonderful gift from you; thank you, Father," he said," but now I must take your leave, for Mother will be quite anxious by now." Then, with a hesitant pause, he added, "Actually, I didn't take her permission for coming here."

"But why didn't you? You should have, you know," said his father's voice.

"You're right, I should have, but then I might not have been here at all."

"But why? What objection could she have?"

"Because she thinks I'm still a child. Can you believe, she puts a kohl-mark even now on my forehead every morning to ward off evil-eye, never letting me out of sight if she can help it! To every request of mine, her stock reply is 'You're still a child, my love!' Now, you can well see for yourself whether she'd have allowed me to come here."

Jagdambii heard his father guffaw. As he stopped laughing, Jagdambii said, "But now I really must leave for KaTkaa."

"All right, son, you may go, but I hope you won't forget that unless you reclaim the *Deorhii* and return to live here, I would be restlessly wandering around in this deserted *havelii*."

"Father, I can't put my finger yet on a deadline for it, but rest assured I shan't let you down. That's a solemn promise. Please accept my *pranaam* before I depart," said Jagdambii, bending down to touch the floor with his fingers and then touching them to his forehead.

"May you live to see a hundred Springtime! I shall await your return to the *Deorhii* to live here.

Turning around, his father's gift in his hand, Jagdambii called out, "*Sakhii MaaN*, are you still here?"

"Yes, my dear, go ahead."

"I'm about to depart and wish to take your leave now. The next time I'm here, my mother will be with me, and we'll come not on a visit but to live here. Please accept my *pranaam*. Farewell!"

"Farewell, my son. Don't forget your *Sakhii MaaN* after giving her the exalted status of *MaaN*, is all I ask."

Having taken leave of the wandering spirits, Jagdambii retraced his steps to the main entrance, found Baadal and left for KaTkaa.

Meanwhile, anxiety levels in the KaTkaa household at Jagdambii's unexplained disappearance – without telling anyone where he meant to go – had been going up by the hour. Mangluu, the syce, being the only person to see him go out, was naturally questioned, but all he seemed to know was that he had overheard Jagdambii whisper into the horse's ear – "Come, let's go for a long ride."

"A long ride? A long ride to where?" Shambhuu Naath wondered, his face clouded by worry for the boy's safety.

After the miracles that people had witnessed on the occasion of Jagdambii's *yajno'paviit* ceremony, first during *Maatri-bhikshaa* and then in the orchard, he had risen in the esteem of everyone in the community. The average village-folk were concerned for him, too. There were many, though, who felt there was no reason for too much anxiety; they believed the boy had obviously gone off somewhere quiet to have a private conversation with *Bhagvatii*. Most others, however, disagreed, saying, he hardly needed to go anywhere for the purpose, quiet or otherwise, for the moment he fervently called out to the goddess, she would appear wherever he happened to be. Opinions were going dime a dozen!

Regardless of their differences, however, they all wondered where the boy had gone. Meanwhile, *Baabaa* had sent his men several times to look for him in the orchard, expecting he would possibly be found under the *mahuaa* tree, but to no avail. He consoled Bhavaanii telling her that wherever Jagdambii was, he would be perfectly safe, that no one could harm him in the least. Bhavaanii herself was sure, too, that her son would be safe, being under such a powerful mentor; she was no less than the mighty *Vana-Durgaa* herself. Still, she was worried beyond words, and vexed that he had not bothered to let her know where he was headed, far less seek her permission for such a long absence.

Baabaa Shambhuu Naath and Kaashii Naath waited anxiously on the front porch, their eyes trained on the path Mangluu said the boy had taken as he rode out that morning.

It was late afternoon when Kaashii Naath spotted him returning astride Baadal in the far distance. *Baabaa* heaved a sigh of relief and came down the steps to the front yard. Dismounting the horse, its coat glistening from the long ride, Jagdambii ran to *Baabaa* and embraced him, whispering, "*Baabaa*, forgive me for having gone off without telling you." Then turning to Kaashii Naath, who was eyeing him with great curiosity, he said aloud, "*Kakkaa Jii*, I didn't know that Baadal is such a rogue!"

"What happened?"

"I thought I'd give him some much-needed exercise, but the moment I was in the saddle, he broke into a gallop like mad; and much as I tried to rein him in, he wouldn't stop, until we were at the doorstep of our *havelii* in Singhwaar."

Baabaa patted the boy's back, saying, "Jagdambii, you ought at least to have told your mother you were going out for a ride. She's been so worried. Do go and see her at once, she's mighty mad at you."

Jagdambii dashed off to his mother. Bhavaanii sat on the *manDap*, praying silently, distraught with anxiety. "*MaaN*, why are you so upset, I'd just...."

Before he could even complete his sentence, she broke in sternly, "First tell me what it is you're holding in your hands, would you?"

"It's a baton."

"Where did you get it, eh?"

"My father gave it to me as a gift."

Bhavaanii could hardly believe she'd heard right, exclaiming in complete confusion, "What? What did you say?"

Jagdambii moved closer to her and said in a grave tone, "Yes, *MaaN*, that's the truth; it's a gift from my father. I'm sorry I went off to take a look at our ancestral home without letting you know. While exploring the *Deorhii*, I got a chance to have a long conversation with my father and your favourite maid, Mohini, my *Sakhii-MaaN* now. That's why I'm so late coming back."

"What are you raving about, son?" Bhavaanii exclaimed, incredulous and alarmed.

"I'm sure you know well, *MaaN*, I would never ever tell you a lie. This baton here is indeed a gift from my father; he gave it to me as a memento of my maiden visit to our ancestral *havelii*." Jagdambii then went on to describe his eventful day in graphic detail to his mother. Noticing her turn rather quiet, he added, "*MaaN*, just stop worrying now, I'll take care of everything. I won't breathe easy until I can return to my ancestral place and bring it back to life. I just can't bear the thought of the souls of my father and *Sakhii-MaaN* wandering around endlessly in the desolation of Singhwaar *Deorhii*."

❋❋❋

Nearly two years had gone by since Jagdambii's visit to the *Deorhii*.

Bhavaanii had just finished her morning *puujaa*. As she came out, she noticed Jagdambii sitting on the verandah, looking rather downcast and asked him if anything particular was bothering him. The boy glanced up at her, saying, "*MaaN*, how long shall I sit idle, doing nothing? I've not been at peace with myself ever since my return from the *Deorhii*, plagued by the echoing pathos of my father's voice pleading for *mukti* from limbo! What shall I do? He must be expecting me to act quickly. I want to travel to Delhi at the earliest, you know, and have it out with that butcher of a contingent commander who murdered my father. I know my father's soul will have no rest until I've avenged him."

Bhavaanii's heart was pierced to the core by her son's agonised voice, her eyes welling up with pride and shared pain. Trying hard to restrain her emotions, she counselled him, "I know how you feel, my son, and I'm proud that you're so alive to your responsibilities. But I'd be failing in my duty if I didn't advise you to be patient just a little while longer; you'll enter into your eighteenth year shortly."

She fell silent for a moment, then, with weary sigh, added, "You don't know what reserves of patience I've had to draw upon, waiting for the day you'd be eighteen."

"Would my father understand the need to wait until then? Would he forgive the delay?" asked Jagdambii as though she knew how he would feel about it.

Bhavaanii looked at her son with pride, and replied firmly, "Of course, he will. Let me tell you something more, son: I'm myself keen that you should avenge your father's murder and regain your rightful legacy, and carry on the good work and name of your forebears. But, at the same time, I don't think it'd be right to deprive you of the time-honoured ceremony that has been observed in the family for generations. My son, that's something I regard as sacred!

Jagdambii responded at once, saying in a tone of resignation, "As obeying you is a sacred duty for me! I guess I'd have to be patient until then, but I can't but keep looking forward eagerly to that day."

Meanwhile, seeing mother and son deep in conversation, Paaro sauntered across the courtyard to join them. Bhavaanii and Jagdambii stood up to greet her, the boy touching her feet as he was meeting her first time that day. She noticed that he was not his usual cheerful self, and asked him directly, "What's wrong with our dear Jagdambii? No smiles for *Kaakii-MaaN* today?"

Even before Jagdambii could think of a polite response, Bhavaanii came clean in his behalf: "He wants to travel to Delhi."

"Delhi? Why Delhi?" exclaimed Paaro, a trifle amazed to hear of the famed imperial Capital so far away. In this remote corner of Mithilaa, people had only heard of it in tales.

"He wants to challenge the Mughal army commander, who killed his father, to a duel," replied Bhavaanii.

"And he wants to go all the way to Delhi alone?" asked Paaro with evident concern.

"Well, *Kaakii-MaaN*, I haven't an army to take with me, have I? Neither am l intending to wage war against the Emperor – I just want my revenge in a duel with my father's murderer, and that, I'm certainly capable of handling alone." Having thus stated his mission rather tersely, Jagdambii rose to his feet and slipped away, saying, "*Baabaa* must be feeling lonely sitting all alone on the front porch. I must go and be with him for a while."

□

9
The Third Wife of Dharaadhar

Jagdambii had left an awkward silence in his wake for the two ladies to tackle. Paaro could see Bhavaanii was struggling with the anxiety pent up inside her, and needed to be diverted.

"Bhavaanii, I've often thought of asking you something, but have been hesitant lest you thought I was prying," said Paaro tentatively.

"What are you saying! You're dear to me as my own sister, how could I misunderstand you? Do feel free to ask anything you like," said Bhavaanii, surprised at Paaro's formal approach.

"Maarkandeya's father told me Dharaadhar *Bhaai* was only a couple of years younger than he. I was surprised to learn that the gap between their age was so small," said Paaro.

"Surprised? Surprised in what way?" asked Bhavaanii, wondering what Paaro was driving at.

"Well, I knew Dharaadhar *Bhaai*'s first wife had died not long after the wedding and he'd remarried soon after. But then, how come you're so much younger than I?"

Bhavaanii did not say anything for a few moments, as if debating in her mind how to reply the question, and then she said quietly, "Actually, *Diidii*, I'm his third wife." "Oh! What happened to the second one then? Was she killed in the *Deorhii* massacre?"

Bhavaanii looked into Paaro's eyes for a long moment, and then replied, "No. It's a long story but there's no reason why I can't share it with you, if you have the time."

"Well, my dear, I'm all ears, if you please."

Taking a deep breath, Bhavaanii launched into her narrative of how Dharaadhar Thaakur had come to have three wives one after another.

"The first of my husband's three wives, Maalatii, was my own elder sister. She was a real beauty, her beautiful eyes and long black hair smooth as silk were truly a gift. Unluckily, though, tuberculosis took hold of her at a rather tender age, and it only got worse with time. My father did his best to get the most advanced treatment available, even taking her all the way to *Benaares* to have her seen by the famous *vaidya*, Trayambak Shaastrii. Everyone declared it an incurable condition. My father was deeply upset as Maalatii reached the customary age of marriage. Though a respected Sanskrit scholar of *darshan-shaastra* in Kaashii, my father however, was...well, he was, I must admit, a rather greedy, self-centred man, capable of anything as long as it served his own ends!"

Bhavaanii paused again, perhaps to regain her composure in the aftermath of the unpleasant admission, and took up the threads again, "In his efforts to locate a suitable match for Maalatii, he came to know of Jagdambii's father, a most eligible bachelor in the community then, and while pursuing the lead went to Singhwaar and met my late mother-in-law. She was rather taken by my parental antecedents and eventually gave her consent. I have to tell you that my father deliberately kept from her the fact of Maalatii's incurable, and by then fairly advanced, condition. Well, the wedding passed off without incident. Jagdambii's father stayed just a week at our home that first time. I don't need to tell you that the bride and groom were allowed no privacy, as is customary, during the first three nights. When they were by themselves on the *Chaturthii*, the fourth night, the first question he asked his beautiful bride was, 'Say, why do you keep...um... Well, sort of coughing all the time? Are you all right?' and then offered to make the customary gift of the gold *kangan* he had brought as a present for the occasion. As he slid the *kangan* on her wrist, however, he was shocked to find her in the grip of a burning fever, and exclaimed,

'O my God! You seem to be running high fever. No need to keep that veil on – do lie down, and try and get some sleep, if you can!' With that, he passed the rest of the night sitting up by her side, keeping vigil. On his return to Singhwaar on the seventh day, *MaaN Jii*, curious to find out how everything had gone, asked him 'So, Dharaadhar, tell me how you liked my daughter-in-law.' He said she was extremely beautiful, but at the same time rather sick, and added, 'I'm not sure what exactly ails her but whatever it is, it isn't something ordinary.'

MaaN Jii, though furious that she had been conned, so to speak, by the girl's father, knew that there was little that she could do now for fear of becoming a laughing-stock in society. She told her son, what was done was done; Maalatii was her daughter-in-law, and that regardless of her condition, they had to bring her home as soon as possible. An auspicious *lagna* was suggested by the family priest for *dviraagaman*, and Maalati arrived at the *havelii*. Her new family consulted the very best of *vaidya*s and *hakiim*s and virtually spent a fortune over visits to far-away places for treatment; even tantra-mantra, special *anushThaans* and talismans from Sufi saints were tried out. However, nothing seemed to work. My father was duly informed of all that was being done but he never said a word, neither in apology nor in accusation. As for *MaaN Jii*, she'd curse my father for his selective memory: while praising his daughter's beauty, he had never even hinted at the scourge that would soon take her away. But to be fair to *MaaN Jii*, she never said a harsh word to Maalatii. Jagdambii's father was always a polite and attentive husband to her, too, doing his duty, and even telling her what he knew to be a lie – that she'd get better soon! In her heart, however, Maalatii knew she was moving fast towards an untimely end.

One day when she'd lost all hope, she took her husband's hands in her own and said, a look of utter despair on her face, 'I'm so sorry I wasn't able to give you the slightest pleasure expected of a wife, and have little right to ask anything of you, yet would you promise me something if I asked." 'I surely will, my dear, if it's something within my means, that's all I can say.'

'Promise me then that after I'm gone, you'll marry again, and mind you, this time a girl not only beautiful, but also healthy.'

Jagdambii's father had a heart of gold: he couldn't bear the pain his dying wife felt and tried to reassure her she'd survive, but this time she brushed it aside and insisted on having him promise, so she could die in peace. Eventually he gave in, saying, 'All right, I promise I will.'

Maalatii died the following day.

A year later, he travelled to *Gayaa* and performed the terminal *Shraadha* rites for Maalatii. On return, he fulfilled his promise to her, marrying a second time. His second wife, Gaurii, a deeply religious woman, was something of a fanatic in her devotion to Lord Shiva. She had worshipped the Lord ever since she was a little girl. She would go to the temple every Monday without fail to offer flowers and *bilva-patra* with elaborate rituals; she'd fast without even water to drink on *Mahaa-Shivaraatri* followed by prolonged rituals in the evening. *MaaN Jii* was duly impressed by Gaurii's devotion, but decided to delay her *dviraagama* until after three years of marriage."

Three years! It appeared too long a wait to Paaro. Anticipating the question in her eyes, Bhavaanii resumed after a brief pause: "I'll tell you why. An instinct told *MaaN Jii* – and it soon turned into a conviction – that while Maalatii, who was brought home within a year, had but a short time here, she herself had come in the third year and had had a long and satisfying life. Well, I won't go into the merits of what she believed, but it meant that Gaurii continued to live with her parents; Jagdambii's father visited her from time to time over the next couple of years, but Gaurii's life style remained unchanged, no matter if she was now the daughter-in-law of a wealthy, noble family.

"On the *Mahaa-Shivaraatri* day the third year, she went into the woods to gather *bilva-patra* for the evening *puujaa*, and bitten by a black cobra there, she died instantaneously. When the bad news was broken to Jagdambii's father, he came to believe that he would never have the blessings of a happy conjugal life, and began to flatly refuse to remarry whenever *MaaN Jii* brought it up. He told his mother in no uncertain terms that if she wanted a daughter-in-law, she'd have to content herself by finding brides for Shri Raam and Raadhey Shyaam. That is exactly what happened. Both my younger sisters-in-law were married and came to the *Deorhii* well before I myself did.

"With Maalatii's demise, our contact with Singhwaar *Deorhii* snapped. My father was seen as someone less than honest, and best forgotten. Greedy as he was, though, he still wanted to ingratiate himself with them whenever he could. So, when the date of the *yajno'paviit samskaara* of my only brother was fixed, he sent a formal letter of invitation to the *Deorhii*, hoping that gifts in cash and kind from the wealthy family would cover most of the expenses. Outraged by the cheek of it, *MaaN Jii* tore the letter to pieces, heaping curses on her son's former father-in-law, calling him a cad and a cheat. Destiny, however, had other plans, as they say. Jagdambii's father was not the one to nurse a grudge even against people like my father. He not only sent a decent *bhaara*, but also surprised us by showing up to attend the ceremony."

Bhavaanii paused for a moment, as though to recall the exact sequence of events before resuming, as Paaro waited for the rest with obvious eagerness:

"I remember it all so vividly, as if it only happened the other day. He arrived at our place in his gorgeous phaeton drawn by two black thoroughbreds, on the day of *Kuma'ram* preceding the sacred thread ceremony. He wanted to leave for Singhwaar as soon as the main ceremony was over the next day. When he came to take leave of my mother, she pleaded with him to stay for at least one more day. As I said, Jagdambii's father was indeed a decent man; he said to my mother, 'It'd be most impolite of me to brush aside such a warm gesture on your part. I'll leave tomorrow,' and postponed his departure to the following day.

"Being a younger sister-in-law, I was closely involved in the arrangements made to see that his stay was comfortable;

as usually happens between such relatives, we exchanged light-hearted banter within limits of decency.

"He was all set to leave after breakfast the following day, his personal baggage already loaded on the phaeton. I can still see myself sitting in front of him as he ate his breakfast, imploring him to have a second helping of this or that.

"I don't know what got into me, and suddenly, out popped a question I least expected to ask, 'You stayed an extra day at *MaaN's* request; wouldn't you stay another day at mine?'

"He looked up at me, clearly surprised by the unexpected question, with an odd expression on his face that made me blush a deep crimson. Then he broke into a smile and said, 'If you ask me, I can stay put for good here!' He postponed his departure again for a day.

"As I was serving him breakfast the next morning, he looked at me quizzically and asked, 'Aren't you going to ask me again to stay over for yet another day?'

'No,' I replied diffidently.

'Why is that?' he persisted.

'Well! I believe people should know their place and act with restraint. That you accepted my request yesterday and stayed over is good enough for me. But if you permit, I can share something in confidence with you.'

'Sure, sure! Why not? Please', he said, looking at my face expectantly.

'I felt very happy that you came, and it makes me sad that you have to go!' I said in a rather subdued tone of voice.

"I cannot quite describe to you, *Diidii*, how his hand poised over the plate suddenly became still and the way he stared at me for the longest time, making me blush again. The awkward silence that fell between us needed to be broken, so I said, rather inanely though, 'A penny for your thoughts, *Jiijaa ji*! Your breakfast is getting cold.'

"I thought maybe he had been reminded of Maalatii, who had remained divinely beautiful until the very end, her terminal illness notwithstanding. Maybe he hadn't managed to get over it. A moment later, he resumed his breakfast without saying anything more.

"When he was finally ready to leave, my parents brought out a pair of *dhotii*s dyed yellow with turmeric, a twirl of sacred thread and five pieces of betel-nut in a red *changeraa* to offer it to him as *Bidaaii*, customary for guests departing after a ceremony. Jagdambii's father protested, saying it was hardly necessary, and that they could deem their offering as already accepted. My mother, who had remained quiet until then, said softly, 'Thaakur *Jii*, you'd do us a great honour if you actually accepted it.'

"To my surprise, he yielded to her without further ado.

"Little did I know that the day had an even greater surprise in store for me! Truth to tell, as soon as I heard my father beginning to make a mention of it, I quickly withdrew to the room behind and stood listening at the door. After he had accepted the *Bidaaii*, my father began apologetically to offer my hand to Jagdambii's father; he had certainly been guilty of deception, he said, and had no moral right to come back to him with such a proposal, but seeing the magnanimity and affection with which his former son-in-law had attended his son's ceremony had raised his hope to atone for his past misdemeanour.

'Thaakur *Jii*, the fact that you've taken the trouble to come all this way is proof enough of how large-hearted and forgiving you are. I'm confident you'll give me another chance,' he said. Jagdambii's father turned deeply thoughtful. I'd be lying to you, *Diidii*, if I didn't tell you that as I stood behind that door, I was dying with curiosity, wondering what his response would be. I tried to take peek into the room, and at the very same instant he happened to glance towards the door. Our eyes met and I blushed in embarrassment, as though I'd been caught red-handed doing something forbidden. Then I heard him gravely declare that the right and proper thing for my father would be to go to the *Deorhii* and place the proposal before *MaaN Jii*, and that he could only help him to the extent that he'd say yes, if she decided to consult him. I have to admit that I could have danced for joy to hear him say that! I've no idea why, but to me, the age difference between us seemed to be of little consequence.

"My father somehow managed to get *MaaN Jii* to see him, and put his proposal before her with great trepidation. As was only to be expected, she rejected it out of hand, but she soon learnt from *Munshii* JaTeshvar Laal that this might be the only such proposal which the Master would not turn down as usual. (Now, who told *Munshii Jii* this, remains a mystery of sorts!) Anyhow, *MaaN Jii*'s desire to see her son happily married again far outweighed her dislike for my old man, and eventually she gave her consent. That's how I came to be the third wife of Jagdambii's father.

MaaN Jii insisted on the three year rule for *dviraagaman*, so I went to live at the *Deorhii* only at the end of that period. It was my misfortune that I could enjoy my husband's company only for a few years, but he gave me everything that one can hope from a loving husband, and before parting, he also gave me my boy who's all I live for now. Well that's my story before we met here, *Diidii*; the rest you already know."

Paaro, who had been listening intently to her, asked, "Such a big carnage took place in the *havelii*, and no one turned up from your parents' family to ask after you! Neither did anyone show up during Jagdambii's ceremony. May I ask why?"

"There's no one who could come."

"Why? Whatever happened to your parents and your brother?"

"Well," replied Bhavaanii mournfully, "as I said, my father was a Sanskrit teacher in Kaashii, while my mother and brother lived in the village looking after family property; they had everything – farmland, orchards, fishing-ponds, decent income, and respectability – you name it...! But who's safe from the unseen hand of Destiny? A cholera epidemic struck the entire region and wiped out half the village population; there wasn't a single family that didn't lose a member or more. Unfortunately, my only brother was one of them. My parents were devastated. My father tried his best to get my mother to go to Kaashii with him, but to no avail. She wouldn't leave the house where her only son had died, and grieved to death shortly afterwards. My father returned from Kaashii to perform my mother's last rites and visited us at the *Deorhii* for a couple of days too; that was the last time I saw him. He had lost the will to live, sold everything he possessed for a song and went away to live the life of a *sanyaasii* somewhere near Haridwar. I've no idea where he might be now, or whether he's even alive any longer."

Bhavaanii just couldn't go on anymore, her voice all choked and eyes welling up at the memory of having lost her entire family on the parents' side as well as her husband's in tragic circumstances.

□

10
Jagdambii Comes of Age

The day Jagdambii entered upon his eighteenth year *Baabaa* Shambhuu Naath's house was all decked up in fresh mango leaves on strings hung over doors, along the eaves and edges of the thatched roof of the *manDap*. The entire household wore a look of joyous festivity with a band of musicians playing on the *rasan'chowkii*.

Jagdambii was bathed with eleven pitchers of water drawn from the old family well by as many *Braahmanas*, after which he was given a fresh set sacred thread and a set of new yellow-coloured clothes to wear. Meanwhile, Bhavaanii had already begun the *puujaa* at the appointed hour with all the traditional rituals to invoke the goddess *Vana-Durgaa*. The ancestral sword, a family heirloom, kept on the *chinvaar* was anointed with holy water. Jagdambii was then seated on a separate *aasana* by his mother's side, the entire family standing around. The rituals over, Bhavaanii stood up and made a sign to Jagdambii to do likewise. She then reached up to tie a kesariaa silk turban on his head with *Baabaa*'s help, and put a sandal-paste *tiikaa* and *akshat* on his forehead. Then she picked up the family sword with great solemnity, and handing it over to him, said:

"Son, had your father been alive, he'd have been the one to hand over this sword to you. In his absence, I give it to you in the hope and faith that you'd keep the family tradition intact. I'm done with the responsibility for your actions and now on you'll answer for all that you do yourself. May the goddess *Vana-Durgaa* and our family deity always protect you! Go forth, now, and seek the blessings of all family elders gathered here to felicitate you."

As Bhavaanii finished speaking, the *Braahmana*s started chanting mantras in unison and showered *akshat* mixed with flower petals and twigs of *duurva* grass on his head by way of blessings.

Jagdambii bowed low to touch his mother's feet, saying, *MaaN*, bless me in cheers that I may be able to wreak vengeance on my father's assassin."

Bhavaanii's face clouded over for an instant only to regain its composure the very next moment as she said drawing him into her arms:

"You're the brave son of a brave father. I'll never stand in the way of your doing your duty. I command you to ascertain an auspicious time and get on your way. May the *Vana-Durgaa* ever be by your side! I have no doubt that you'll accomplish your mission."

"I expected no less of you, Mother!" said Jagdambii gratefully and went forth to touch the elders' feet for blessings. As he greeted *Baabaa* Shambhuu Naath, the elderly patriarch drew him into a warm embrace, and said, "May the goddess *Durgaa* help you to achieve your heart's desire. May you always be victorious, Jagdambii!"

"*Baabaa*, do me the favour of looking up the *Panchanga* yourself, will you? I want to launch my campaign in the auspicious *muhurta* ascertained by you personally."

"But do you want to travel to the Delhi all by yourself, Jagdambii?" *Baabaa* asked, watching his face expectantly.

"I haven't decided on that yet, *Baabaa*. Do you have anyone in mind to accompany me?"

"If you have no objection, may I go with you?" asked *Baabaa* hopefully.

"You *Baabaa*! Would you be able to take the strain of such an arduous journey?" Evidently, Jagdambii was surprised by *Baabaa*'s offer, wondering whether his old bones could take the punishing journey to Delhi.

"Don't worry about me. To tell you the truth, I have lived all these years since you were born in the hope that I'd have the privilege some day to witness your exploits. But for it, I might have joined my forefathers by now," said *Baabaa* with conviction.

The moment Jagdambii was assured of *Baabaa*'s keen desire to accompany him, he broke into a brilliant smile, and said jubilantly, "I must admit, *Baabaa*, this is what I secretly wished for too, but considering your age I didn't think it'd be right for me to suggest you undertake such a long journey. By volunteering so emphatically, you've solved my problem – who could I find better suited than you to accompany me? Your delightful company would not only lighten the monotony of such a long journey but also afford me the benefit of your experience guiding me at every step."

The tradition of handing down the family sword was akin to the custom in royal houses of anointing the eldest prince as the heir-apparent. On such occasions, it was customary to feed *Kumaariis*, *Braahmana* men and boys, and also distribute food and alms among mendicants, wandering *saadhuus* and faqiirs. All such obligations out of the way, Bhavaanii felt hugely relieved that the ceremony had gone off without a hitch. She could not, however, help feeling her heart skip a beat every time she remembered, or someone mentioned, that Jagdambii would soon be leaving for Delhi on a perilous journey with an even more daunting task.

On the day the two were to leave, the entire family gathered again in the *Puujaa-ghar* of *Baabaa*'s home, and after offering *aartii* to the family deity, Bhavaanii adorned Jagdambii's forehead with red-sandal paste *tiikaa* and blessed him, "Farewell, my son, may you return in triumph with the blessings of the most Benevolent *Vana-Durgaa*!"

As usual, Jagdambii touched his forehead to the edge of the *chinvaar* for a long moment and took the elders' blessings. They all came out to the front yard where Mangluu the syce waited for them with their horse ready for the day's ride. They were to be accompanied by a cook and three other trusted men for miscellaneous duties including taking turns to be their night-guards. They all stood by their respective horses, with their satchels and weapons, ready for departure.

The porch and front-yard were packed with village folks come to bid farewell to them, all filled with a sense of pride mixed with curiosity to see the handsome young lad, already a bit of a celebrity, leaving for Delhi to avenge his father.

"*Baabaa*, we ought to leave now," said Jagdambii when there arose a farewell in chorus from the gathering:

"Go, Jagdambii, go! We'll await your triumphant return."

In a matter of minutes, the party of five men bound for far-away Delhi, more than eight weeks of gruelling ride at the time, were little specks on the horizon and then out of sight altogether.

Bhavaanii had indeed put on a brave front at the time of departure but her heart was full of foreboding at the dangerous nature of his mission. She returned to the *Puujaa-ghar* and sat down to pray for her son's safety. She lost sense of time and knew not how long she sat meditating, deeply immersed in seeking divine blessings for her son. Paaro and Saavitrii came and peeped in several times but had to retrace their steps as quietly as they had come.

Then, Bhavaanii had the sense of a deep, seemingly familiar voice addressing her:

'Bhavaanii! Take heart, I'll be with him every step of the way?'

Bhavaanii opened her eyes and put her head on down on the *chinvaar* floor, saying aloud, "*Maatu*, please keep Jagdambii from harm!"

□

11
At the Great Mughal's Court

The long ride to Delhi on horseback took the usual number of weeks, including scores of overnight halts in unfamiliar caravan-serais, *dharma'shaalaas* and temple precincts, and sometimes with a hospitable household when they could find one. They had to cover a distance of hundreds of *kosa* through unknown habitations, small towns and cities, interspersed with long stretches of dense forests crawling with outlaws and infested with ferocious wild beasts. The small party from KaTkaa, however, managed to cover the huge distance without incident, arriving at the outskirts of the imperial capital at sundown some eight weeks later.

As the small group from distant rural Mithilaa entered the city, the sights and sounds of Delhi, the splendid Capital of the Mughal empire, with its bustling streets teeming with fine carriages; its gentry in stylish attire, exchanging greetings with great refinement; its imposing buildings in red sandstone and marble, decorated with domes and minarets; its crowded bazaars and its myriad other novelties took their breath away and left them gaping in wonderment.

Quickly emerging from his state of awe, however, Jagdambii reminded his mentor:

"*Baabaa*, we'd better stop ogling at the sights and find a suitable place to stay before it gets dark. We really don't know yet how long we might have to stay here."

"You're right, my dear, but now that we're here, let's familiarise ourselves with the place; while we do that, we might also find a place to set up our *Deraa*," said *Baabaa*.

So, for a while they roamed around the streets and by-lanes but *Baabaa* could not find the kind of place he had in mind for setting up camp. He wanted a quiet location, away from the hubbub of the city; finally they crossed over to the other side of the city and found themselves in another part of its suburbs. Here they came upon a Shiva temple set in a large meadow covered with rank grass. The spot had the very kind of serene quietude that *Baabaa* had been looking for. He found it so heart-warming that he reined in his horse to turn towards it, saying, "Why not explore the possibility of setting up camp around the *Shivaalaya*?"

"Your wish is our command, *Baabaa*," said Jagdambii, following his lead.

They found that evening *puujaa* in the temple was in its final stages, with the *sandhyaa-aaratii* still on. A large gathering of devotees stood at the entrance in the *pranaam-mudraa*, waiting for *aaratii* blessings. The KaTkaa party joined in, noticing straightaway that the local congregation was well up on the ritual, some blowing on the conch-shell horn while others sounded handheld gongs and played the *Damaruu*, all so involved as to seem in a trance in motion.

Just as the *Aaratii* concluded, *Baabaa* Shambhuu Naath sat down in padmaasana in the temple *jagmohan* and began to recite *Panchaakshara shloka*s in praise of Lord Shiva:

To the One who has for garland
The Lord of serpents,
To the three-eyed One;
To the One who has for his limbs
The powder of ashes,
To that great Lord of lords,
To the Pure, the Eternal
One who wears the quarters, the naked one
To the One spelt with 'N'
To that Shiva I bow down!

So compelling was *Baabaa*'s sonorous chanting, so perfect his diction and cadence, that it at once grabbed the attention of the devotees, who began to irresistibly gravitate towards him. Impressed by his devotion, they stood around him listening while *Baabaa* went on fervently:

To the One who's adorned
With sandal-paste prepared
With waters of the Mandaakini,
To the One who rides
The bull Nandii, as his Lord;
The Lord of the Desire-god,
To that great Lord of lords,
Adorned with myriads of Mandaar blossoms,
To the One spelt with'M'
To that Shiva I bow down!
To Lord Shiva
Who's the sun to Paarvatii's lotus-face,
To the destroyer of Daksha;
To the blue-throated One,
To the One who carries
The banner of the Bull;
The One who's spelt with 'Shi'
To that Shiva I bow down!

By now, most of them squatted around his seated figure, listening intently, under the spell of his person; they were captivated no less by the glowing countenance of the handsome young man by his side. They all waited for him to complete his reading, eagerly looking forward to finding out who the newcomers were, as Shambhuu Naath went on with his chant from memory, his eyes closed:

To the One whose head, adored
By the lord among the Sages,
By VasishTha, Agastya, Gautam;
The One who has for his eyes
The sun and the moon,
And Agni, the fire-god,
To the One who's spelt with 'Va',

To that Shiva I bow down!
Whoever reads this five-lettered hymn,
Filled as it is with merit,
Dedicated to Lord Shiva,
He rejoices for ever and ever
In the Lord's company, close to Him!

Having completed his chanting of the *Panchaakshara Stotra*, *Baabaa* rose to his feet, and then lay down in *danDavat pranaam* to the *lingam*. As he stood up again, an elderly man from the gathering stepped up to introduce himself to him:

"I'm Shivaanand Upaadhyaaya of the *Kaashyap gotra*; my family for generations has looked after the *Shivaalaya*, taking care of the worship on a daily basis. You seem to be new to this place. Would you be so good as to introduce yourselves?"

"We've come to Hastinaapur, renamed Delhi, on a special mission from the ancient land of Mithilaa. My name is Shambhuu Naath Thaakur and this is my grandson, Jagdambii Thaakur."

The moment *Baabaa* mentioned Mithilaa, the expression on Shivaanand's face changed into one of great welcome touched with reverence, and he said:

"Oh sir! I'm greatly honoured; it's my privilege to receive guests from Mother *Jaanakii's* birthplace. You're worthy of adoration for that reason alone! Allow me to have your blessings." With those words, he bowed low and touched *Baabaa*'s feet, and turned towards Jagdambii, who stepped back at once, saying, "No, no; You're way older, it wouldn't be right for me to let you touch my feet. May you have the blessings of Lord Shiva!" Much taken by Jagdambii's courtesy, Shivaanand pulled him into a warm embrace. As he did so, he felt a huge wave of peace wash over him; and as he withdrew, with his hands still on Jagdambii's shoulders, he felt captivated by the young man's presence. *Baabaa* Shambhuu Naath broke the spell, exclaiming, "Now, isn't he someone special, Shivaanand *Jii*? My grandson is a favoured devotee of *MaaN Jagdambaa*. He's come here to present himself before the Emperor, Mohammad Jalaluddin Akbar, with a special petition, you see. I'm here only to keep him company."

While Shivaanand was still absorbing that piece of information, *Baabaa* made his request:

"We may have to stay in Delhi for quite a while in that connection. Would we inconvenience you in any way if we were to camp in the *Shivaalaya* premises?"

"Oh, absolutely no problem at all. On the contrary, it'd be a great pleasure for me to be able to make your stay here comfortable. Perhaps it may also give me the chance to have greater access to your esteemed presence," replied Shivaanand humbly.

Baabaa smiled his satisfaction at Shivaanand's response, raising his hand to ward off more eulogy from his prospective host, and added, "Shivaanand *Jii*, grateful as I am for your generosity, let me make it clear at the outset that we'd only use the temple premises to set up camp; we won't accept any *Prasaad*."

Shivaanand looked at him, rather bewildered, and asked, "But why? I thought you're an ardent devotee of Shiva."

"I certainly am one, but we in the Mithilaa region are mainly devoted to *Shakti* worship and abstain from the *Prasaad* of Shiva shrines, except *Baidyanaath-dhaam*, as part of a time-honoured tradition. I do hope you won't take it amiss!"

"No, no! I won't mind anything at all where you're concerned," assured Shivaanand. *Baabaa* further explained, trying to assuage his feelings, "That's why we in Mithilaa always worship Uma-Maheshvara, Shiva and Paarvatii together, as *Ardha-naariishvara*, you know."

"I understand," Shivaanand reassured *Baabaa* again, then went on to add as though wondering aloud, "but if you won't partake of *Prasaad* here, how are you going to manage your meals in a place that's altogether new to you?"

"Well, it's kind of you let us use the temple premises for our camp, and that's enough; we wouldn't like to impose on your hospitality any further than that. It won't be difficult for us to cook our meals as we have a professional cook in our party."

Despite *Baabaa*'s reluctance, Shivaanand insisted on opening a room at the back which they could use as a kitchen, providing them with firewood and utensils, and reassuring them again that he was honoured to be taking care of such distinguished guests.

Thanks to Upaadhyaaya taking such good care of the KaTkaa party, they began to feel quite at home in practically no time.

However, a couple of days passed without any progress towards their real mission. Everyone was worried, but Jagdambii was particularly restive. He had really no clue where to start, who to ask for help in this unfamiliar city where they were total strangers, or how to go about the task in hand: to manage an audience with the Emperor. Like all powerful rulers of the time, the Great Mughal lived behind several layers of tight security. Indeed, he was quite out of reach of a common petitioner from a nondescript principality in a remote backwater of the realm, particularly a petitioner who was a claimant to an estate already seized by the authorities.

❋❋❋

It was past midnight. *Baabaa* was fast asleep by Jagdambii's side, but he was unable to go sleep; he stepped out on the verandah, wondering whether he would have to return home disappointed and in disgrace. If so, what would happen to his father's wandering soul? And his *Sakhii MaaN's*? Would all this effort have been in vain? Overcome by despair, Jagdambii broke down, calling out aloud in an anguished voice, "O *MaaN*! Am I to return without my revenge then? Is that what's fated?"

All of a sudden, Jagdambii's eyes were drawn up to the clear, star-spangled night sky, as though commanded to witness a most unusual movement of celestial bodies. He saw countless brilliant points of light beginning to come together.

Electrified, he focused hard to make out the image forming in the middle of the massed light-points, but he found his eyes blinded by their massed brilliance. Just then he heard a soothing feminine voice speak to him from, apparently, not very far from where he sat, "Jagdambii, there's hardly any need for you to be so dejected. Everything happens in the order pre-ordained by destiny! The time for your heart's desire to be realised is close at hand. You shall undoubtedly succeed in your mission. I'm with you as I've always been!"

As the voice stopped, Jagdambii saw the massed luminosity up above in the heavens vanish out of sight, in the blink of an eye, as it were. He involuntarily cried out, "*MaaN*!" running out into the temple yard and looking in vain for the massed light that only moments ago had been there in the sky.

Baabaa woke up with a start as he heard Jagdambii's cry. He saw him standing in the yard looking up at the sky, walked over to him and asked softly, "What are you looking at, Jagdambii?"

"*Baabaa*, look, there it was!" said Jagdambii, pointing his index finger above. *Baabaa* looked up too, but all he could see was a lone star up there, twinkling faintly in the inky night sky.

❋❋❋

It was a dreary routine, tiring and frustrating in equal measure, strangely back-breaking with little activity. Every morning the last two days, Jagdambii and *Baabaa* would be up at dawn, get ready for the day and walk out of the temple area, to the point near the gate of the imperial fort beyond which common folk had no access. He would stand over there, under the shade of some tree, and wait until dusk fell; he did not know what else to do. His pleas for entry into the fort with the burly, stony-faced sentries had so far fallen on deaf ears; he did not know a soul in the huge, faceless city he could turn to for counsel or assistance. He and *Baabaa* had both racked their heads for a way to move forward out of the impasse, but had not been able to come up with anything at all. They would return to their camp in the twilight, exhausted, having done nothing much except standing and waiting for something to happen, without quite knowing what exactly it was they were waiting for.

Call it a coincidence, a stroke of luck or divine intervention as you will, but their fortune seemed to turn on the third day.

It so happened that the carriage of Raajaa Maan Singh, the chief of staff of the imperial army and the Emperor's relative, passed that way. Rather unexpectedly, too, the Raajaa noticed the elderly man with sandal-paste *tiikaa* on his forehead alongside a striking, handsome youth just standing under a tree by the paved roadside, glancing rather wistfully at every passerby. Who knows what moved the Raajaa, but he ordered his carriage to halt, and beckoned to them to approach him and asked them what they waited for. They introduced themselves as *Braahmans* of *Shaandilya gotra* from Mithilaa with a petition to present to the Emperor about atrocities perpetrated at the behest of the Nawaab of Waariaul.

The Raajaa fell silent, as if pondering on the matter. Eventually, he told them to wait there and moved on towards the gate with his colourful retinue. Neither *Baabaa* nor Jagdambii had any idea who he was, but they guessed he must be someone important to have such a fancy carriage and so many armed escorts. The twosome, however, had gone up quite a few notches in the esteem of the sentries who had witnessed the scene. One of them, himself curious as to their identity, told them it was Raajaa Maan Singh, wondering aloud why he had chosen to come that way today rather than using the North Gate as was his wont.

The anticipation of something concrete emerging from the chance encounter with Raajaa Maan Singh made Jagdambii and *Baabaa* impatient; every moment felt like hours. In reality, though, it was only a short while later when a Guard Captain came out of the gate and asked them to follow him.

Baabaa smiled encouragingly to Jagdambii who was thrilled – they were after all going to get inside the fort. They silently thanked their *IshTa-deva* and the *Vana-Durgaa* as they followed the Captain quietly.

The Emperor, Mohammad Jalaluddin Akbar, sat on an ornate golden throne set with precious stones, placed on a high marble platform. It was a full court with the famed *navaratna*s and other distinguished courtiers in attendance. Raajaa Maan Singh had a seat in keeping with his status. A number of heavily armed guards stood behind the courtiers, alertly watching from side to side. Having heard of the elaborate protocol at the imperial court from Shivaanand, the two petitioners from Mithilaa greeted the Emperor with *farshii salaams* three times over, stood up and waited. The Emperor looked long at them, as though appraising their credentials; then he asked them to state the reason for having made such a long and arduous journey.

Standing upright, Jagdambii summoned all his courage, and said:

"Your Majesty, I've heard it said that the Emperor of Hindostaan, Mohammad Jalaluddin Akbar is not only a brave warrior but also a doyen of Justice. I've come all this way to knock at Your Majesty's door, confident that justice will be done in my case as well."

"Justice will most certainly be done! You may state your case without any fear," said the Emperor.

Having repeated the *farshii salaams*, Jagdambii stood up to make his case. Beginning with the imbroglio over LaaDlii and Pyaare, he went on to recount the way Nawaab Salaamat Khaan and Ghulaam Sarvar had conspired to get the Mughal contingent over on false pretences to attack Singhwaar and massacre its innocent populace and reduce the village to a heap of rubble; and then, he described the brutal murder of his father, Dharaadhar Thaakur, who had been taken captive, and could have been charged with sedition and given a fair trial rather than being hacked to death in cold blood. Anticipating the possibility of awkward questions about Dharaadhar taking up arms against imperial troops, Jagdambii argued, "My father was fully aware of the consequences of taking up arms against the large, highly trained contingent of the imperial army, equipped with far superior weaponry: certain death! He knew that they would all be slaughtered like sheep. And yet, that's the option he chose over surrender! Doesn't that tell Your Majesty that the real story lies hidden between the lines? My father could see that surrender was not an option since he knew well that the Nawaab and his Vizier had so poisoned the ears of Your Majesty's commander as to believe that an example needed to be made of the Thaakur of Singhwaar, or else they'd soon see him leading an army of Hindu insurgents. Your Majesty has only to look at the sheer gore of his brutal murder to know that I'm not telling a lie! So, Your Majesty, my father and my uncles could also foresee the kind of fate awaited them or their women and children. In order to save them from it and fight valiantly to the bitter end, they went so far as to put even their innocent families to the sword. I'm sure Your Majesty can well imagine the horror of such despair! My father and his men fought hard but the outcome, as I said, was a foregone conclusion, Your Majesty. They were massacred to the last man, and my Singhwaar was laid waste, but the worst was indeed reserved for my father."

Jagdambii took a deep breath and plunged in to conclude his narrative:

"For a rag-tag group of un-trained warriors, the Singhwaarians fought fiercely, and it's true many of Your Majesty's soldiers were killed, or maimed for life, but then it was all in the heat of a battle for survival, I assure you! In the sequel, however, the imperial *Subedaar* of Paataliputra ordered the confiscation of our family estate as compensation for damages even though all of it happened owing to the machinations of the greedy Nawaab, aided and abetted by his Vizier. My father acted in self-defence; he was forced to take up arms against the imperial army since he was taken unawares by the wiles of Ghulaam Sarvar, but surely nothing can remain hidden from you, mighty Sire of the world, even about things that happened many years ago. Your Majesty can have the whole sequence of events investigated and if I'm found to have lied, you can have my head, but *JahaaNpanaah*, say this I will: my late lamented father was not only a loyal subject but also a practical man of the world, so aware of his limitations to a fault, he wouldn't even dream of sedition, far less of waging war against Your Majesty. Those were all lies fabricated by Ghulaam Sarvar to remain in the good books of his vile master. I've nothing more to say; it's all up to you, Your Majesty!"

Jagdambii's words left a stunned silence in the Court at what everyone saw as a lot of plain-speaking on the part of a brash young man. Much as it was couched in polite speech, what he'd said could easily be misconstrued as wild allegations and undue hostility against imperial officers. Of course everyone waited with bated breath to see the Emperor's reaction. A good half-minute passed before he spoke:

"*Braahmana-kumaar*, we're very sorry to hear of your father's misfortune. You'll certainly be restored to your family estate."

Once again Jagdambii bent low, his head almost level with his knees, and offered three *farshii-salaam*s to express his gratitude to the Emperor. Then he stood back tall, drawing himself up to his full height, and said firmly:

"Your Majesty, do kindly excuse my candour that some might say smacks of insolence, but I have to say this: I'm indeed a *Braahmana* but not one given to asking for alms!"

The young man's confidence did seem dangerously close to insolence. The Emperor frowned and said, a degree of irritation beginning to creep into his voice, "What precisely do you have in your mind then, young man? You did seem to be asking for your inheritance to be restored to you."

"Yes, Your Majesty, I do want it back, but only after fighting a duel with my father's murderer in your august presence."

The Emperor, evidently taken aback at Jagdambii's request, turned thoughtful. Once again a hush fell over the Court. No one stirred. Then the Emperor said with apparent concern, "You do appear to be a courageous man, but courage alone doesn't necessarily make one an expert swordsman. The army commander you wish to fight happens to be a veteran warrior; you'd likely lose your life in a duel with him. Wouldn't it be far better to accept my offer and return home to your ancestral estate? Think about it."

"Your Majesty, may I submit that you needn't worry for my safety. If I returned home having simply accepted your offer – indeed a generous one – I should never for a moment be at peace with myself for the rest of my life. Neither would my ancestors ever rest in peace. Do please allow me an opportunity to avenge my father, Your Kind Majesty! I beg of you to grant me this one favour!"

Visibly impressed by Jagdambii's impassioned plea, the Emperor said with the shadow of a smile on his lips, "Well! You're indeed a brave young fellow; you've the courage of conviction to stand firm for what you see as right. That's the attitude we like to see in men. The duel is on! And we shall witness it too, but I'm afraid it cannot take place today. We'll have it tomorrow, same time, and same place."

With that, the Emperor rose to his feet, the courtiers hailing His Majesty's health and prowess in unison before the assembly was dismissed for the day.

❋❋❋

The following day, when Jagdambii and *Baabaa* arrived at the entrance to the fort, they were expected. A Guard Captain, already waiting for them there, led them deferentially inside. A large open area in the Palace complex inside the fort had been identified for the duel, and those who normally attended Court were already assembled there. Behind them stood a contingent of heavily armed soldiers from the elite Imperial Guards. All eyes were riveted on Jagdambii, standing tall and debonair, in the middle of the arena. There were many who admired the gall of the young man who'd challenged a veteran swordsman of the imperial army, putting his life at risk, but nearly everyone thought he was stupid and would soon pay for his stupidity with his life. But the lad showed no sign of nerves as he stood waiting out there in middle.

Presently, the Emperor escorted by his personal guards arrived on the scene. Everyone stood up and hailed the ruler, bowing low to offer the traditional greeting. As soon as he was seated, the Emperor asked, "*Braahmana-kumaar*, are you ready for the duel?"

"Just waiting for Your Majesty's signal. I'm at your command, Sire," replied Jagdambii, stepping up to greet the Emperor ceremoniously.

"We're pleased. Let the contest begin," said the Emperor, with a quick wave of his bejewelled hand.

As Jagdambii moved back into the centre of the arena, the contingent commander, who had so mercilessly slain his father and the rest of his family eighteen years ago, came forward and stood facing him. Jagdambii drew his sword, touched its blade to his forehead with his eyes closed in a moment of silent invocation. Then he raised his head and looked his adversary in the eye. Hardly had their eyes met, the commander seemed to quake with an unknown fear; he had the sensation of a hungry lion looking into his eyes. Within moments, the veteran of countless campaigns was drenched in cold sweat, and so dizzy, that he was barely able to stand on his feet anymore; eventually, he fainted, falling to the ground without a blow having been exchanged.

Jagdambii could not help laughing in amusement at the ungainly sight of a much-vaunted veteran warrior swooning from fear.

"Hey, look at that! Imagine a warrior fainting away in fear," he exclaimed.

Everyone watching the scene, beginning with the Emperor himself, was aghast at what had happened. A hush had fallen over the gathering, but it was soon broken as the Emperor, enraged by the apparent cowardice of a decorated commander, thundered, "Get this unmanned heap of a nincompoop out of my sight at once, someone!"

A couple of soldiers scurried to do his bidding and carried out the unconscious man from the arena.

Presently, another veteran stepped forward, bending low to offer *farshii salaams*, and said obsequiously, "If *JahaaNpanaah* commands, I'll challenge this arrogant boy!"

The Emperor now looked at Jagdambii and asked him, "Are you willing to accept the challenge?"

Jagdambii looked the challenger in the eye. Once again, the moment their eyes met, the burly man seemed to tremble in a sudden onset of panic. Jagdambii turned to the Emperor, "May it please Your Majesty to excuse my speaking frankly again. Why this single challenger alone, I'm prepared to take on ten such at a time!" he said, in a polite, yet firm, voice.

Baabaa Shambhuu Naath, who had been listening to all this, frowned. He thought Jagdambii was needlessly taking things a little too far. Even though he enjoyed the protection of the Benevolent One and was unlikely to come to harm, there was hardly any point in escalating the confrontation. He looked at the Emperor and sensed that he had not liked Jagdambii's boast, either. It was soon evident that he indeed had not, as he chided Jagdambii:

"Young man, don't you think you're shooting your mouth rather too haughtily for your own good? Showing off a dare beyond a point can be dangerous."

Jagdambii bowed to the Emperor again and replied with great humility, "Your Majesty, I'm fully cognizant of my capacity as well as my limitations. I'm also aware that showing off in the august presence of *Shahashaah-e-Hindostaan* would be unpardonably foolhardy. I'd never make that mistake, Sire!"

He paused for just an instant, as though considering if he should go on, then added, "But if Your Majesty would please to give me the opportunity, I shall prove that I haven't spoken in arrogance."

The Emperor shot back, "You can have that chance later. For now, fight the one challenger who stands waiting for you!"

"I'm at your command, Sire," said Jagdambii, and as before, he touched his sword to his forehead for a moment of silent prayer. Then he raised his head and looked at his opponent. Meanwhile, at the Emperor's unspoken sign, a soldier called out aloud, "Fight!"

Jagdambii jumped up in a flash at the word, and roaring fiercely like a tiger, began raining blow after blow on his opponent in such a seamless, electric succession that all the poor fellow could manage was to somehow escape being decapitated or cut up bad, stumbling backwards cringing and taking Jagdambii's blows on the round, thick-metal shield in his left hand; indeed, on several occasions a denouement seemed imminent. The Emperor was so thrilled by the lively duel, one-sided though it was, that every time the challenger teetered on the brink, he would appreciate Jagdambii's blows with a 'Bravo!' or 'Well done!', hardly caring that it was his own man at the receiving end. After the duel had gone on for a while, Jagdambii suddenly spun his heavy, double-edged sword close to the veteran's right hand, crying out "Beware!" to forewarn him. What followed was such blur of flashing feints that all the audience could see was the sword flying out of the challenger's hand high into the sky. As it came plummeting down, it was embedded into the ground in front of the Emperor's podium, precisely at the point beyond which no one was allowed to go towards the royal enclosure. The Emperor could not help applauding the manoeuvre that had given Jagdambii a clear advantage, "*Kyaa khuub*!" he exclaimed smiling broadly, patting his thigh lustily.

The disarmed commander now felt as though he stood naked and helpless, as a thousand pair of eyes including the Emperor's ogled at him in amusement. He did not know which way to look. To make things worse the 'arrogant boy' had now begun to add insult to injury, openly hurling ridicule, "What are you looking at, Sir? If you've even an ounce of gumption left in you, find another sword and come, get me! You dared to mislead His Majesty calling me an arrogant boy: this time I'll have that arrogant head of yours rolling on the ground here!"

To think that this young lad, barely out of his teens if that, had made him look so helpless and contemptible in front of His Majesty in full court made him go berserk with fury. He lunged sideways to snatch a sword from one of the soldiers on sentry duty and rushed madly at Jagdambii. Already anticipating some such move, Jagdambii took his blow on his sword and pushed him several steps back by sheer force, then released the pressure abruptly, moving niftily to a side. Taken by complete surprise, the challenger fell forward awkwardly face down on the ground. Jagdambii laughed at him in scorn. The commander, hopelessly demoralised by now, struck out wildly at Jagdambii, but it turned out to be simply the wayward sword-waving of a desperate man. Jagdambii let him vent his frustration for a while, as though granting the last wish of a man about to die, then shouting a warning to him, "Enough! Now beware!" he struck out, beheading the challenger in one flowing swipe of his sword. The severed head of the dead man rolled a few paces to come to a stop not far from where his first sword lay embedded in the ground. The headless body convulsed awhile, spraying jets of blood before growing still. The audience had gone very still too; everyone wondered silently to himself if things had gone a bit too far!

Baabaa Shambhuu Naath stole a furtive glance at the Emperor, but did not find his face reflecting any regret at having lost one of his commanders. In all probability, he had not even imagined that a veteran of the imperial army, a professional sword-fighter, could be killed in a one-on-one combat with a young civilian, and the realisation was yet to sink in.

Anyhow, he now turned towards Jagdambii and said, "Young man, you're not only brave, your fencing skills are unique as well. No praise would be too high, but now tell me, are you still firm on your challenge of taking on ten soldiers at a time?"

Jagdambii bowed and said, "If it pleases Your Majesty, I'm perfectly willing to do so, but I have a submission to make, Sire."

"Go ahead. You have my permission," declared the Emperor.

"Your Majesty, I do not wish anyone to lose his life unnecessarily...."

The Emperor interrupted him before Jagdambii could complete what he'd begun to say.

"Are you afraid of taking on ten of them at a time for fear of losing your life?"

"Your Majesty, I really wonder what sort of a fight a scared man, fearing for his life, could put up against ten guys coming at him all at once!" replied Jagdambii.

"Well said, young man! What would such a man be capable of indeed. All right then, you tell me what sort of ground-rules have *you* in mind," said the Emperor, eyeing Jagdambii with appreciation.

"Your Majesty, I'd suggest that once a combatant is disarmed, he should be deemed to have been killed or vanquished, and must then withdraw from the arena."

The Emperor found the suggestion reasonable and agreed readily. Meanwhile, the fallen commander's body had been removed from the arena and the ten soldiers meant to fight him simultaneously had been identified. As Jagdambii saw them prepare to march in to the middle, he walked hurriedly over to the periphery where *Baabaa* stood alongside others in the audience, and bending quickly to touch his feet, whispered to him, "*Baabaa*, quick! Give me your sword with your blessings so that I may fulfil my mission."

"I'm sure you will, with the blessings of the Benevolent *Vana-Durgaa*. My blessings will of course be with you, as they've always been," said *Baabaa*, taking his sword out of the scabbard and handing it over to him.

Jagdambii jogged back to the middle and now stood there with a sword in either hand, his ancestral sword in his right and the one *Baabaa* had just given him, in his left; he was surrounded by the ten Mughal soldiers on all sides. When it was nearly time for the combat to begin, he raised his hands, crossing the two swords and touching them to his forehead, his eyes closed again for a moment's meditation. As he opened his eyes, he saw the soldiers instinctively take a step backwards.

As on the last occasion, a soldier barked out the command at the Emperor's hand-sign; and the combat began in a flash. As many as ten highly-trained professional soldiers on the one side and Jagdambii all by himself on the other, never mind if he held two swords! – to all intents and purposes, it was a hopelessly unequal contest. But spinning like a top in the middle of the circle formed by the soldiers, Jagdambii deftly fended off their blows with *Baabaa*'s sword in his left hand while feinting and slashing incessantly with the heavier, double-edged sword in his right. Once again a hush had fallen over the audience; they all watched spellbound; particularly the Emperor, himself an expert swordsman, looked on keenly with the fascinated smile of a connoisseur. The contest no longer appeared to be so unequal after all!

Anyhow, it went on in this manner for quite a while, till at one point it appeared as though Jagdambii, swaying and dancing like a veritable phantom, fending off blows while giving it back good, had vanished in the blur of frenzied sword fight. Suddenly, one of the soldiers lost his sword; it flew skywards to fall down and got embedded in the ground where the other sword still stood upright. The Emperor, thrilled by the unbelievable spectacle, shouted "*Kyaa khuub*!" again and yet again.

The miracle of the dancing phantom appearing and disappearing in a whirl of frenetic feinting and cut-and-thrust went on repeating itself at regular intervals. Every time it grew invisible or nearly so, another of the remaining nine soldiers lost his sword in exactly the same manner as the one before, and retired from the arena as agreed upon. Before long Jagdambii was the lone combatant left standing in the middle. Strangely enough, he looked none the worse for all the frenetic activity; it seemed to have left no mark of fatigue or weariness on his quiet cheerfulness.

The imperial staff overseeing the arrangements at the contest site and high ranking officers of the Mughal army, all battle hardened veterans, muttered and mumbled grudging appreciation of the young civilian's performance, incredible as it was, against such heavy odds. There was little else they could do other than that, for they had been witness to something that they could not have even imagined only a while ago.

The Emperor now beckoned to Jagdambii to approach the imperial enclosure and said admiringly:

"*Braahmana-kumaar*, we're enamoured of you, for your incredible gallantry, virtually bordering on self-abandonment;

and the feats you've performed today are nothing short of the miraculous. Even though born a *Braahmana*, your *Kshatriya*-like attributes are highly commendable indeed." The great Mughal paused as though considering a suitable reward before going on, and then added solemnly:

"I, Mohammad Jalaluddin Akbar, *Shahanshaah-e-Hindostaan*, confer on you the hereditary title of Chaudhary, and hereby order the release of your confiscated family estate and properties. We are also pleased to reward you with a thousand gold sovereigns in cash and the grant of proprietary title to all land from Kamtaul to Kanojar GhaaT in kind. You're welcome to stay on in Delhi as our guest for as long as you wish."

Having declared the reward and the grant of title, Akbar rose to his feet, and took off a string of grape-sized gold globules, set with nine different varieties of precious stones, he was wearing; then coming to the edge of the imperial podium, he placed it around Jagdambii's in a spontaneous gesture as though to highlight his appreciation. Jagdambii expressed his gratitude by offering the *farshii salaams* to the Emperor. As he straightened, the latter smiled and said, "Our government will arrange for you all to be escorted back to make sure you face no inconvenience on the long journey home to the east."

With that the Court was dismissed for the day with usual fanfare and the Emperor left for the Palace with courtiers close to him and his personal attendants. The gathering came alive at once in a buzz of openly articulated amazement at the incredible scenes they had just witnessed, everyone curious to know where and how the *Braahmana* boy had acquired such fantastic skill in sword-fight.

Even though they were in the midst of strangers, *Baabaa* Shambhuu Naath could not restrain himself: he ran up to Jagdambii, embracing him with tears of joy in his eyes and said, "Son, my long-standing desire to see your exploits for which I have waited and prayed and worked so hard has been fulfilled to day. I wouldn't mind if I were to die now!"

"*Baabaa*! Please don't utter such inauspicious words for heaven's sake. All this has only been possible thanks to the years of hard training you gave me in our hideaway in the KaTkaa c*haur* where you first saw me with *Vana-Durgaa* watching over me, and of course her special blessings to me."

Just then Raajaa Maan Singh joined them; profusely praising and congratulating Jagdambii, he asked him, "Young man, tell me something, where and from whom did you acquire such amazing skill at fencing?"

"My revered *Guruu*, my mentor, my friend, philosopher and guide – he is right here, Your Highness!" replied Jagdambii pointing to *Baabaa*, "All I know of scriptures or mythology or art of warfare, I owe it all to him alone."

Baabaa, overwhelmed by his emotions, rejoined modestly, "It's his goodness that he's giving me the credit for his success. The fact of the matter is simply this: he's a favoured son of the Benevolent *Vana-Durgaa*, without whose protection and patronage the Singhwaar branch of our family would've been annihilated. As it happens, he's the sole surviving heir of his line now. The rest, as he described in the court, were all killed in the midnight massacre at the *Deorhii*."

The Raajaa, expressed his deepest sympathies and added, "Jagdambii, your parents are truly blessed to have had a son like you. One must rejoice for them!"

□

12
Homecoming

Having made the best of the hospitality extended to them as imperial guests for three days, Jagdambii and *Baabaa* decided to leave for KaTkaa on the fourth, an auspicious date according to the *Panchaanga*. Before their departure, Jagdambii was given the imperial *farmaan* that applauded his awesome performance, with the great Mughal himself as his witness, and specified the details of his reward in cash and kind, and the actual sackful of a thousand gold sovereigns. A contingent of fifty soldiers led by a veteran commander waited outside the imperial guest-house to escort them back home.

Jagdambii came out dressed in *chuuDiidaars* and a velvet *shervaanii* embroidered in gold and silk thread, sporting a pearl necklace. His now famous family sword tied with a golden cummerbund hung along his left flank. Accompanied by *Baabaa* Shambhuu Naath, he got onto the *haudaa* of the richly caparisoned elephant provided by the imperial *fiilkhaanaa* and departed for home. Jagdambii had told his escort commander that before leaving Delhi he would like to visit the *Shivaalaya* where they had stayed on arrival in the city.

After Jagdambii and *Baabaa* had paid their obeisance to the deity, they turned to Shivaanand, "*PanDit Jii*, the memories of your spontaneous hospitality to us, strangers though we were to you, will forever remain with us. I have no words to thank you enough for what you did for us," said Jagdambii.

Shivaanand, who had already heard of Jagdambii's miraculous feats at the Court, was so overwhelmed by his humility, he could barely speak, far less express his appreciation. *Baabaa*, keen to be on the way without further delay, sought to take leave of their erstwhile host. Finally, Shivaanand found his voice; turning to Jagdambii, he said, "*Kumaar*, all of Delhi is agog with the tales of your bravery. That you gave me the chance to be of service to you is enough reward for me. May the Wielder of the Trident grant you all a safe journey home!"

A short while later, they were on the highway that another great emperor Sher Shah Suri had had built some forty years ago.

The return journey, seated comfortably in the *huadaa* on elephant-back and the well-equipped imperial escorts taking charge of their security and other needs, passed off like a dream when compared with their outward journey only a few weeks ago. They arrived at the outskirts of PaaTaliputra in record time. The commander of the escort-party apprised Jagdambii respectfully – as was indeed expected of him when addressing an imperial guest – that they were about to reach PaaTaliputra and here they would have to cross the holy river *Gangaa* on barges and country-boats to her north bank in order to head towards Mithilaa.

"But Commander, before we make the crossing, I'd like to see the provincial *Subedaar* at PaaTaliputra," said Jagdambii.

"As you wish, Sir," said the commander, heeling his mount to move ahead of the imperial guests' train to inform the *Subedaar* in advance. The latter had already received intelligence of the likely arrival of Chaudhary Jagdambii Thaakur, recently decorated by *Zill-e-Ilaahii* in person, under an imperial escort. The guests of the Emperor were warmly welcomed. The *Subedaar* quickly went through the motions of taking note of the contents of *Shaahii farmaan* – the imperial scroll – formally restoring Jagdambii to his family estate and the *havelii* at Singhwaar and the grant of additional lands as reward. Deferring to the *Subedaar*'s advice that it might not be a good idea to attempt crossing the swollen river after sundown, they decided to camp at PaaTaliputra for the night.

At dawn, however, they were on their way once again. The barges, eagerly offered by the imperial naval outfit at PaaTaliputra to the guests of the Emperor, had no difficulty taking them across the river.

Once on the north bank, the Hindus took a dip in the holy river and observed the ritual of offering flowers, lighted earthen wick lamps placed on plantain leaves and prayers to *Gangaa*; then they embarked on the last lap of their journey.

As their caravan reached the bifurcation for KaTkaa and Singhwaar, Jagdambii said to Shambhuu Naath, "*Baabaa*, I want to first go to the *Deorhii* where my father's wandering soul anxiously awaits my return. It would surely be comforted to learn of our success." *Baabaa* instinctively knew Jagdambii was only asking him for the sake of form, and that he had already made up his mind to first visit Singhwaar by himself. He was in two minds whether to try and persuade him to first go and meet his mother, or just let him have his way. The old man would have liked nothing better than to take him straight to KaTkaa first and make him over to Bhavaanii, saying, "See, *Bahuu*, I've brought your son back, victorious and safe!"

Jagdambii was quick to read *Baabaa*'s mind, hastening to reassure him, "*Baabaa*, don't worry, I'd probably make it to KaTkaa too, by the time you arrive there; I just happen to be going via Singhwaar. And surely, you know that I'll be safe!"

Finally, *Baabaa* agreed, exhorting him not to take too long at the *Deorhii*. Jagdambii got down from elephant-back, and commandeering a horse from the escorts' spares, galloped away on the Singhwaar trail. As he was lost to sight behind the cloud of dust he left in his wake, the rest of the party continued on to KaTkaa.

Meanwhile, an advance team of the escorts had reached KaTkaa to inform the family, anxiously awaiting their return, of the likely time of their arrival. The good news sent a huge wave of relief and joy through the family as well as the close-knit village community. A gathering began to form outside *Baabaa*'s house to welcome them back, and soon packed the village square with people.

When the elepahant carrying *Baabaa* and the cavalcade of the imperial escorts arrived, they couldn't believe their eyes: *Baabaa* sitting in the beaten-silver *haudaa* atop a huge, richly caparisoned elephant, escorted by a contingent of Mughal soldiers led by a knight commander in full gear! They hadn't seen anything like this ever before in their lives. *Baabaa*, dressed in a silk *dhotii*, a *kimkhaab* mirzai and the ceremonial *saaThaa paag* – a traditional Mithilaa turban with sixty folds – and wearing a string of real pearls in addition to his usual *rudraaksha* beads, made for an impressive picture as the Mughal commander deferentially helped him down from the *haudaa*. His two sons and grandson stepped up to touch his feet for blessings. Affectionately stroking their heads to bless them, *Baabaa* turned all around smiling jubilantly, his right hand raised in blessings to all the rest in the gathering as well. Then he said to Kaashii, "Take the soldiers to the school and make the best possible arrangements for their stay you can – they have come escorting us all the way from Delhi! Do make sure they aren't inconvenienced in any way."

"As you wish, Father," said Kaashii, but unable to restrain his curiosity, he asked, "But where's Jagdambii?"

"He went off to Singhwaar to visit his ancestral homestead on the way. Don't worry; he'll be here any moment now."

With that, *Baabaa* turned to walk to the front porch where the village elders sat waiting for him with questions without count. The first to go was Kaaliicharan Upaadhyaaya, the astrologer who had made Jagdambii's horoscope all those years ago.

"I can hardly wait to ask if any of my predictions about Jagdambii proved to be on target," he said.

"Oh Kaalii *Baabuu*, the miracles of Jagdambii have far exceeded your predictions," replied Shambhuu Naath with evident pride.

"Do be more forthcoming, Shambhuu Naath *Jii*; you don't have to talk to your friends in riddles," said the old astrologer.

"You had only said he'd avenge his father and be restored to his family estate. Well, he did all that, of course, but so pleased was Akbar Baadshaah with him, he conferred on him the hereditary title of Chaudhary and also gave him a whole lot of additional land grants and gold, and can you believe – his own *navratna* necklace he was wearing as well. He even declared us his personal guests and sent us home with armed escorts, as you saw!"

"Well, what did Jagdambii do to earn so many accolades?" asked Kaalii *Baabuu*, gaping in wonderment.

Baabaa then recounted to them the details of all that had happened since the time they reached the imperial capital.

Just as *Baabaa* was concluding his account, someone yelled excitedly, "Look, there he comes!" They all looked up and there he indeed was – the strapping young hero of *Baabaa*'s tale! The assembled village folk craned their necks, jostling and pushing one another, to get a better look at him – though he had lived all his life in their midst except for the last three months! As Jagdambii, smiling broadly, rode into the front yard, the crush of people happily parted to let his horse walk in. Hundreds of them together hailed him with a chorus of blessings, wishing him a long life and well-being. Jagdambii, overwhelmed by their warmth, raised his hand, turning the horse a full circle, to return the greetings of each one of those cheering him.

As Jagdambii approached *Baabaa*, the patriarch embraced him joyfully and said, "I was beginning to worry a little about you."

"*Baabaa*! You still see me as a child, don't you? It's not you but your affection for me that leads you to all this fussing and worrying."

"No one can win an argument with you," said *Baabaa* patting his back affectionately, "but all's well that ends well. Now, do run off straight to your mother. She's been longing to see you."

When Jagdambii entered the inner courtyard, he found a maid waiting with an earthen pitcher of holy water to wash his feet. Paaro put a *tiikaa* of sandalpaste and *akshat* on his forehead and welcomed him with a garland of fresh flowers while Saavitrii, who stood on the other side with a metal thaal of lighted earthen wick-lamps, stepped in to make an *aaratii.* Jagdambii feeling a trifle bashful at such an elaborate formal reception by family women, could not help chuckling in amusement as he said, "What are you all making such a fuss for?"

"Well! Our son has come home robed in such glory, we're doing this simply to ward off an evil eye, that's what!" said Paaro smiling.

"In fact, it's I who should be doing *aaratii* in your honour for having brought me up with such great care and love," said Jagdambii deeply humbled.

"*Baabaa*'s right, you have to have the last word! But enough! Let's go and see your mother who's been waiting for you so long at *puujaa.*"

Just then, Bhavaanii emerged from the *Puujaa-ghar.* Jagdambii ran up to her and flung himself into her waiting arms. Mother and son stood there for a while in a silent embrace; then Bhavaanii whispered softly, "Oh, how I've missed you, my son!"

"*MaaN*! I'm back having avenged my father, but meantime, what have you done to yourself? Look at you! It seems as though you haven't had a decent meal in a long time! Rarely have I seen you looking so pale and haggard."

"Really! Am I looking so bad?" asked Bhavaanii smiling, though her eyes were moist.

"Indeed, it appears that if I hadn't returned for a few more days...."

Bhavaanii interrupted him hastily, "No, no! Don't even mention it. I have yet to fulfil many a heart's desire."

"You do? Then why don't you go right ahead and tell me what they are so that I begin to take care of them. I promise I'll not pause for a moment's rest until each one of them has been realised," said Jagdambii innocently.

"Oh, forever playing the innocent, Jagdambii my boy! Don't you get what your mother's hinting at – you bringing her a daughter-in-law, perhaps even the prospect of having a grandchild to play with, eh?" said Paaro smiling. Jagdambii, suddenly bashful, started laughing, and replied with mock seriousness, "Well, no matter how weary I am from the journey, I'll go out this very moment and bring her here if you'd just give me some idea of who you have in mind!"

Everyone laughed merrily.

"Mothers of all grown-up sons have such dreams, but mine are a bit different," said Bhavaanii quietly in the aftermath.

All of them looked up with curiosity towards her, but before she could say anything more, Kaashii and Sadaashiva walked in and caused a change of topics by beginning to describe the arrangements made for the stay of the Mughal soldiers, mostly for Jagdambii's benefit.

Later that evening, *Baabaa* joined the rest the family for a chat.

"Bhavaanii *Bahuu*, do you now see how I'd foreseen the shape of things to come as far back as eighteen years?"

"All of it has only been possible because of your support, *Baabaa*!" said Bhavaanii earnestly.

"No *Bahuu*, I've had no hand in it – it's all owing to the grace of *Vana-Durgaa*," said *Baabaa* with genuine modesty.

"How could I ever deny her blessings, but nothing would've been possible without you taking us under your wings during such difficult times."

"Well, quite frankly, I'm surprised that you appear to be still not convinced of the *Devii*'s special favour on Jagdambii. If you'd only seen what I did at the imperial court in Delhi, you'd never doubt it!"

"You're right, *Baabaa*; many years ago the *Devii* herself told me as much. Her words are still clearly etched in my memory: that it was she who inspired Mohini to persuade me to flee the *havelii*; that it was again she who guided me to your place, a safe haven for the two of us; and that she'd forever look after my boy," said Bhavaanii.

"Well, there you are! And yet you are bent on giving me the credit for it all?"

Suddenly noticing Jagdambii smiling mischievously, *Baabaa* added, “Do you see how he smiles? That’s what he wanted, too – to heap all the credit for his victory on me.”

“Haven’t I been telling you for years?” said Paaro.

“What?”

“That Jagdambii’s a mischievous fellow!”

Everyone laughed; Jagdambii alone remained quiet. Bhavaanii couldn’t help asking him, “Anything the matter with you? Why have you suddenly turned so glum?”

Now, Jagdambii turned to *Baabaa*, and said with exaggerated earnestness, “*Baabaa*, I want you to be the judge: If someone’s being dubbed as ‘mischievous’, is it something to be happy about?”

Everyone laughed merrily once again. It turned out to be a most pleasant evening, full of light-hearted banter and easy-flowing conversation and plenty of laughter; soon Jagdambii was also laughing along with the others, despite the niggle of a new anxiety beginning to slowly take hold of him.

❋❋❋

When mother and son found a quiet moment to themselves, Jagdambii said, “*MaaN*, I’ve something to tell you.”

“Then why don’t you go ahead and tell me what’s bothering you?”

“With *Baabaa*’s consent, I visited the *Deorhii* on our way back from Delhi. I had a chance to commune with my father’s and *Sakhii-MaaN’s* spirits once again. While my father’s soul has been set free now, *Sakhii-MaaN’s* is still bound to the *Deorhii*. I want to have hers released as soon as possible, too.”

“Well, this is something I myself want badly. I still remember your exact words after that first experience of yours. I know Mohini will be in limbo until my return to the *Deorhii*, and now that your father’s been released, it would be most unfair to leave her wandering any longer.”

"That's exactly how I feel, but how could I possibly go and tell *Baabaa* that we want to leave here and return to the *Deorhii* after all that he's done for us since I was born, and so soon, too, after our triumph at the Court. It'll break his heart!"

Bhavaanii could sense Jagdambii's dilemma as it was very much her own. She silently pondered over it as she sat facing her son, his head bowed and forehead creased by a frown.

Meanwhile, *Baabaa*, who'd been looking around for Jagdambii, chanced upon them, and asked, "What are you two looking so dejected about?" He noticed they had risen to receive him and offer an *aasana* rather too hurriedly, as if taken unawares in the middle of something private.

"Before I sit down, you must tell me if I've interrupted something personal," he queried.

"Please, *Baabaa*, don't be so formal; we've nothing to hide from you. As a matter of fact, you've come by exactly when you're most needed. Do sit down please, will you?" pleaded Bhavaanii.

As *Baabaa* sat down, others began gravitating towards them and soon it turned into an impromptu session of the family council.

"I was actually looking for Jagdambii to find out how his visit to the *Deorhii* went off, you know," said *Baabaa*.

That set Jagdambii recounting his detour earlier that morning:

"The last time I was there, the place was all covered with rank growth everywhere, the buildings infested with spider-webs, the forecourt under layers of rotting leaves accumulated over time, balconies lurching under their own weight and verandahs overlaid with layers of dust and pigeon-droppings – it was a perfect picture of neglect and desolation. But this time around, there was a sea-change; the precincts are now clean and tidy and the courtyards have a fresh coat of mud-paint; a good deal of maintenance effort has been made."

Bhavaanii, a little alarmed at the implication of what Jagdambii had just said, asked, "But who's brought about this change? I'd the impression no one could go in and touch a thing there. It seems the place is no longer safe from intruders!"

"Don't worry *MaaN*! It's only JhagDuu who can go in to clean up the campus from time to time, and that because he has the guardian-angels' permission to enter the *havelii*. You do remember JhagDuu, don't you? – The guy who came herding *Deorhii* cattle here and met you, remember? He's the son of Parameshvar, my father's trusted manservant, and a reliable fellow himself."

Apparently still not convinced, Bhavaanii said, "It follows that in time there will be others who will lose their fear and begin trespassing at will. Who knows which of them will turn greedy and start exploring? How can I not worry, son?"

"But at least stop worrying for now, and hear me out, will you?" said Jagdambii, almost pleading with his mother.

"All right, carry on."

"Towards the close of my earlier visit to the *Deorhii*, I went to the *Puujaa-ghar*, and was horrified to see it littered with the rotting skeletons of two trespassers who had met their end there several years ago. No one had cleaned it since. I was literally in tears to see our family deity so grossly defiled and called out to my father with whom I had communed long only some time ago. He responded immediately; after listening to my submission that JhagDuu be authorised to clean up the *Puujaa-ghar* and also enter the premises from time to time for upkeep, my father's spirit granted permission with the conditions that he was never to bring anyone else to assist him or for any other reason and never be on the premises except daylight hours. I explained all this to JhagDuu, and only retained him for the job after he had taken a solemn oath to never let greed overwhelm his loyalty. What I saw of the *Deorhii* this time makes me implicitly trust him as the right man. Mother, I'm sorry I must have assumed you'd approve of the arrangement, already granted by Father's spirit, and forgotten to mention it in all that excitement of showing you the baton my father had gifted."

"It's all right, son. What you did seems to be perfectly in order in the perspective I now have, but let's hear something of how your recent visit went," said Bhavaanii.

"Well, this time I first went to the *Puujaa-ghar* and thanked the family deity for her special blessings during my mission to the imperial capital. When I came out and called to my father's spirit, there was no response at all. I went round the premises despairing of ever again being able to be in touch with him, finally ending up in the personal apartment where my father had gifted me the baton on my previous visit. There, I could suddenly hear him speak to me,

"Come my son, I was waiting for you."

He sounded very happy to see me. When I sought his blessings, he blessed me, saying:

"*Kuliinam vaa, kuliinam vaa*
Veer purusha bhaavinam!

Son, you proved yourself famously. Any father would be blessed to have a son like you. The day I've waited for is finally here, it's time for me to go. I don't know if the efficacy of a son making *pinDa-daan* for his departed father, as depicted in the *Puraanas*, is really true; you'll only offer it later at *Gayaa*. But it brings me great peace that you've avenged your father." He paused for a moment, then I heard him again, "Son, I've very little time now, but before I go, I want you to make a solemn promise, will you do so?"

"Father," I replied, "anything you wish, I'd do it even if it were to cost me my life!"

"Do not forget Mohini," he said, "she's still wandering around in the *Deorhii*. Never forget, she laid down her life to save our line from extinction. You must help her out of limbo at the earliest."

"Father," I assured him, "Mohini is like my own mother to me. I shan't let her suffer a day more than the time needed to make the *havelii* livable for my mother."

"I agree with you," he said, "and I trust you to live up to your promise. So long, son! It's time for me to go."

I felt as though that moment would wrench my heart out as it passed, for I knew it in my bones that this was the last time we should commune with each other. But, as someone wise said, there's a certain inevitability to such things that's inescapable! So, I made my last *Pranaam* to him, and heard him say:

"Diirghaayu bhava! Kiirtimaan bhava! Yashasvii bhava! Sarvatra vijayii bhava!"

Presently, I felt a gust of icy breeze pass me and go out the door! Before I could fully grasp its significance, I heard the voice of my *Sakhii-MaaN's* spirit address me:

"I'm left alone and truly in limbo now. When will it be my turn, son, or am I doomed to remain in this state for ever?" she asked.

"Never! Surely, you heard the solemn promise I just made to my father. It's only a question of a little time – even you wouldn't want your mistress to return to live in ruins of a *havelii*."

"I agree with you, my son! As long as you don't forget me altogether, I'm prepared to wait patiently. But now I must not keep you from returning to KaTkaa where your mother waits for you anxiously."

So, then I left the *Deorhii* to get on my way here."

For a while no one spoke, each one of them silently working out the implications of Jagdambii's account of his recent visit to Singhwaar. Finally, he himself broke the uncomfortable silence; turning to *Baabaa*, he said, "*Baabaa*, the love and affection that you've given us for long years, and, in fact, the very air of KaTkaa and the lovely scent of the earth here will remain with us until the end of our days. But my sense of duty to the legacy of my forebears compels me to consider moving back to my ancestral homestead and to try and bring the *Deorhii* back to life once again at the earliest. Left to myself, I would've loved to spend some more time with you, *Baabaa*, but I'm afraid there's no way I can postpone fulfilling my solemn promise to the departed soul for any longer than absolutely necessary."

Everyone listening to Jagdambii could sense the firmness of his resolve to return to the *Deorhii* in the near future. However, before anyone could voice a discordant opinion, *Baabaa* hastened to reassure Jagdambii, "Much as your departure will leave a void in its wake and this household will never be the same again, I'll never allow sentiments to stand in your way, my boy. Who knows, I might even lose my will to live much longer, but I know – this had to happen sooner or later."

As if to prove that he had spoken in right earnest, *Baabaa* sent for the *Panchaanga* from his room right away, and having studied it thoughtfully, as was his wont, (perhaps also giving himself time to get a hold on his emotions) he looked at Bhavaanii and said, "*Bahuu*, as far as I can see, the first day of the *Shaardiiya Navaratra* would be an auspicious day for your re-entering the *Deorhii*. After all, it's not a new house, you'll only be returning to the *havelii* where you've lived before. Still, if you so wish, we could consult a *jyotishii* to confirm this or suggest another date."

"No *Baabaa*, I don't think we need consult anyone else. The date you've suggested is fine, but it's only three weeks away and I wonder if it'd be enough time to restore the *Deorhii* to a reasonably livable state."

"Why not? I'll put Sadaashiva on the job full time," said *Baabaa*, turning to ask him whether he thought it was doable at that time.

"Sure, we have as many as twenty days in hand. I think it can be done," said Sadaashiva, rising to the challenge.

"Well, that's final then. We'll set your return to the *Deorhii* on the *Kalash-sthaapan* day of *Durgaa-Puujaa*," said *Baabaa*, taking turns to look at Bhavaanii and Jagdambii.

❋❋❋

Sadaashiva was about to enter the *Deorhii*, with a number of masons and handymen in tow, when he remembered the two black cobras that he had encountered there some eighteen years ago. He decided to explore first; asking the workers to wait for him at the entrance, he went in by himself, moving warily, watching out for possible danger at each step he took. The place was indeed much better kept now, as Jagdambii had said the other day. As Sadaashiva approached the *manDap*, he saw JhagDuu sweeping the other side of the courtyard, apparently without any fear. JhagDuu placed him instantly despite the fact that he was seeing him after eighteen years, and beaming a toothy smile, exclaimed aloud in surprise, "Master Sadaashiva, you here?" Sadaashiva beckoned to him to come closer and told him the purpose of his visit. JhagDuu's heart danced for joy at the good news and it showed on his face.

When asked, JhagDuu told Sadaashiva that lately he had been sighting only one of the two cobras, which made sense in the light of what Jagdambii had revealed. JhagDuu said he had mostly seen the lone cobra in the *Puujaa-ghar*, facing the *chinvaar* with its hood up, as though it were praying.

Letting JhagDuu carry on with his work, Sadaashiva went and stood on the front verandah of *Puujaa-ghar* in the *pranaam-mudraa*. He could not see any serpent but decided to make his submission in absentia:

"O *Naag-devataa*, listen to me if you're somewhere around here. I'm Sadaashiva, son of Shambhuu Naath Thaakur of KaTkaa, here in the domain under your protection, to carry out renovations to the *havelii* at its Mistress's behest, but I would like to have your permission before I bring in the workers."

There was no response at all!

After waiting and watching for a considerable amount of time, Sadaashiva decided to try again:

"I'm Sadaashiva; you've seen me before. I'm here alone. The workers are sitting idle outside the *havelii* for want of your consent. How can the Mistress come to live here unless it's been renovated before the *Kalash-sthaapan* day?"

As he made his second plea, Sadaashiva could hear the hissing sound a cobra makes when its hood is up, even though he could not see a snake this time. He continued to stand, his hands folded, hoping for the best, and said in a tone of supplication:

"O *Naag-devataa*, being only an ordinary mortal, I can't understand you; I'd been favoured with a *darshan* by you en paire the last time I was here. Why not this time? How can I get on with the task at hand?"

All of a sudden, a large cobra appeared, as if out of nowhere, before his eyes; it was so fearsome it took his breath away. Trembling all over, he somehow mustered enough courage to address the apparition:

"O lord! How can I, an ordinary mortal, grasp your mystery, but I wonder what happened to your companion?"

As soon as he had spoken, Sadaashiva realised he had made a mistake: the serpent began hissing evermore menacingly, its tongue flicking in and out rapidly and eyes red as hot coals. It was visibly incensed. Sadaashiva dropped down on his knees and put his head on the stone threshold in abject surrender, saying:

"Lord, I have no right to question; I do beg, forgive me for once!"

The apology seemed to work; Sadaashiva sensed that the serpent had calmed down and, presently, it disappeared as fast as it had materialised. He knew then that his prayer had been granted and at once headed for the *chinvaar* and put his head down on it, addressing the family-deity:

"*MaaN*! You'll no longer go without worship. Jagdambii will soon be here to resume *puujaa* on a daily basis. I pray you to grant me strength and speed to be able to renovate the *havelii* by the stipulated *tithi*."

□

Epilogue

On the first day of *Nava-raatra*, the freshly renovated *Deorhii* of the Thaakurs of *Dighvae'Sannahpur* at Singhwaar stood decked up like bride on her wedding day. Indeed, it was nothing short of a complete transformation of the *havelii* that had remained abandoned for close on two decades. Its forecourt that had until recently evoked nothing but fright and aversion, was packed with village folks in a festive mood. The very air around the *Deorhii* spelled joy and gaiety. Evidently Sadaashiva and his team of workers had done a marvellous job of it well within the stipulated time. The *havelii* looked as good as new!

Jagdambii's triumphal party led by *Baabaa* Shambhuu Naath had left KaTkaa at first light and was about to arrive at Singhwaar, well before the *muhurta* chosen for re-entry.

Baabaa elegantly dressed for the occasion, his *rudraaksha* beads and recently acquired pearl strings on his neck and the three sandalpaste marks on his forehead, was smartly astride his horse, his sword gently swaying along his left flank. Chaudhary Jagdambii Thaakur was also dressed in his ceremonial best: a *kimkhaab achkan* and a silk *dhotii* and a red *paag* with colourful feathers on top, in keeping with the title conferred by the Emperor; he rode his father's favourite horse, Baadal alongside *Baabaa*, and had on around his neck the nine-gem necklace won during his now famous contest at the imperial court; the ancestral sword *'Mahishaasura-mardinii'* hung on his left flank. Behind them the huge palanquin of Bhavaanii Bahuu carried by sixteen *kahaar*s, moved at a stately pace; it was followed by another one carrying Paaro and Saavitrii. Kaashii Naath, and Raam

Iqbaal, specially invited on the occasion, rode behind them. Maarkandeya, also on horseback, flitted at will from one end of cavalcade to the other. The rear was brought up by the entire village folk of KaTkaa on foot – everyone was invited for the big occasion at Singhwaar.

As the cavalcade arrived at the *Deorhii* entrance, two rows of *singha* players trumpeted in unison to announce the triumphant homecoming of the owners of the *Deorhii*, followed by a variety of musical instruments bursting forth in tandem to form an orchestra of sorts, playing cheerful, popular tunes. A group of *PanDit*s standing by began at once to sprinkle holy water, *akshat* and *duurva* grass-twigs on the returning family, chanting Vedic hymns in blessing to Jagdambii for a long and productive life.

Surviving members of a large number of Singhwaar families had returned to the village after news spread of Jagdambii's exploits at 'Dilli darbaar' and his triumphant return with a much larger estate granted by no less than Akbar Baadshaah himself. Most of them decided to stay on, and had flocked to watch the homecoming of the young Master and the dowager Mistress, and showered flower-petals of welcome on them. Jagdambii, quick to acknowledge their gestures, looked all around smiling, his hand raised in salutation. His upright stance and the quiet dignity of his smile, reflecting his genuine goodwill towards all and sundry, reminded the assembled village-folk so much of Dharaadhar Thaakur, their hearts ached a little even in this moment of joy.

Jagdambii's horse negotiated its way slowly through the crowds, and as he dismounted in the middle of the forecourt, he was greeted by Sadaashiva, who had been supervising final touches to the renovation work until the previous evening, and had decided to stay on and join the party at Singhwaar. Meanwhile, Bhavaanii Bahuu's palanquin had also arrived at the huge arched entrance to the *Deorhii*. She now emerged from the parting in the drapes and stood a while, turning around to take in the surroundings of the old *Deorhii*. Myriad images from the past came crowding into the moment, flashing past her un-seeing eyes; she felt overwhelmed by the sudden upsurge of emotions, but only for a passing moment. Her eyes had indeed welled up in that instant; Paaro and Saavitrii had both noticed her emotional strain and came to stand near her, but were discreet enough not to speak to Bhavaanii just then. Jagdambii had noticed it, too, and well understood what was going on inside his mother's head; he tried to draw her back from her reverie, whispering softly to her:

"*MaaN*! What are you doing standing here like this for? Let's go inside the *Deorhii*, I say! Or we'll have missed the *muhurta*."

Bhavaanii, who had indeed been transported to another time for those few moments, was startled right back into the present and trying to get a hold on herself, ascended the short flight of steps and entered the outer courtyard.

The moment Bhavaanii stepped in, a small but powerful whirlwind arose from the point where she stood. It soon grew in size, enveloping and very nearly blinding her. People standing around could barely make her out inside the dusty little hurricane, as though she had suddenly turned invisible. In her panic, Bhavaanii flailed and pushed at the veil of swirling dust to break out of it, but it would simply not let go of her. No one had a clue what was happening or how to help her out; everyone merely looked on, bewildered and helpless.

Meanwhile, in addition to its circular motion, the whirlwind had begun to move forward horizontally, dragging along Bhavaanii trapped inside; it took her across the courtyard to the private quarters she had earlier occupied with her husband; having made her take a couple of rounds of her old bed-chamber, it emerged back on to the verandah, then moving through a smaller courtyard into the narrow corridor at the back of the *Deorhii*, it brought her out to the exact spot on the riverside where Mohini had parted with her all those years ago. And then, the dusty veil of eddies enveloping her seemed to subside and sort of vanish under her feet.

Family members, who had followed Bhavaanii helplessly, were now even more amazed to see her standing in the *pranaam-mudraa*, her eyes closed; there was not the tiniest speck of dust anywhere on her person!

Baabaa at once relieved and concerned, stepped up, asking, "*Bahuu*, are you all right?"

Jagdambii, the only one to have remained unruffled through all this, now filled in for her, "*Baabaa*, don't worry, she's fine. It was just Mohini, receiving her Mistress and bidding her a final farewell at the exact spot where they had parted on that fateful night eighteen years ago."

Tear drops trickled down Bhavaanii's cheeks as she opened her eyes, remembering that night when her old life had been shattered and the sights that Mohini had just shown her inside the dusty veil. But determined not to let all that cast a shadow on the big day of her son, she quickly wiped them off her face, and said to *Baabaa*, "Jagdambii's right *Baabaa*, I'm fine."

Presently, Sadaashiva, who had been supervising the arrangements for the rituals of *Kalash-sthaapan*, marking the commencement of *Durgaa-Puujaa*, hurried over to tell them it was time to move to the *Puujaa-ghar*.

Jagdambii approached her mother, and putting his arm tenderly around her shoulders, whispered to her, "*MaaN*! Let's go now and worship the family deity we were forced to leave abandoned all these years!"

Bhavaanii walked alongside Jagdambii without saying a word. As they approached the *Puujaa-ghar*, they could hear the bitter-sweet notes of shahnaai from the *naubat-khaanaa* 'atop the *Deorhii* entrance – while closer to them the *Vaidikas,* standing outside the *Puujaa-ghar,* chanted:

"Om Ganan'naantvaa Ganapati gvam havaamahe
Priyaan'naantvaa priyapati gvam havaamahe..."

□□□